W9-BQS-895

Sam Coale
August 3, 1990
Lahore

BREAKING THE CURFEW

Emma Duncan studied politics and economics at Oxford and for two years worked at Independent Television News. She moved to *The Economist* where she wrote on business, science and foreign politics and travelled widely in the Gulf and the subcontinent covering, among other things, the Iran-Iraq and Afghan wars. Since January 1986 she has been *The Economist's* South Asia correspondent based in Delhi. This is her first book.

E = 7

SPECIAL PRICE
IN PAKISTAN

Rs. 180

BREAKING
THE CURFEW

A Political Journey Through Pakistan

Emma Duncan

— money, breakdown, fears, chaos, influence

ARROW BOOKS

Century Travellers

Arrow Books Limited
20 Vauxhall Bridge Road, London SW1V 2SA

An imprint of Random Century Group

London Melbourne Sydney Auckland Johannesburg
and agencies throughout the world

First published by Michael Joseph in 1989
Arrow edition 1990

© 1989 Emma Duncan

This book is sold subject to the condition that it
shall not, by way of trade or otherwise, be lent,
resold, hired out, or otherwise circulated without
the publisher's prior consent in any form of binding
or cover other than that in which it is published
and without a similar condition including this
condition being imposed on the subsequent
purchaser

Printed and bound in Great Britain by
Courier International, Tiptree, Essex

ISBN 0 09 973790 6

CONTENTS

BREAKING
THE CURFEW

INTRODUCTION

THE KING FAISAL mosque in Islamabad, built out of Saudi Arabian money and Islamic brotherhood, is huge, white and hard-edged against the soft blue backdrop of the Murree Hills. Its design is based not on a dome but on a pyramid, so the sun batters the triangular white marble faces that reach up to a point topped with a twenty-foot golden crescent. On the day of President Zia's funeral, a couple of hundred of the half-million who attended edged their way slowly up the roof and balanced along its steep edges. A handful made it up to the crescent and stood, grasping it for security, watching the foreign dignitaries damp with heat in their dark suits, the rows of soldiers in pagris – turbans with stiff-starched ornamental fantails – and the off-white sea of Pakistani civilians, all dressed in the baggy shalwar kamees pyjama suit that disguises divisions of money, class and power. The only splash of colour was the coffin, draped in gold tinsel and silk flowers.

George Shultz and Geoffrey Howe got it wrong. As the coffin approached, preceded by a double row of black pagris, they marched forward from the VVIP's stand and coincided unfortunately with midday prayer time. As the mullah droned the call, they were brushed aside by important Pakistani people emerging from their stand to pray. The foreigners retired, the protocol men squirmed, and the Pakistanis, turning their backs to the coffin, bent towards Mecca. When the prayers for the newly-designated shaheed – martyr – ended, Shultz, Howe and a stream of white, brown and black ministers and ambassadors came forward with their wreaths. The laying of wreaths is not an Islamic practice, but these had been adapted with tinsel and bright ribbons to extravagant Pakistani taste.

The Pakistanis returned to their stand, and the jostling and

1

intriguing amongst those who aspired to power began. General Fazle Haq, the chief minister of the North West Frontier Province, sat in the front row, with his arm round the shoulders of Nawaz Sharif, the young businessman chief minister of Punjab, and whispered into his ear. Behind them, Mohammed Khan Junejo, the prime minister whom Zia had sacked three months earlier, stood stiff and silent, either disapproving or unsure how to start his own intrigue. Makhdoom Qureshi, the bulbous-nosed landlord whom Zia had made governor of Punjab, was hovering to get a word with the large, grey, Shultz-lookalike bureaucrat, Ghulam Ishaq Khan, who had slid into the presidency in the crisis that followed Zia's death; but Ishaq walked off with Illahi Bakhsh Soomro, the dapper minister of information, water and power.

The hawk-nosed foreign minister, Sahabazada Yaqub Khan, was not in the business of intrigues: a migrant from India, with no Pakistani constituency, he has no place in the power structure other than that accorded to him by his superior intellect. He sat in a back row and seemed to be crying. Ghulam Mustapha Jatoi, Bhutto's old right-hand man, who had dissociated from the opposition and was waiting to be made prime minister, was giving his telephone number to Western journalists. The politicians who were not edging between rows and exchanging whispers were watching others doing it.

Benazir Bhutto, the leader of the main opposition party, has her own martyr, her father, Zulfikar Ali Bhutto, who was executed by Zia. She, therefore, was not present; but she was all over the West's television screens, looking pale and serious and trying to avoid saying how much she hated the dead president. Plenty of other opposition leaders were there, eager to make it clear that, whatever their previous views about Zia, they were with the establishment on this day of national mourning.

Above the public political intrigue, at the back of the stands, were the people who really mattered. Against the loose comfort of the shalwar kamees their khaki uniforms looked stiff and smart. Their chests flowered with medals, their backs were straight and their eyes watched the politicians like adults checking the antics of a school playground.

Outside these small dramas, neither audience nor actors, were half a million people. Perhaps they were there for the party; perhaps they were mourners; perhaps they were gloating at the dictator's death; perhaps they were wondering what this sudden

2

earthquake in their country's government would do to their futures. Those inside the roped-in enclosure wouldn't have been interested in their thoughts unless the half-million had started rioting; but those outside were sufficiently involved or curious to stand for three hours in the soggy August heat-bath or edge their way up 500 feet to the golden crescent on top of the mosque.

When I first started working on the subcontinent at *The Economist*, there was an immediate option of a trip to Sri Lanka or Pakistan. I chose Sri Lanka, which sounded soft and luscious and manageable, like an avocado pear; Pakistan sounded bitter and tough, an underripe mango of a country. But there was news brewing in Pakistan – elections seemed at last about to happen – so, reluctantly, I prepared to go there.

It was 1985, and most of the big men from Bhutto's government were in exile in London. I took them to lunch in expensive restaurants, and watched them tear bread rolls and pick each other to pieces. I was charmed by their brightness and bitterness, and slightly shocked by their mutual hostility. It hadn't occurred to me that an opposition might grow to hate itself more than the government. I mentioned this to Mumtaz Bhutto, a cousin of the dead Zulfikar's, and a former chief minister of Sind. He smiled a fat, V-shaped smile. 'Our biggest mistake,' he said, 'was to build a presidential palace in Islamabad. Now we all want to live in it.' I admired the skill of satisfying journalists by giving them fragments worth quoting while neither endangering yourself nor helping them understand what is going on. I stored the quip for subsequent use.

When I arrived, Mumtaz's wife Mariam took me round. It was her job – she was holding the political fort while her husband was in exile – but that made me no less grateful. I watched her friends exchange small bits of political news amongst pink silk and Moghul miniatures and began to get a feel for the fragmentation and regrowth of political groups. A cool young man with an American degree was assigned to introduce me to angry trade unionists who explained to me how it was impossible to be a trade unionist and to Sindhi nationalists who showed me the marks from their lashes in jail.

In Lahore, a slower, more thoughtful city, it was all explained to me. Karachi, centre of trade and industry, minds its own business, but Lahore's part-time and full-time intellectuals develop theories about other people's. A friend of a friend came to my hotel. We sat in one of those uncomfortable little alcoves they design for your comfort in the rooms of expensive hotels, ate the packets of pistachios from the fridge and drank the whisky that nobody had stopped me bringing through customs while he explained Pakistan to me. By the end of the bottle I had that flash of exhilaration that comes from the realisation that you understand everything. It had gone by the morning, but I was in love with the place.

Pakistan is a forty-two-year-old country of about 100 million people between Iran, Afghanistan, China and India, with a coastline that stretches from just east of the Strait of Hormuz, the mouth of the Gulf, to India. It has a gross domestic product per head of $350, which puts it between Haiti and Lesotho, and $60 above India. It exports cotton, heroin, labour and a favourable geopolitical attitude to the West, which do not quite pay for its imports of consumer goods and machinery. It has four provinces, Punjab, Sind, the North West Frontier Province and Baluchistan, as well as some Tribal Areas (only partially under the control of central government), the Northern Areas (ex-princely states) and Azad (Free) Kashmir, from which Pakistani soldiers shoot at Indian soldiers in Occupied Kashmir.

No Briton is quite free of the romance of the Raj. Although India has acquired a monopoly on imperial nostalgia, at the time it was the area that is now Pakistan which stirred the British imagination and won their respect. Kipling represented a Raj prejudice, not just in favour of the pugnacious Muslims against the educated Hindu traders and lawyers, but also for the hills and mountains of the north against the endless, dry plains of central India and the soggy luxuriance of the south. His patch ran from Lahore, home of the Zam-zammah gun that Kim plays on as the story starts, and centre of the shady dealings that drive the book's plot, to the northern borders where lonely, embattled political agents in his stories made war and friendships amongst the Pathan tribes. Real-life civil servants considered it a privilege to get one of those jobs – to be allowed to leave your wife and family and risk your life in the remotest, most dangerous part of the Empire.

Kipling's admiration for the area is partly to do with the effect of hardship, danger and responsibility on the green young men who either grew up fast or died. But the root of his passion, it seems to me, is sensual. He loved the rich texture of the place, overloaded with smells and colours and small dark mysteries glimpsed in veiled windows: India was a rich fruit-cake heavy with spices, to England's bland Victoria sponge.

4

The country is hot, bright and intensely varied. I carry a mental album of images that give me pleasure. On Manora Island, Pakistan's Brighton, the beach-donkeys are camels, labouring up and down the beach with their peculiar loping grace and permanent weary smiles, carrying whole families on their bright saddle-cloths embroidered with bells and bits of mirror. The water is pale turquoise, breaking into white near the shore. Further out, rocks and seaweed are mapped in dark blue. The beach stretches away, turning as white as the waves with distance and disappearing round a corner a couple of miles on.

Arid Baluchistan has oases with date palms to the south and orchards around Quetta where the cold sweetens the apples and apricots and hardens the nuts. But those are blobs of relief in a range of colours that varies from grey to sharp pale yellow to ochre to brown, flattened into desert or creased up into folds and ridges of chiselled mountains. In fertile Punjab there is a rich softness to the landscape that is best at evening when the sky has gone pale, the tractors have ground their way home down the straight tarmac roads, and smoke from the villages rests, in perfectly horizontal strands, over the cotton, the sugar-cane and the maize. Going north, hills harden into yellow mountains. Swat valley, its slopes striped with terraces of luminous rice and persimmon trees, is their soft centre. At the top of the northern areas, on the Chinese border, is the climax of Pakistan: K2, the second highest mountain in the world, a neat black and white marbled pyramid, dusted with thin cloud, set against the eye-wrinkling brightness of the blue.

History is central to the richness. In the interior of Sind, you drive past neglected tombs left by the Arab invaders in the eleventh century. The Hindu temples are mostly – nervously – tended. In Lahore, the Sikhs' second holiest city after Amritsar, a gold-roofed Sikh shrine stands beside the Emperor's mosque, whose three white marble domes are silk against the rough tweed of its red sandstone courtyard. Across a tree-bordered lawn from it is the fort, sandstone again, with green parrots streaking among the gardens and marble rooms and courtyards laid out on top of it. Lahore has looked after its Moghul wonders well; more surprisingly, the white neo-classical grandeur of the best the British built has been glisteningly restored.

The buildings are old, but the country is new. Pakistan, like Israel, was an idea, born in the mind of an eccentric student at Cambridge, and taken up by a cold legal genius whose brilliant oratory turned the fear and confusion among the Indian Muslims into a demand for land, and founded a country. That, to me, is its initial oddness. Where I come from, companies, social clubs, intellectual movements are founded; countries are the accidental results of rivers, seas, mountains and the squabbles of forgotten kings. Like families, nobody asks for them; they're just there – to be loved or ignored, defended or betrayed.

Pakistan's strange origins have given it a tendency to national self-analysis which initially attracted me to the place. A country based on an idea has an ideal, however confused that may be; at least, different people in it will have some sort of ideal that the place is supposed to be living up to. I have no ideal vision of Britain, so the country does not disappoint me; but too many of the Pakistanis I talked to seemed disappointed. It was not just disappointment that they were not as rich as they should be or that their children were finding it difficult to get jobs; it was a wider sense of betrayal, of having been cheated on a grand scale. The Army blamed the politicians, the politicians the Army; the businessmen blamed the civil servants, the civil servants the politicians; everybody blamed the landlords and the foreigners, and the left and the religious fundamentalists blamed everybody except the masses.

More than anywhere I have been – much more than India – its people worry about the state of their country. They wonder what went wrong; they fear for the future. They condemn it; they pray for it. They are involved in the nation's public life as passionately as in their small private dilemmas. I did a small experiment with an English friend who does not believe that politics matters much to people. A chatty hotel waiter sat down with us to share a bottle of local whisky. My friend asked him questions about his family; I, about the dead president. I won hands down. My friend got monosyllabic answers, and I got florid, threatening images of the vengeance which mistreated children wreak on a dictatorial father. To a political journalist, a politicised country is thrilling. You begin to believe that what you are writing about matters not just to a small coterie of heavy-lunching politicians and journalists but to everybody who lives there.

If the rest of the world didn't care, that would begin to be depressing. But Pakistan gets headlines because it is at the centre of some of the world's biggest uncertainties, involved in them as an actor and a potential victim. To the west there is the Gulf, whose underpopulated countries Pakistan supplies with workers and soldiers. You can see the scale of the labour trade at Karachi airport any day: queues of men who look too poor to be in an airport, punctuated by neat accountants with their briefcases and plaid suitcases. The soldiers and pilots you do not see; but they have provided the bulk of Saudi Arabia's trained military manpower. Rumour has it that there are thirty airstrips on Pakistan's south-western coast, ready for use by an American rapid deployment force in defence of the Gulf, and that the port at Pasni is being developed as a base for nuclear submarines. The Pakistani government and the Americans wearily deny it, saying that the airstrips do not exist, and the harbour has had its jetty repaired to help Baluch fishermen offload their catches.

The invasion of Afghanistan changed everything for Pakistan. It brought around three million refugees, and sudden, large, quantities of aid from the West. It brought generals and prime ministers and foreign ministers and droves of members of parliaments to the Khyber Pass, where they could gesture conveniently at commu-nism, and make commitments to freedom, of which Pakistan, despite being under martial law, had become a bulwark. It brought Swiss doctors and French nurses and Australian surgeons and American agriculturalists to Peshawar, the grubby capital of the North West Frontier Province, where they bought carpets and started clubs and put up the price of property and employed people. It also brought bombs, planted by Afghan agents, to the bazaars and the airline offices, and worries about future instability. The Russian withdrawal has heightened, not allayed those fears: at least the guerrilla war against the Afghan and Soviet troops was a known quantity. When the Russians started to pull out, Pakistan began to buzz with fears — that Afghanistan would get a fundamentalist government that would bring a similar revolution to Pakistan, that the Pathans would once more start demanding their own home-land and slice up both Afghanistan and Pakistan, that an Afghan civil war would be fought inside Pakistan.

Iran's unstable politics — rival theocrats jockeying for the succes-sion, anti-government guerilla groups — mean more Pakistani uncertainty. An Indian financier, the sort of man you listen to because he has his ear to the world's bank accounts, questioned me about Pakistan and listened sceptically to my answers. 'Of course,' he said picking a piece of cork out of his glass, 'there will be terrible blood-letting in Iran within a couple of years, and that will determine Pakistan's future.' I wanted to know why this was self-evident; but he went to find a clean glass and another conversation.

Pakistanis are, by and large, more nervous of India, the local giant, than of Russia. Nobody has forgotten that Pakistan was created against the wishes of the Congress party that usually runs India. There have been three wars, now; and in the course of the last one, in 1971, India helped break the original state of Pakistan into two, creating Bangladesh. Most Pakistanis believe they would like to do it again, by helping separatists in Sind, or in Baluchistan or the North West Frontier in partnership with Russia. Wherever they see a crack, people say they'll try to prise the country apart.

The risk posed by these regional unknowns is incalculably greater if Pakistan has the bomb. It has a uranium enrichment plant at Kahuta, twenty miles south-east of Islamabad; but the government says that uranium is not enriched beyond five per cent of the fissile isotope, uranium-235, the level needed for civil reactors. Foreign doubts about the truth of this claim have been heightened both by the arrests in America and Canada of Pakistanis buying pieces of equipment specific to nuclear weapons, and by an interview given by the chief scientist at Kahuta, Dr Abdul Qadeer, to an Indian journalist. Dr Qadeer said that Pakistan had already developed a bomb, and subsequently denied it. Whatever the truth is, any Pakistani government which signed the nuclear non-proliferation treaty would have a short life. Everybody, except for a few intellectuals whose disapproval of bombs balances their fear of India's nuclear capability, wants the bomb.

Internal uncertainties complement the external ones: the more unstable a country is, the easier it is for outsiders to destabilise it. Compared to Pakistan, India, where I lived for a year and a half, has got its domestic affairs settled. It has its Sikhs, Gurkhas and a whole vocabulary of separatist movements demanding their own countries, its communists who march on Delhi, its daily skirmishes between Hindus and Muslims, but the basic question of how the country should be run seems to have been resolved. Perhaps India's democracy will not survive; but, for the moment, people are reasonably secure in it. The matter does not occupy many minds, so there is more intellectual room to worry about smaller, duller things like child labour, canals and corruption scandals.

Nothing is settled in Pakistan. The country has spent twenty-four years out of forty-one under martial law or a state of emergency. It has had three national parliamentary elections, one of them under martial law. Only two prime ministers, Zulfikar Ali Bhutto and his daughter Benazir, have come to power as a result of a process which anybody in the West would recognise as a democratic election.

It may be that the country will now settle down to a comfortable, dull sort of political life, where governments change through elections and people stop caring and voting. It may be that the place will end up balancing between martial law and anarchy, and people will lock their brains away in despair and stop thinking about it. It may be that the country will split into pieces, in which case there will be no Pakistan to worry about.

Because the plot has yet to be resolved, the audience stays interested. Every small event may hold the key to the denouement. Political or economic snippets are dissected, analysed into their constituent parts, fed into the various equations and their results mulled over. If one of the generals was heard to express private disapproval of General Zia's policy of Islamising the legal system it might have meant that the Army brass was lining up against him and plotting another coup. If the prime minister got bypassed by a visiting American general it might have been that the Americans had suggested to the president that he should change political horses because the prime minister had been insufficiently enthusiastic about supporting the Afghan mujaheddin. These sorts of calculations go on around any polity; but the strange thing about Pakistan is that everybody does it. Because political change is not just a shuffling of names at the top, because it happens through strikes, arrests, violence, people mind about it.

To say 'nothing' is settled, and then to talk about martial law and democracy, is to imply that the business of representation and the transfer of power is everything. I anticipate the objections: this is an occidocentric view, which ignores the fact that governments and changes in government have little effect on most people. So I qualify: it's not everything, but it is basic to the way a country works, and a lot of people seem to mind about it.

Who gets power and how isn't just a matter of placating greedy élites, nor of fine theories imbibed by the children of the upper classes at British universities. It makes a difference not just to the sort of governments that run a country, but also to how life is lived. It is to do with avoiding strikes, riots and people getting shot on the streets. Those things, and the possibility of those things, send money abroad, close shops, and leave people with a fear of the future that does things to them not easily measurable on economic indices.

9

Just after a riot in Karachi, I drove round one of the areas on the fringes of the violence. The shops were closed, there were a few cars and some bits of glass on the streets, and small groups of people on the pavements, mostly silent, waiting for something. I asked the taxi-driver what they were expecting. Nothing, he said. They were, it seemed, in shock: unable to believe what had just happened, and yet, for the moment, unable to believe that it wasn't going to go on.

But those people, and the crowds at Zia's funeral, are usually victims rather than actors; and journalists are mostly interested in actors. That is why I have written this book as I have. It is about the powerful people in the country – the people who have determined what it's like, and who will continue to have a big say in what the country becomes. I have divided people into classes not because I have a particularly Marxist view of the country's past and future, but because land, or tribal clout, or religious influence, are the common political link between otherwise dissimilar individuals. Those are the things which determine the say that those people have in national life.

The first part is a couple of essays on what makes Pakistan, to my foreign eye, peculiar and interesting. The third chapter is a quick history which I think useful, but, because I wasn't there, out of kilter with the rest of the book. The second part is something like a map of power in the country; but the analogy does not quite fit. The place is changing too fast. Families who used to run things four centuries and even twenty years ago have watched martial law and money erode their influence. People whose parents sat in cupboard-sized shops now have big parts in the national drama. The boundaries are shifting, and the rivers changing their course.

Those changes mean clashes – between new and old, between guns and institutions, between money and authority. They force the visitor to wonder who is running the country. That isn't a question which has a clear answer; but I've tried to give an idea of which way I think things are going.

I've written the book through individuals mostly because illustrations are better copy than generalisations. But I've also done it that way because I enjoy the place because I enjoy the people. Most of my eight months in Pakistan have been spent listening to people talk about themselves and their country and trying to fit these disparate individuals into general propositions. I'm still not bored with it.

Part One

1

FOREIGNNESS

SITTING IN A garden on a winter morning, drinking milky coffee and shading my eyes from the bright sun, I mentioned to the man I was talking to, one of the central figures in the country in the past couple of decades, that I found Pakistan a hypocritical place. I said it partly as a provocation, but he, to my surprise, agreed with me, and had a theory to explain it. I might not like his theory, he said, but I should be patient while he explained it.

There are two sorts of nations, he said – those rooted in the soil, and those rooted in ideas. India belongs to the first category: it has grown gradually out of the things that have happened to a particular bit of earth. When Nehru died, he asked for his ashes to be scattered over his native soil. Pakistan, on the other hand, was created by the descendants of people who thundered into the area from Tashkent, Afghanistan, Iran, Saudi Arabia, with a sword in one hand, the Koran in the other, and an idea in their heads – an idea of conquest, expansion or conversion.

India's Muslims have always been susceptible to ideas. The Khilafat movement which brought Indian Muslims out on to the streets in revolt against the British in the 1920s was the result of the defeat of Turkey in the First World War, and the harsh terms imposed by Christian victors on the Muslim loser. It wasn't anything to do with Indians, yet the idea of the defence of the Umma (the international Muslim community) shook the subcontinent.

At partition, the Muslims came from India to Pakistan in search of an idea of a homeland. The people who lived in Pakistan were not stirred by the cry: local grandees had mostly either supported the British or allied themselves with the Congress party. Still, the locals were quite happy to get rid of the Hindus, because they could

13

wipe out their debts to the money-lenders and get hold of abandoned property. When Pakistan was almost a reality, they voiced
their support. 'It was a piggy-back ride,' said the theorist; 'though
you mustn't ever say so in this country.'

The fanfare of idealism that brought the new country into being
didn't change the nature of the place selected to make it a reality.
Islamic morality and egalitarianism were laid over a tribal society
with normal rural sexual and alcoholic habits and a rigid hierarchy
of power. The old world persisted, paying lip service to the new.

'And this,' said the theorist, 'created a fundamental hypocrisy, or
maybe an ability to kid ourselves, in Pakistan. Look at the way the
country was set up. The idea of Islam was so strong that it seemed
to us perfectly reasonable to have a country where the decision to
build a culvert in Dhaka was made 2,000 miles away, across the
width of India. The absurdity of it! Then, in 1971, after the war,
Pakistan ceased to exist. East Pakistan became Bangladesh, and
West Pakistan . . . called itself Pakistan. We never talk about it. We
pretend it didn't happen. We're masters at pretending that things
aren't happening.'

I liked his idea, but I wanted to throw in some more confusion.
The British left their mark, too, in all sorts of areas of life, from the
legal and administrative systems and the language to the chicken
cutlets and the Scotch. The country's official language is still
English, the upper classes speak to each other in a confusing patois
that slides between the two. London, not New York, is still the
second home of the rich Pakistanis, and they are only now
beginning to shift their children to American universities, as the
British ones get too expensive.

Most important, the measures of how a country should be run
come from Britain. There is still a lot of respect for their incorrupti-
bility, for the railways and roads they built, and for the depth of the
research they did into the languages and customs of a people
strange to them. The legal system is British, and barristers win cases
by drawing on centuries-old British precedents. Parliamentary
procedures are – when there is a parliament – basically British.
Political debate centres around the degree to which Pakistanis will
be allowed British (or, more generally, western) political freedoms.

The force of British ideas has its own contradictions: British
writing taught the youth of the colonies a theory of politics which
the rulers did not practise. Freedom of speech is central to the idea;
yet during the 1857 mutiny, Mr Roberts, Commissioner of Lahore,

wrote that 'with the exception of . . . the summary execution of a Meerut butcher who . . . made a very dubious and threatening speech to the Bazaar Sergeant, nothing of moment occurred.' British governments played on tribal and religious divisions as ruthlessly as any subsequent set of rulers. Yet in the minds of many, time has whitened the behaviour of the British, and the hold of their intellectual tradition remains strong.

The contradictions, the confusions, the hypocrisies seem to me to stem from the same root that makes Pakistan such an interesting place to observe. It has three sets of history, and three sets of standards. It has the baggage of ideas that go with Pakistan, Urdu and Islam; it has the British package; it has the ancient local base of Punjabi, Sindhi, Baluch and Pathan culture. The different layers fit badly together; and when they contradict each other, people start telling lies to others and to themselves. That comes out in the gap between sexual morality and behaviour; when governments stick to the letter of the law and abuse its spirit; when civil servants take bribes and decry the country's immorality.

For a foreigner, the place can seem shockingly deceptive. It welcomes the visitor with familiar ways, then shows an alien face to shatter the sense of easy intimacy. It presents itself neatly on paper, but a glimpse of the divergence between the official and unofficial versions of the country invalidates the explanation. It draws the journalist into attractive generalisations and intellectually pleasing pattern-making, then contradicts itself and destroys the thesis.

There are three stages of acquaintance with the place. At first it is wholly mysterious. The visitor wanders through the narrow alleys of bazaars, his senses confused by the strangeness and excess of everything. There is too much noise, and a greater variety of it than in developed-country cities: motor bikes, rickshaws with their silencers removed, horse-drawn tongas, people shouting louder than they do in the West. The foreign nose, which has inured itself to the strong smells of spices and sweets, is suddenly assaulted by the odour from a row of old sheep heads staring out of a butcher's shop. There is more colour everywhere, partly because warmth opens doors and brings life on to the streets, and partly because Pakistanis like their clothes, their buckets and their lorries bright. A couple of hours of all this drives the newly-arrived foreigner, dazed with the heat and the oddness of it all, back to his hermetically-sealed room in the Lahore Hilton where they swear they boil the water.

The foreigner with a few contacts then embarks on the next stage.

A telephone call to a friend of a friend usually produces a dinner invitation that night, where in London it might yield an offer of drinks a week next Thursday. The dinner is at a house in one of the more central suburbs – the subcontinental equivalents of Hampstead or Kensington – furnished as the house of a much-travelled Londoner might be. There are four or five good Persian carpets, curious carved wooden antique chairs, some delicate geometrical Baluch embroidered shirt-fronts used as cushion-covers, and maybe some Koranic calligraphy framed on the wall next to the antique water-colours of the Punjabi landscape.

There is quite a lot of whisky to drink, or gin and lime – no tonic – and bowls of peanuts or spiced dried lentils. There are a couple of businessmen there with their wives – one of whom teaches in the girl's college in the university – a politician who is a nearby landowner, and a couple who are both civil servants. The civil servants were both at Cambridge, and the other men at American universities of varying qualities. The language is English, with occasional anecdotes and bits of reported speech in Urdu; the films, plays and books are all British, American or European. The humour and the conversations are familiar; the manners better. The edge of snobbery in the social gossip is slightly sharper than in London. The political gossip is odd only in that there is so much of it, and most of the guests seem to be related to some of the protagonists. The foreigner returns to his hotel-room a little unsteadily, with a couple more invitations and a comforting sense of finding himself amongst fellows.

The third stage is the most uncomfortable. The visitor discovers that the politician, a sensible man with an economics degree and a vision about the development of his constituency, was elected mostly because he is a living saint. The businessman who was talking about the profitability of his ultra-modern textile mill is said to be one of the country's main heroin traders who is allowed to carry on his operations because he is in partnership with a general. Two bottles of the civil servant's whisky – at 1,000 rupees each – were drunk, his marble floor is covered in silk carpets and his son is at university in America, yet his official salary is 9,000 rupees (£300) a month. His wife, with whom the visitor had a fascinating conversation about tradition and superstition and its oppressive effect on the women of Pakistan, has refused to allow her daughter to marry a boy who is not a Sayyed, a direct descendant of the prophet. The man who proclaimed himself an atheist and despised

16

the government's fundamentalism beats himself in the Shia processions at Muharram. The visitor then feels duped: why do they pretend to be in twentieth-century Europe when they're in seventh-century Asia? How can educated people justify benefiting from superstition and ignorance? Why do they complain about the state of their government and their laws when they're profiting from the anarchy? Why do they criticise the Army's power when they're working with the soldiers? He may choose to take the next plane out, or he may stay to watch how the people live and try to unravel the contradictions and the inconsistencies.

Women provide the oddest contradictions. You see few enough on the streets. Many of those are shrouded from head to foot; the more modern and the poorest show their faces. A horrified American in Peshawar said to me that the way the South Africans treated blacks had nothing on the way the Pakistanis treated their women. Many Pakistanis are disgusted, publicly as well as privately: a supreme court judge, for instance, published a long article in the *Nation* in 1988 (before Zia's death) on 'Crimes against women in Pakistan', discussing not only common practices like cutting off the noses of women suspected of adultery, but also the new Islamic laws brought in by Zia which he considered both discriminatory and open to abuse. 'It is said', he began, 'that most law suits are caused by women, money and land in Pakistan. This reduces the position of a woman to chattel and makes her a symbol of respectability and social status like money and land. These are the characteristics of a retrogressive, feudalistic, male-dominated society.' His article ends up on Islam, as such discussions so often do: pious Pakistanis worry how it can be that a religion which is supposed to promote good for both sexes is abused and twisted to oppress one.

Yet the self-assurance of so many women I met – mostly rich ones, I grant you – suggested something far removed from oppression. At dinners, I felt like a clumsy adolescent who has not yet learnt how to dress or behave. Those women had an immediate, direct friendliness that did not suggest familiarity, but was merely what was due to a guest. There were none of the gestures or tones of voice that imply confidences to be shared, which western women use as a way of establishing friendships; but then there was no coldness either. They just had very good manners, and an economy of movement that seemed to be what is called grace.

The perfection of their clothes and make-up seemed to support my prejudice that they would be indolent and ignorant because Islam would limit their educational and professional ambitions. I had forgotten that, in a country of servants, you can tell little about the occupation of the middle and upper classes from the state of their clothes. When the maid leaves the silks cleaned, ironed and shimmeringly ready, half an hour at the make-up tray can turn a businesswoman into a sleek socialite.

The women at those parties turned out to be more intellectually confident, as well as far better groomed, than their London counterparts. The evenings never took the shape of London dinners where, during the main course the twosome and threesome conversations drift to a close, and the men are, one by one, pulled into a general, forearms-on-the-table conversation while the women sit back. These women stayed, out of habit but not effortlessly, in the front of the conversation, and won their points with an economy of voice that paralleled their movements.

A decade of Islamisation has not halted the rush of women into the workplace. I went to a women's advice centre, and the women running it said that many more were working in 1988 than in 1978. They were even becoming secretaries, a job that has been a male bastion since the British days partly because of the intimacy it involves with the boss. Of course, they said, women in the countryside had always done agricultural work. In the towns, the lower middle classes tended to be most conservative about their women – they were those poor black burqa-shrouded ghosts I saw around the bazaar streets – but they are beginning to work too, although some of them just did piecework sewing at home. Almost all daughters of the upper middle and upper classes – graduates and plain matriculates – were working, the bulk of them as teachers. The newest vogue was for women to set up their own businesses: the advice centre was plagued by aspiring entrepreneuses wanting help. The only women who would certainly not work, said the upper-middle-class graduate at the centre with some malice, were the wives of newly rich businessmen. They took up charities and committees, the poor and the arts, and were constantly occupied without soiling their hands with labour.

Working women have problems, of course. A woman without her own transport, for instance, sometimes finds it difficult to get to work. Buses are reluctant to stop for a single woman because the conductors worry that, since it isn't done for a man to sit next to a strange woman, the seat beside her might remain unoccupied and the bus thus lose a fare. The advice centre was doing a study of employers' unwillingness to take on women. Some said they didn't know how to talk to them: they couldn't be as rude to female employees as they were to their male ones or to their wives, but they didn't want to be polite to them because it would sound like deference. Some said that female receptionists attracted too many people who weren't serious customers. Still, to the horror of the fundamentalist lobby, women have made it to the workplace, and there are women in offices so brazen that they do not even cover their heads.

Qualified women have an advantage not just in the job market but also in the marriage market. 'There's a big premium on the cow with a certificate round her neck,' said a graduate. She told me that a boy in love with a BA would probably abandon her if his parents found an acceptable MA – but only if he were an MA or better. A boy would want a girl to have educational qualifications on a par with his or slightly lower, but not higher.

Arranged marriages are still the norm, amongst rich and poor. Only in a very thin slice of rich, westernised Karachi are love marriages frequent. The first cousin is usually the parent's choice. Having noticed a surprising incidence of what looked to me like subnormal people amongst those I met, I asked a woman from a landed family whether she thought the practice was messing up their genes. She said that, odd though it might seem, while she was pretty sure it was affecting the upper classes, the peasants seemed unharmed. Her wet-nurse's parents were first cousins; the nurse married a first cousin whose parents were first cousins; all their children had married first cousins, and the grandchildren were all perfectly intelligent and healthy. Clean air and good country food, she concluded.

I found the acceptance of arranged marriage hard to reconcile with the strong smell of romanticism and sensuality about the country, and the mournful Urdu love poetry and the Punjabi folk-tales of passionate fornication ending either in blissful union or in murder; but perhaps the contradiction heightens the intensity of the romance. A girl told me that it was compulsory to be in love at school: she had carried with her, and swooned over, a photograph of a friend of her brother's to whom she had spoken once. The most admired girls were those who were married to somebody of their parent's choice while harbouring a secret passion for another.

Arranged marriages seem to work, on their terms, better than our romantic ones do. Nobody expects much from them: the best a girl can hope for is friendship and support, and if the marriage is merely a sharing of a house, money, and children, then she will not be disappointed. But these days, amongst the rich, things are not so clear. There are good love marriages, and they lead others to aspire to wedded fulfilment. In the course of a few visits, I watched a young man trying to get married. His parents were happy to arrange something for him, but he wanted a bit of romance in it. He found a girl he liked, and tried to date her. They met a couple of times to play squash, but her parents were wary, and stopped her going out alone. He lost interest, and agreed to an arranged marriage. His parents found him another girl, a fairly westernised teacher, and he married her. After a while she became discontented: he was providing no romance, and was allowing her less independence than she had expected. Soon there was talk of divorce.

But despite creeping westernisation, marriage in Pakistan remains a duty, not a pleasure; and if it goes wrong, the misery is not personal property, but belongs to the couple's family and friends as well. Many of the rich still live in large houses with a selection of cousins and in-laws – not because they cannot afford more houses, but because they prefer it. Marital rows are team efforts with referees and spectators, partly because people are always in each other's rooms and houses, and partly because Pakistanis mind each other's business more than we do in atomised Britain. At first I thought that the sudden crowds of fifty or a hundred people you see in the streets were small political demonstrations, and then discovered that they were just car accidents. Everybody stops to check out what's going on, the way the cousins wander in to take sides in the family row.

Compulsory involvement in other people's affairs seemed to me tedious. People have to go to the weddings of distant relations and slight acquaintances. 'Condoling' is an important word in the social vocabulary. If somebody dies, their close relations stay at home for anything up to forty days while people come to condole. Every day there are newspaper snippets, something like *The Times* Court Circular, of politicians condoling somebody's death. A Pathan, the day after the festival of Eid, was complaining of exhaustion. I asked what he was doing all day. 'Receiving congratulations,' he said. 'Some people come, they give you congratulations, you give them congratulations, then some more people come.' Nobody enjoys the formalised sitting around, yet offence is taken if a relation fails to perform his social duty.

But to a self-centred westerner, the family support system is impressive. I was with a couple late at night; we were hungry, and going out to a restaurant, when the wife remembered that she had heard that her aunt was not feeling well that day. She asked to be dropped at the aunt's house, although she would get no food there, so she could sit with the old lady for a bit. It wasn't a sacrifice, it was just the ordinary thing to do. Their deference to their parents amazes me. I sat with a heavy-drinking politician and his father. The father offered his son some of the beer he was pouring for me, but the son refused: he had never, he explained to me, drunk or smoked in front of his father.

I have no defence in the face of their criticism of our treatment of the old; and I suspect that much of the generalised disapproval of western morality is a fear of losing the sense of family duty. People will tell you it's gone — their children, they say, criticise them without fear, whereas they used to tremble before their fathers — and they may be right that it's going, but the remains of their respect for seniors and concern for relations still put westerners to shame.

The religious fundamentalists' main specific grounds for opposition to the West is our sexual licentiousness. The extremity of their fear of illicit sex is measured by the punishment for it — death by stoning — yet there is a thick atmosphere of latent sex. There is sex in men's eyes as they follow women — locals as much as foreigners — down the street and in the *doubles entendres* of their conversation. Men try to turn apparently innocuous professional encounters into sexual ones: this unsuspecting foreigner found herself propositioned a number of times by people she was interviewing on cold political topics. It feels like a paradox that in a country so concerned with holding back the tides of lust, sex should hang so heavily in the air; but I suppose the second follows from the first and reinforces it.

I had to admire some people's ploys. An opposition politician who was 'underground' came at night to a house where I was staying. He left in the early hours. Half an hour later, as I was undressing, the door of the ground-floor room I was sleeping in burst open. It was the politician, ashen-faced and panting. The police had surrounded the house he was staying in, he said, and he needed sanctuary. Hastily covering myself, I said I would wake my

21

hosts. No, no: he didn't want me to bother them. He made it clear that he would find it comforting to get into bed with me; so I said he could sleep on the sofa or leave, which he did with a tragic flourish. My host discovered the next day that the police had never come.

It can be embarrassing instead of funny. A top dog – known to have a long-term girlfriend as well as a wife – took me to dinner, loaded his conversation with *doubles entendres*, and afterwards in the car clutched for my knee and my hand. I said I would rather he didn't; he apologised and stopped. Later I said carelessly to somebody who asked my opinion of him that he was a flirt. This got back to him, and his face was stiff with anger when we next met. Never, he said, had his reputation been so damaged – and so unjustly.

I found the juxtaposition of protectiveness and rapaciousness shocking. Given a sleeper compartment all to myself on the train from Peshawar to Lahore, I rejoiced at being in a country that looked after single women. Waking up to a torch-beam directed at my legs through the hole where the door-handle was supposed to be, I spat mentally on Pakistani manhood.

Mostly, I just felt sorry for them. A young accountant I met, a deeply religious young man troubled by his own failings, defended the conservatism of his society until I mentioned the matter of sexual frustration. That, he said, was a very big problem. He was twenty-nine, and not yet earning enough for a decent girl to want to marry him. It might be five years before he was acceptable marriage-meat. What was he to do? He used to go to Liberty market, the smart shopping area of Lahore, to watch the women there; but he was always bumping into friends of his mother's.

Perhaps the accountant's guilt kept him pure; but in the country-side, amongst people less affected than townies by the ideology of Islam, there seems to be a great deal of sex going on. A Pakistani who had recently returned to the country from Britain told me with relish the ongoing saga of his servants. They had got a girl from a friend's village to cook for them, and had left town for a while. On their return, they discovered from the gardener's enraged wife that the girl was conducting an affair with the gardener in the study, and with the watchman from next door in the living room. Fearing murder or pregnancy, they sent her back. The next girl, a thirteen-year-old, was told to sleep beside the gardener's wife. The first night she was there, the gardener's wife woke them to say that the girl had disappeared. She was found in

22

the gardener's brother's bed. They asked her why she was there, and she said she was feeling horny. The gardener thrashed his brother, and took up with the girl himself. They sacked her too, and were looking for a cook with a low sex drive.

I tried to persuade adherents to strict Islamic morality that, in order to reduce sexual thought and activity, licence was the answer. People in London, I told them with conviction, were much less obsessed with sex than people in Pakistan. But, reading an interview in the *Herald* with a renowned TV-mullah and controversial conservative, Dr Israr, I thought perhaps I had missed the point. The interviewer asked him why he was so keen that women should be locked up. He replied, 'Freud says sex is a very potent factor. Women hold an attraction for men. Their presence before men will only decrease that attraction. What I want is that this attraction should increase . . . In the present situation, men have become used to women. They are attracted to women only in extraordinary circumstances, not generally.' Purdah, therefore, was intended not to reduce the danger which sexual licence posed to society and the family, but rouse the lust of limp men. It certainly works.

Alcohol is the other main symptom of corruption that the fundamentalists blame on the West. The Koran fairly clearly bans the stuff – although some whisky-loving scholars try to exempt the grain by arguing that the book speaks only of sharab, which generally translates as wine and which, in the prophet's day, was certainly made only from grapes. The lawmakers, however, have been unsympathetic, and any Muslim caught drinking grape, grain or any other sort of hooch is liable to eighty lashes' punishment.

Drinkers are, therefore, reasonably careful: I have only rarely drunk with people in restaurants, and always with the bottle in a plastic bag, under the table. But the law is not enforced against private citizens drinking at home. On the rare occasions when somebody is done for possessing drink, there is a political motive behind the harassment.

Alcohol is freely available. Vodka, whisky, gin, rum and beer are legally brewed locally by a Parsee, a former minister for religious minorities. Non-Muslim locals and foreigners can buy it with a permit, on which they have to declare their religion. The number of units granted to an individual depends partly on his income, on the grounds that a poor man given the maximum six bottles of spirits or ninety-six bottles of beer a month will sell it; but the premium on local spirits – which sell officially for around 600 rupees a bottle – is

23

not that profitable since better-quality imported stuff is always available.

With the smuggling premium the price differential between higher and lower quality imported whisky is less significant, and since the host who served Red Label might appear mean or impoverished, Black Label is favoured. In Karachi, it costs around 1,000 rupees (£30) a bottle. Although Scotch is the commonest drink, English gin, French and Italian wines and Russian champagne are available. The cheapest thing around is Russian vodka, which retails from 120 to 800 rupees, depending on how far you are from the Afghan border.

I have drunk gin in gardens under canopies, by swimming pools and bonfires; Scotch in a general's drawing room; wine on businessmen's soft sofas; vodka on a tribesman's carpet. After a while, I was as surprised as I would be in London if I went round to somebody's house in the evening and they didn't offer me a drink. Some people, of course, don't drink; but many of those keep drink for their guests.

A businessman who had disturbed our interview to perform his evening prayers said as he rolled up his carpet, 'Someday when you see me drinking a glass of whisky, you may think I am a bad Muslim. I do not think so. I worship my God, but I like my whisky.'

'There is no moral consensus against it,' said a civil servant at a Karachi party. 'If we thought it was bad we might stop, but we don't think it's bad, so we go on. Look at all these people!' He waved his whisky glass at the bright silks and pale shalwar kamees. 'They're all at it. The volume is large enough for margins to be quite low, so the price is still reasonable.' On the whole it's moderate: one stiff drink for the women, three for the men, who develop a back-slapping cheerfulness by the time dinner arrives. But because smuggling premiums make the import of high-volume, low-alcohol-content drinks uneconomic, prohibition imposes spirits – the most dangerous form of alcohol – in Pakistan.

People who are against alcohol vigorously deny that there is large-scale drinking. Talking to General Zia, I slid it into a question on whether laws against drinking led to national hypocrisy. He told me six times that my presumption or premise was wrong, and denied that restrictions meant hypocrisy. He said that there was some drinking, because 'as long as we are human beings, we should know weaknesses', but distinguished that natural human frailty from 'some people who behave in an unnatural manner, those who drink and they pretend to be as pious as anybody could be'. I can't see how those succumbing to human weaknesses can avoid being hypocrites, since nobody can publicly admit to drinking.

Widespread drinking goes straight back to my theorist's argument on the historical origins of hypocrisy. Alcohol was common and accepted in the place that is now Pakistan before the country was created. The British added whisky and beer to the range of local liquor, and those who wanted to copy the sahibs learnt to drink as well as them. Sobriety as nationalism and virtue is a recent idea.

Language provides a similar illustration of the tension between the country's three histories. Urdu, the national language, was created by the Moguls. Its name comes from a Turkish word for Army, which travelled south into Persian and west into English, becoming the world horde. *Urdu ka zaban* was the language of the Army, a mish-mash of Persian, Arabic, Sanskrit and local languages, which enabled the Moguls' multi-national armies to understand each other, and was adopted as the court language. It spread all over India, and the Urdu spoken in Lahore is the same language as the Hindi spoken in Delhi. The governments are trying to distinguish them – the Pakistanis adopting more Persian and Arabic words, and the Indians more Sanskrit words – but the people still understand each other.

At partition, people in some of Pakistan's cities would have spoken Urdu, but most would have known only Punjabi, Sindhi, Pashtu, Baluch, Brahui or Seraiki. Urdu was spoken more in the Hindu-majority areas of India, because it was a language common to the Muslims that drew on the glorious past when they ruled the subcontinent. The refugees from India brought it with them. Like Islam, it was to unite Pakistan.

The story of the attempts to turn over the educational system to Urdu illustrates the gap between paper and reality, and the power of the upper-class and military lobbies. The campaign has been about as successful as the attempts to change Lahore's road names. Anybody asking for Captain Anwar ul Shaid Road will meet blank faces; if he asks for Montogomery Road, he may have more joy. Nobody has heard of Sir Sultan Mohammed Shah Aga Khan III Road, but anybody will point you to Davis Road. The Mall, Egerton Road, Lawrence Road, Nicholson Road all have heroic Islamic names, but nobody knows them.

In Bhutto's days, when some schools taught in Urdu and some in

English, there was a vague policy to switch to Urdu, but nobody did much about it. In 1978, Zia committed the country to a ten-year switch-over, at the end of which all education would be in Urdu. He also reversed Bhutto's policy of nationalising education, and allowed private schools to blossom.

Whatever the government may want, people want their children to be able to speak English. It isn't useful just as an international business language, or only for children likely to go abroad to university: it is also the language of social and professional advancement. People are taken more seriously if they can speak English. They may be ignorant fools, but they are assumed, until they prove the contrary, to be educated people. So it isn't just the upper classes who want English as a pas-devant-les-domestiques code to distance them from the rest of the country: the lower orders want English to improve themselves. People practise their English on you as you wander around. As I stood peering at a poster of Benazir Bhutto in Lahore's old city, a man came up to me. 'My daughter is Mr Bhutto,' he explained.

After Zia's takeover, private English-medium schools, for the middle classes as well as the rich, sprang up all over the country. The smarter residential areas are spotted with signs for Model School and Cambridge School. Many of the names reflect the days when good education was associated with Christianity: amongst the bigger English-medium schools in Karachi are St Peter's, St George's and St Andrew's. There are English schools in the not-so-rich areas, too. My favourite sign, in Lahore's old city, advertises:

   Dr Sir Iqbal English Nursery School
   Our students ambassadors of the good and manners
   Aim to be grand and respected as name

The pro-English lobby is strengthened by anti-Urdu feeling. People who are determined to preserve their native language against the spread of somebody else's go for English as a preferable lingua franca. The Sindhi separatist movement is pro-English in so far as it is anti-Urdu. Even in Punjab, where there is no political correlative, an intellectual and literary pro-Punjabi, anti-Urdu movement exists.

The small anti-English lobby combines leftists who are against English as a bastion of the upper classes with Islamic fundamentalists who dislike the language because it is connected with the West and therefore carries with it the smell of corruption: Zia sympathised with the second group, and prodded the government towards getting rid of English. The government, manned mostly by civil servants educated in English, has been moving slowly. The army objected to being Urduised, so the cadet schools were exempted. The upper classes objected, so after some confusion their schools – Aitchison, the Karachi Grammar and a handful of institutions patronised by the rich – were exempted. Apart from those, no schools teaching in Urdu were to exist by 1988. Officially, they do not exist. Unofficially, they continue to mushroom.

Despite the attempts to abolish English, it remains the official language. Amazed when I discovered this, I rang the press man at the embassy in London to check. Certainly, he said: after all, he, a Pathan, spoke English better than Urdu. And when were they going to change it? 'Haste means waste. Rome was not built in a day. But the government is doing its best . . .'

Compared to the local languages in Pakistan, Urdu is courtly and polite. I met a man on a plane whose parents had come from Lucknow in India, home of the purest Urdu, and who had a paper-making factory in Punjab. I asked him to insult a business partner who had cheated him, first in Urdu, then in Punjabi. He pondered, and said in Urdu, *'Mujhe tumse ye umid nehi thi'* – I had expected better from you. And in Punjabi? He didn't want to say it. I begged him. Well, he said, he would probably call the man a *harami*, a bastard, and a *bhenchud*, a sister-fucker. He and I argued, during our flight, about religion and the prophet's marital practices; 'Of course,' I said with a smile after the young man had defeated one of my arguments, 'the prophet only really liked his thirteen-year-old wife, didn't he?' 'Ahha,' he said, 'Now you're really speaking Urdu.' I was wrapping a piece of malice in bland words.

Urdu loads speech with deferential forms of address. Like French, it uses plural verbs and pronouns for formal politeness; and *aap* ('you' plural) may be combined with *sahib* or *ji* as a suffix to the person's name, denoting respect. Debasing himself further, the speaker may call the addressee *jenab* (honoured sir), *huzoor* (your reverence – a term for the prophet), or even *huzoor e aqdas* (your exalted reverence). Letters are still more deferential and formal. A lowish employee, writing to the boss, might well start his letter *'Ba khidmat e aqdas, izzat ma'ag, jenab e ali'*: 'I humbly present to your sacred person, the highly honoured . . .' The employee need not know the proper forms. Outside the courts are rows of scribes learned in the art of writing crawling petitions in an almost illegible formal script.

I don't think the forms of deference in Urdu imply any real feeling of inferiority: I think they go straight back to the Mogul court, when the emperors wanted to shroud the brutality and insecurity of political life with a pretence of civilisation. Courtliness and poetry, glossing over the realities of murder, torture and intrigues that kept them in power, gave their rule an aesthetic acceptability. Formal deference and titles with religious connotations were encouraged to mask the emperor's vulnerability to siblings and princelings and to keep the image of the God-king polished. It retains that role today. According to a Punjabi journalist, 'If we impose Urdu, rather than Punjabi, on our household, it is to achieve a level of civilisation.'

The forms of politeness may bear little relation to somebody's feelings or intentions, yet they matter to people. Bhutto was a rude man, and his failure to observe the forms alienated people. One of the people who fought in the separatist war in Baluchistan in the 1970s told me that he was certain it wouldn't have happened if Bhutto had been politer to the Baluch leaders. Zia's manners made a great impression on the country. I was constantly told about the way he stood up when visitors come into the room and pulled their chairs out for them. When they left, he often saw them to their cars, and opened and shut the door for them. His courtesy seemed to be a palliative even to those who opposed his acquisition of power by force: he may have been an absolute ruler who retained his position by the grace of the gun, but at least he behaved as though he depended on the goodwill of the people.

Urdu is not a language well-suited to political discussion. The principal literary form in Urdu is poetry, mostly love lyrics: they are both passionate and so formal that, traditionally, the masculine gender is used for the beloved, because it would be too intimate to refer to her femininity. There is political poetry: at political rallies, a youth will usually take the microphone before the speakers start, and intone something for or against the government. But the genius of the poetry is not rousing or collective. It is individual, introspective stuff, which, according to aficionados, leaves the reader gloomy and lethargic. A poetry buff told me of introducing two mostly English-speaking Pakistani girls to the art. They were quite cheerful at the beginning of the evening's reading; 'by the end, it was like a funeral party.'

The prose is new: it was only about a century ago that people started writing essays and stories in Urdu. It remains formal and eliptical, reliant on metaphor and symbolism. For political journalists under tight censorship, this is a boon. Because readers of Urdu are used to writers working through metaphors and implying, rather than stating, their meaning, it is easier to write between the lines in Urdu than in English. Columnists during Zia's martial law would often refer to General Pinochet, or discuss the performance of historical tyrants, secure in the knowledge that their audience would immediately know who they were talking about.

English is better than Urdu at logical argument. An editor from a newspaper group which publishes both Urdu and English papers told me that they had tried translating leading articles from the Urdu papers for publication in the English ones. They sounded ridiculous, he said. Urdu wins arguments not through logic but by the use of successful metaphors, often religious, that sound intuitively right. An Urdu leader may clinch its point by closing with a couplet. Conversely, the cool, plodding logic of English leaders would not convince an Urdu audience.

Zia himself gave me an enjoyable example of the knots people can get into talking in one language while thinking in another. On the matter of the harshness of Islamic punishments, he said, 'There is nothing much that I can do. My Holy Book says this is the punishment, and there is no logic. Whatever is written in the Book, you can argue it out, but basically two and two make four and you can't make it five.' The English cliché that illustrates immutability is based on mathematical logic, yet he used it to explain the power of a religious dictum which denied the force of logic.

Translation causes particular problems. I was mystified that, when I asked in English if I could have a railway ticket, or a cup of tea, the person I spoke to would often reply 'Why not?' A friend and I puzzled out the reason. In English, the request form is a question: may I have a cup of tea? In Urdu, it is a command: give me (very kindly, sir, your reverence) a cup of tea. To formulate it as a question is to suggest that there are likely to be large and possibly insurmountable obstacles between you and the cup of tea – hence the polite query as to why these might occur.

Much of the political discussion in Pakistan centres round the applicability of western ideas about how to run a state. It is, therefore, necessary that political concepts central to western

29

theory should be translatable into Urdu: if they cannot be spoken about, they cannot be argued over and accepted or rejected.

One of the main battles is about the role of religion in the state; yet Urdu has no word for 'secularism'. The nearest equivalent is '*ladeen*', which means without religion. It is one of the worst things you can say about anybody. A good man is a good Muslim; a bad man is *ladeen*. '*Ladeen*' cannot be used neutrally. A writer told me that people used to use the word 'secularism', written phonetically in Urdu characters, when they wanted to write about the idea; but the religious lobbyists disapproved, and in the past ten years the word has disappeared from the Urdu papers. So nowadays, you cannot write about secularism in Urdu, even though the Islamisation of government and laws is one of the hottest political issues around.

Theoretically, Pakistan's press is fairly free: after the lifting of martial law there was plenty of fairly rude comment about the prime minister and the government, and even criticism of Zia. To a visitor picking up the morning's papers it therefore seems mysterious that the journalism produced by a country with a good supply of talented, well-educated people passionately aware of their country's failings should be so poor. The real stuff of journalism, the reporting on corruption and government abuses, riots and bomb-blasts, heroin-traders and bank defrauders, hardly exists. The news pages are full of reports of chief ministers condoling deaths, announcements of new schemes to benefit the poor, and statements put out by opposition leaders. They are, by and large, boring compilations of press releases.

The weakness goes back to the Raj. Before independence and partition, Hindus, better-educated than Muslims, dominated the newspapers. The Muslims confined their political writing to pamphleteering: they didn't make use of reporting as a tool for exposing a government's failures. Circumstances since then have not encouraged journalists to investigate.

There have been periods of unusual toughness that have wiped the papers clean even of serious comment. In 1978 four journalists were flogged. In 1979 Zia closed two newspapers and imposed pre-censorship: papers had to be sent to the government before they were printed. Editors tried leaving white spaces in place of the articles they were told to cut out, but were banned from doing that. In 1982 pre-censorship was lifted, but Zia made the press's position quite clear: 'I could close down all the newspapers, say, for a period of five years, and nobody would be in a position to raise any voice against it. If they try to organise a meeting or procession, I will send them to jail.' Self-censorship with 'press advice' – phone calls from the ministry of information – was encouraged.

Even in less repressive times, the government can choose from a selection of curbs. There is the Press and Publications Ordinance of 1963, under which the government can ban newspapers which print things that 'tend directly or indirectly to bring into hatred or contempt the government established by law in Pakistan for the administration of justice in Pakistan or any class or section of the citizens of Pakistan or to excite disaffection towards the said government.' The government controls the allocation of newsprint quotas, and, most important, government advertising revenue, which makes up anything from thirty to seventy per cent of a newspaper's income.

The government's task has been relatively easy, because, although some journalists have been brave, the newspapers have not been militant. In 1985 the Council of Pakistan Newspaper Editors agreed to a 'code of ethics' according to which 'the press shall not publish news or comment, photographs or advertisements which may undermine the security or solidarity of the nation and its ideology . . . the press should refrain from involving the defence forces in politics and offer only fair comment on its performance and conduct.'

The acceptance of such a code might seem extraordinarily submissive, but editors have not been left with much self-esteem. Since the newspaper proprietors are pure businessmen – like Khalil ur-Rehman of the huge Jang group – or businessmen with political connections and ambitions – like the Haroon family of the Dawn group – they tend to be fairly careful to ensure that their papers do not step out of line. Owners pay close attention to, and frequently interfere with, the content of their papers. They have become editors-in-chief, reducing their editors to office managers. When editors cease to be professional journalists they give up setting reporting standards and their subordinates' work suffers.

There are plenty of tasty stories which nobody will touch. Popular during one of my visits was the one about a provincial chief minister who had bought a large slice of wasteland and subsequently declared the area a tax-free industrial zone, thus increasing the value of his purchase nearly 100-fold. I asked an editor why he had not covered it. Such matters, he said, touched the proprietors' interests too closely: the provincial governments provided nearly as much advertising revenue as the central government. Besides, 'If I investigate this matter, who's going to protect me? If the police take me, they are not interested in my rights. I am very much in doubt about the independence of the courts. In your country, maybe a member of parliament would defend me in the last resort. But here, the chief minister controls the assembly.'

Good journalism is allowed where it doesn't matter. The Dawn group, whose papers are mostly bland, publishes the *Herald*, an excellent magazine staffed mostly by young women, which does about the only serious investigative social and political reporting in the country. Its circulation is tiny, so the government isn't bothered; and as a quality showpiece, it's worth the risk for the Haroons. But, spending the day in May 1988 when Zia suddenly sacked his government and parliament with one of its journalists, I felt the insecurity of the job. I was full of excitement at the political earthquake, but my companion was quieter. She said that they might drop her long piece on the political violence in Karachi from that month's magazine, which was just about to be printed, and use the fashion story as the cover.

'Nobody knows what's going to happen now. He might do anything to the press.' I told her I'd be in tears if my work was going to be wasted. 'I was upset last night,' she said. 'But it seemed silly when the whole country's at stake.'

Pakistan at first appears to be an extraordinarily open country, a joy to a foreign journalist. People talk to you: officials expound theories, politicians give you interviews. The telephone books are a pleasure in themselves. Under the entries for most businesses and government departments is a list of the names of all the officials, their jobs and their home telephone numbers: even that of the director-general of the Inter-Services Intelligence, the most powerful and secret of the secret services, is offered. Sadly, that seems to be disappearing: the 1988 Karachi book is less liberal with its information. It retains, though, my favourite phone book entry in the world: 'Bhutto, Z.A. (Late), 70, Clifton Road.'

The landlady of the Canadian journalist I stayed with in Karachi noticed a man hanging around outside the house for weeks on end. Eventually she asked him who he was. He introduced himself politely as an employee of the intelligence section of the police, explained that he had to watch the journalist, and gave her his card. After a while he disappeared, then she saw him again a few weeks later in Clifton Road. He greeted her warmly but wearily, and said that he had just been put on to Benazir Bhutto.

But the openness is deceptive: unimportant things and people are easy to get at, but big things are very secret. That is partly why the reporting of them is so weak. In the past decade, even when there has been a parliament and a cabinet of elected politicians, most of the big decisions have been taken not by them but by generals and bureaucrats. People collect snippets of rumours, and try to piece them together into a theory: it is one of the country's principal conversational entertainments, enjoyed by people at all levels of society. Everybody is an amateur conspiracy theorist, and nothing is taken at face value. When Pakistan was knocked out of the cricket World Cup in the semi-finals, it wasn't just because the Australians were better than the Pakistanis. There were various theories: one of the Pakistani players had been betting against his own team; the English umpires had favoured Australia because if England won its semi-final it would have to play against either Pakistan or Australia, and Australia was weaker; one of the Pakistani players was an employee of the company sponsoring the game, which had foisted him on to the team.

Conspiracy theories are also a useful way of avoiding believing the worst. Politicians, civil servants and soldiers have argued to me that the riots in Karachi and the gangs of armed men terrorising the countryside in Sind are caused by the Foreign Hand. They mean the Indians. Maybe the Indians are involved; but, as any sensible foreign hand knows, that sort of chaos can be exploited but not created.

It looks to me as though something much more serious – what people call a 'breakdown of law and order' – is going on in bits of the country. When people start killing each other quite often; when kidnapping is common and armed robbery something that can be expected in the smarter suburbs of town; when the police do nothing much about crime or are promoting it, and people cannot redress their grievances in the courts, then the government, whose prime responsibility is to ensure the safety of its civilians, has failed.

I started at the beginning of the 'communal violence' file in Dawn's library. Lahore, 15 September: Shias demonstrated after Dr Israr, the ex-television mullah, said something tactless about one of their Imams. Bahawalpur, 15 September: in an 'untoward incident' during a religious festival, one person was killed and forty seriously injured. Lahore, 17 September: 'the city was tense after sectarian clashes in which three people died and six were hurt.' Day after day, there are bits of blood-letting between Sunnis and Shias, mohajirs and Pathans, Pathans and Pathans, mohajirs and Sindhis. Mohajirs are those who came from India at partition and their descendants. Karachi, with a rich population mix and the whole gamut of political and administrative problems, suffers most.

The state of the universities is one of the most depressing aspects of the violence. I talked to a man at Karachi University's Applied Economics Research Centre, who blamed most of it on the student wing of the right-wing Jamaat-i-Islami, the IJT. Firearms were first used in 1979, when IJT members shot at the crowd cheering the electoral victory of a rival student's union. After that, guns became commonplace, hand grenades appeared, and people were killed.

The IJT, he said, also harassed academics it disapproved of. Earlier in the year, teachers from his research centre had been playing cricket by their building, with women watching. IJT boys had attacked them, saying that the women should not be there. While the teachers were in a meeting deciding how to protest, the IJT had vandalised their cars. Recently, one of the IJT boys had told him to watch his step if he didn't want to be kidnapped. He reported it to the vice-chancellor, who said it was probably a joke.

The most obvious reason for the growing violence is the number of guns in the country. The Pathans have always had guns, but since the beginning of the war in Afghanistan supplies sent mostly by America to the Afghan guerrillas have been sidetracked by Pakistani administrators and soldiers. The whole country has been saturated with them. People started using rocket-launchers in ethnic riots in Karachi. The government apparently sees the spread of weapons as something to be encouraged: the chief minister of the NWFP (North West Frontier Province) presented the deputy commissioner of Peshawar with a Kalashnikov – a prohibited bore, incidentally, despite being the commonest weapon in the country – to reward him for his services to tax-collection.

The police seem to be part of the problem, not a solution to it. An old Air Force officer was telling me about the armed robbers who came into his house in the rich Defence Society area of Karachi. 'They were very disappointed. Nothing but books.' He was fairly sure, he said, that they were Eagle Squad – paramilitary police – boys. How did he know? Well, he said, after forty years in the services, you learnt to tell. Everybody believed it, anyway.

I half-believed him, and found plenty of press cuttings to support the prejudice, such as:

'An investigation ordered by the Inspector General police, Malik Mohammed Nawaz, has revealed that eight police officers and constables of Karachi Ferozabad police station were directly involved in a robbery committed at the house of a superintendent of police . . . The so-called anti-burglary staff of the Ferozabad police station picked up a prostitute . . . They later took her to the vacant house of the SP who was at that time on vacation in his native village. After enjoying themselves with the prostitute, the policemen searched the house for valuables and decamped with cash and jewellery worth tens of thousands of rupees.'

I don't think there's anything particularly odd about the police. Lawlessness goes all through society. The robberies, kidnappings and riots are the extreme fringes of it; but people don't much obey the traffic laws or the tax laws either. Maybe, as somebody argued to me, it is because Muslims have religious laws, so they do not believe in the validity of laws enacted by governments. That doesn't, however, explain why they don't obey the religious laws – for instance the bans on alcohol and fornication – either.

I suspect the 'breakdown in law and order' is also to do with another useful cliché: 'bringing the law into disrepute'. There are too many people around the top of the ladder of power who are cheating too. The *Herald* devotes a whole page to small official and political scams. A minister of the Sind provincial government was robbed at Heathrow of a briefcase containing fifty million rupees in cash: he didn't report it to the police. Another Sindhi minister employed a dacoit who escaped from Sukkur jail as his personal bodyguard. A politician-businessman increased the duty on all scrap except the sort he imported.

There are less amusing sides to it. Politicians have political opponents harassed, jailed and tortured. Civil servants are told to fiddle election results. Generals take power in violation of the constitution, the crumpled document that is supposed to set an immutable framework for all law and government.

There is always an attempt to make it appear legal. The police will produce a spurious charge, the magistrate will sign the order for continued detention every time it comes up. The torture never happened, because the man has no evidence. Instead of burning ballot boxes, the civil servant disqualifies opposition candidates through an established legal procedure. A court is persuaded to justify the general's coup. It looks nicer on paper; but nobody is really fooled.

2

MONEY

LOOKING AROUND Karachi with the eye of an economic journalist, the place seems very much like any third-world country prospering on the back of the green revolution and the earlyish stages of industrial development. Presumably its exports of agricultural commodities and manufactures made with cheap labour are doing very nicely, because the streets are full of smart foreign cars, and the shops of foreign luxuries associated with a place which has plenty of foreign exchange to spare and can therefore afford a lax import policy. Presumably the entrepreneurial class is reinvesting its profit in industry, because there are factories going up around the edges of the city. It looks like a richer version of India.

Most of the statistics support that picture. Economic growth has been running at six to seven per cent a year for ten years, while industrial output has been growing at nine to ten per cent over the period. Agriculture is doing pretty well and the service sector is booming. The big foreign earner in the statistics books – but not on the streets – is labour exported to the Gulf which, at its peak, was bringing in – officially – $3.2 billion a year, more than the rest of Pakistan's exports put together.

But there are strange things about the figures when you look at them more closely. The oddest thing is that while industrial growth is quite fast, the Pakistanis save very little: their domestic savings rate is around five to seven per cent, compared to the Indians' twenty-two per cent. If they don't save, where do the industrialists get money for investing in industry?

They borrow, you discover when you go to see a banker. The industrialists do not invest their own money, and the Karachi stock exchange, through which they might invest the public's money, is a stunted dwarf compared to India's burgeoning exchanges. They borrow from the foreign banks, who are fairly careful about who they lend money to, and from the nationalised banks, which are not, since the money belongs to the government or the foreign loan agencies. Anybody who wants to set up an industry and manages to get a loan from one of the government financing institutions can make a profit immediately. He can borrow up to seventy per cent of the value of the investment; if it's judged to be a 'priority' industry he can get another twenty per cent from the institution in equity; and by overinvoicing imported machinery he can get the government to pay more than the cost of the whole investment as well as stashing away some foreign exchange in London or Switzerland.

It may take years to get one of these attractive financing deals; you may never succeed. Politically influential people get their loans processed more quickly than other people, sometimes with better terms: one such businessman, for instance, managed to get his chain of ice-cream stores categorised as a 'priority' industry, and thus benefited from the equity as well as the loan. Some of the people who have borrowed money do not pay it back. In 1988 some thirty billion rupees worth of the banks' loans were classified as 'non-performing', when their total credit to the private sector was 100 billion and their capital base ten billion.

Investment in industry, therefore, isn't quite the statement of confidence in the country's future that it looks. India's industrial base, which is growing more slowly and produces shoddier goods, seems solider. The capital comes mostly from the businessmen and the millions of small savers who are pouring their rupees into the stock markets that are growing up all over the country.

Those foreign-exchange earnings are not quite as they seem on paper, either. The $3.2 billion – falling slowly, now, as the workers are sent back from the Gulf – were certainly there. But they were the dollars or dirhams that went through the official channels, the banks with branches in the Gulf states. A great deal more money came through the *havala*, or black, market: according to a banker I talked to, probably as much again as went through the white market. The havala market is an intricate network of money-men all over the Gulf, with contacts – branches, almost – in the remotest bits of Kashmir and the tribal areas, anywhere that labour has migrated from. It has many advantages over the legal routes. It is quicker – legal money can take over a week to get from Dubai to Attock, whereas the havala market can transfer credit in under two days – and it enables the recipient to avoid questions from the income tax man. One might think that Pakistan's workers were taking a risk by entrusting their earnings to unlicensed, illegal money-traders; but that is not, apparently, the case. The havala market has a reputation for absolute integrity.

The other big industry and export that the statistics do not help with is heroin. Over the past ten years, according to the Americans' figures, Pakistan has been producing between eighty and 800 tonnes of opium a year, depending mostly on the government's variable enthusiasm for the official anti-heroin policy. Opium refines down to a tenth as much heroin. In 1988, the street price in London for a kilo of heroin was £100,000, and Pakistan was producing about twenty tonnes of the stuff – a bit under $4 billion worth. Nobody really knows how much of the trade the Pakistanis control, and how much of the money they earn from heroin is sent back home; but it seems likely that heroin was earning them more than cotton, by far their biggest official export, which brought in around £300 million in 1985–6.

Even the figures of legal, visible exports are, according to the customs men, quite misleading. Pakistan probably exports rather less than the statistics would have one believe. The government wants to increase foreign exchange earnings, so there are incentives to export: exporters, therefore, overstate the value of their consignments. According to a customs man, badly-sewn rags which will never be sold masquerade as high-value garment exports. All the exporter has to do is persuade, or pay, customs to certify that his rags are worth what he says they are.

The Pakistani economy is probably much richer than it is on paper. It certainly looks like a country with a gross national product per head of more than $350, which is where the World Bank puts it. Great chunks of the economy do not officially exist: people are understandably keen not to get their businesses involved with officialdom, because that involves them in all manner of taxes and levies. I met a chairman of a district council, which is empowered to raise small taxes locally for the uplift of the area. The council decided that the shopkeepers in town should pay 100 rupees each towards building a sewerage system. The chairman discovered a year later that the taxes had not been paid: the shopkeepers had each paid the local tax man 300 rupees not to collect them. She asked the shopkeepers why they had shelled out three times the proposed tax in order to avoid it. To keep off the books, they said.

There are also large economic problems that do not officially exist. The country's official external debt is around $11 billion – serious, for a country with an official GNP of around $35 billion, but not Latin American. However, according to a civil servant at the top of one of the ministries that worries about these things, that figure relates only to money borrowed for civilian purposes. He reckoned that the external defence debt – which he called, in an economist's metaphor, invisible – was around $15 billion. He said I'd never be able to find out quite how big it was, not just because it didn't officially exist but also because nobody really knew the size of it.

The gap between the figures and the reality isn't just a difficulty for confused foreign journalists: it creates an economic problem. The government is painfully short of money, to the point where development schemes proposed by the international aid agencies cannot be carried out because although the foreigners will provide the dollars, the Pakistani government does not have the rupees. The government does not know how to raise more taxes. Increases in customs duties are offset by increases in smuggling, and only about a million people pay income tax. Agricultural incomes are exempt from tax, and because landowners dominate the political scene attempts to make them pay up have failed. The exemption helps non-farmers avoid tax, too: a businessman I talked to had, with the connivance of a landowner, put down most of his year's profits as payment received from the landowner for shares in his company, so no tax was paid on the money.

I like talking to foreign bankers: they provide some sort of touchstone in a place like Pakistan that seems at once to be a vibrant boomtown and an imminent disaster. But I expect them to be more impressed by short-term visible prosperity than by long-term worries of the sort that local commentators voice, so I was suprised by an American I visited. 'Certainly,' he said, 'the economy is grossly understated on an official basis.' He wasn't, however, too impressed by all the money.

'This is an economy without any depth. India is a totally different deal: there has been massive capital accumulation. Here, everybody is geared to the hilt. They just roll their money over as quickly as they can.' And, I wondered, were people siphoning their profits abroad more than they tend to in other third world countries? Much more so, he said. He could understand it, though: the place was so insecure. The multinationals seemed to agree. A country with 100 million people that looked as though it was getting rich quickly should be a good investment; but a lot of foreign companies, he said, had checked the place out and decided against it because they, like the Pakistanis, were worried about what might happen. India was poorer; the bureaucracy worked more slowly; but the foreigners were investing faster because there was a certain economic and political solidity about the place.

But it wasn't really the lack of investment that he was worried about. It was the corruption that amazed him. Locals endlessly complained to me about corruption but, assuming that westernised Pakistanis were unreasonably comparing their country to Britain and exaggerating the scale of it through their general disillusion with Pakistan, I had discounted much of what they said. I asked the banker how Pakistan rated internationally. 'Getting close to Nigeria,' he said. 'India's small shit compared to this place. You're talking about major political figures charging fixed fees.' He reeled off a list of small stories about his clients. One was owed thirty-five million rupees by a government corporation and got the organisation to pay after negotiations with the man who was to sanction the payment. The man was to get seven per cent cash. Another client had a large income tax bill which he avoided by paying twenty per cent of it in cash to the tax man. 'This,' said the banker grimly, 'is the major problem in Pakistan. It is on a scale that is totally disfunctional.'

There is an argument that corruption is efficient: that it is simply the market asserting itself in the face of government inefficiency. That seems a reasonable description of some sorts of corruption – a lot of what I saw in India, for instance. Regulations and a drowsy bureaucracy might mean that a businessman's consignment of raw materials would take a couple of months to clear customs unless he paid a few thousand rupees. But a lot of corruption is extremely inefficient – it prevents governments from collecting taxes, allows people not to pay for utilities, enables people to buy jobs and to pocket government spending.

I went to see a businessman friend in his office to ask him what sort of payoffs he made. There was excise duty, he said, levied according to what and how much he produced. He made a deal with the excise boys to declare half his production, and gave them a third of the value of the tax he would have paid on the rest. Then there was the old age benefits tax, which depended on the number of employees in an industrial establishment of over ten people. Again, he would agree with the taxman to understate the number

41

of employees. There was a similar deal with social security tax. His cousin, he said, spent at least 20,000 rupees a month in international telephone charges. By paying the telephone men 1,000 rupees, he reduced his bill to 2,000. For electricity, there were three levels of charges – residential, commercial and industrial. Residential was cheapest, so people paid the electricity man to register their business consumption as residential.

It was a pity, he said when I next saw him, that I hadn't stayed in his office ten minutes longer. The electricity man had come, and pointed out that he was paying an unnecessarily large bill – 5,000 rupees a month. The summer months were coming, the bill would be going up. If it was convenient to my friend, the electricity man would arrange to halve the bill. My friend was worried: the meter was sealed; wouldn't somebody find out? No, said the electricity man, the glass could be taken out carefully with a screwdriver. And what, said my friend, if he was transferred? Then the electricity man would introduce his successor to my friend. They made a deal.

Corruption results in widespread, small-scale privatisation. Everybody has their man in the telephone corporation who mends their phone; some of the men have business cards and headed notepaper. On the pavements outside the post offices are men selling stamps of every denomination. The men inside the post offices may not be able to supply you with what you want, and will direct you to the men outside who charge a fifteen per cent mark-up, of which the men inside the post office get five per cent. If you want a passport, the men in the office may not have the form, but will direct you to the men on the pavement who sell you one for fifteen rupees.

Then there is the corruption that damages the business of government. A Pakistani I met had returned after twenty years in Britain, and was trying to work as a consultant to government. He had put up a proposal for a contract and had been offered it for ten per cent cash to the man in the ministry. He hadn't taken it, and was upset by the idea of paying for a contract. He felt it devalued his work: he wanted to get a contract because he was good. He thought he was going to end up mostly working for international organisations, which would enable local lefties to sneer at him as a paid agent of economic colonialism; but then he wasn't at all sure he wanted to stay in Pakistan.

I was surprised by the shamelessness. Civil servants are unembarrassed to be seen to live beyond their means – rather, they show

42

off their wealth. The man in the ministry doesn't couch his demand for a percentage in euphemisms: like a businessman, he asks for it outright. Customs officials laugh at old-fashioned bribers who conceal their 1,000 rupee note in their passports.

Locals also seem to find the scale and frankness of it offensive. Within twenty-four hours, a banker said to me, 'this is an entirely cynical country', a politician said, 'this selfishness is eroding all the good in our society', and an economist said, 'this is a country without remorse of guilt'. They seemed to see corruption as a symptom of some larger amorality that they were groping towards; but I, as usual, wondered whether it wasn't just that they expected too much from the place.

I have to agree with them, though, that the get-rich-quick ethic is stronger than anywhere else I have been. Over the past ten years, a lot of Pakistanis have seen a few Pakistanis become suddenly very wealthy from the Gulf, heroin and smuggling; and the speed of their rise, perhaps combined with the national insecurity that makes long-term investment seem pointless, leads people in all sorts of walks of life to want to emulate the nouveaux. A reasonably well-off friend of mine recounted a conversation between his elderly mother and aunt:

'I do need a new car,' said the mother.

'You don't have enough money,' said the aunt.

'Why not? Everybody else does. Where do they get it?'

'I think they smuggle heroin.'

'Perhaps I can do that too. Do you know where I can get some heroin?'

It might be a joke, if it weren't for the number of people of that class who had tried it and are now in British and American jails. My friend told his mother off stiffly.

The appeal of quick money explains the strange success of rip-off investment companies in Karachi. For three years, from 1985, companies offering investors sixty to 100 per cent a year mushroomed. The companies could survive so long as the new investments were higher than the interest payments. But by 1988, when around five billion rupees had been invested in about 300 companies, they were beginning to go bust.

Some of the investors were uneducated workers who, one might argue, were ignorant enough to be conned. But plenty were retired Army officers, bank employees, and civil servants who must, if they had thought about it, have known that the bust had to come. Yet the customers closed their eyes and put their savings in. The call of quick profits apparently silenced their common sense.

To me, the modestly wealthy look extremely rich because even they can afford what in Britain is now the monopoly of the very few: labour. Most middle-class Pakistanis have a servant, while a rich family would have a watchman, a gardener, a cook, a bearer, a driver, two or three women to look after the children, a couple of cleaners and perhaps a few hangers-on from the ancestral village who are looking for a job in town. Then there is outside labour: most women have their clothes made for them, which to me is an astounding luxury, but in Pakistan is cheaper than buying them ready-made. The proliferation of ready-made boutiques in the smart cities is nothing to do with cheap mass-production: the boutiques provide trendy new shalwar kamees designs beyond the imagination of the backstreet tailor.

Cheap labour helps explain the intense social life. The people I know seem to be out at dinners and parties every night. They say there isn't anything else to do. Martial law has driven most of the interesting theatre out of public halls, though it persists in a small way in people's drawing rooms. Twenty years ago the upper classes used to go to films, but television and then the video provided them with home entertainment, so the lower orders monopolise the cinema halls, which are therefore dirty and show bad films. People don't read books much; but they also socialise furiously because they can afford it, as the British upper classes could fifty years ago. With an army of servants behind you, it is no trouble to invite ten people at four hours' notice, or forty people in two days' time.

Labour is so cheap that it has no value as a status symbol, the way the British butler in America does. In Pakistan, imported goods are a favourite way of showing off money. I went to the bazaar with a friend to buy a Thermos jug. The Japanese one was twice as expensive as the Pakistani models. She asked the man why: 'It's Japanese,' he said. The Japanese evidently know their market, because the Made in Japan label could not be removed. Discovering this, my friend hesitated, but still bought it.

A Pakistani who had been abroad for a long time tried to explain how amazing the spread of imported consumer goods was to him. He remembered, twenty-five years ago, that his father had kept in a cupboard a pile of boxes of Wilkinson Sword razor-blades. They were for civil servants from whom he needed a favour. A lowish civil servant, or a small favour, rated one box. A top man, and a big favour, got five. These days you can buy six imported brands in any shop. In the Agha supermarket in Karachi's smartest area, Clifton, you can get a box of twenty-five Davidoff No 2 cigars for 3,250 rupees (£100). In London, they cost £150. Barbican non-alcoholic beer must be the ultimate in Pakistani conspicuous consumption: bottled for Saudi Arabia, it costs thirty-five rupees (£1.10; or one and a half days' pay for a servant) and tastes like the inside of a tin can. The man in the shop said it was selling quite well.

Officially, all such luxuries attract duties of up to 500 per cent; in fact they mostly don't. Some are smuggled, some are provided through the exemption certificates given to foreign embassies for the needs of their staff. Some of the embassies sell the goods, some the exemption certificates. A customs man I spoke to had been called in to inspect a diplomatic consignment of foodstuffs that was five times heavier than it was supposed to be: it was for the Embassy of the Holy See which, he assumed, had sold a certificate to a businessman keen to stretch its value. The Brazilians seemed to be using their exemptions to boost coffee exports. They had requested a certificate for a tonne of coffee. My customs friend queried it, the foreign office insisted, and the Karachi coffee price crashed soon afterwards. Alcohol is the most profitable import: there was a time in Islamabad when anybody caught short of drink late at night was told to go to the house of a certain Thai diplomat, turn their car lights off and wait. A servant would come to take the order. I asked the customs man if all the embassies did it. Everybody, he said, except the Americans, the British, the Germans and the Chinese.

The big Karachi and Lahore parties – 200 to 300 people, any sort of alcohol you wish, staffed by uniformed servants handing round drinks and managing the open-air kitchen where whole fish simmer in four-foot-long pans – are one of the most popular ways of showing off money. They are difficult evenings for an unaccustomed foreigner to manage: the spirits are not much diluted, and food arrives at eleven-thirty at the earliest, and sometimes not till one-thirty. I asked why: somebody said that the guests all arrived very late on the grounds that the most important person always gets there last, another said that party-givers wanted to demonstrate how much alcohol they could afford, and somebody else said that since the measure of the success of a party is how late it goes on, the hosts kept their guests trapped as long as they politely could.

Women are another way of demonstrating wealth. Rich women

45

tend to wear obviously expensive clothes and a lot of jewellery. Most of it is far too elaborate for my taste – filigree-work encrusted with tiny rubies, emeralds and diamonds, reminiscent of the decorated buses, frilled with bright steel cut and perforated into delicate patterns, and set with brightly-painted scenes of rural idylls and F-16 jet fighters. Right at the top of the social scale, however, women are developing a taste for expensively-designed simplicity.

Their clothes are a miniature of the past fifteen years of political life. Everybody, these days, wears the shalwar kamees. 'They were such ugly things in the seventies,' said a friend of mine, 'that nobody would be seen dead in one.' Smart men wore trousers, shirts and safari suits; smart women wore skirts and dresses. Then Bhutto, the man of the people, took up the shalwar kamees, and was seen in one in the Sind Club. It became the uniform of populist politics and symbolised the rejection of the anglicised upper classes. Rich PPP men were happy to be seen in public in one, though in the Bhutto period their women stuck to western couture.

The shalwar kamees fitted President Zia's political vision, too: it was indigenous therefore anti-western therefore Islamic. Civil servants were instructed to abandon their trousers and wear the shalwar kamees to the office. Zia's emphasis on Islamisation changed the atmosphere on the streets. Women were nervous of showing their legs and arms, so they too took up the shalwar kamees. Smart clothes designers realised this and started a shalwar kamees industry: expensive materials, new fashions every few months, styles that could fit easily into London and New York. It's amazing what you can do with what is basically a baggy pyjama-suit. I quote from one of last summer's fashion articles in the *Herald*:

'Voluminous Turkish shalwars teamed with asymmetrical knee-length jackets, snappy cowgirl kameeses and elegant bead-encrusted sheaths, a potent mix of leather, snakeskin and metallic net silk, oversized double-lapel jackets and an inspired range of shalwar variations that set the imagination on fire.' All of which, while retaining the essentially modest, demotic pattern, enables the Pakistani women about town to look exotic, slinky, and very rich.

In the more central suburbs of Lahore and Karachi, new money is asserting itself loudly in bricks and mortar. The current favourite design looks very like the White House, though I am not sure whether the model is the American version, or the neo-classical mansions that the British built for their officials in the mid and late nineteenth century. These days, regular water and electricity supplies to rich areas have made the floodlit swimming-pool a common accessory. The cars – a couple of Mercedes and a Pajero Jeep – are also an important part of the outfit. One newly-successful Lahorite had the architect change the design for his house so his guests could see the inside of his garage from the dining room.

The ostentation is particularly odd in comparison to India, where wealth is manifested privately, if at all. There are old reasons for that difference. Long before the Indian government took up socialism or Gandhi first sat down to his spinning-wheel, simplicity and poverty were Hindu virtues. The Congress party turned them into a political creed: wealth is both slightly immoral and proof that its possessor has been ripping off the masses.

Neither Jinnah nor any of the creators of Pakistan were much interested in the renunciation of worldliness – maybe because the idea has a smaller role in Islam than it does in Hinduism and plays no part in the political mythology of the Indian Muslims. I suspect that the Moguls are partly to blame for the Pakistanis' ostentation. You have only to look at a miniature of one of the kings to see how they used the show of wealth as a political tool. Flipping through a book, I stopped at one of Shah Jehan seated on a balcony. Rubies and pearls hung round his neck in ropes and glistened in a spray on his turban. Behind him, the walls were inlaid with the flower designs in lapis, cornelian, jasper, onyx and topaz whose remains you find in Mogul monuments. The walls and pillars were marble, and above him was a canopy of red and gold embroidery. Around his head was the halo of gold he introduced into court painting after seeing western religous art: he was the God-King, an idea started by Akbar and promoted by descendents who needed to assert unquestioned superiority over the squabbling princelings around them. The Moguls' ostentation was a visible expression of their power, a constant reminder to dazzle anybody who doubted their supremacy. I suspect that people still associate a show of money with authority.

Some people gave me a more prosaic explanation – insecurity. 'What else should we do with our money?' they asked. 'There isn't much point in saving when we have no idea what will happen to us in ten years' time.' A quiet lady at a dinner said that, when she thought of investing some money, she always remembered the people arriving from East Pakistan, in 1971, during the civil war.

Some had been big businessmen, with millions of rupees in their companies and bank accounts, and they had fled to West Pakistan with nothing but their briefcases.

Either way, the show is another deception. Sir Thomas Roe, the British ambassador to the court of Shah Jehan, wrote that the Mogul emperor on his balcony reminded him of a Player King in a London theatre. Modern ostentation strikes me similarly: it is meant to imply power, solidity and status, but it doesn't necessarily mean any of them. It is just money, often unusually liquid money.

As in Britain, there is money and there is class, so my generalisations need to be qualified. Old money's large, marble-floored houses are less garish, are filled with antique furniture instead of the popular eighteenth-century silk-covered repro, and have miniatures and good modern paintings on the walls instead of the cinema-poster school of art. Old money is almost always landed, so, as in Britain, it goes off to its estates for the weekend. Unlike in Britain, it is almost always involved in politics, with an uncle or a cousin in a ministerial job. It is extremely snobbish. Mimicry seems to be a national talent, and old money amuses itself imitating the thick accents of new money trying to speak English.

There is a large, embarrassing book called the *Biographical Encyclopaedia of Pakistan* which explains some of this. It has 120 pages of 'notable families'. Their members are mostly zamindar, landlord, by occupation. I chose one at random: 'He is scion of famous Gardezi family which is reputedly known by the sway of the sanctity of Hazrat Shah Yusuf Gardezi, who migrated to Multan about a thousand years ago from Gardez in Afghanistan . . . He joined the Grammar School in Bournemouth and Horley; there he qualified with the gratifying merits in the previous examination of Cambridge University and was given admission in Kings College at Cambridge for the distinctive features of his family.'

Pakistan snobbery is quite different to the Indian version, which is integrated with the caste system. Indian social hierarchy is so immutable that it never need be mentioned: it is always visible, to the practised eye, in tiny gestures and expressions of deference. Pakistani snobbery is a manifestation of insecurity. There is, in bits of the country, the remnants of a caste system left by cohabitation with Hindus, but it no longer has much power to keep the lower orders down. The country has been shaken up too much, people are too mobile, money circulates too freely and the masses are insufficiently deferential.

You can watch the difference on the streets. Indian traffic does not obey the official rules, but it is relatively well organised. It operates according to a hierarchy based on size and power: trucks take precedence over buses, buses over Ambassador cars, Ambassadors over Suzukis, Suzukis over taxis over rickshaws over motor cycles over draft animals over push bikes. Pakistani traffic does not obey the official rules, nor any other set of rules. The buffalo cart thinks it has as much right to the road as the Mercedes, the rickshaw as the Pajero Jeep. The result, in the clogged backstreets of the big towns, is a lively and often abusive disorder.

The new rich are to some extent susceptible to snobbery. Their cars betray them: not content with the Mercedes, entirely urban people will buy themselves a Pajero, which implies an ancestral estate with bumpy roads. Marriage into one of the older families is considered advantageous, but, these days, their social cachet has limited power. Money speaks loudly and freely, and the power of its voice leads old money to say, with monotonous frequency, 'Pakistan is an absolutely materialistic country. Our people are interested in nothing but money' – which also means, 'People don't pay enough attention to ancestry, land and a good English accent.'

Karachi, the hot-house of new wealth, has two clubs which illustrate the social divide. The Sind Club is the city's most exclusive. It is a grand, rather austere establishment, dating from soon after the British capture of Sind in 1843, of yellow-brown stone with a front of high arches and long windows. Huge trees shade the lawn, and the herbaceous borders are a little out of control. The food in the almost-empty restaurant is a degeneration of Raj cuisine – chicken cutlets and caramel custard – and the waiters' white aprons are grubby. The great bar-room is empty, and serves only as a corridor to the ladies'. 'Every night we were at a cocktail party, then on to the Sind Club till the early hours,' reminisced an old *grande dame*. 'It's all finished, now. This town is just a dump. It used to be so gay.'

The Gymkhana Club, considered socially second-rate, is rather gay. The businessmen who couldn't get into the Sind Club joined it and have spent a lot of money on refurbishing it and improving its facilities. Its 1930s buildings have just been restored, and sparkle with white paint and new red tiles. The card-room's tables are covered with new green baize, and the verandah spruced up with new cane furniture. The lawn is crowded with tables and garden chairs occupied by families eating good local food and sipping their cokes, and girls in tracksuits saunter by, tennis and squash-rackets in hand. Beyond the neatly clipped hedge is a floodlit swimming pool which girls sometimes venture into after dark; beside it, a bar with black-tied waiters sells soft drinks and an open-air cinema shows American films. The *grande dame*, I discovered, was applying for membership.

The energy of new money matters because snobbery isn't just a social entertainment. All through society, what a politician described to me as the pecking order has traditionally determined who runs things. You get glimpses of it in the newspapers: 'the chief minister visited Alipur Tehsil and met local notables' – the men at the top of the pecking order. They will get the largest soft loan from the agricultural development bank, the concession to sell fertiliser there, and so on. The politician explained how he was selecting candidates for the ruling party in the local elections according to the village pecking order. It was determined, he said, partly by what family you came from. The smartest local families were those which the British had selected to mediate between them and the locals. To qualify for high status, you also had to belong to one of the three largest tribes in his area – gujjars (originally shepherds), rajputs and a tribe of weavers – which give you a weight of support. Then your network of relationships mattered – how many siblings, cousins and offspring were married into other important families. Piety was a help, and knowledge counted – 'though please,' he said as I took notes, 'keep that at the lowest priority'.

But then, he said with an expansive sweep that implied large-scale devastation, so much of this had been swept away in the past ten years. These days there was so much corruption that power was determined less by the old ranking and more by the ability to hand out money. 'Quite important people are being insulted by people who can give bribes.' What did they give bribes for? Oh, anything, he said vaguely. Getting things done. Under martial law, say, the soldiers would announce that the shops were dirty, and make the shopkeepers close down. The notables would go to them and ask them to be reasonable. Nothing happened. Then somebody would pay them some money, and suddenly the shops could be opened again. In his area, I guessed, there would be a lot of that: it was on the Indian border, and the heroin trade was said to take advantage of the hollow parts of the surgical instruments that were manufactured locally to facilitate the export of their product.

The old money, new money division doesn't have much basis in history. A lot of the money that pretends to age is really quite new – the product of British favour, being enjoyed by a third generation – and the grandchildren of today's new money will be as snobbish as the old money is now. They meet already in Lahore at Aitchison, Pakistan's Eton, a fantasy in Mogul-Gothic red brick surrounded by cricket lawns striped by buffalo-drawn mowers and dappled by ancient overhanging trees. The British established it as Chiefs' College for the sons of the local grandees, most of whom, in Punjab, were the Sikh remnants of Ranjit Singh's empire. The Sikhs left at partition, so there were forty-two people left in the school in 1947, including employees. There are now 2,545 boys. The gurdwara – the Sikh place of worship – is a library, and the Hindu temple is the accounts office.

It costs 20,340 rupees (£678) a year for a boarder in the senior school, which puts it within the reach of a great many parents. Admission, therefore, depends on who you know: what sort of sifarish – the magical, crucial, recommendation from a higher being – you can get. These days higher beings are often beholden to lower beings with financial clout, so people whose parents were never on nodding terms with a chief are getting their children into Aitchison.

A man at a dinner – two landlords, two businessmen, one general, all Aitchisonians except one newly-successful businessman – wished to explain this to me. The Pakistani upper class, he said, used to be a tightly-knit operation. Of the twenty-one boys at Aitchison at partition, fourteen were related to each other. So who, I asked, went there these days?

'Just a load of slobs. Anybody.' Clearly I looked at him in surprise, for he went on, 'You British think you know a bit about snobbery. I tell you, we've polished up your act.'

Despite the insecurity and blurred borders of the upper classes, they still manage to give the impression of being a close little world. It happened ridiculously often that, if I was with two people who did not know each other, they knew each other's cousins. The network makes the upper classes' lives easier. If anybody in that world wants to get something done, there is a quick calculation of whether there is a friend or relation around

51

the top of the ministry in question. If not, a friend or relation probably knows somebody. Then the complex business of the exchange of favours starts.

Favours have a great deal more weight in Pakistan than anywhere else I have been. I suspect it is probably to do with tribalism. Until recently central governments have left tribes to manage their own affairs, and when local chiefs were fighting and allying against each other, it must have been necessary to be able to trust somebody to repay a financial or social debt when you knew that you couldn't go to court to claim it. These days, everybody still carries an unwritten balance sheet of favours. A large favour – like, said a civil servant, if the prime minister got me a job with the United Nations – may leave the receiver in debt all his life, with the giver demanding a stream of smaller favours.

The system can lead to bitter hatreds. Somebody who has got a favour and doesn't settle up – maybe because he thinks the original favour incommensurate to the request – may earn a lifetime's resentment. The political world resounds with angers born of the conflict between the compelling social requirement that favours must be returned, and the thoroughgoing fickleness of most Pakistani politicians. 'Loyalty', a much-prized virtue in Pakistan, simply means keeping your balance-sheet in order.

When the tiny world of the upper classes has such a large hand in running the country, genealogy becomes politics. A foreigner I know who is interested principally in government has taken up family trees as a sideline. He showed me his masterpiece – Pakistan on a single sheet of paper in the 1960s. Ayub Khan, the president, is at the centre. The web of family relationships around him includes many of the characters the reader will meet later in the book. From Ayub Khan, it is two steps to the Haroons, the country's most prominent newspaper-owning family, one of whom is a minister of Zia's; one step away from them is General Yacoub Khan, Zia's brilliant foreign minister and a member of one of the old Indian princely families. Starting again from Ayub, it is two steps to the Qureshis, and they are directly linked to the families of Abida Hussein and Fakr Imam: that bit of the web ties up three of the most important political forces in Punjab.

It's a lovely piece of work, which becomes an amusing board game. How many steps from the Nawab of the Bugti tribe to Zulfikar Ali Bhutto? Would it be quicker to get from Illahi Bakhsh Soomro, minister and Sindhi landlord, to the Khan of Kalat or the

Mir of the Talpurs? In the top left-hand corner, the genealogist has even managed to get in the Guinesses, through the Aga Khan.

It doesn't quite work any more, though. The Bhuttos are on the map, but Zia wasn't, and nor are most of today's generals or much of today's money. The landscape has changed, and is changing still.

3

HOW THEY GOT HERE

PAKISTAN IS built on layers of conquest. To start at the beginning, I took a subsidised flight – the government is half-heartedly trying to encourage tourism – to Mohenjodaro on the banks of the Indus. At 4,000 years old, it is one of the world's oldest known cities.

It was a yellow maze of brick with a concrete shop, a guest house, and an empty museum with little pottery bullock carts with wheels that go round, the relics of Indus Valley toddlers. There were no other tourists there; the foreign archaeologist had gone away for six months leaving a pile of empty whisky bottles; the workers were playing basketball by the bank, which wouldn't change any money. Years of excavations had piled bricks up into the places they might have been in, cleared out the narrow drains running along the narrow streets and opened out the ovens and rebuilt their tall chimneys. One hillock had been reconstructed; but stretching down below it, to the dry riverbank where the Indus used to run, were piles of ancient rubble, and there were brick-covered hillocks all around waiting to be picked over and rebuilt like Lego. I wanted to know why it had stopped, not grown, layer on layer, through the centuries, so I bought the only copy of a book by Sir Mortimer Wheeler from the boy selling tickets for the museum.

Sir Mortimer was not sure. It might have been that the civilisation collapsed in on itself, he thought. The archaeologists had noted that the upper layers of houses were worse-built and smaller. That might have happened because the town's population grew too large, and the surrounding area was overgrazed. But shoddy building did not explain the unburied bodies found in the streets when the town was first excavated. The Mohenjodarans, he believed, were normally assiduous about cleaning up their dead. The bodies made him feel that Mohenjodaro had been evacuated,

54

probably because it had been attacked. The vague date for the fall of Mohenjodaro coincides with the vague date set on the Aryan invasion of India. So, Sir Mortimer thought, it might just be the case that the Mohenjodarans, weakened by city life and too many children, had been finished off by the white hordes from the north. Maybe Aryans camped there, leaving no architectural trace; anyway, others came back later. The main hillock is topped by the remains of a Buddhist stupa, a broken bell of thin brick.

Written history provides an extraordinary record of invasion, failure and retreat. Cyrus the Achaemenid arrived from Persia sometime around 530 BC, quelled the local tribes and press-ganged them into his armies. From Greece Alexander came, conquered Persia in around 330 BC, and moved into the eastern bits of the Persian Empire. He got as far as the five rivers of the Punjab; but his soldiers had had enough and refused to cross the fifth. To British schoolboys, the arrival of the Huns in western Europe is a fearful historical watershed; but in India, where they finished off the Gupta dynasty at the end of the fifth century, they disappear amongst the waves of northern aggressors, pale armies driving energetically south, setting up their kings, losing the dynamism of conquest, and disappearing back northwards. Some left buildings, some only genes.

In the seventh century the Arabs came from the south-west with the energy and discipline of a new faith. But it was not the easy, necessary victory of a force driven by a mission to convert a degenerate, caste-ridden society: it was a long fight, won after seventy years by a nineteen-year-old Arab general, Mohammed Bin Qasim, who brought the faith that was to dominate the area ever afterwards. After 150 years, however, the Arabs lost their military grip, and the old pattern of northern invasions returned. The most destructive was Mahmud of Ghazni, son of an expansionist Turkish nobleman, who, starting in the year 1,000, invaded India seventeen times, principally to fill the Ghaznavid coffers.

Babur, the first Mogul, wanted not wealth, but a kingdom. He was a stray, a descendant of Tamberlaine and Genghis Khan who inherited a small province east of Samarkand but was deposed at fourteen by his twelve-year-old brother. After several failed attempts to capture Samarkand, he turned his attention southwards and, in 1526, at the fifth try, defeated the army of Shah Ibrahim, the last of the Afghan Lodi dynasty, at Panipat. Babur's son, Humayun, hurried on to Agra, the Lodis' capital, where the treasury was kept. There, the Raja of Gwalior's family gave the conquerors 'the famous diamond which Alaudin must have brought. Its reputation is that every appraiser has estimated its value at two and a half days' food for the whole world ... Humayun offered it to me when I arrived at Agra. I just gave it back.' That is probably the first mention of the Koh-i-Noor.

Babur succeeded, finally, for two reasons. He brought with him a supply of firearms – guns had arrived on the subcontinent, through contact with the Turkish and the Portuguese, but they do not seem to have been in regular use in warfare in the north – and he found that Shah Ibrahim's nobles were ready to betray their king. Babur's diary for 1520–5 is lost; but Annette Beveridge, his translator, fills the gaps from other sources. Babur was at a wedding in Kabul when Dilawar Khan, son of the Lodi governor of Punjab, arrived. 'When admitted, he demeaned himself as a suppliant and proceeded to set forth the distress of Hindustan. Babur asked why he, whose family had so long eaten the salt of the Lodis, had so suddenly deserted them for himself. Dilawar answered that his family through forty years had upheld the Lodi throne, but that Ibrahim maltreated Sikandar's amirs, had killed twenty-five of them without cause, some by hanging, some burned alive, and that there was no hope of safety in him. Therefore, he said, he had been sent by many amirs to Babur whom they were ready to obey and for whose coming they were on the anxious watch.' They knew Ibrahim was on the way out, so what was the point in defending him? By changing the man at the top, they could hope to live unmolested. The report reads eerily like the attitude of the rich families to the British, to Bhutto, and to General Zia when it was time for Bhutto to go.

Extravagance and intolerance finished off the Moguls. Aurangzeb, who died in 1708, was a religious bigot who tried to enforce a rigid version of Islam on the Hindu-majority empire. As a result he drained his coffers fighting wars against the Rajputs, the Hindu warrior and princely caste, and Shivaji, the bandit patron saint of Bombay who gives his name to the present-day right-wing Hindu party in India, the Shiv Sena. In theory, the Mogul empire survived for another century and a half after Aurangzeb; in practice, succeeding emperors were at the mercy of battling factions.

Out of the chaos, the only strong leader to emerge was Ranjit Singh, the brilliant Sikh general who took Lahore in 1799 and ran the Punjab as a personal fief. The Sikhs had started off as a small devotional sect in the sixteenth century, but had metamorphosed into a militantly anti-Muslim fighting force; and Punjab's Muslims had a tough time under the Sikhs. Factional fighting after Ranjit Singh's death, however, destroyed his kingdom; so it was the turn of the British, by then the strongest force in the subcontinent, to take over.

The British had just been disastrously defeated in Afghanistan: in 1842, retreating from Kabul, the entire British force, with the exception of a doctor, was wiped out by Pathans. Feeling the need to restore their military confidence in the north-west, they captured Sind from the ruling Amirs in 1843. Mountstuart Elphinstone, one of the great Indian adventurers, said that the annexation was done in the spirit 'of a bully who was been kicked in the streets and goes home to beat his wife in revenge'. The conqueror, Sir Charles Napier, said it was 'a very advantageous, humane, useful piece of rascality'.

Punjab was annexed in 1848 after a couple of small wars. The Sikhs, who had attacked the British army, were to pay an indemnity of a million rupees. There was no money in the treasury in Lahore, but a local chief offered to pay it in return for Kashmir, so the British, who had no particular claim to the place, sold it.

The British made Punjab – which then stretched nearly as far north-west as Peshawar – easier to run by setting up an administration. The two Lawrence brothers, Henry and John, were responsible for establishing a system of land revenue, to be paid in cash, and a school of civil servants soon seen as the archetype of the British administrator in India. Their men trekked the countryside on horseback, learning about tribes and castes, adjudicating in disputes, building canals, schools, jails and courts. The government provided material improvement and tough reprisals against political troublemakers.

The strong central government that the British set up found that it could rely on the local nobles' loyalty, much as Babur could. The account I have of the Indian mutiny, or first war of independence, in the potted history of Pakistan published in the National Hijra Council's book on *The Muslim World* tells me that 'in 1857, the people of Indo-Pakistan made a Herculean effort to throw off the British yoke and rose from Peshawar to Bengal but some treacherous elements led to the failure of this war of independence'. And in Punjab, the huge province next to Delhi that might have made the mutiny succeed? Punjab was quiet. Punjab waited to see which way the revolt would go, the British waited to see which way Punjab would go, and the revolt collapsed for lack of support. For the next ninety years the landlords of Punjab were among the government's most faithful supporters.

Two themes there still run through Pakistani politics. The local rulers' narrow horizons made it easy for the conquerors. The invaders were up against a collection of small kingdoms or republics whose consuming interest in plotting against each other prevented them from establishing the sort of defence that could block the way from the north. Armies were for maintaining kings and princes against their relations, neighbours, or people.

Then there is the weary pragmatism of the local chiefs. Perhaps millennia of invasions have had their impact on the land's political reflexes. Perhaps too many successful conquests led to a collective understanding that invaders were not worth resisting, that it was better to lock up your women and your animals and pay your dues to the latest arrival. The process becomes circular: the less resistance, the easier the invader's job, and the easier the conquest, the less worthwhile resistance appears. Anyway, there was much to be gained from the conquerors. The local clients found that, provided they signed up with the new rulers, they had powerful backing for their authority. The conquerors found that the chiefs were useful underlings happy to share in the profits of power.

Under the British, Punjab did handsomely in material terms. But in the rest of India, the Muslim minority was lagging behind. It had few of the middle-class people who, among the Hindus, were climbing up the ladder of advancement: the Muslims were, by and large, landlords, craftsmen or poor people who had at some point converted to Islam to escape the stigma of being at the bottom of the Hindu caste system. There were Muslim doctors – hakims – and lawyers, but the Muslims showed a reluctance to learn English, apparently from a fear that it would lead them away from their religion. The Hindus, who had learnt Persian to prosper under the Moghuls, had no such qualms.

A remarkable man, Syed Ahmed Khan, led a reform movement at the end of the nineteenth century to stir the Muslims out of their decline. In 1875, he set up the first great Muslim university, Aligarh College. He argued for making terms with the British – Islam and Christianity, he said, were not so far apart – recognising earlier than most that partnership with the British was necessary to the Muslims, because of the problems the religious minority might encounter in an independent democratic India.

His movement was swept aside after the First World War, when the defeat of Turkey reversed the Muslims' shift towards the British and spawned the anti-government Khilafat movement. Gandhi, that consummate politician, harnessed the Muslims' anti-British fervour to his own movement; but the alliance crumbled after Turkey's new dictator, Attaturk, abolished the Caliphate, and India's Muslims had nothing left to fight for.

Jinnah first emerged politically as an ambassador of Hindu-Muslim unity. Born in Karachi, he was brought up in Bombay and trained as a lawyer in London where filial duty only just prevented him from taking up a career as an actor. In 1906, Sarojini Naidu, the Indian poetess, left a touching portrait of the man without whom Pakistan would probably not have happened:

> The calm hauteur of his accustomed reserve but masks, for those who know him, a naive and eager humanity, an intuition as quick and tender as a woman's, a humour as gay and winning as a child's – pre-eminently rational and practical, discreet and dispassionate in his estimate and acceptance of life, the obvious sanity and serenity of his worldly wisdom effectually disguise a shy and splendid idealism which is the very essence of the man.

As the movement for independence gained speed, and the Congress began to get down to specifics about elections and governments, Muslim fear of marginalisation took over. The British, pursuing their successful policy of dividing to rule, helped the split along. For Jinnah, the final breach came in 1928, when Congress rejected his demand that there should be separate electorates for the Muslims and Hindus.

The Muslim League gained strength from the tension between the two communities. Having started off as a movement mostly of rich landlords, it began to recruit more members from the small but crucial middle class of lawyers, doctors and civil servants. Where the Muslims were in a minority, and therefore afraid, the League was strongest. The results of the provincial elections in 1935 demonstrated its weakness in the Muslim-majority areas that became West Pakistan. In the frontier, Dr Khan Sahib and his Pathan nationalist Redshirts, allied to Congress, won. In Punjab, the pro-British Unionist landlords' party romped home, and Sind was a confusion of factions. Baluchistan did not exist.

In 1940 the League formally adopted the idea of Pakistan. 'The areas in which the Muslims are numerically in a majority, as in the North-Western and Eastern zones of India, should be grouped to constitute Independent States in which the constituent units shall be autonomous and sovereign.' The British and Congress hailed the idea as ridiculous; but by 1946, feeling among Muslims was so strong that the government began to believe that something would have to be conceded. By early 1947, when the violence had got serious, the British had decided that they would have to slice up the subcontinent and get out; although in April Mountbatten still said to Liaqat Ali Khan, Pakistan's first prime minister, that partition 'would be the worst service I could do to India, if I were her enemy or completely indifferent to her fate'. Then the massacres started up in earnest, the borders of the west wing – Sind, the NWFP, half of Punjab and a collection of princely states – and the east wing – east Bengal – were quickly negotiated, and the deed was done on 14 August.

The last invasion into the area that is now Pakistan came from the south and the east. There was more bloodshed than in any of the previous episodes, but no conqueror, except perhaps Jinnah. The troops marching on the new nation were refugees from the old. About seven million arrived in West Pakistan, most from eastern Punjab, Delhi, Uttar Pradesh, Gujerat, Bombay, Hyderabad, though every province and every city contributed some of its people. They brought the features, languages and food of the places they came from; but the identity they clung to was their religion. They lived first in barracks, camps, and in the Hindu and Sikh property that was not grabbed by local Muslims, and slowly began to settle down to become citizens of their new nation.

Troubles came fast. Within two weeks, Jinnah, the Governor General, sacked the pro-Congress government in the NWFP. The brother of the chief minister, Abdul Ghaffur Khan – who died in 1988, over a hundred years old and still opposing the Pakistani government – was arrested and several people were killed in the ensuing violence. The Pathans started muttering about Pashtunistan, their own state, and the Baluch about Greater Baluchistan. Jinnah said that Urdu would be the only official language of Pakistan, so the Bengalis, most of whom spoke no Urdu, were up in arms.

Riots against the Ahmadis, a sect which mainline Muslims claim is heretical, broke out in 1952, and in the next year, the governor general, a Punjabi bureaucrat, sacked the Bengali prime minister on the grounds that the government could not keep order. That was partly an excuse. The civil servants and the generals were disgusted by the faction-fighting amongst the politicians, and thought they could do a better job themselves. Many writers maintain that that episode was a decisive point in Pakistani history: the military and civil bureaucrats established their hegemony, and the politicians would never have much of a chance again.

The Muslim League had been taken over from the middle-class refugees by the landlords of Punjab and Sind who were reasonably content to work as junior partners to the civil service and the army. Politics therefore began to diversify: the middle-class Muslim Leaguers and the few progressive landlords who had hoped for something better left the party. Most turned to the National Awami [People's] Party, the Khan brothers' left-wing movement in the frontier, which gained a national base.

There was no question, however, of elections, since Pakistan still did not have a constitution. The constituent assembly had been arguing over the matter since 1947, although the problem was a simple one. East Pakistan was more populous than West Pakistan, but the West Pakistanis, who dominated the civil service and the Army, and were richer and racist, did not want to be run by dark-skinned Bengalis from the East. In the rush to create Pakistan, nobody seemed to have noticed this mathematical difficulty.

The solution came not from a politician but a general. Ayub Khan, soon to be Pakistan's first military dictator, came up with it while pacing a London hotel room. West Pakistan's provinces would be abolished, and the remaining provinces – East and West Pakistan – would have equal representation. This neat formula, which with military logic ignored its inherent political difficulties, was steamrollered through the protesting provincial governments.

But before elections could be held, the military moved in. In 1958, Generals Iskander Mirza and Ayub Khan abrogated the new constitution, dissolved the government, abolished political parties and imposed martial law. The generals' only excuse for taking over was the normal sort of disorder that had characterised political life for the previous eleven years, and a view that democracy did not 'suit the genius' of the people. They seem to have been motivated by their contempt for politicians, combined with a lust for power. Ayub decided that power, once acquired, was not to be shared:

61

with the support of the Army, he immediately ousted Iskander Mirza and established himself as president.

Ayub's ten years get variable, but, for a military dictator, fairly favourable reviews. He was not particularly oppressive. He introduced a careful sort of democracy, in which people voted for 80,000 'Basic Democrats' who in turn voted for the president and the assemblies. They were more easily bought or otherwise manipulated than the regular electorate, and so Ayub ensured that he would not lose power.

English-language commentators, mostly in favour of secular politics, applaud his stance on religion. Like Iskander Mirza, who said that 'if the learned maulanas [Muslim scholars] try to dabble in politics there will be trouble', he thought religion was not the business of government, and vice versa. His Muslim Family Laws Ordinance is seen by present-day feminists as a bulwark against the fundamentalist lobby. That, and his decree that Basic Democrats should have the right to solemnise marriages and prohibit or arrange divorces, infuriated the mullahs.

Ayub brought prosperity to many. Pro-business policies helped industry to boom; and although raw material prices were kept down to boost industrialists' profits, agriculture did reasonably well through the technological benefits of the green revolution. Middle-class businessmen and traders prospered, and land reforms benefited middle-sized farmers. Western support for Ayub's government ensured him a ready flow of aid.

But the government's economic strategy in the end helped bring it down. Mahbub ul Haq, Pakistan's most resilient economic bureaucrat, argued that developing countries should 'shelve for the distant future all ideas of equitable distribution'. Following this logic, the government concentrated on making the economy as a whole grow and ignored inequality. The poor remained poor, and levels of government spending on education and other social services were pitiful. Resentment grew amongst the poor and not-very-rich. In 1968 people started to come out on to the streets, protesting against inequality and Ayub's refusal to allow them any real participation in government.

Zulfikar Ali Bhutto, a young Sindhi landlord who had been one of Ayub's ministers and was sacked in 1967, harnessed the rising political feeling. He set up the Pakistan People's Party, whose socialist rhetoric appealed to the young disenfranchised idealists protesting against Ayub. He won popularity in the villages and the

towns' poor industrial areas with a slogan of basic economic rights –
'*roti, kapra aur makan*': bread, clothes and housing – and with a
crude, humorous showmanship that won him his audiences'
affection as well as their votes. The PPP had the right message at the
right time, and a talented demagogue to put it across. It soon
became the most serious political challenge to the government in
West Pakistan.

Ayub's biggest problem, however, was not in the metropolis but
in the bit that had come to see itself as a colony, East Pakistan. Since
the arguments between the two wings started over the Bengali
language just after the country's creation, they had never stopped.
The influence of the East Pakistan wing of the Muslim League
crumbled as dissatisfaction with rule by West Pakistan grew. By
1954, there was serious violence in East Pakistan, centring on jute
and paper mills. At one jute mill belonging to the Adamjees, a
family from western India that had moved at partition, 400 people
were killed in a riot between Bengali and non-Bengali workers.

West Pakistan, particularly the Punjab, dominated both the top
civil service jobs and the Army. The British had not considered the
Bengalis to be a 'martial race', and Ayub, trained by British
generals, shared their ethnic contempt. 'East Bengalis,' he said,
'probably belong to the very original Indian races . . . they have all
the inhibitions of downtrodden races and have not yet found it
possible to adjust psychologically to the requirements of the
new-born freedom.'

East Pakistanis could see little to choose between their treatment
by the British and by the West Pakistanis. Like the British, the
businessmen from the West bought their jute at depressed prices,
processed it and got fat on the profits from exporting it. In 1959–60,
national income per head in East Pakistan was about three-quarters
that in West Pakistan; ten years later, it was about two-thirds.
Despite having more than half the population, East Pakistan got less
than half of government spending.

A strong political movement grew out of East Pakistan's discontent: the Awami League. Sheikh Mujib, its leader, led strikes and
protests in support of its demand for greater autonomy. Accused of
taking part in a conspiracy to assassinate Ayub, he was jailed for his
pains; but that didn't stop the disturbances.

Faced with trouble on the streets in both East and West Pakistan,
and a strike in Karachi in March 1969 that paralysed the city, Ayub,
a sick man, handed over to another general. Yahya Khan promised

to hold regular, no-messing-about elections. Rather surprisingly, given the performance of Pakistan's generals, he did so. There was no good reason for anybody to be shocked by the results, but West Pakistan, at least, was horrified. The Awami League won 160 seats – all but two – in East Pakistan; the PPP won eighty-one out of 138 in West Pakistan. The rest went to the remnants of the Muslim League, the NAP, and small religious parties.

West Pakistan was faced with the logical outcome of the way the country had been designed at partition – Bengali rule. Although Yahya seemed prepared to accept Sheikh Mujib as prime minister, the politicians were not. Bhutto, who planned to be prime minister himself, ordered his party members to boycott the assembly, and said that he would personally break the legs of anybody who attended it.

Sheikh Mujib proposed that the two wings should solve their dispute by giving each other greater autonomy: they should set up a confederation with two sovereign states, two constitutions, and common defence, foreign affairs and currency. Egged on by Bhutto, Yahya refused to accept the suggestion. The Awami League organised strikes and protests in Dacca, the capital of the east wing, which was by then in a state of anarchy and revolt. The army moved in, Sheikh Mujib was arrested and taken to West Pakistan, and the soldiers indulged in brutality against their countrymen and co-religionists so ghastly that Pakistani writers today avoid the episode: phrases like 'it is unnecessary to go into the gory details . . .' explain as well as mask the horror.

The generals, it seemed, thought the situation could be controlled. Even though they had evidence from the election results, they failed to understand the strength of political feeling; but military logic should have made it clear that the Indians were bound to intervene and that the Pakistanis would never be able to defend an area 1,500 miles away by land, with an air link that the Indians could cut at will, and as far away by sea as France, since the ships would have to go all the way round the Indian coastline.

It was a short war. The Indians invaded on 23 November, 1971. As Bhutto addressed the United Nations in New York, saying that the Pakistani Army would fight for 'a thousand years', tearing up the resolution that called for a cease-fire, and storming out, Dacca fell. The Pakistani army surrendered on 16 December. The world's television networks broadcast the scene of a Pakistani general being stripped of his badges at the ceremony at Dacca racecourse. Bhutto returned from the United Nations, and was sworn in as chief martial law administrator and president of a truncated and humiliated country.

The circumstances of Bhutto's accession to power made the task of running the country both easier and more difficult. The loss of assets in East Pakistan, now Bangladesh, made for economic problems; there were refugees to be catered for and prisoners to be extricated from India; national self-confidence needed to be rebuilt. But the Army's humiliation made it less of a threat to an assertive civilian politician than it might have been. When he sacked the two generals who had called him back from New York to take over, there wasn't a murmur.

His biggest advantages were affection and optimism. He was genuinely loved − not so much by those who dealt with him directly, but by the poor. Their response in the election had given him an unchallengeable majority in parliament. His young party workers and the trade unionists and student leaders that supported the PPP believed in the 'New Pakistan' that he promised them.

Bhutto drew up a constitution: the first constitution that Pakistan had had which guaranteed equal political representation to all Pakistanis through direct elections, and which recognised that the provinces' identities mattered. Contrary to his wishes − he would have preferred a presidential system − parliament was to be sovereign, and the prime minister the chief executive. All the fundamental rights you could wish − freedom of expression, freedom from imprisonment without trial, freedom of religion − were guaranteed. It was passed in 1973, by which time the government was already abusing it in on a grand scale.

To start with, Bhutto's rule went according to his socialist colleagues' plan. He had a left-wing cabinet − people like the trade union leader Mairaj Mohammed Khan, and the finance minister, Dr Mubashir Hassan − which pushed ahead with the policies that his socialist manifesto had promised. Huge chunks of industry, the banking system and life insurance companies were nationalised. The civil service was shaken up. Land reforms were passed. Bhutto taunted the foreign capitalist governments who were alarmed by the enthusiasm with which the Pakistanis greeted socialism.

In the early days, before and after coming to power, Bhutto encouraged the amorphous, but enthusiastic, left to organise itself. The PPP was born out of a collection of activists; militant workers who formed trade unions, students who joined student unions.

65

They asserted themselves on their own little patches, and fought other – mostly religious – organisations that grew up in opposition to them.

But by 1972 it became clear that Bhutto was alarmed by the growth of these partly-autonomous groups. He began to take action against them on a scale, and with a viciousness, that amazed former supporters. Trade unionists were jailed and tortured, newspapers' independence curtailed, and organisation even within the PPP was discouraged. Bhutto, it seemed, wanted all power to rest in, and all benefits to spring from, himself. To ensure his independence from the Army and the police, he set up the Federal Security Force, a paramilitary organisation answerable only to himself. The FSF was responsible for most of the attacks on party members who were too left-wing and on opposition politicians.

Loyalist PPP members also joined the lawlessness. Asgar Khan, a retired air marshal who led one of the main opposition parties, the Tehrik-i-Istiqlal, records trying to speak at a rally in Lahore in 1972. It was broken up by a raiding party, armed with revolvers, sten guns and iron bars, led by PPP national assembly members. The guests and organisers were beaten up and a lot of people injured, but nobody was killed. Usually, he says, the police had been intimidated by party members: once, however, when the PPP was causing trouble, a police officer took the microphone, and said that Asgar Khan had as much right to speak as Bhutto, and that if any bastard dared interrupt the police officer would skin him alive.

When he came to power, Bhutto had made terms with the left-wing, nationalist parties that had won the provincial elections in Baluchistan and the frontier. But, unwilling to share power even with those who had been legitimately elected, he found a pretext to sack the Baluch government. The NWFP government, run by Abdul Ghaffur Khan's son Wali Khan, resigned in protest. The leaders of both provinces were imprisoned for the rest of Bhutto's time in power and their parties were banned. That move sparked a civil war with separatists in Baluchistan. The Army was sent in and, between 1975 and 1978, nearly 10,000 people were killed. Echoes of Bangladesh began to rattle round the heads of civilians and soldiers alike.

As Bhutto discarded the left, he started recruiting the rich landed politicians into his party. They came willingly, always glad to be with government; but it was too late for Bhutto to build himself a political constituency strong enough to back him against those he had alienated. He faced the anger of the businessmen whose businesses he had taken away, the religious leaders whom he had ridiculed and harassed, and the old left-wingers who hated him as only ex-supporters can.

The people did not desert him. He won the 1977 election with 58 per cent of the votes and 80 per cent of the seats. The opposition claimed the election was fixed. Certainly, there was some fiddling, either because Bhutto was determined to get a two-thirds majority in parliament or because he felt the need to obliterate his opposition; but most observers reckon that he didn't cheat much, and that he would have won anyway.

Popularity, however, was not the issue at that stage. By 1977 all the opposition parties had lined up against him in the Pakistan National Alliance. It included the religious parties, who tend to be the organisations best-equipped to get people out on to the streets, and was backed by the resources of the businessmen he had alienated. Money procures people, buses to transport them and, if necessary, violence.

From February 1977 onwards, there was a crescendo of protest in the streets. In April, twenty-five unions called for a general strike: Bhutto declared martial law in Karachi, Hyderabad and Lahore on the day it was scheduled, but Karachi was nevertheless paralysed. The PNA leaders were arrested, all except for Pir Pagaro, one of Sind's living saints and the leader of a faction of the Muslim League. He embarrassed the others by bringing tubs of ice cream to the house where they were detained, a fact widely reported in the newspapers when their followers were being gunned down around the country. Somewhere between 250 and 300 people were killed during the six months of the PNA movement.

Forced to accept that things were getting out of hand, Bhutto started negotiations with the PNA. He agreed, in principle, to hold another set of elections in October, though the PNA leaders were still suspicious. Asgar Khan maintains that PPP members were still being given guns, and PNA members were being arrested. They wanted evidence of his good faith; but the matter was soon taken out of their hands.

With martial law in force in the main towns, the Army was increasingly involved in Bhutto's troubles. He kept in closer touch with the generals than with the politicians during that period. The chief of Army staff, Zia ul Haq, whom Bhutto had promoted over the heads of others largely because he seemed entirely loyal and none too bright, was in effect in charge of law and order. The PNA leaders had been calling for the Army not to obey orders to crush the demonstrations.

On the night of July 4th, the Army surrounded the houses of all the main PPP leaders. The government was ousted, and Zia announced the next day that the Army would restore order.

'I want to make it absolutely clear,' he said, 'that neither I have any political ambitions nor does the Army want to be taken away from its profession of soldiering. My sole aim is to organise free and fair elections which would be held in October this year.' The Army's intervention was widely welcomed.

Bhutto was put in a comfortable house in Murree, the hill station above Islamabad, and the PNA leaders were kept in detention for a few weeks longer. The election commissioner announced that elections would be held in October, and the PPP said it would take part. When he was freed, Bhutto signed his death-warrant: vast crowds attended his meetings, suggesting another electoral victory. According to the 1973 constitution, Zia was guilty of high treason for abrogating it by force, and could be condemned to death. Bhutto was therefore arrested and, in 1978, convicted by the Lahore High Court of being the 'arch culprit' in the murder of one of his opponents. He was executed in 1979.

Bhutto's years set a tone for Pakistani politics that had been barely audible before. His ruthless treatment of the opposition was reminiscent of the Mogul emperors, who liked not just to wipe out their opponents, but to demonstrate publicly the scale of their military victories. Babur records in his diary that he raised 'great pillars' of the skulls of Pathans he had killed. Bhutto, similarly, could not live with a whisper of opposition, either within his party or outside it. Criticism invited brutal reprisals. In the end that weakens a leader: he does not hear what others are saying, because nobody dares tell him, and he creates in those who survive his harassment a bitterness greater than that harboured by enemies who were never his friends.

The pillar-of-skulls attitude to politics is a manifestation of insecurity – not real insecurity, perhaps, but perceived insecurity – and it also creates instability. If a leader harasses and crushes the opposition, he is less likely to stand down quietly when his time has come, for he will fear revenge. The pattern, once established, repeats itself. Those whom Bhutto victimised were, in turn, happy to victimise the PPP when it was out of power. His death was a shock, but not a surprise: those who live by violence can expect to die violently. Less dramatically, once the fixing of elections becomes normal practice, standards of freedom and fairness are hard to restore.

Zia did not hold elections that October. He said that the previous government needed to be made publicly accountable, and that there was no point in holding elections until the 'bad elements' had been cleansed from politics. Some of the PNA leaders who had welcomed his intervention began to shift nervously away from Zia, while some – particularly those from parties which tended to do badly in elections – moved closer to him. The Jamaat-i-Islami made its support clear; Pir Pagara said publicly that it might be wise to delay elections. The Jamaat and the Pir's Muslim League were, initially, well-represented in Zia's government; but he soon dispensed with the politicians, relying instead on bureaucrats like Mahbub ul Haq and the veteran Ghulam Ishaq Khan, as well as a sprinkling of landlords to represent the country's hereditary politicians.

The civilians were there as administrators, however, not policy-makers. The real stuff of government was done by Zia and the generals whom he had appointed as governors of the four provinces. Of those, General Gilani, governor of Punjab and former head of the military Inter-Services Intelligence, and General Fazle Haq of the frontier, were the country's most powerful men. With an obvious nose for politics, Zia avoided seeing the cabinet *en masse*: he tended to see ministers individually, and to set up small think-tanks on particular subjects.

Again, in 1979, Zia promised national elections; but politically attuned ears pricked when he held local elections instead. It looked as though he might be taking Ayub's route, giving them a stunted form of democracy to release some political frustration while avoiding the threat that a national, popularly elected government might pose. Then the beginnings of the Islamisation programme, with the establishment of an Islamic Ideology Council, suggested that Zia was planning to stay awhile: he was setting himself up with the task of pulling the country back on to the true path which would clearly take a long but undefinable time.

In October 1979, he banned all political activity and ordered that the parties' offices should be closed and their funds seized. The inevitable symbols of military efficiency signalled the beginning of the real martial law: lime was sprinkled in the drains, the soldiers ordered restaurants to clean themselves up, butchers were instructed to put gauze over their meat, and the army tried to control prices, with the result that goods started disappearing from the shops.

Zia was blessed with luck, and in 1979 he had his biggest break. The international community was down on him for executing Bhutto, and introducing Islamic punishments – flogging, amputation and stoning to death. America had cut off aid because of suspicions about Pakistan's nuclear intentions. Suddenly with the Soviet invasion of Afghanistan in December 1979, Zia changed from being a medieval tyrant to a bastion of the free world holding back the flood-tide of communism. The foreign money started to flow.

The West was therefore better able to ignore the repression which started in earnest in 1979. The 1,500-or-so detentions in 1977 had mostly been short, polite affairs. In 1979, around the time of Bhutto's execution, about 3,000 PPP leaders and workers were jailed. Some were still inside in 1988. Then, in 1981, when the rump of the PNA, along with the PPP, formed the Movement for the Restoration of Democracy, around 15,000 were imprisoned. The jails were flooded: people were being kept in tents. 'They arrested 460 lawyers,' a lawyer told me. 'If you were known and you weren't inside, people assumed you were a government stooge.' Even some members of Pir Pagara's party were jailed, because the police were given orders to pick up anybody involved in politics. The press said not a word: there was complete censorship at the time.

The biggest wave came in 1983, when the MRD launched a movement of protest that took off in Sind and, according to somebody in government at the time, shook even Zia. Some 21,000 people were arrested then. The authorities had learnt a bit in six years. First of all they picked up not the top leadership but the local politicos, the people without whom the movement wouldn't get on the streets. They didn't bother too much about the big shots, most of whom courted arrest and ended up in Karachi jail.

Bhutto's and Zia's methods of repression were quite different. Bhutto's opponents, famous and obscure, were tortured. Mairaj Mohammed Khan, a minister in Bhutto's government till 1972, can no longer see properly in one eye because of the beatings he got in jail. If the FSF's target had disappeared, its thugs would pick up members of the family, male or female. Given Pakistanis' attitudes

70

to their families and their women, that is remembered with particular bitterness.

Zia's approach was more tactful, more military, more efficient. The better-known political leaders whose stories would get about were better treated. Low-level party workers were abused, but they mattered less. I couldn't get figures on the number who died, but a human rights activist who, jailed by both governments, has no particular bias, said that while fewer people had been tortured under Zia, more had been killed in detention.

Zia, a good tactician who moved as circumstances did, seems to have decided after the 1983 movement that he should allow the country to let off a little political steam in less violent ways. He announced a programme for elections, which took place in 1985 after a referendum which inquired of the country whether it approved of the Islamisation programme. Some ten per cent voted, the answer was a resounding yes, and Zia judged that it was a vote of confidence in himself which gave him grounds for remaining in power for the next five years.

The election was a gamble. Parties were not allowed to contest, but MRD members could have stood as individuals with a common slogan. They misjudged, and called for a boycott of elections. The populace, which knows that elections are not just about policies, but about getting a representative in parliament who can distribute some of the benefits of government, ignored the MRD: fifty-three per cent of the country voted. Before the new assembly met, Zia amended the constitution so that he could dismiss parliament almost at will.

The prime minister, Mohammed Khan Junejo, was a nominee of Pir Pagara's who did little of note, some of which annoyed the president. The National Assembly members sat, in their smart white building on a slope just above the rest of Islamabad, and debated many matters. They did some things that Zia needed – passed the eighth amendment to the constitution, for instance, which indemnified the martial law government of responsibility for all its actions, legal and illegal – but not much else. It was the sort of parliament that you would expect from those sort of elections, there to extract money and favours for itself and its constituents.

Zia sacked it in 1988. Nobody expected its dismissal, since it caused him so little trouble, and many conspiracy theories evolved from the mystery. But it seemed to me, watching the sad reluctance on his face as he fulfilled what he said was his regrettable duty, that his motive for getting rid of it was much the same as Ayub's for taking over in 1968: he despised the politicians, liked the everyday exercise of power, and had missed his daily dose of that exhilarating tonic in the previous three years.

Zia's political game showed a strange regard for form. I do not expect a man who holds absolute power to bother with appearances, yet he did – not just in his deference to visitors, but also in legal matters. Nobody seriously expected a judge to take a stand against him, but his constitutional amendments sewed up every possible loophole, down to the point where all the actions of the martial law government were not only unchallengeable in any court, but also where 'all orders made, proceedings taken, acts done or purporting to be made, taken or done by any authority or person shall be deemed to have been made, taken or done in good faith and for the purpose intended to be served thereby'. That was after any dissenting judges had been – legally – got rid of.

According to one of the ministers in cabinet before the 1985 elections, nobody was allowed to speak of democracy, because Zia did not like the word. Yet the forms of it were observed; the ballot boxes not tampered with; nobody prevented from going to the polls. His opponents could not credibly deny that the elections had been free and fair. Entirely legally, however, he managed to set up a parliament that, while it had the structure and the manners of a democratic assembly, lacked the content of argument, ideology and opposition that gives those messy, discreditable bodies life.

To the westerner, it was confusing. Here was a parliament; here were elected representatives; why wasn't it the real thing? It wasn't the real thing because, although the format was pretty much the same as anything you get in the West, the content was different, and the content was different because the history, the culture, the economy and the people were different. In those circumstances, a man who knows how to manage the system can make of a parliament a deformed and handicapped creature.

Because Zia's manipulation of the system was so personal – he even wrote his name into the constitution – his extraordinary death in August 1988 in a plane crash that wiped out much of the Army top brass as well as the head of the American military mission and the American ambassador left the country in confusion. Of course, there was a constitution which could be followed but, because of the way Zia had played his game, nobody was prepared to assume that the people who mattered were really, in the long run, prepared to play it by the rules.

Pakistan, therefore, treated the promise of elections in November 1988 suspiciously. Every muttering from GHQ was construed as a threat of martial law. Every statement by the Army chief, General Aslam Beg, confirming the soldiers' commitment to free and fair polls was picked apart for possible *doubles entendres*. When gunmen in Sind killed 200 people, fearful observers said Vested Interests were trying to stop the election happening. But it happened, quite quietly, and there was much rejoicing and distribution of sticky sweets throughout the land.

Part Two

4

BUSINESSMEN

Arif Zahur was at the stage when youthful energy ceases to hold off creeping plumpness. His white shirt bulged slightly over the edge of the trousers of his fawn suit, and his brown silk tie followed the curve outwards and hung over its edge. There was no sign that his dynamism was flagging, though. With a seriousness that implied urgency he dealt simultaneously with the meeting of the All-Pakistan Textile Manufacturers' Association and some Japanese visitors. Genuine preoccupation with work commands respect, so even though I had an appointment I was more apologetic than he when he asked me to wait awhile and took me through his white offices, past the pot-plants in brass bowls and the tinted windows, and turned me over to an aunt who was reading magazines in his waiting room, instructing her to entertain me.

She did. She was a thin woman of fifty with a sharp face, fierce eyes and plucked eyebrows redrawn in supercilious arches. A navy blue silk chiffon scarf swept around her shoulders, in the manner more of Parisian chic than Islamic modesty. She wasn't really his aunt: the relationship, she explained, was rather distant. Her grandfather was Sir Somebody Somebody, her father an intellectual and a poet. They had both been at the same Oxford college as me – the best possible introduction.

Her conversation buzzed angrily. Jinnah used to come to their house a lot, she said. He liked a sip of whisky, although he was a moderate drinker. She drifted into a reminiscence of Jinnah's treatment of a drunken secretary, then remembered the point.

'He was interested in political and economic freedoms for the Muslims,' she said furiously. 'Not religion the way these people are doing it! Can you imagine, my friend who was the women's tennis champion in 1942 played in shorts! Can you imagine that today?

That's why these young men, they feel . . .' She slipped her hands up to her throat and mimed throttling herself. She was a member of the Women's Action Forum, she said; and I could see her in their protests, threatening policemen with her handbag. She did not surprise me, but my lack of surprise did. The oddness lay in her normality in Pakistan – a country where archetypal upper-class mothers, the sort whose political involvement in Britain stretches no further than opening the grounds of their houses for Conservative party bring-and-buy sales, can be found abusing not only a conservative government but also the police.

I wanted to know more of how the world seemed to her, and she needed no prompting. We were quickly on to drugs. 'There's a lot of it about,' I said, to punctuate the conversation.

'You don't need to tell me! Why, in my family . . . well, all Lahore knows . . .' Her brother, she said, had been caught with his wife at Heathrow with some heroin. He didn't know anything about it, but he had taken the rap for his wife, and was still in a British jail. I was disappointed when summoned by Arif Zahur. I thought I'd probably learn more about life from his not-quite-aunt.

The point of Arif Zahur was his dramatic rise to business stardom. I was interested in the speed of mobility in Pakistan, the sudden appearance in the halls of wealth and on the lists of social acceptability of people whose names nobody had heard of two years before. I liked that. It was a change from the stagnation of the Indian business world, where almost all the big names had been names before the British left.

Arif Zahur's origins weren't quite as humble as I would have wished – after all, the relation I had met had had a knighted grandfather – but he was certainly middle class. His father had been a provincial civil servant and Arif had started life at 350 rupees a month in an insurance company. After it was nationalised he took a room in a hotel, started trading, went into contracting and got his first big job, to build a textile mill. He often worked, he said, until one-thirty in the morning, directing the labourers by his car headlights. He started in 1977, and by 1981 he was big enough to begin his own development projects – like the office complex we were sitting in. Then he had built his own textile mill. He told me his story with a speed and earnestness that made me both pay attention and feel guilty for taking up his time.

How did he account for his success? Hard work, of course; but there was the matter of dealing with government.

'It's a very personalised system. Your file is there, you have to push it along. You want to borrow money – it's easier if you're known. I can walk into a bank and ask for a million rupees in cash, they'll give it to me straight away. But my first limit, I remember, was 10,000 rupees.

'One day a government official came to this office and said, Why have you done all this landscaping? Where's your permission? I'm going to have you arrested. I told him to go to hell; and the next day I talked to some high people, so that was all right.'

A man came in to sell Arif some yarn. He was in the better position, since yarn was in short supply, but Arif treated him as though it were a buyer's market. I watched him beside me at Arif's curved wooden desk, designed so you couldn't put your knees under it. His right hand twisted his loose watchstrap round and round, and his Adam's apple bobbed up and down like a cork on water.

A fat little boy came in, his face puckered into a sulk. 'Say hello to aunty when you come in,' said Arif sharply. (Grown-up women are automatically honorary aunties.) 'Hello,' mumbled the boy at his sneakers.

Arif had just got back from abroad, and wanted to check on his mill. He agreed to take me along. The fat boy demanded to come too, and bounced down the stairs in front of us. Arif, still shouting instructions to his staff as he left, came last.

By the time we got on the road night had fallen, and the boy went to sleep at once in the back of the car. It was one of those cars where you can't find the handle to wind the window down, realise it must be a button, and fumble around the door hoping that the driver hasn't noticed your incompetence. Arif put Lionel Ritchie on the tape.

We went out of town along the canal, and on south towards Multan. We passed trailers and trucks loaded with hay and maize stalks, held down by huge white tarpaulins which bulged over the sides of the vehicles like rising dough. The car lights caught the glittering silver and coloured plastic decorations on the lorries and buses.

Arif asked me what my book would be called. I didn't know. He hoped I wouldn't call it The Rich and the Poor; and I assured him I wouldn't.

'The poor are doing quite well, you know. The people who have difficulty, they are the middle classes. The poor can live in any small

79

house, and it doesn't matter. The middle classes, they have a status to keep up. They have to socialise, and belong to some club.'

Half an hour outside Lahore, past the pink and mauve strip-lighting round a roadside restaurant and the single red bulb inside the wooden box of a cigarette stall, came the stretches of white street-lamps illuminating long buildings behind barbed-wire-topped brick walls. It was the new industrial zone, Arif said, where you got all manner of tax breaks and incentives. Everybody was putting up mills there. The four new ones on our right belonged to Nawaz Sharif, the chief minister of Punjab.

I had expected a mill to be full of colour and limbs shining with sweat. Arif's was air-conditioned and white, except for the grey-green of the machines, and strip-painted the same colour, to machine-height, all round the walls. Beyond the room with machines winding thread on to six-foot cotton reels, there were 108 twelve-foot grey-green looms, the newest shuttleless looms from Switzerland, battering cloth out thread by thread. There were about thirty people working in the huge space, most of them sweeping up the thin white snow that covered everything. I put my ear close to the manager's mouth to catch his explanation of this new technology, but I still couldn't hear; so I nodded, and taking a fingerful of the snow, rubbed it into the tiny clots that were presumably collecting in the workers' lungs.

In the next room, the creamy-white cloth was loosely piled into soft mountains. Two men were standing watching an unfolded bale pass like tracing paper over a lighted box. Hardly any faults with the new machines, Arif said: the shuttleless looms meant that there were far fewer breaks in the thread. Beyond, bales of cloth packed in white plastic were piled high, waiting to be despatched to Manchester and Spain. Oddly, after the efficient grandeur of the world's best textile machinery, they were addressed in badly-written blue felt pen.

Arif was buying more machines: he wanted 200 altogether. They cost two million rupees each, so, I worked out quickly, that was a capital cost of around $25 million. Where was the money coming from? The World Bank, at fourteen per cent. So that meant interest payments of $3.5 million. And if there was a slump in demand for cotton cloth next year? That was his problem, he said. Or the World Bank's, I thought.

He left me with the manager, an elderly man who had come from a nearby factory. I asked him about the workers' pay. The minimum was 1,300 rupees, he said, and the average 2,000; and they all got accommodation. I felt a twinge of embarrassment as Arif returned and listened questioningly to the manager's answer. I had already asked him about pay, and was just checking. They said the same. On the way out he pointed to the workers' cottages, rows of plain pale concrete, behind the mosque and the guest house surrounded by tall rose-bushes and a lawn with ghostly long-legged birds picking their way over it in the dark.

On the other side of the workers' houses, Arif's expansion programme was under way. The second mill was still only a huge cage of scaffolding, around thick cement pillars and a brick wall growing up them. Beside it were piles of sand and gravel, pipes and hoses, a small cement mixer, and twenty workers with wheelbarrows. The site was lit by a single bulb, loosely tied to the branch of a single, leafless tree.

The site manager argued with Arif. He was smaller, slighter and without the advantage of a suit; but he showed no subservience. The workers crawled over the emerging building, and queued up with their wheelbarrows to pour sand into the cement mixer, or take cement out of it. One man wheeled his barrow over towards the scaffolding, on to a metal plate between vertical runners. He stood bent over, holding the handles of his barrow and facing the mill. Somebody pressed a lever, he shot up twenty feet, and wheeled his barrow on to the building's roof. The fat little boy demanded to be taken in the lift too. 'I want to inspect the roof,' he said petulantly; so up he went.

The wheelbarrow queue stared at me as it waited, with those downtrodden male stares that mix curiosity, hostility, misery and lust. Then I realised there were two women, one wearing an orange shalwar kamees that looked like a 1920s pyjama suit, one with a dark blue shalwar kamees glittering with a sweeping pattern of silver and coloured sequins. They watched me blankly. I tried a smile, worried that it wouldn't work; but it did, and they giggled at each other.

On the way back Arif said that, after two days in London, he couldn't stand it and had to come home. I tried to remember the answers and excuses I had had to use too often in response to Pakistani complaints about growing racism in London. I'd never come up with anything satisfactory: I usually resorted to 'It's a tiny minority, most of us aren't like that', which I wasn't sure I believed and which is easily refuted by the *Sun*'s circulation figures. But Arif elaborated.

'You have to do everything for yourself there,' he complained. 'Here, somebody opens the door for you. You go home and your dinner is prepared. You get up in the morning, and everything you like is on the table.

'You must think this is a strange place.'

'Why?'

'In London, you do everything properly.'

'And here?'

'Here . . .' he laughed, 'We do everything wrong.' He didn't mean that, so I asked him what he did mean.

'Here things are informal. You can walk into my office, maybe you have a recommendation from a friend, so here we are after four hours driving from my factory and I have told my wife you will have dinner with us. In London, you make an appointment for some days' or weeks' time, you have your time, and that is finished. This country is very personal.'

Arif, I thought, was beginning to feel the downside of success. He complained about his foreign trips. He worried that he didn't see his son, so the boy clung to him when he was at home. He seemed uncomfortable in the restaurant we went to, though we had to go to a place that looked expensive because he was entertaining an American buyer. The restaurant had black and white walls, mirrors, black tablecloths with white napkins and, through french windows, a lighted rock garden built as a decoration for the room. With the waiters in black tie, the only colour in the room was Mrs Zahur's blue satin below her diamonds.

Personal – one way of describing it. Tribal, cliquish, nepotistic are others. You could also say that rules and laws no longer apply, any semblance of system has disappeared, and these days it only matters who you know – personally. But it is a complicated business, this 'informality'.

In a sense, they run a class system and a tribal system simultaneously. You can be 'in' either by being, say, an Arain (the tribe of hard-working Punjabi small farmers that Arif and President Zia belong to) and tying yourself into the Arain network in the banks, the civil service, the judiciary, to get your loans, or your file passed on, or your case settled. Or, if you have been to the right school or university, or you now get invited to the right parties, you can tie into the old-boy-and-new-friends network.

One effect of this is the help and hospitality offered to me all over the country. Being white, I immediately qualified for the second group. If you are running a system of exclusivity, you can afford to be generous to those who are accepted; and generosity is a way of keeping the club strong. But the class clubbery isn't as tight as it was in Britain when Britain was at a comparable economic stage – say 150 years ago. Partly, the pedigrees of those claiming class are not long enough; and partly, the tribal network, weak though it is in towns, cuts through the class network.

Tribal and feudal duties – though nobody would ever talk of them like that – force you to look after not only the people who went to school with you, but also a lot of people who never could have. A young woman friend of mine complained that she had become an employment agency for all the people on her parents' estate; and I would listen to her telephone conversations about whether Rafiq's brother could get a job at that hospital, and whether anybody knew anybody who could ring the administrator.

The tribal network means that it is easier to become Arif Zahur than if the old boy network alone operates. Everybody belongs to something: even the mohajirs, uprooted from India, have brought their tribalism with them. A Memon – a community of very successful businessmen from western India – is more likely to help a Memon than a non-Memon. The Arains, it is said, have done well during Zia's rule.

It is also much easier to be Arif Zahur than it was twenty years ago. Ayub Khan ran a pro-industry policy which made a few industrialists very rich, and which was partly responsible for his downfall. The managing agency system, introduced by the British, meant that industrial families could run huge empires unconstrained by monopoly legislation or rules on shifting profits and losses between different companies. Those families owned the banks, and were accused of using their financial power to keep out competition.

People were aware of, and angry about, the concentration of money in so few hands. In 1968, Mahbub ul Haq, then the government's chief economist and finance, planning and commerce minister under Zia made a notorious speech attacking the 'twenty-two families' who, he claimed, owned about two thirds of the country's industrial assets, eighty per cent of banking and seventy per cent of insurance in the country.

'In the past,' he said, 'modernisation was foisted on a basically feudalistic structure in which political participation was often denied, [the] growth of responsible institutions stifled and free speech curbed, and where all economic and political powers gravitated towards a small minority. There is not much that can be done to save development from being warped in favour of a privileged few in a system like this unless the basic premises of the system are changed.'

Nobody is quite sure who the twenty-two families were supposed to be. Lawrence White, an American academic, trying to put figures on the concentration of wealth, found thirty families who controlled a little over half the assets on the Karachi stock exchange in 1968. Rashid Amjad, a Pakistani academic, found forty-one industrial houses which controlled eighty per cent of the assets, and ranked them slightly differently. But everybody includes, within the first ten families before 1970, the Saigols, the Habibs, the Adamjees, the Sheikhs, the Fancys and the Dawoods.

The lists of the successful testify to migrant power. Most of the top families were not native to the area that became Pakistan. Before partition, Hindus monopolised trading and there was hardly any industry. The cotton which Pakistan grew in abundance was exported to Britain or to Bombay, not processed in Karachi. Some of the prominent business families which did originate from Pakistan went elsewhere to make money. The Saigols, for instance, were in Calcutta before partition, running the leather business which the Hindus despise .

The Memons, from Kathiawar and Jetpur in western India, made up the single most successful business community in Ayub's time. The Dawoods and the Adamjees, who rank first and second on most people's pre-1970 lists, are both Memons. They are not a religious group, but a caste, like the Patels or India's dominant business caste, the Marwaris. I asked one of the younger Adamjees, Iqbal, to account for their success:

'I suppose we do nothing else,' he said. 'You'll hardly ever find a Memon doctor, for instance. We talk business at breakfast, lunch and dinner. But we're unusual for a business community. We spend a lot of money. We like to have good homes, we travel a lot.' I got some measure of the resilience of these people from the Adamjees' history. Most of their business, he said, was originally in Burma. That was all nationalised, so they moved to Pakistan. Two thirds of their business was in East Pakistan, and they lost that in 1971. Then half the rest was nationalised by Bhutto.

The small religious communities did well, too: Bohra Muslims (the Karims from Bombay) and Khoja Ismailis (the Fancys, who

84

were in East Africa before partition) feature on the lists. Certainly, the migrants prospered partly because they moved to Karachi, the country's only port, and the obvious place to set up new businesses; but the ability to move to the right place at the right time is part of the economic virtue of the migrant.

Almost all of the indigenous families that did well under Ayub were Punjabis, and almost all of those were from a little town called Chinyot. They are, unusually for Muslims, a community which for centuries has done business by habit and tradition and has continued to do so – perhaps because they were relatively recent Hindu converts to Islam. They tend to say they converted under the Moguls, while non-Chinyotis whisper that it was much more recent. When the Hindus and Sikhs left at partition, the Chinyotis were among the few Muslims who had experience of making money.

One of the few non-Punjabi houses that did well under Ayub was Gandhara industries, owned by General Habibullah. Like Ayub, the general was a Pathan. He was also Ayub's chief-of-staff, and the father-in-law of Ayub's son Gauhar. The president's family connections with oligopolistic wealth heightened the resentment against a system that allowed its increase and prevented its spread. Bhutto spotted the political potential of this resentment, and played to it at all levels. He wrote in *Political Situation in Pakistan* in 1968:

'A new class, small in number, of capitalist barons, is unabashedly plundering the nation's national wealth. The disparity between the rich and the poor keeps on growing. There are no anti-cartel or anti-monopolistic laws to prevent the abuse of privilege. There is not the slightest pretence of giving the system the appearance of humane capitalism, as is done by the more intelligent capitalist governments. Here, in Pakistan, there is free loot.'

Then the protestors, the students, trade unionists and professionals started coming out on the streets, forming the nucleus of what was to be Bhutto's PPP and, in the process, bringing down Ayub. When they brought Bhutto to power, they expected policies which followed logically from his speeches and writings, and they got them. The 'basic premises' which Mahbub ul Haq wanted changed were shaken up radically.

The private sector was no longer allowed to let rip. It had a role, Bhutto said; but its needs were to be subservient to those of the nation, not vice versa. Butto thought that government should own 'basic' industries, so in January 1972, it took over iron and steel,

85

heavy engineering, car and tractor manufacture and assembly, chemicals, cement and a whole spread of heavy industries. The big families reeled, stopped investing and kept their heads down or started up abroad.

As the new year of 1974 struck, Bhutto announced that he was nationalising the banks and life insurance. He said it would help the businessmen get over their hangovers. Since the industrialists had convinced themselves, through the warmth of a speech he had recently made, that Bhutto had promised no further nationalisations, they felt betrayed, and began to hope for revenge. Certainly they helped to finance his downfall and are blamed for it by his left-wing loyalists. But it doesn't seem that, by themselves, the big businessmen would have got rid of the government.

The far more numerous small businessmen, with their flour, cotton-jinning and rice-husking mills, were more dangerous. Bhutto earned their hatred in 1976 when he nationalised those businesses; and that step struck terror into the hearts of the pettiest businessmen. If he could take over the tiny operations of small men, where would he stop? The rice-huskers and the flour-millers had the street-level contacts to organise strikes and protests; and, with their full backing, the movement to overthrow Bhutto took off.

Private investment virtually stopped during the Bhutto years. After 1977, when it became clear that Zia's government was friendly towards the private sector, it picked up again, and industry has grown energetically in the past ten years. The warm business climate – which may be to do with good harvests, or with heroin and smuggling money churning round the economy and increasing demand for imports and domestic manufactures – cannot really be set to the government's credit. But a few measures, like the return of a few enterprises to the private sector, and the delicensing of industries and imports, have made it easier for the businessman to expand confidently. And, of course, there has been not a sniff of socialism in the air.

Business after Bhutto, though, was different to business before Bhutto. Hardly surprising: you cannot expect to blow up a house and find the pieces all settle in the same place. But both the form of growth, and the sort of people who were doing well, were unfamiliar. There were some involuntary changes, and, it seems, some decisions that businessmen made consciously or half-consciously, which were designed to ensure that the same thing did not happen to them again.

Some of the business houses disappeared, others never recovered their prominence. Whether they lost their confidence in the country, or in themselves, or whether the new environment gave others a chance, is unclear. Only their decline is obvious. There are names on those old blacklists – the Fancys and the Valikas, for instance – which are rarely heard these days. The Adamjees, survivors of Burma and Bangladesh, are still a big name, but they haven't begun to recover their pre-1971 position. 'We've got very tired of taking these knocks,' said Iqbal Adamjee. The family had been so shaken up, he said, that it had stopped working as a unity. There was so much uncertainty in the air that the family members couldn't agree on a joint course of action, so they decided to split up. He and his father were one unit, located up the sidestairs of Adamjee House. This grand building on Karachi's main business street, Chundrigarh Road, has a vast sign above its main door for the state-owned Muslim Commercial Bank, which occupies most of it: that was the Adamjees' bank before nationalisation.

The Saigols – somewhere in the top four of everybody's pre-1970 lists – are still there at the top. But they are now just a group of powerful individuals: the family no longer exists. It split, not just for future security, but also because of rows. Maybe it got too big: there probably comes a point when the organism is too large to continue, and has to break up and grow into separate new empires.

Naseem, although he looks only forty, is probably the biggest of those individual Saigols. He is a small, very clever, pixieish man who watches you closely. I met him at his house, which was designed for him, and rises and falls in a sequence of rooms at different levels leaving a geographical confusion and an impression of marble, rich carpets and silk-covered cushions and women. Around the walls are tables with collections of curious antiques or small pieces of modern sculpture.

The party was by the swimming pool, with circles of chairs and tables and uniformed men carrying trays standing discreetly by guests and waiting for their attention. On one side of the pool was a grove of the type of palm trees whose symmetry and straightness make them look plastic; on the other was a grove of eucalyptus, their pale trunks, ethereal in the spotlights, leading to the expectation of distant half-seen nymphs flitting in and out of the further darkness. In the foreground, men in blazers and white jackets leant their heads together, and women kissed, moved on, perched on the edges of chairs, rose and kissed. Naseem oiled the party's wheels, introducing people, breaking up sterile conversations and muttering orders to the uniformed phalanx.

His office, where I arranged to meet him, fitted his history. I couldn't find it at first. He told me the road it was in, and the buildings it was near; but I was looking for something large and imposing, in keeping with the Saigol wealth. Then, through a gate that looked as though it led to a private house, I found an unobtrusive grey concrete building, mostly covered in bougainvillea. It was an office keeping a very low profile.

Naseem Saigol was in a spacious room furnished with not much except two (imitation, I thought) antique globes. He wore a cream shalwar kamees and a fawn waistcoat, indistinguishable from most of the male population of Pakistan, except that his were clean and ironed, and out of his waistcoat's breast pocket bloomed a cream silk handkerchief.

The family was, unusually, from Chakwal, a part of Punjab famous not for business but for the soldiers it bred. They went to Calcutta and built up their leather business, which expanded into shoe-making and tyres. They decided to stay in Calcutta after independence, but Jinnah contacted them, as one of the few successful Muslim business families, and asked them to help build up Pakistani industry. Along with the Dawoods, they built the first cotton mills, then expanded into cement, established a big chemical complex outside Lahore and started the United Bank in 1952.

Ayub Khan, who had more in common with businessmen than with the landlords, encouraged businessmen to go into politics. He brought in a Dawood and A.K. Sumar, another leading Memon, and invited Rafique Saigol, Naseem's elder brother, to join. Rafique became the member of the national assembly for the textile town of Faisalabad, minister of communications and treasurer of the Muslim League.

'I think it was a major mistake,' said Naseem. 'When Mr Bhutto came to power, we were among the first to be selected for his attentions. He was afraid not only of our economic power, but also of our political power. Soon after the election, I met him in Lahore. I told him I was building a house – that house you came to. He said you don't need a house, you need to leave the country.

'Then he came to Faisalabad and made a speech. He said he wanted to caution the workers in our mills to keep a close watch on the owners. How could we go to our factories after that? We managed them by remote control, never entering them.'

Of course, he said, Mr Bhutto asked them to join politics. And Rafique did join him: he ran Pakistan International Airways for two years. He discovered he was sacked when he read it in the newspapers. But that was Bhutto all over, said Naseem: he liked to have his enemies close to him, so he could victimise them.

Naseem thought it was difficult for businessmen to know how to manage politics. They didn't really have time to cultivate politicians, because the ministries changed hands too often. Mostly, they concentrated on public relations and on influencing the bureaucrats, but that was getting more complicated, too.

'The same set of bureaucrats has been working under Zia for eight years. Now, as you know, they are not very happy with the political government. You ask them for something, and they say let the minister take the decision. The minister doesn't know anything, so politics comes into it. You have to get a member of the national assembly on your side . . . and all the time, the bureaucrats are sitting back and smiling, waiting for the politicians to fall on their faces.'

Was it, I asked, any better under the generals? He shrugged. 'They were more systematic. We didn't like Ghulam Ishaq Khan [king of the bureaucrats and Zia's finance minister before he became president after Zia's death] but he was a strict budgeter, and a disciplinarian. Now it's all erratic: suddenly there's a duty, then an extra duty . . . you can't make economic policy like that.'

How, I wondered, did businessmen get their political views across, if they were wary of politics these days? There was the Chamber of Commerce, he said; but really, there were somewhere between fifty and a hundred opinion-formers, who were always in contact with each other about any important issue. They would have a view, and that was the view of the business community. And were those people set against Benazir? Yes, he said with a wry smile. She has moderated her views since she came back, but . . .

The trouble was, he said, that Pakistan needed the sort of set-up Turkey had, where the Army's role in government was written into the constitution. But the people of the subcontinent were very politically aware. They might accept, pragmatically, that in a country like Pakistan a military government was the answer, but they wouldn't accept it intellectually, so martial law met with protests.

The politics of businessmen like Naseem Saigol, and the government's reaction, is neatly summed up in two quotations. Bhutto was sent a report, in April 1977, which said that,

'Among those who have contributed large sums of money to the PNA fund in Lahore [is] Naseem Saigol.'

Bhutto answered:

'The Income Tax Department, the Excise and Taxation Department, etc, may be asked to take care of these industrialists so that they are engaged elsewhere and cease taking interest in the agitation. The Commerce Ministry may also be asked to blacklist these persons for the time being and not to issue any import-export licences to them until the agitation ends, so that they may give more attention to their business problems and less to the political agitation.' Harassment on the street, therefore, was to be met with harassment in the ministries, the shouts of demonstrators with the bureaucratic cold-shoulder.

But while Bhutto did no favours to the big families, it may be that his policies in the end helped business grow. I found Sultan Lakhani in the family's new development in central Karachi. He is the eldest of four brothers who in less than ten years have built Laksons, a group with a turnover of $200 million which makes cigarettes, soaps and detergents, surgical instruments and paper and board. The two towers of Lakson Square, honeycombs of concrete rooms, were still being built; but the atrium of the partially-occupied one was impeccable, with white marble, trailing plants, and a sound-proofed quiet that blocked out the background Karachi noise.

I thought perhaps my difficulty in making an appointment with Sultan Lakhani, and his reluctance to talk once I met him, might be to do with being an Ismaili. I had met it before amongst that community, and it struck me as probably wise. For such successful businessmen with, in the eyes of mainstream Muslims, unorthodox religious views, they have been remarkably free from persecution or even hostility; that may be not just because of their notorious philanthropy, but also because of their political discretion.

Mr Lakhani, a thin man with a reluctant smile, said one thing that surprised me after all I had heard from businessmen of the good old days of Ayub, and the horrors of the Bhutto years. He thought he would never have made it if the banks had not been nationalised.

'In Ayub's times, the banks just wanted to go for the big names, the good names. My father's credit limit was peanuts compared to

90

ours. These days, if you can persuade the banks that you'll work hard, you can get the money.'

The Ismailis have had some quiet business successes, lately. Apart from the Lakhani brothers, Sadruddin Hashwani has established himself as the biggest hotelier in the country, with the Holiday Inns and the Pearl-Continental chain, formerly Pan Am's Intercontinentals, to his credit. But the fastest-rising community in Karachi is the Punjabis who, after the disruptions of the 1970s, look as though they may be taking the mohajirs' place. I asked Sultan Lakhani why this was so. 'They work harder than the rest of us,' he said without humour.

In a country like Pakistan, the rise of the Punjabis isn't just a matter of modest sociological interest, like the fashions in Mancunian or Scottish accents on British television. Their success under the Zia government arouses passions. Since the Army is ninety-five per cent Punjabi, and the civil service is heavily Punjabi, Punjabi businessmen are accused of benefiting from eleven years of rule by the civil and military bureaucracy.

In the sort of tribal or racial atmosphere that has developed in Karachi over the past two years, this impression is a dangerous one. Those successful mohajir businessmen, the Dawoods and the Adamjees, are certainly not on the streets yelling against Punjabi domination; yet the visible Punjabi business successes have certainly heightened the anger of the protesters amongst the mohajir middle classes.

When the protests have turned to violence, Punjabis have not much been involved in the fighting: the shooting has been between mohajirs and Pathans, who are seen as taking jobs away from locals, and infecting the city with drugs and arms. But the growing alliance between the Punjabis and Pathans (sanctified in a political party, the Punjabi-Pakhtun Ittehad [union]) has heightened the divisions in the city, increasing the hostility between them and the mohajirs.

This 'tension' and 'hostility' is not just the stuff that stops people going to each other's parties, and results in the odd scrap between groups of youths. Too many lives have been lost and too many shops and houses burnt for people to talk of it lightly; yet I was still surprised how defensive people were who lived miles, geographically and economically, from the riot-hit areas.

I went to see Tariq Shafi, whose family, still united, runs what is probably the biggest private business group in the country, and waited outside his office in a back room of a Chundrigarh Road building. His secretary had permed hair and the half-starved look of girls in London advertising agencies that in Pakistan is prized only among the very rich or fashionable. She had a black jumper with a pair of huge red lips on it and matching fingernails. I asked where she bought the jumper. She had knitted it herself, she said with a devastating smile.

Tariq Shafi has a quick but welcoming handshake. He is an expansive young Chinyoti, good-looking in the open muscular style of a sportsman, with mischievous eyes and a grand moustache that creeps up his cheeks towards his temples in the manner of Victorian whiskers. His shirt was crisp, pure white cotton, his tie grey-and-pink striped silk, and his blue woollen blazer with brass buttons hung on a coat-stand. He was irritated already, answering the telephone and trying to send a test-message on his new mini-fax to his brother in Faisalabad; then I told him I was interested in the Punjabis making it big in Karachi.

'Shit,' he said, 'You want to kill us? Look, we've never before thought about being Punjabis or anything else. That phone call, that was from Iqbal Adamjee, one of my closest friends. Now people are saying we shouldn't be here, we should go back. Because of all this, there has been no new investment in Karachi for a year.'

His father and three brothers had started tanneries in Calcutta, Madras and Delhi. At partition they got a ginning mill in compensation. Their house was inside the mill in Faisalabad. His father got up every morning at four; and Tariq would automatically wake up and turn off the air conditioner, which his father disapproved of.

By the time Bhutto came to power, they were already among the lower ranks of the big families. They kept their heads down during the seventies, but have been expanding fast since, mostly in textiles. Tariq reckoned that their group turnover would be around 2.5 billion rupees. The family stuck together: the firm is still run by the youngest of the four brothers, and about sixteen cousins are in charge of different bits.

He took me down to the industrial area. The road was lined with high walls; behind the walls, the roofs of mills. They were all the old mills, he said, the ones that boomed in the fifties and sixties. The slump in the seventies was partly Bhutto's fault. Labour scared away the owners, mills closed and they were only just starting to be reopened, with this new cotton boom. He had bought an empty mill, was refurbishing it, and had imported some second-hand

Swiss shuttleless looms from a factory in Italy. They were much cheaper, he said, and good as new; but most people didn't want second-hand machinery because you couldn't get the loans from the government or the foreign agencies.

So it wasn't quite true that there was no investment? 'You always have to have some investment,' he said with a flick of his hand, 'just to keep things going. But there isn't nearly as much as there should be. I bought plots of land in the new industrial estate at Nooriabad. Great mistake. I can't do anything with them, and they're lying empty.'

'Why?' He looked at me in surprise. 'The place is miles out of town. With the law and order situation, the kidnappings and the riots, nobody is going to drive there.'

The green machines were waiting in giant plastic bags in the stripped warehouse. Three men were smoothing cement on a square of the floor as though it were a high art. Tariq checked the place, and moved quickly to the factory next door, which was up and running. After Arif Zahur's mill, this one felt crafted out of years of economy and ingenuity. The machinery was a hotch-potch built up, I suspected, with a lot of thought. There was clumsy old Chinese machinery for breaking up the cotton bales that arrived, smart new British ones twisting the cotton wool into a thick rope, Japanese ones for thinning the rope. Spinning was done by German machinery, and a lot of Japanese machinery that Tariq had picked up in a mill in Baluchistan that had gone bust, the weaving by ancient Pakistani and Japanese machines. Tariq said with admiration that they were as fast as the most modern; but the second-hand Swiss ones with which he was replacing them made higher-value cloth with fewer faults. Beyond them was a relatively quiet room of Taiwanese ones, a quarter of which were working. They, said Tariq, were a disastrous buy. 'Never trust the Taiwanese. You can't get the spare parts.'

In the car on the way back, I asked if he had ever thought of being anything but a businessman. He pondered, as though it were an unusual question. Sometimes he regretted it, he said; but he was born to it. There wasn't really any choice.

'Look, over 300 years, nobody from our family has gone into the Army, the bureaucracy or politics. We Chinyotis are just businessmen. In Punjab, the feudal lords sneer at us because we're just shopkeepers, we've got no class and no taste. Now we're getting it in Karachi too.' We ate chicken tikkas at his desk, while he signed papers when his hand was free.

'I am a mohajir too, you know. I have migrated from Faisalabad. My household is a real United Nations. The cook is Bengali, the maid Sri Lankan, the driver is a Pathan and the gardener a Sindhi. My children speak Urdu, not Punjabi. I put on a tape of Punjabi songs in the car, and my four-year-old son told me to take it off. I asked him why. He told me that only dogs speak that language.' He was worried about his children. He used to play with the boys in the street in Faisalabad; but the only contact his children had with people of another class was with the servants.

'We're not living in Pakistan. We have our air-conditioned cars, our videos, our satellite antennas. We've lost touch with the country.'

That isn't just because of the wealth capsule that the upper classes in all third world countries build to insulate themselves against the ugliness and violence around them and to provide them with some of the goodies of the rich world. It is also the effect of their political insecurity. Nawaz Sharif, the chief minister of Punjab with the four new textile mills next to Arif's, is one of the very few businessmen prepared to endanger their livelihood for political power. He was also, until he went into politics, fairly small fry, so he had less to lose than the big families, and a great deal to gain.

At thirty-six, he became one of the most powerful men in the country and an unusual chief minister for a province run by the landed. His rise was a consequence of the Zia years. Like Ayub, Zia was of the middle classes, and more at home with them than with the landlords. Although Nawaz Sharif came to power after the elections of 1985, he was picked up before then by the all-powerful military governor of Punjab, General Jilani, because he was bank-rolling the opposition *Tehrik-i-Istiqlal,* and the military government thought it would be useful to have a young man like that on their side. Since Zia wrote into his constitution that the president was to choose the provincial chief ministers as well as the prime minister, the generals had no trouble in putting Nawaz Sharif in power after the 1985 election.

I was summoned for breakfast at the chief minister's residence, a white colonial bungalow off Lahore's wide, tree-lined Mall. It was too early for me, but my arrival was eased by a chauffered limousine accompanied by a neatly-coiffed press man. The beauty of the winter morning woke me: the sunlight was pale through the trees, and there was one set of footprints in the dew on the long lawn beside the house. I was ushered by the whispering press man and two silent bearers into a room of white sofas, gilt-edged mirrors, and vases of floppy red roses.

Nawaz Sharif, a plump, pale young man, bald on top, gave the impression of wearing a cravat, although he was in shalwar kamees. He was uncomfortable and suspicious: who was sponsoring me to write this book? Why was I writing it? I began to wonder why he had agreed to see me. He had brought his protection: a tiny press man who hardly ate any of the four-course breakfast, and concentrated on echoing Nawaz Sharif's sentiments, annoying the chief minister as well as me.

Nawaz Sharif told me that the government was deeply concerned about the uplift of the poor. Unemployment and homelessness were their main priorities. (Shelter for the shelterless, said the press man; Nawaz Sharif ignored him.) The only real solution to unemployment, though, was industrial investment. (Industrial investment, nodded the press man. Nawaz Sharif glared at him.) I was concentrating on the waiters in white pagris, who were bringing round plates of food which were evidently coded: if you took the scrambled eggs, you were supposed to take the toast from the next plate, if you took the spiced omelette, you were supposed to take the parathas, and if you took the chick-pea curry, you were meant to have the light, buttery puris. I tried to eat bits of all of them and make notes.

There had been a great industrial expansion recently. He thought, to be fair, that the credit for this should go to the martial law government. General Zia gave back industry to the owners, and they had repaid by investing.

How, I asked, was his business doing these days? He frowned slightly, and waved his hand.

'I hardly have time to go there . . . I believe some expansion has taken place, but my family takes care of that. I have a very heavy schedule.' ('Very heavy schedule,' said the press man.) In fact, Nawaz Sharif said, leaning forward with his first sign of animation, he was in favour of having a tax holiday for business investments all over the country. In which industries? All. 'Let us,' he said with conviction, 'let capacity grow. Afterwards, we can tax it.' It struck me as an irresponsible thing for a chief minister to say when the government was on the edge of an economic crisis brought about by its failure to generate enough resources; but Nawaz Sharif was apparently pleased with it, because the next day it appeared on the front page of all the major newspapers.

He was less happy when I asked him about an article I had enjoyed in the previous day's newspaper:

'The Chief Minister said that victory and defeat in the elections was in the hands of God Almighty, and by the grace of God Almighty the Muslim Leaguers would win. He said that these elections were being held strictly on non-party basis and it was unlawful to use name or platform of any party. The law was there and it would be enforced, he added.'

I had laughed aloud reading the story, wondering whether the journalist who had written it had juxtaposed these two statements for his readers' amusement. Mr Sharif also, it seemed, noticed the contradiction. He denied that he had said it and asked, in a manner that suggested our interview was at an end, whether I enjoyed Pakistan, and how long I would be staying.

To find out how Mr Sharif's business had been getting on since he had come to power, I dropped in on Ittefaq Industries, and found a Mr Amin in the overcrowded offices on the ground floor of Ferozesons Building on Empress Road. Mr Amin was proud to explain how much expansion there had been recently. In 1981–2, according to the company report, turnover had been 337 million rupees. The report's figures only went up to 1983–4, when turnover was 537 million. But Mr Amin said that by 1986–7 it was at least 2,500 million. The group had had little more than the foundry and a textile mill five years earlier. Since then, it had built the biggest sugar mill in Asia, four textile mills (and another on the way), and a private hospital in Lahore. Mr Amin explained the phenomenal growth. The chairman, he said, was a very religious man: God had rewarded his devotion.

Evidently Nawaz Sharif's business interests were not suffering from his involvement in politics. Yet money-making is not a sufficient reason for going into politics: any reasonably canny businessman can do well under a neutral government by knowing a few of the right people. Politics is a serious risk to a family like the Sharifs: their financial problems start when they are out of power. Then, as the businessmen who made the mistake of being seen to be too close to Benazir suffered under Zia, the Sharifs can expect bad times. When I next met Nawaz Sharif, just after Zia's death, he was a worried man.

Like Tariq Shafi, the biggest businessmen wouldn't touch politics with a barge-pole. That isn't just because they have been brought up to have nothing to do with it; experience and observation have taught such men that they are more vulnerable than landlords are to changes in government. Governments have no difficulty in making life hard for businesses, using the methods which Bhutto suggested should be used against those he had heard were financing the PNA: questions about their tax returns, rejections of applications for licences, detention of imports at customs. Professional businessmen are not, by and large, interested in taking those risks. Those who do, like Rafique Saigol, may learn to regret it.

You might argue that it is a good thing if money keeps out of politics – that if capital gets too strong a hold on Islamabad, there will never be social progress of the sort that educates the poor and starts to raise their incomes. I think I would disagree. I couldn't help feeling that the country's future would feel safer if its wealth-producers felt they had more of a stake in it. Too many people muttered to me about the financial 'parachutes' they had set aside abroad for themselves: they were ready to bail out.

If the businessmen are insufficiently involved in running the country, it isn't really their fault. A few of them, particularly under Ayub, did try; but Bhutto's measures against them decreased their corporate clout, and his treatment of them seems to have warned them off. Pakistan's history, in which successive governments have wreaked easy and devastating vengeance on their predecessors' supporters, doesn't encourage people to test the political waters – particularly people as vulnerable as businessmen, who governments can make or destroy. Landlords are less easy to hurt: they, I thought, would have the security to play politics.

5

LANDLORDS

THE PAJERO JEEP swung out of a steep alley into a sloping village square surrounded by windowless twenty-foot high walls that gave it the air of a prison exercise yard. Before the driver could get to Chandi's door, a boy had appeared out of the dusk to open it. Chandi put her black embroidered dupatta, which had fallen onto her shoulders during the journey, back over her head and stepped out. A little group of people surrounded the jeep and greeted her, bowing low, arms outstretched to touch her knee or her foot. She, talking to the driver, made a small attempt to raise the nearest woman; but the woman ignored the pressure of the hand and carried on with her obeisances.

We walked away from the reception committee up a narrow street, to a carved gate. It opened inwards and two women came out with a flower-patterned sheet. They stood on the far side of the gate, each with an arm stretched up holding a corner of the sheet, which became a screen. I asked Chandi what that was for.

'My modesty,' she replied shortly; then seeing I wanted more, explained. 'You know the chador we wear on our heads? That means sheet or curtain, and this is the same idea. At the end of the street is the village bazaar, and unless they put up a chador for me, there is a risk that a man might see me. I am the first woman in my family not to be in purdah. They know that I make speeches to hundreds of men; but . . .' Without resolving the contradiction, she passed into a high-walled garden.

Under the verandah of a long house that faced onto the garden, Chandi hoisted herself up onto a three-foot-high, ten-foot-long platform and sat on an embroidered cloth, leaning on sausage-shaped cushions. The dais was arranged so that the sitter, silhou-etted against the trees and flowerbeds, should face the audience on the verandah. A man and two women brought an oil lamp and an ancient telephone, put the telephone beside her, and squatted round the lamp on the floor, while she talked to them. I remembered where I had seen the platform before: in the Red Fort in Delhi, in the emperor's diwan, his audience hall; only there, it was white marble carved into flowers and arabesques of stems. The semi-precious stones that should have inlaid the carving had been taken away, probably by British soldiers during the mutiny. There the emperor Akbar and his descendants had held court, as Chandi did in her village, legs tucked under her, leaning on silk-covered bolsters like a dictionary illustration of how the Persian word for audience had, in English, become a sofa.

On the outer wall of the house were photographs of racehorses: a gallery of glossy, undifferentiable animals held by a man with a moustache, a trilby and a severe long face whom I took to be Chandi's father. She appeared by his side in a couple: a very young, very sixties-looking Chandi, with bouffant hair under her dupatta and the serious expression of a girl who is beginning to go about in public.

Lower down in the village, drumming started. It wasn't drumming for its own sake, the skill of interplaying a vocabulary of rhythms that catches your heartbeat and takes your breath away; it was monotonous, one-beat drumming-for-a-purpose, moving slowly about the village as though gathering people. It tugged at me through my tiredness, and I wanted to follow it, to find out what mysteries it was playing out. Above the slow waves of drumming, small contributing choruses of barking rose then died back again, while the drum went on. Then another drum answered, on the opposite side of the village, moving to and fro and catching, then losing, the beat of the first drum. A third started up, destroyed the rhythms and turned the drumming into a great throbbing circle.

The question she had been discussing, Chandi explained as we bumped down through the village, was whether she herself should stand in the local elections. She didn't really want to: she was already a member of parliament and had served for long enough on the district council. But she was worried that, if she stayed out of the race, her Wicked Cousin and his allies might snatch control of the council. So she was waiting to see whether he would stand, and he was waiting to see whether she would stand . . .

In the middle of the explanation, she fell suddenly silent. She stared downwards at the hands folded in her lap. I started to speak at the same time as she did, and withdrew.

'We just passed my ancestor's grave. I had to make a small prayer to him.' In the darkness, I could just make out the shape of a hill, on top of which were two uncertain white lights, one above the other.

Chandi is Abida Hussein, a landowner and thus one of the class known as feudals, the ruling élite, or just ordinary farmers, depending on who you talk to. They are blamed for many of the social and political ills of Pakistan, because they have had a lot to do with the way things have gone in the country. Their business is farming, but they tend to concentrate on their hobbies of shooting and politics.

There are probably only 5,000 or so Pakistani landed families that matter, but their political importance is disproportionate to their numbers or even their wealth. Any slice of Pakistani history has the big names playing their part: the Qureshis, Gardezis, Noons, Tiwanas, Soomros, Khuros, Bhuttos, Jatois and a social and political Who's Who of families. The landowners have dominated any sort of parliament in the area, even before Pakistan was created; they have held on to a fat slice of every cabinet, and have provided the last two prime ministers of Pakistan, Zulfikar Ali Bhutto and Mohammed Khan Junejo. In this, Pakistan is quite different to India. Important Hindus have been businessmen more than land-lords; and the Congress party has been dominated by Brahmins who, by tradition, do not own land. Land reforms since partition have helped wipe out large estates.

The British are usually blamed for creating the classes and encouraging the failings that prevent Pakistan from living up to Pakistani ideals; but the foundations of landed estates were built long before the Raj. They are the result of conquest, and the conqueror's need for loyal barons to run the countryside. The Moguls turned pragmatism into a system of administration, and land and revenues from land were given out as prizes in victory or as payment for the job of putting together troops when the king needed them.

According to J.M. (later Sir James) Douie, expounding the principle of land revenue at the beginning of his *Punjab Settlement Manual*, the handbook of land revenue assessment written for British civil servants, land revenue is more like a rent than a tax: it qualifies the landlord's absolute title to land. Insecurity of tenure, particularly among the rich, is a useful piece of leverage for any colonial ruler, Mogul or British. The emperor giveth, and the emperor taketh away. 'The Native Governments which preceded our own found it convenient to secure the swords of the brave, and the prayers of pious men, to pacify deposed chiefs and to reward powerful servants, by assigning to them the ruler's share of the produce of the land in particular villages or tracts. The system . . . was too deep-rooted for a foreign government to destroy. Prudence dictated its continuance.'

Being British, the colonisers wanted the revenue system, which had fallen into some disrepair by the time they were getting round to administering India, properly organised and written down. So starting with the Permanent Settlement of Bengal in 1793, they allocated title to land.

The settlements helped consolidate large estates. Previously, land revenue had been set at about the same level as, or sometimes higher than, the rentable value of land. Land was therefore not much in demand: there was a shortage of tenants, rather than of cultivable acres. The British set land revenue lower than the 'Native Governments' had, which made it immediately more valuable. When the settlements came round, therefore, landlords were keen to establish their sole proprietory rights. Sir Charles Aitchison, Lieutenant-Governor of Punjab in the 1880s, pointed out this problem in his biography of John Lawrence. 'Some of the officers entrusted with the revision of the revenue settlement had imbibed extreme views of ownership and were disinclined to recognise a double right in the soil . . . In one division of the province, out of 46,000 heads of agricultural households who had been recorded as occupancy-tenants, more than three-quarters were, by a stroke of the pen, reduced to the position of tenants at will, liable to eviction or rack-rent.'

Irrigation, Britain's most solid economic contribution to the subcontinent, increased both prosperity and the potential for patronage. Most of Punjab and Sind were salt deserts in the mid-nineteenth century. In order to raise agricultural production, the British started building a huge network of canals which are still the spine of Pakistan's irrigation system: great concrete headworks, with three or four canals maybe a hundred feet across cutting away through the countryside, branching out, turning once-infertile areas green. Land thus became suddenly valuable; and a grant of land was a gift of an income for the family for ever.

Sind had, and still has, the highest concentration of large landholdings. Earlier and more intensive irrigation in Punjab made the difference. Although the British handed out some of Punjab's newly-irrigated crown lands as patronage to the already-rich, the bulk went in smallish plots. Peasants from the overpopulated areas in east Punjab – mostly Sikhs, who were thought to be strong, hard-working fellows – were imported, given small farms, and told to grow food. Selection was simple: men were lined up, the fine physical specimens chosen, the weak rejected. One Mr J.A. Grant, settlement officer in Amritsar, recorded his method in 1893: 'walking down the row I could easily see the men who were physically unsuitable . . . His colour would often betray the habitual opium-eater, and his general appearance (more especially his hands) the shaukin [fop] and jawan [young man] who . . . had never done a hand's turn of honest work behind the plough . . . A show of hands is a simple method for discovering the real workers amongst the community.'

Ayub Khan, the middle-class soldier, tried some land reforms, but they had little effect. Bhutto, the people's man, promised more: 'The remaining vestiges of feudalism,' he wrote, 'require to be removed.' But less land changed hands under his reforms than under Ayub's: knowing that Bhutto the landowner was unlikely to push them too far, people put land in the names of their distant relations, their loyal retainers, and even their peasants without telling them. The vestiges of feudalism clung on.

Money, and the power of eviction over tenants, are useful resources for those who wish to influence governments, because governments need the support, and fear the opposition, of people who have those things. But in Pakistan landlords have authority which goes way beyond their economic clout. Most are the heads of braderis, which are manifestations of a sort of diluted tribalism, rather like the Scottish clans of two hundred years ago. A braderi is not ethnic, linguistic, or religious: it is just a club that you were born into whose solidarity is based on the legend or fact of distant, shared ancestry.

A member of your braderi who gets into a position of power is likely to attend to the interests of his fellow-members before the national interest, so even the poorest person in the clan will tend to want the richest fellow-member to become a minister. Thereafter, if the system is working properly, jobs, promotions, electrification, canals, land grants, contracts, subsidies, should flow, preferentially, to the braderi members. Whether an impoverished sharecropper thinks it out that carefully when going to vote for the zamindar who represents his clan is irrelevant: in the countryside, collective clan voting clearly has a huge – but not always reliable – impact on election results.

The landowners' other source of power is religious. Not all of them have it, but those who do make use of it – even if Chandi, in the presence of a foreign friend, brushed away the obeisances of her spiritual followers. Religious power among the landed gentry has two origins. One, in Islamic terms, is reasonably legitimate: the spiritual authority that accrues to those who are directly descended from the prophet (or who claim to be, and are believed). They are the Sayyeds, who trace their genealogy back to a migration either directly from Saudi Arabia, or through their ancestors' wanderings through Iraq, Iran and Afghanistan. Around the world, the significance of Sayyed-ness varies from a vague aura of aristocracy to sizeable political clout; and in Pakistan, it tends towards the latter.

The second source of religious power is pir-dom. Pirs are saints, or, since holiness seems to be hereditary, the descendants of saints. They have no place in mainstream Islam, which abhors the notion not just of the worship of men, but also of intercession between man and God; but Pakistani Islam has some eccentricities. The great pirs – like Chandi's ancestor – were mostly Sufi mystics, men whose extreme holiness enabled them to perform miracles, and whose shrines and descendants are thought to be able to achieve the same effects today. Most people have their own – living – pir, whom they will ask for advice, and for charms to sort out health, income tax, and family problems. As a result pirs become wealthy people, since the only restrictions on the amount they charge for charms are the poverty and scepticism of their followers. Poverty has always been there; scepticism comes slowly. Sir Malcolm Lyall Darling, a British civil servant, wrote about Chandi's area early this century, 'The peasantry, almost to a man, confess themselves servants of the one true God and Mohammed is his prophet, but in actual fact they are the servants of the landlord, money-lender and pir. All the way down the Indus from far Hazara in the north to Sind in the south, these three dominate men's fortunes; and though they are found in greater or lesser degree all over the province, nowhere are they so powerful.' The money-lender has gone, with the departure of the

103

Hindus at partition; in its place is the Agricultural Development Bank of Pakistan, whose rates are less extortionate. The other two persist.

Democracy demands that people should be divided into camps, and tribalism and religion are one way of doing it. Pakistan's tribalism is too disparate and diluted to lead to the kind of politics that can be found in bits of Africa, where the biggest tribe will, unless the other grabs military power, always run the country and discriminate against the smaller tribes. Yet even the Pakistani system seemed to me to have distinct disadvantages. As Chandi and the other landlords I met proved, either because of what they said or what they were, politicians are selected not because they are clever, or they have intelligent policies, or even – unless you get a man like Bhutto who stirs imaginations – because they promise to improve the lot of the poor, but because of the number of followers who think they will do better if their own man is in power.

But Pakistani society is at an interesting point where tribal and religious pulls are no longer reliable. Villagers are getting choosier about the people they are prepared to elect. The families themselves split, put up rival candidates, and find that competition, combined with an increasingly discerning electorate, requires them to perform. More alarmingly for the landlords, at times ancient loyalties can be swept away by a new enthusiasm or hatred.

In the twenties and thirties, the Punjabi landlords' party, the Unionists, was the strongest party in Punjab, and took the British line on all matters of importance. But the Muslim League's call for Pakistan stirred Punjabis, and in the 1940s the Unionists crumbled. The ascendancy of the Muslim League did not force Punjab's landlords into opposition: instead they joined the new ruling party. An old left-wing landlord I went to see in Multan, the only person I met who talked willingly about the now conveniently-forgotten Unionist period, told me (extracting a promise that I should not use names) the story of a still-prominent neighbouring family, loyal Unionists, in the 1940s. The head of the family got a call from the governor's house, telling him that partition would happen, so he should join the Muslim League. His son, he was told, would be arrested, taken to jail, and there should slap the superintendent, shouting Pakistan *Zindabad* (Long Live Pakistan). These things came to pass, and the son was sent into solitary confinement, with fans, servants, and food from home. The story of his bravery echoed round the town; and after twenty-one days, when he stepped out

104

of jail, the people shouted British *Murdabad* (Death to the British) and placed garlands round his neck.

With few exceptions, the landlords have been with every government since partition. Policies often favoured industry and the towns against the land, yet the landlords rarely took themselves into opposition. They preferred to be with the government, even if the government was not with them: like their ancestors under the Moguls and the British, they are better at functioning in government than in opposition. They have never pretended to offer their people ideological comfort: what they can provide is a share of the benefits of power, in return for which they expect support.

Bhutto was a shock to them. He was a landlord himself, but a Sindhi; to start with, some of the Sindhi landowners were with him, but the Punjabis were not. He rejected the usual method of gathering support in the countryside, the making of deals with landlords, braderi and religious leaders, for a direct appeal to the masses. When he won the 1971 election, Punjab's landlords were, by and large, excluded from power; though a few families, like the Noons and the Qureshis, had insured themselves by offering up candidates to the PPP, and so managed to keep a family member in the governing party. But, like stray sheep, the landlords returned to the fold of government: through the 1970s, the vestiges of feudalism drifted into the PPP.

Bhutto's demise did not mean the fall of the landlords who supported him. Zia started off with a lot of ministers and advisers from middle-class backgrounds similar to his own – like Javed Hashmi, whom the reader will meet later. But uncertain dictatorships tend to go for ready-made power bases, and the landlords, offering a phalanx of strong rural support, edged their way in, and, from the 1985 elections onwards, dominated the polity. Three-quarters of the members of the senate, the national assembly and the provincial assemblies were landlords.

Even the economics currently in vogue in the World Bank, which is not hugely bothered about the distribution of wealth (on the grounds that the market will sort it all out in the end) complains about the survival of large farms. Economic studies suggest that middling farms produce more per acre than do large farms. But, talking to landlords in Pakistan, it seems to me that overall figures mask a big difference between two sorts of landlord – the 'vestiges of feudalism' and the new, competitive capitalist landlord. The first you find more of in Sind, the second you find some of in Punjab.

If they bother, large farmers are good at getting their hands on the inputs needed to go for high-intensity Green Revolutionary agriculture: they know the bank managers to get loans from, they know how to import tractors, they know where the fertiliser is being handed out. They are rich enough to take risks, they know how to operate the system, and are beginning to look like the professionals who farm vast acres of Europe and make their profits from understanding the Common Agricultural Policy. Their domination of politics helps: despite decades of constant pressure from bureaucrats like the planning minister, Mahbub ul Haq, for the imposition of an agricultural income tax, they still pay none. Even military governments have not dared take the one step that would unite the country's most powerful class against them.

I sought Chandi out soon after the election of 1985. I had heard of her as a dynamic woman, a member of parliament elected in her own right (most of the women are nominated to the twenty reserved seats) and the wife of the young Speaker of the National Assembly. Oppositions are usually more interesting than governments to journalists, who tend to try to find out what is wrong with what the government says, and Chandi was part of a group that seemed to be gelling into an opposition. Not the real opposition, of course, since most of the political parties had boycotted the election; but the opposition among the people who knew a bit about what was going on.

She is a small, round, bright-eyed woman with the expression of a determined child. Jibes from male parliamentary colleagues about her plumpness are usually answered with sharp insults about their physical or mental failings; so those comments have been abandoned in favour of complaints about the quickness of her temper. She has an acute, magpie intelligence, picking up small bits of information and ideas and building them into her latest campaign.

Her background is a convenient combination of class and money. The story goes that her maternal grandmother was in love with one of her cousins, who was already married. When his wife died, they expected to be allowed to marry; but the great-grandfather, angry that the cousin seemed relieved by his wife's demise, said they would do so over his dead body. Instead, he would give his daughter to the first man who asked for her. The next day, a young man with a patched coat, who said he was a Sayyed (an immutable requirement) asked for the girl, and was given her.

He became Sir Maratib Ali, who made millions contracting for the British, principally as the main caterer to the Army in Punjab, and thus launched one of Pakistan's biggest business families. Along with the Nawab of Kalabagh he financed the Unionist party and, like any *nouveau-riche* aspirant to class and power, married his children off to some of the better landed families in the province. One daughter was married to Chandi's father, who had land around Jhang in central Punjab; another to Chandi's husband's father, whose estates were in southern Punjab, near Multan.

Chandi was educated in Pakistan, then sent abroad to finishing school in Switzerland. She returned with a fashionable 'sixties hairstyle and a desire for independence, but her family decided that she should marry her first cousin, and, after a fight, she acquiesced. Cousin-marriage guarantees that the Sayyed blood-line stays pure. Chandi and her husband, who was a minister in Zia's first military government, have turned out to be good political partners, fighting and winning their respective district council and national elections in their hereditary constituencies, and working together in parliament. Her quick acerbity complements his diligence.

She commutes between her estate, her family in Lahore, politics in Islamabad and conferences abroad (women politicians from Islamic countries, being in short supply, are in international demand). Her two jeans-and-T-shirt-clad teenage daughters and her eleven-year-old son don't get much of her time; but one of her daughters still wants to be a politician. The son wants to be a geologist, but watches his mother's politics carefully. When Chandi's Wicked Cousin was made a minister, she derided his appointment on the grounds that he had never won an election. 'But Mama,' said her son, 'Abu (Daddy) was not elected when Zia made him minister.' That, said Chandi, was quite different.

I drove to Jhang to watch her campaigning for the district council elections. Going west out of Lahore, towards Faisalabad, we crossed the Ravi, drained by the drought that hit the whole subcontinent in 1987. By European standards it was still wide; but on either side were great grey mud flats with buffalos wallowing in shallow pools and small boats dragged up on them like a row of dead insects. I wondered how many canals there were downstream which were not being properly fed; how many fields were therefore not being properly watered that season; how many labourers and tractor mechanics unemployed ... Nothing can push the whole of a western economy into depression the way failed rains can destroy a year of an agricultural country's growth.

The land was flat, the farming neat and rich: thick fields of sugar cane, as high as a man and shining green in the sun, maize, waving feather flowers, carpets of potato leaves and bright yellow fields of what might have been mustard. Every few miles was the red splash of a brick kiln, with a forty-foot-high chimney spouting black smoke, and workers dark with sun piling up <u>newly baked bricks</u> in blocks. The road was good and straight. The buses, glittering with their shiny metal decorations, travelled, like us, at sixty m.p.h., and so were less of a danger than the buffalo carts lumbering along, laden with families, at five m.p.h.

I passed the time counting tractors. I saw ten in twenty kilometres, most of them herded around workshops in the villages we passed through. Were they necessary or useful in a country with a growing population and growing unemployment? They implied an impressive amount of capital, but whose was it? Their existence did not prove their utility, only that somebody in government or an aid agency had decided that it would be a good thing to lend people cheap money to buy them. The ancient simplicity that rural life appears to have preserved, with workers in hand-woven cloth driving their buffalo-carts full of sugar cane at dusk, and rising at dawn to tend the cotton, is deceptive. Agriculture in countries like Pakistan is hardly less dependent on civil servants than it is in Europe. There is always a tractor policy, a handloom board, a sugar support price, a cotton purchasing corporation.

Arriving in Jhang, we drove through thick gateposts into a curved drive leading up to an old bungalow, the pillars of its verandah almost hidden by pink and orange bougainvillea. There was a crowd and a commotion between the Pajero parked in the drive and the front door: thirty men pushing towards a central object, with a few small groups around them in concentrated discussion. Then the crowd broke, and flowed in towards the house behind Chandi, who had been invisible in the middle of the tall, well-built crush.

I poked around the main room while she did her politics. The desk, with a misty, professional photograph of a younger Chandi that might have come from the just-engaged page of *Country Life*, was piled with papers and reference books – Pakistani women, statistics books, the *Jhang Gazetteer* of 1936, which Chandi told me she used as an election reference manual since it was the best source on local families, tribes and customs. The courtyard behind the bungalow was full of the noise of schoolchildren from the other side of the bougainvillea-covered wall, and the sun, which had crept under the roof of the verandah, was warming me to sleep; but Chandi's energy, when she joined me, shamed me into wakefulness.

She, like everybody else, had joined the PPP after it won the 1971 election and had got a seat in the provincial assembly. She had found Bhutto warm, idealistic and brutal. The only time she met him alone he ripped her to trembling pieces for some critical comments that had been passed on to him, then asked her whether politics would be too tough for his daughter Benazir. In 1977, when everybody was scrabbling to be allowed to stand as a PPP candidate, she was not selected. Instead, Bhutto chose her cousins, the Bokharis, themselves landowners in Jhang – according to Chandi, because he wanted to make sure that there was no female competition for Benazir on the political scene.

That was the beginning of the battle with her Wicked Cousin. Her people had won the district council in the first local elections under Zia in 1979, and since then the Wicked Cousin had been trying to unseat them. He had a good chance of winning this time round, she thought, since his father-in-law, Makhdoom Sajjad Hussein Qureishi was the governor, and the bureaucracy would therefore go out of its way to help him. The PPP was not much of a threat. Their man was a nice young fellow, another cousin of hers, by some complex relationship on both the paternal and the maternal side; but his group could not match hers or her Wicked Cousin's.

'These groups,' I asked, 'what exactly are they?'

'Supporters.'

'Yes, but . . . are the people supporting you now the same as those who supported you when you were in the PPP?'

'Of course,' she said impatiently; then, understanding, laughed a little. 'My dear, we have no ideology here, except in the Islamic parties. It's all clan rivalry.' Again I didn't understand: she and her cousins must be in the same clan.

'Of course,' she said, as though I had questioned a privilege. 'We can have intra-clan as well as inter-clan rivalry.'

That confusion between actor and critic worried me. These people spoke of themselves as examples of a type written about by left-wing academics, decried by Bhutto, abused in five-year-plans. They used the same vaguely Marxist socio-political terms – the feudals, the ruling classes, the vested interests – which, in developing countries, have strong moral overtones. Yet having, by implication, condemned their class and the superstitions and inequalities that perpetuate their privilege, they continued to live those despised lives with no apparent psychological ill-effects. Maybe, I thought, it was the only way that lives which stretched from New York to Jhang could be lived. If Chandi did not play Jhang's politics on Jhang's terms, she wouldn't win elections; but if she didn't observe the game with a certain scepticism and distance, she and I could not be friends. There had to be a flaw, though – a point where theory and practice failed to meet.

The saintly origins of politics seemed to me the oddest part. Her father's family, she said, had travelled from Arabia, through Iraq and Iran to Afghanistan, and migrated to Punjab centuries back. It was said to be able to trace itself back to the prophet; but when I smiled in sympathetic scepticism, she said, as though weighing up scientific evidence, that the genealogy seemed fairly reliable.

One of her ancestors, Shah Jewna, was a wandering Sufi saint. Part of Sufism entailed exercises to prove the control of mind over matter; so Shah Jewna had stood on one leg in the Chenab river and recited a verse of the Koran 124,000 times, tying a knot in a cord for each verse. Fish ate most of his body but he went on until he had finished. Because of his holiness, people made pilgrimages to see him, and gave him tributes of money and land in the village that is now named after him. His shrine and the three or four thousand people descended from him were believed to have healing powers.

'Can the descendants,' I asked, 'live off being pirs?'

'Yes,' she said, 'depending on their reputation. Pirs can charge anything for a charm from one rupee to a thousand. One of my cousins, whose amulets are thought to be effective, makes a hundred thousand rupees (£3,500) a year, which is enough to live quite well on in the countryside.' I didn't want to ask how much of this she believed: that would be pressing too hard at the join.

The local election campaign started the next day, under the ubiquitous canopy of red, yellow, blue and green geometrical cut-outs of material sewn on to each other that graces all weddings and political meetings, Chandi gave a forceful speech to the council members and around 100 of her supporters who turned up for the promised meal. I understood enough to know that I did not need to understand more. It was the stuff of campaign speeches: this administration's achievements ... further progress ... a glorious

110

future. It went down well. Chandi's speeches are made with such conviction that it is hard to imagine anybody having the audacity to doubt them.

But when she sat down, things turned a little difficult. Her secretary approached and whispered nervously to her: lunch was not ready. She snapped at him, and he scurried away. People started to fidget and whisper; then a man with fantastic Victorian whiskers levered himself out of his chair, hobbled over to the microphone, cleared his throat and started singing.

It was a rollicking Punjabi song that sounded much closer to Irish or Scottish folk than to the subtle, mournful Urdu love-songs I think of as subcontinental music. The old man tapped the beat with this stick; some of the audience laughed, some swayed with him; and I fancied I could hear him describing the pleasures of amorous pursuit among the haystacks. 'What's it about?', I whispered to Chandi. 'The Agricultural Development Bank,' she muttered. 'He's narrating the troubles of the farmer's life, and blaming them all on the bank.'

Lunch, at last, was in the courtyard at the back of the house in metal dishes on waist-high stands, with piles of tin plates and mugs and plastic bags-full of flat bread. The predictable chicken curry was covered with a two-inch layer of grease which I tried to drain off my portion, while others took extra spoonfuls to mix with the rice. There were bowls of plain rice, and bowls of sticky yellow rice with bits of green and pink sugared fruit, raisins and nuts. The meal was over quickly, but Chandi's duty had been done. Food is an important part of politics.

The press was there, and a delegation approached me. The international fraternity of journalists is a little like a freemasonry: in the subcontinent, at least, the sign of the press card opens a world of hospitality and comradeship to you. The *Pakistani Times* correspondent, a smooth, grey-haired fellow in a jacket and tie, gave me a beginner's guide to Jhang politics. There are too many big families here, he said. They are feudals, having some saints in their ancestry. The people are mostly uneducated, so they are voting for the people from these families. I asked whether they would vote for Chandi in the forthcoming election.

'Of course,' he said. 'Her group will get maybe seventy per cent of seats.'

'Why?'

'She is very popular, and especially the women like her. She has done many things for Jhang.'

'If she had not done these things, would she be re-elected?'

'No, maybe some Muslim League feudal would be.'

'And who are the Muslim League people here?'

'The people who were PPP in 1977,' he said without hesitation, looked me in the eye, and laughed. 'You see they are big people, they cannot afford to oppose government. Look what is happening to Abida Hussein's farm.'

So: the man from the sycophantic government newspaper complimented the opposition. The oppressive feudals were having to compete with each other for the people's favours. And the press, while displaying the universal journalistic cynicism about The System, took me that afternoon through the crowds of plump traders and grubby peasants registering themselves as candidates to prove that democracy was in action in Jhang.

As we drove out to Chandi's farm down straight tree-bordered roads reminiscent of France, I asked her what the journalist meant about her farm. The government, she said, was trying to cancel her lease on the land. She had taken the case to court, claiming that the government was acting illegally, since the leases could be cancelled only if the farms were incompetently managed, and independent assessors had praised her management. The government had sent police onto the land to keep the workers off; Chandi organised three or four thousand of her people into pickets around her land, and they kept the police off.

Down bumpy lanes between fields, we stopped at a white colonial bungalow. Darkness had fallen, and the arches of its verandah were lit from under the bougainvillea, so that the flowers glowed pink in the night. It was the house of the Dane running her experimental cattle-breeding station. He came free from the Danish aid budget; she had to pay the rest of the costs. I slotted Chandi into my category of efficient capitalist landlords.

The Dane was on the verandah to meet us, walking a little stiffly, his face creased like a farmer's and his soft white hair shining in the light. Inside, his wife was putting the two-bar fluorescent battery lamp on the mantelpiece. It was just about time for the evening power cut, she said; so nice that you knew when they were coming. She wanted us to have coffee before we went to see the cows, but it took a long time: the gas cylinder was running out, and there was not so much flame to make the water boil. She moved very slowly; she had a little bit of bad back, she said, but looked

half-crippled as she walked. Her husband watched her difficulty
with passionate tenderness.

Chandi and I sipped tepid powdered coffee and the Dane spoke of
the farm with serious enthusiasm. The cows were doing beautiful,
he said, and the calves were putting on weight faster than in
Denmark; but there was difficulty, because with all the policemen
in the fields the fodder was short, and they would need to buy some
in. This politics was most disgraceful. He had written to the Danish
authorities, and certainly they would be making some complaint.

The power was still off when he went to the cowshed, so we left
the car lights shining down the walkway between the two cow-
pens. The light caught two rows of curious eyes and wet noses,
sticking out from between the bars. The Dane walked us to his
pride, one of the eldest of the Jersey-Zebu half-breeds he was
working at which were designed to combine the richness of Jersey
milk with the toughness of the Zebu animals. The young bull's
features had the solidity of Jerseys, without their gentleness, and
the fierceness of the Zebus, without their haughty elegance. With
rough pride, the Dane rubbed the cheek of this mean-looking
animal, which rocked its head from side to side and groaned.

I was aware of the silence around only when it was disturbed.
Jackals started up, first in a canon, then louder into a chorus, then
stopped. I looked at Chandi in mock horror.

'It's the desert of northern Punjab,' she said, 'just a few miles
from here. You're on the edge of civilisation.'

I drove south with Chandi, to her husband's constituency near
Multan. She had to attend his grandmother's funeral. Only the
men saw the burial: the women of the village, two hundred or so of
them, sat on the ground in the yellow, earth-floored courtyard of
the ancient family mansion of baked mud, stone and carved
wooden gates. Around the outside were the poorest, with faded
cotton clothes and sun-wrinkled faces that had passed straight from
childhood to old age. In the centre of the circle was the family, their
high-heeled shoes snagging on each other's synthetic shalwar
kameeses. One would wail, another join her, and they would clasp
each other in a dying paroxysm of grief. A plump girl in black and
white, with a black handbag, white shoes and black and white
bangles, turned to me and smiled.

'This is hypocrisy,' she said.

In the cool of the house I talked to a pale, silent girl who had taken no part in the mourning, but had sought me out with her eyes. She came from St John's Wood, she said. Her father was a banker. She had been sent to Multan a few months earlier to be married. She missed St John's Wood, and her friends, and London . . . so much. She wanted to talk of London streets and shops and theatres, perhaps to reassure herself of the reality of life outside Multan.

Two tombs on a hill dominate Multan. They were built by Tugluq emperors for themselves in the fourteenth century, but used to house local saints. They are hexagons in fine brick and blue tiles capped with white domes, the beauty in the subtlety of colours: stripes of darker brickwork on pale that emerge as you step back, and blue tiles set in bands in the brick and frames around the arches which, as you approach, separate into arabesques of blue from aquamarine through sky to ultramarine. The tombs have none of the opulence of the Mogul's marble and semi-precious stones; and the architecture is solider, less exuberant, with, somewhere in the buttresses leaning towards the dome, the memory of a tent.

The smaller of the tombs belongs to Hazarat Bahauddin Zakariah, a saint of Arabian origin and the ancestor of the Qureshi family, which produced the governor of Punjab who was Chandi's Wicked Cousin's father-in-law, and Shah Mahmood Qureshi, the young Muslim Leaguer who represented Multan in the Punjab assembly. The Qureshis, as their name suggests, are of the clan of the Prophet, and among the biggest landowners of Punjab. Their support has therefore been sought by successive governments: Shah Mahmood's uncle was governor and chief minister of Punjab in Bhutto's time, and Shah Mahmood himself – Aitchison and Corpus Christi, Cambridge – had been chosen by the Muslim League to win the Multan district council back from Chandi's husband's faction.

It wasn't Shah Mahmood I was interested in, though. I had had enough of saintly origins and foreign educations. I was after his rival, whom I had met at a party in Lahore. Javed Hashmi had been standing awkwardly, clutching a plate with the nervousness of a man who does not know how to involve himself in any of the small conversational groups around him. I went to talk to him, and found myself being given a lecture about partition in clumsy English. It wasn't a bad lecture, but I didn't want it, so I left on pretence of getting some pudding. Later I learnt that he was an example of a type I wanted to meet – the middle-class politician on the rise.

Punjab is the place to find Javed Hashmis. Economically and

socially it is decades ahead of the rest of the country, and its middle classes have the self-assurance to edge their way into what had traditionally been the monopoly of the landed rich – politics. As Javed Hashmi's story illustrates, though, they are vulnerable.

I caught up with him in Multan during the election campaign. The battle lines were drawn as they had been for the national elections: the Qureshis with the Gailanis, another big local family, against the middle-class-feudal alliance between Javed and Chandi's husband, Fakr Imam.

He came round to Fakr's house, where Chandi and I were having tea with plates of uneaten iced cakes, and greeted us with a boyish, pink-cheeked enthusiasm. But, he said, would Chandi please go away while he talked to me? His English – which had improved since I had last met him – was always worse when she was there.

His family had a bit of land. By the standards of his village, it was rich; by the standards of the outside world, it was poor. He was educated at the village school, did well, got a place at university and, in the late sixties, joined the PPP. When the Qureshis and Gailanis went over to Bhutto, he left, and joined the student wing of the Jamaat-i-Islami. He was apologetic about that period, explaining the Jamaat as the only strong organisation that was anti-Bhutto and anti-feudal. He went to jail fourteen times under Bhutto, he said; once, in Lahore fort, they put him naked on ice blocks in January. The government registered 167 different cases against him, including a murder charge, for which he was tried. It seems to me odd that, in a country where killing is part of politics, murder charges against opposition politicians – like that which hanged Bhutto – are always cited as proof of the government oppression. Whether the murder actually took place or not seems irrelevant.

Zia picked Javed up and made him a minister. Javed accepted because he needed the position to give him the clout to stand up to the Qureshis and Gailanis. It worked: in the district council elections in 1979, for the first time in fifty years, the Qureshis and Gailanis were both defeated, and Javed and Fakr Imam's group won. Then in 1985, he got his National Assembly seat and, since the Qureshis were the Muslim League, was back in opposition.

Opposition, he said, was a big disadvantage. I had an idea of what he meant, but wanted to know what the reality was like.

'Our politics,' he explained gently, as to a child, 'is not a very mature politics. The people who elect us do not elect us for giving speeches, but for their own protection against the police, the criminals, their opposite clans. The police, you know, they are a fascist force. Even I am scared. In colonial times, this was the need, but now it should not be so.

'I will give you an example. Four or five days before, there was an inquiry about the death of a woman. They were opening the grave, and they called the notables of the area, including my brother-in-law. They arrested him, and kept him for three days. We went to the magistrate, but he has connection with my political enemies and refused to give a verdict on the application for bail. Then we had to go to the Multan bench of the Lahore High Court, and they came to our rescue. Why do the police do this? Because I am fighting elections against the governor's son, and if the voters see that I cannot protect my family, they will know that I cannot protect them.'

'But you can get protection from the courts?'

'Sometimes, sometimes not. There were two judges on the bench. One we knew would not help us, but the other is the son-in-law of the ex-attorney-general, and has contacts with Zia.'

'That means he would help you?'

'It means he can help. He is not vulnerable.'

The next morning we went to his village, Makhdoom Rashid, a few miles outside Multan along roads bordered by cotton-fields and populated by small donkeys wobbling under bursting sacks of cotton. Its mosque shone homogeneous blue from a distance; but close up, had the tombs' elaborate delicacy of a paletteful of blue tiles. Behind it was a huge field of graves: long humps of smooth mud growing out of the earth and throwing curved shadows.

As Javed walked me through the bazaar past the heaps of sweets like yellow marbles, people came out of their shops and wrung his right hand with both of theirs. I was touched by the welcome they gave their local hero. No doubt he had raised the prestige of Makhdoom Rashid far above that of neighbouring rivals. Some people followed us down the village, and as we toured, the crowd grew. A man with a box camera preceded us, running backwards to get a distance. When Javed stopped for a picture, men pushed in at the sides and stretched on tip-toes behind us, and small boys struggled for a place around our knees.

Most of Makhdoom Rashid was mud. Houses with mud walls, no windows and a door grew out of mud streets. Javed pointed to a collection of tiny one-roomed houses: those, he said, were the scheduled castes. That floored me: scheduled castes is the Indian euphemism for untouchables, yet Muslim Pakistan is not supposed to have castes.

'Until partition mostly the village was Hindu. These people do the low jobs – cleaning and washing.'

'But are these scheduled castes Hindus?'

'They are scheduled castes.' The only explanation I could hope to grasp at was that they were untouchables, who saw no advantage in going to Hindu-dominated India, but were despised equally by the caste-tainted Islam of Punjab.

At the end of the village was the rich-smelling buffalo-pound; beyond that, a scene for a Pakistani Constable. Women cotton-pickers lounged on mountains of newly-picked cotton, their skins dark and their pink, purple and orange clothes brilliant against the white heaps. They had dupattas slung over their heads as a concession to modesty, but there was nothing modest in their stares and their lazy postures. Javed shouted at them; there was a gust of laughter, and they yelled back. I reckoned they must make the mullah shudder; but how do you impose Islam in an agricultural society? Women's labour is needed, and labour, the great liberator, demands freedom of movement and vision.

Javed's women were inside: he could afford to keep them there. He had the biggest house in the village, with *Hashmi Manzi* written in concrete letters above the metal gate, and a yard full of women. The façade of the house was in the style of a 1930s cinema, with elaborate concrete mouldings of vases full of flowers, stars, stylised plants winding arabesques around each other. The cavernous front room was half-full of charpoys. Five daughters were lined up in front of me, the elder three serious with self-consciousness, the younger two giggling furiously.

'Five daughters,' said Jave disapprovingly. 'This is what happens in a male-dominated society when everybody is crazy for sons. And this is how you have the population problem.' And there again was this strange gap between thought and action: Javed the man producing a bevy of daughters, and Javed the thinker disapproving of such backwardness.

Javed lost the district council. Shah Mahmood, with the protection of government behind him, won it back in the election in November 1987. Javed's Muslim League opponents started proceedings to dislodge him from his national assembly seat, through petitions claiming electoral malpractice. Many of those are filed against any successful candidate; but if they are ruling party candidates or otherwise powerful people the election commissioner doesn't get round to investigating them for years, and probably not until the government has been unseated. In Javed's case, things moved along, and in 1988 the laborious process of recounting all the votes polled for him in 1985 had started. The matter took up so much of his attention that his cotton-ginning business was suffering. People who have to earn their living cannot hold out long against that sort of harassment.

Chandi was better placed to fight back; but the local elections hurt her. Although she won a majority of the seats, traditional wheeling and dealing, promises from the Muslim League and a little tactful harassment by the bureaucracy meant that between the date when the council was elected and when it was due to elect its chairman, enough of her supporters had been won over for an opponent to get the chairman's post. The only consolation was that the Wicked Cousin didn't get it either; but Chandi attributed the sudden resumption of hostilities against her farm to his appointment as a minister. Then the wheel of fortune turned again: in 1988 the government and the entire parliamentary system were sacked and Chandi, the Wicked Cousin and Javed were all out again.

Another revolution of the wheel in the November 1988 election. Old battles forgotten, Javed and Chandi both linked up with the Muslim League. Javed was crushed by a PPP landlord; Chandi swept back in. Her cousins, like most of the big Punjab families, tactfully divided their loyalties between the PPP and the Muslim League's alliance; but they were beaten anyway.

The PPP just got a majority of Punjab national assembly seats, but the real winners were the landlords. Both parties played it safe and chose candidates for their wealth, their braderi and their pir-ness. In the long term, tribal clout and saintly ancestry are deteriorating assets: as people go to the Gulf, watch television and make money the memory of distant miracle-makers fades. But for now, and a longish time into the future, they remain useful to governments. Nobody can manage the countryside like they can. Maybe there will never come a time when they find that the Punjabi countryside is no longer manageable, as seems to be the case in some of Sind.

The evening I arrived at his house in the interior of Sind, Junaid Soomro announced that we were going to supper with some friends of his a few miles out of the little town of Shikarpur where he lives.

We would eat outside, by the light of the moon, and roast goats on a fire. His younger brother, uninterested or uninvited, went on fiddling with the video to stop *Top of the Pops* disappearing into a grey storm of electricity.

Down the narrow stairs, the waiting cars were blocking the alley. Three watchmen stood around a small fire, staring at us. Junaid and I got into the front seats of one Suzuki, with two gunmen in the back, and another six gunmen tried to get into the other.

You cannot get six men with Kalashnikovs in one Suzuki. They tried four in the back and two in the front; three in the back and three in the front, then switched around so the fatter ones should be in the back. An argument began, the pitch rose, and Junaid leant out of the car window and yelled at them. Two stood back, the other four fitted neatly in, and we drove off down the alley with the abandoned guards watching indifferently.

In the main street, shops were still doing business, but most of the clientele had shifted to the restaurants, eating kebabs and spiced roast chicken in greasy fingers. A couple of soldiers walked down the street hand in hand, as indifferent to the street as it was to them. At the next corner were two Army lorries, the bored, pale faces of soldiers staring out from their depths. Down the side-road a knot of uniformed men stood by a dark blue Suzuki van advertising itself as the property of the Narcotics Police.

Junaid took another sideroad, stopped at a house, went in, came out, took the car round another set of narrower streets that turned into alleys, and as he stopped by a watchman's fire, I realised we were back at his house. The abandoned guards were still there. Too many soldiers, he said.

Junaid is a young landowner, and was a member of the Sind assembly until Zia dissolved his parliaments. His family are the heads of the Soomro tribe or clan. Soomros are scattered all over Sind, but their headquarters are in the north-west of the province, near the Baluchistan border. They are waderas – as the landlords are called in Sind – and politicians: when I met him his family boasted two members of the National Assembly, two members of the Provincial Assembly and a senator.

Junaid has a thick beard, a big nose, a farmer's face that would have been handsome but for crooked teeth. He had trained as an engineer, and worked in a fertiliser factory in Lahore, but as his father aged, returned home to be trained up as head of his branch of the family.

Since the midnight picnic expedition had failed, we returned to *Top of the Pops*, and the room off the upper courtyard where the younger brother was sitting silently. The room had a television and video-recorder, a fridge and a couple of plates on the wall with pictures of Mecca painted on them in bright green and blue. The walls were plain, but for the holes where the plaster had crumbled and a long, dangerous-looking diagonal crack along one side of the room.

Top of the Pops was as mesmeric as an illicit glimpse of a tribal ritual, building up to some unknown and probably brutal end. The camera stared upwards through enlarged thighs and bottoms; girls pulled their painted lips away from their white teeth, shoved their noses into the camera lens, and fawned on the priest of jollity, the middle-aged disc jockey pretending to love it all still. I went on watching long after I realised that the same tape was repeating itself.

Junaid wanted to talk, so I asked him about his land. What crops were grown? What were the yields? He didn't really know much about it, he said with an innocent smile. The land was farmed by sharecroppers. He went to look at it about once a month, and at harvest time the money came in. Why didn't he farm it properly? Didn't he want to make money? He gave me a laugh of real amusement at my failure to comprehend. Money-making, he said, was time-consuming.

'Most of the feudals are too busy with their politics; and you can get things with politics that you can't get with money.'

'Like?'

'People.' Businessmen, he said, got kidnapped, and their families didn't have the network or the manpower to get them back. But, I said, I had heard that a Soomro had been kidnapped recently, so even they were not immune.

'That was me,' said the younger brother, through a mouthful of pistachio nuts.

I became suddenly interested in the plump, bespectacled young man with the air of a junior academic who has not been given tenure. It was a mistake, he said modestly. He was driving past when a gang was hijacking a lorry, so they took him along too. When they discovered who he was, they were terrified, and kept him for a week while they extracted a promise from Junaid that he would take no reprisals. Junaid grinned at his power to instil fear.

'Why then,' I asked, 'do you need all these gunmen around you?'

'Just now,' he said, 'I have a little trouble.'

It was a story florid with details of treacheries, rivalries, and government incompetence; but a fairly standard feud. A dacoit called Kabil had captured two Soomro women, whose husbands had come to Junaid. He had organised a raid into Baluchistan, in collusion with some of the government's tribal levies, and killed a couple of Kabil's gang, but had failed to get the women. A few months back, he located the gang in Punjab, carried out another raid, and killed six or seven of them, but the women still evaded him. Kabil had sent Junaid a message saying that they were now personal enemies — meaning that it was Kabil's duty to kill Junaid. He must, Junaid reckoned, have at least ten men left in his gang, because any self-respecting dacoit has a minimum of twenty, and Junaid had to match his firepower. 'But,' he said seriously, 'it is not so bad. I have three brothers. If he kills me, one of them will get him.'

Bored of talk, he said he would take me to see what the feudals' life was really like. He led me through the courtyard, down backstairs, across an alley and into a room filled with smoke and men. The room was a sickly green, with a white strip light that flickered unpredictably. There was a small table covered in ash-trays, chairs crammed round it, and a bed with a man on it. Cramped into the chairs and squatting on the floor were fifteen-or-so others: one in a pink embroidered Sindhi hat whose vast belly lay across him like an animal at rest, an adolescent with absurdly long, thin, legs in spray-on jeans and an anorak, a small, tense-looking man with sharp eyes and the frizzy hair of residual African slave genes.

The man on the bed sat up slowly when we came in. He looked at us, as though trying to focus, slumped over again, and sat up once more, holding the edge of the table to steady himself. His eyes were red and his skin had fallen off the bones in folds, though he was probably not more than forty-five. Junaid introduced me. I put out my hand to shake his, and he tried to grasp it but missed. The men sitting around him watched attentively.

'This is my uncle,' said Junaid. 'He has destroyed himself. But he is a learned man. Look at his books.' There was a small shelf of books on the wall. I could make out the title of Sidney Sheldon, but nothing else. 'Also,' Junaid said quickly, 'he knows about politics.'

The uncle, who had been staring in wonder at his glass, looked up. 'I want to ask you a question,' he said slowly and deliberately; and, as though reminding himself of what he had just said, 'I want to ask you a question. This is the question. How do you think the matter of Palestinians should be solved? Have they the right to land?' I hedged; he glared at me and told me that my sympathies were with the American-run Zionist conspiracy that was depriving Muslims of their rights around the world, including in Pakistan. There were mutterings of approval from the rest of the room. The uncle looked up to acknowledge them with the air of an actor who is weary of applause because his performance always pleases, and slid down once more on to the bed.

Sind is a century behind Punjab. Although the province had a network of inundation canals built by the Moguls and other local rulers, which channelled the water of the Indus during the flooding season, the British did not turn their attention to building year-round canals in Sind until just before they abandoned the subcontinent. For the engineers, the Indus was too hard a beast to tame: its tributaries in Punjab were smaller, and easier waterways to manage, so the British concentrated first on the smaller task and built Sind's huge Sukkur Barrage in the thirties.

Irrigation is the great moderniser. Not only does it bring more intensive cultivation and therefore greater prosperity: the process of irrigation demands and leads to the modernisation of society. Building canals means marshalling large labour forces, making roads, educating the local population for engineering and maintenance; it generates small industries to supply engineering requirements and services to cater for the newly-arrived population. And, in central Punjab, the canals led to a *de facto* land reform: the import of peasants who got their small slices of newly-cultivable land.

The modernisation of Sind started in earnest only when Bhutto pushed roads through to previously inaccessible bits of the province that had been stuck in a primitive barter economy and had virtually no contact with the cities. Sind therefore is only now developing the resource that political scientists sometimes argue is essential for education, industry, science, administration, democracy and revolution – a middle class. You can find it now, in towns like Shikarpur, selling fertiliser, taking the cash at its petrol pumps and teaching in the schools that are coming up. For the moment, though, Sind is still dominated by two groups of people: the waderas and the haris – the landless sharecroppers. Haris take the possessive pronoun, as in 'my haris'.

The British found the Sindhi landlords more backward and less reliable than the Punjabis. They owned great tracts of land, and, without exaggeration, the haris that lived on the land; but their land was poor and they spent too much, so they borrowed heavily from the local Hindu moneylenders, mortgaging their estates and eventually losing them. The British found this inconvenient. The *Gazetteer of Sind* of 1907 pointed out that, by 1896, forty-two per cent of cultivable land had fallen into the hands of the Hindus, and worried about the trend:

'The wholesale ruin of hereditary landholders soon became too serious a matter to be ignored, whether regarded from the standpoint of justice or policy . . . as a wheel in the administrative machinery they are almost indispensable.' It is not surprising that many Sindhi landlords became vehement supporters of partition.

Modernisation in Punjab has largely replaced sharecropping with more efficient land use – tenancy, self-cultivation and wage-labour. Sharecroppers are unlikely to invest extra labour and money in their land when they have to hand over half of their extra produce to the landlord. Still, for what baffled economists call 'non-economic considerations', and which Junaid tried to explain as the loyalty that money could not buy, sharecropping still predominates in Sind.

People blame Sind's social and economic set-up for holding the province back in all sorts of ways. Literacy in Sind is even worse than in Punjab – fifteen per cent, according to the 1981 census, against Punjab's twenty per cent. Among women, five per cent in Sind can read compared to ten per cent in Punjab. And Sind has failed to take advantage of the job-opportunities in the Gulf. Among those homesick-looking Pathans and Punjabis at Karachi airport preparing for three years in Dubai, there have been virtually no Sindhis. It seems reasonable to blame their lack of initiative on a paternalistic system which provides them with a thin livelihood and a certain security in return for most of the attributes of freedom.

Javed Hashmis are hard to find in Sind. Even more than in Punjab, the running of Sind has been the monopoly of the landed. Its chief ministers and governors have been Khuros, Soomros, Bhuttos, Jatois; the leaders of its political parties, both government and opposition, have been from the same sort of families. They ran their areas both administratively – in collusion with the civil servants – and politically, in competition with each other.

But since Bhutto's demise they are beginning to look less firmly in control. In 1983 the opposition grouping, the Movement for the Restoration of Democracy, organised a protest against martial law throughout the country. It took off only in Sind: the Sindhi landlords, as requested by one of their number, Ghulam Mustapha Jatoi, the head of the PPP in Sind, took processions out of their villages, and offered themselves up for arrest. The Army moved in, things turned violent. Unofficial accounts suggest that there was large-scale killing: in one village, where the soldiers seem to have panicked, it is said that 200 people died.

The landlords got scared. They called a halt to the movement, but, it seems, things had moved out of their hands. The processions, and the whole movement, were taken over by some smallish, left-wing parties which have begun to take root in the towns in Sind. They decided that the confrontation with the government should continue, and it did, despite the waderas. The protests were, eventually, put down – but through suppression by the Army, not as a result of the waderas' orders.

Since the 1983 movement, there has been a massive increase in dacoity – the subcontinental word for banditry – in Sind. The commonest manifestation is kidnapping, but there is bank robbery, hijacking of lorries, and the usual range of armed crime. People do not travel at night in Sind if they can help it, and they avoid some areas altogether.

Dacoity is hardly new to Sind, but it has changed in scale and nature. 1983 seems to have encouraged its growth because the size of the movement and the difficulty the authorities had in putting it down encouraged the view that the government was impotent. If the police were unable to manage unarmed protestors, they were unlikely to be able to deal with armed, professional criminals.

These days the dacoits seem no longer to be under the authority of the landlords. They are freelancers, armed with their own Kalashnikovs, walkie-talkies and all the modern gadgetry a criminal could want – freely and cheaply available in the arms markets in Karachi. They kidnap businessmen, professionals, and weaker landlords, and deal with the stronger ones on equal terms: they are equally well armed, they can make their own agreements with the police, and they no longer need the protection of salaried employment. Business is booming, and they have overtaken the old firms.

To an outsider, the breadth of the waderas' control over life in the countryside is more striking than the decline in their power. But when the Pakistani government, as much as the British, relies on the landlords to run the countryside, whatever happens to the waderas is of concern to Islamabad. The heavy presence of the Army around Sind suggests that the civilian arm of government can't quite manage any more.

In 1985, when General Zia, in consultation with Pir Pagaro, was looking around for a prime minister among the newly-elected members of the national assembly, the name of Junaid's uncle, Illahi Bakhsh Soomro, was floated alongside that of Mohammed Khan Junejo, who got the job. Illu, therefore, aligned himself with the opposition in parliament. The strategy paid off. When Junejo was sacked in 1988, Illu came back in as minister of information, water and power.

He lives in Jacobabad, down the road from Shikarpur, as well as in Shikarpur, Karachi and Islamabad. Jacobabad is his constituency. He is boyishly, cheerfully handsome, with floppy black hair, and claims, incredibly, to be sixty. His youthfulness, I suspect, springs from his permanent air of amusement and the unshakeable ease born of a large inheritance. London's merchant banks used to be full of people like him.

I met him when he was out of government, and fighting to keep his district council. I expected him to be a little bitter, and tense; but when I arrived, two days before the election, he was relaxing with a cup of tea, a tin of biscuits and a cashmere cardigan over his shalwar kamees. The district, he explained, had been pretty much sewn up. By agreement between the PPP, the Muslim League, and his own people, with the help of the deputy commissioner, two thirds of the candidates were unopposed. There was still a fight in the town, and a few small problems to be sorted out in the countryside the next day, but in his area the constituencies were mostly 'pocket boroughs' so there wasn't much need for energetic electioneering.

There were a couple of meetings to go to that evening. As we drove through the town, Illu pointed out the cubicles dotted around the streets, made out of coloured canopies and housing a few plastic chairs and a few men. They were the candidates' headquarters. Most had a poster of their symbol – usually an animal or an agricultural implement – hanging from the overhead canopy; but the man with the camel symbol had a life-size stuffed model with uneven legs leaning drunkenly into the street.

I asked him why everybody had these canopies. He said that Section 144 was in force. Section 144? A British provision of the

Pakistan Penal Code which made street meetings illegal; at least, meetings had to be held in confined spaces. So they hired canopies and confined bits of streets under them. It was good business for the canopy-makers, anyway.

At the first meeting, we sat facing a couple of hundred people in a tiny crowded courtyard, in front of the pillars of an old verandah. On the wall opposite, behind the audience, children hung off the banisters of a diagonal staircase. The little mirrors in the audience's embroidered hats glinted from one strip light loosely fixed on to the verandah above the panel's heads. Many hands garlanded Illu with strings of strong-smelling red roses. After the Bismillah e Rahman e Rahim and a loud monotone prayer from a ragged old man with the red dye growing out of his white beard, Illu gave a small speech endorsing his harmless-looking candidate.

The audience was all male, of all ages and, by the look of the crisp shalwar kamees mixing with tatty turbans and torn shawls, of all income levels, but it was uniformly attentive. Illu's unremarkable speech held them as the rhetoric of a revivalist preacher might. The wondering bright eyes of little boys and the old eyes whitened by cataracts watched him as though he might disappear if they looked away. A donkey walked past outside, braying loud enough to drown his voice, and a boy sitting on the floor in the front tittered. The man behind the boy knocked his head sideways with a blow.

Tea and sweets, one of a candidate's main expenses has to come round at the end. Everybody got a small cup of stewed sweet tea; but the plates of sticky bright pink, yellow and green sweets were put in front of the panel. Nobody took one. Illu called a little boy in the front row. Staring at him in terror, the boy grasped an old man's leg and tried to hide behind it. The old man scolded him and pushed him forward, but he wouldn't go; so another little boy was ordered forward. Keeping his eyes on Illu as though approaching a dangerous animal, he took a sweet without looking at it and ran.

'All Soomros?' I asked. But of course.

'Soomro candidate?' Yes.

'Won't they vote for him anyway when they know he's your man?' Yes.

'So why do you bother with the meeting?'

'After the councils have been elected we ignore them for four years. The least we can do is to come in person and ask them for their vote.'

'Why do the people come?'

126

'For the tamasha,' (something like the French *spectacle*), he said. 'There's not so much to do in Jacobabad.'

Characters from the various meetings we went to that evening turned up during supper at Illu's house, and the fat, hobbling servant laid places for them resentfully as they arrived. The local PPP man stomped in, and glared at me. He was a short, wide man, unshaven, eyes red and face angry. Illu said he was the main muscleman in town. He yelled briefly at Illu about a candidate who had promised to withdraw, but had not; and Illu massaged him with smiling charm while he ate handfuls of bread and chicken curry, his chin almost on his plate, his eyes staring suspiciously at the company.

We retired, after dinner, to Illu's bedroom. I felt awkward; but there was nothing else to be done. In Pakistan, the bedroom is where you sit, receive guests, watch television, talk, argue; the sitting room, if there is one, is left unused, like the Victorian parlour, except for formal occasions, its curtains drawn to keep the light off the furniture. The fat servant, looking angrier than ever, brought green tea. Watching me watching him, Illu chuckled.

'He's a little confused. I think you are the only woman who has been in this house.'

Illu had been good friends with Bhutto, he said, and best man at Bhutto's second wedding. But Illu's father opposed the PPP, and when Bhutto came to power Illu was thrown out of his job as director of the Karachi Development Authority and had a murder charge slapped on him. He was in jail for six months before he was given bail; when he came out, Bhutto offered a truce, and sent him to the embassy in London. Zia sacked him from that job; but 'subsequently I found my way into his cabinet. I was said to be very close to him,' said Illu modestly.

I asked whether people like him could run their areas the way they used to. Not really, he said. The waderas used to control the roads, and thus, supplies and the movement of people. The police used to operate through the ten to fifteen waderas in their area, who would tell them what was going on, where anybody they were looking for was, and would negotiate with the police for people. That wasn't really working so well any more; maybe there was too much going on that the waderas didn't know about, maybe the police were getting greedy and didn't want to share their pickings with the waderas. All the police, he said, had a gang of dacoits they were in league with.

'Does anybody know who these dacoits are?' Illu smiled at my stupidity.

'Everybody knows.'

'Are they the waderas' retainers?' He laughed slightly.

'Maybe. We waderas need muscle. Sometimes we use them for protection, sometimes we tell them to go off and commit some crime.'

The next day we drove out to the villages. The rice had been harvested, and the fields of stubble were gold in the low sunlight. Underneath the stalks, the earth was frosted with salt. We bumped along bunds between fields, and through a maze of ten-foot-high stacks of rice straw. In an opening in the middle, heated by captured sunlight, a buffalo lumbered round a pole, threshing rice. Three men squatted by it, one with a stick which tapped the buffalo's legs as it passed. The buffalo ignored the stick; the men ignored the Pajero.

Why, I asked, did Illu still have sharecroppers? Wouldn't it be more profitable to have tenants paying cash? No, he said. The haris were illiterate, and didn't have the money or the education to be good farmers. Anyway, how would he collect his rents? Nobody in Sind paid anybody else unless they were forced to. It would be a lot of botheration.

He knew the bent of my argument – inefficiency combined with injustice – so, skipping several steps, he said that the haris needed the waderas. The waderas dealt with the outside world for them – fixed the police, negotiated with the deputy commissioner – and lent them money. A young, healthy wife cost around 40,000 rupees: if a hari wanted to borrow that sort of money only the wadera could provide it.

We were on a canal bank and in a new land. A coating of salt on uncultivated fields looked like a thin snowfall on frozen earth. Round the pools of dark green standing water there were thick drifts of bright white salt, the greatest danger to Sind's economy. Largish areas of the province, made fertile through irrigation, are becoming useless once again. Irrigation has raised the water-table; the water sits on the land, then evaporates, leaving a patchy white crust stretching to the horizon. Unless the government or the landowners are prepared to invest in some means of draining the water away, more and more land will become as uncultivable as when it was virgin desert; but the government is short of money and not, in general, much good at large-scale public investment,

128

and the landowners are, by and large, too careless about their estates.

The fields were dead to farming, but, around the flats where the salt was thinner and the earth browner, alive with birds. White herons with black legs and yellow feet picked their way delicately through the pools. Plump black and white kingfishers sat on fences and wires. Dull brown birds sifted the water, turning white when they stretched their wings to fly. It was spectacular, in a grim sort of way; but I realised I had developed an economist's eye: it wasn't beautiful because it wasn't useful.

There were small problems to be sorted out in the villages: Illu's candidate was unpopular, one of his relations had confused the villagers about whom they should vote for, a headman was offended because nobody had come to ask for the village's votes. The villagers were always grouped, hands behind their backs, in a reception party; and we sat on charpoys, drinking tea and eating dried fruit, watching thin old men scratching themselves, little girls with ten silver rings pierced into the length of their ears, and distant women behind woven palm-leaf fences carrying on with their silent work among the buffaloes.

They would be difficult to get out of, those villages. They were out among the fields and the salt, miles off the road along bumpy tracks. The women, of course, could not leave; but neither could the children, because the school was too far away, and the men, without transport, could not go to look for work in Jacobabad.

'They're much better off than they were,' said Illu as we drove back to town.

'How could they have been much poorer?'

'They wouldn't have been able to offer us dried fruit before.'

We stopped on the way back at the big 1930s-cinema-style house belonging to Illu's main political ally, a wadera of the Jakhrani clan and a member of the left-wing Pakistan National Party – also brother of the PPP muscleman. Clicking down the black and white flower-patterned tiles in the hall, the house seemed empty and closed: his family, like others I had come across, had bought a big house not to live in but to make a statement. Illu's friend evidently confined himself to his bedroom, with a table, a bent metal ashtray, a bed covered in papers and one bare bulb. He wore an orange Sindhi hat, and had fat, stubby fingers and toes and the sleeves of his kamees rolled up over muscular forearms which, in England, would have been tattooed. His face had the brutality, but not the dissipation, of his brother's.

129

On the bed was an English-Sindhi dictionary and a copy of H.T. Lambrick's biography of General Jacob. 'You read that,' said Fat Fingers. 'You find my grandfather, Turk Ali Jakhrani.' I did, and was surprised that his descendants should want to boast about him. With the Marri and Bugti tribes he had launched a campaign against Jacob and General Outram. Defeated, he joined the British, then defected. Forgiven, he joined up again, defected again, surrendered again, and passed out of Mr Lambrick's narrative.

The PPP brother arrived. Under a bright light, his ugliness was remarkable. His fat, flabby face was pock-marked, the henna in his hair had grown out, leaving the rest dirty grey, and his jowls had a week's growth of beard. He stared at me.

'Is she married?' he asked Illu in Urdu.

'No,' I said. He started, then smiled, as though a parrot had spoken.

'He's a typical wadera,' said Illu as we left. 'A hard liver. Any money he has, he'll spend. Anything he wants, he gets; if he has to fight for it, he will. That's why Karachi hated Bhutto. When he came to power, the waderas came to town. They took their gunmen to the nightclubs, they got drunk and fought each other, they bought women in lots. Karachi thought them very unpleasant.'

There was a tap on my bedroom door as I sat writing notes. 'I am Mr Keshowlal,' said a smooth-faced man with an uncertain smile. 'I am Mr Illahi Bakhsh's best friend, elected unopposed to reserved Hindu seat in municipal council.' The election, he explained, had already taken place. There were four reserved Hindu seats and twenty-one candidates. The heads of the Hindu community met at the temple, chose four of the candidates, and the other seventeen withdrew. This was a good system, he said; it meant peace and no botheration.

'But how do people get a choice? Elections are supposed to be about choice.'

'Then there is argument and botheration,' he said mildly. His chest purred, and he pulled out a cordless telephone. Replacing it, he said,

'You are coming to my home. Mr Illahi Bakhsh said you like to drink whisky with me.'

It was an old house, just over the street, of small rooms with three-foot-thick walls, twenty-five-foot-high ceilings, and plaster dropping on to the floor. On the table was whisky and poppadums; a silver Kali dancing in a circle of fire, and a fat, comfortable

Ganesh. On the wall was a picture of the Sikhs' holiest shrine, the Golden Temple. I asked him why he had it.

'It is Allah's house.'

'But I thought you were a Hindu.'

'Ram, Allah, same thing. Up there is only one God.'

Unusually for a Hindu, he was a wadera as well as a trader. It was getting difficult, he said: with all the dacoity, it was dangerous to go to the lands . . . especially for a minority community. And all the haris were dishonest – they stole the fertiliser, cheated on their share of the crops. Ten, twenty years ago, they were good people. I wondered what had changed. Respect, he said. People had no respect for the law, any more, no respect for their elders.

'I have four members of council in my hand.' He made a fist.

'Why?'

'I am community leader. I have contacts with DC, police, Mr Illahi Bakhsh, all these people. All four members are with Mr Illahi Bakhsh. He is a good man, loyal man. My brother-in-law is at Karachi airport customs, the only Hindu there. This is thanks to Mr Illahi Bakhsh.' I began to appreciate Illu's political skills.

At six o'clock on election morning, the sounds of a riot woke me. Over parathas and chilli omelettes, I asked Illu what it was. Just a delegation, he said. Some problem because a few leading people were switching their votes and taking their vote-banks with them. Why, I wondered, should they do that? He shrugged. Maybe financial considerations. That brought us back to a democracy argument we had been having off and on: me angrily for, Illu holding that, in present-day Pakistan, it was a waste of time and money. He returned often to the argument more, I think, because it amused him to watch me struggling to maintain that my case was a rational one than because he believed what he said.

'In Jacobabad,' he said, 'There are fifty thousand voters. Out of those, I tell you, fifty know who they are voting for and why. The rest are tied up like battery farm chickens and taken to the polls. I tell you this as a beneficiary of the system.'

'What about 1970? The lower orders in Punjab didn't vote for the landlords then.'

'Punjab is better-educated than Sind.'

'Elections are an educative process.'

'And how long did this learning take in Britain?' he asked innocently.

'Maybe eighty years.'

131

'We haven't got the leisure.'

'Offer me an alternative.' He half-smiled, and suggested we should go to see the polling stations.

The schoolyard used for the women's polling station was full of clouds of burqas, brown, blue and black ones billowing around women drifting, children in tow, towards the crowds around the schoolroom doors or, their civic duty done, chatting in groups. Voting, it seemed, was difficult. Each schoolroom had fifty aspiring voters outside, pushing each other towards the door, and, inside the door, women shoving to get out. In the middle, a policeman was shouting and waving his stick above their heads. They were stuck as a lump of putty in a crack. Illu squeezed out of one of the rooms, his smooth black hair ruffled, looking flustered for the first time since I had met him.

'All the lists are wrong,' he said. 'Nobody knows where to vote. These are the elections you like so much.' It was not, as far as I could see, rigging: it was unorchestrated chaos.

Back in Karachi, and still annoyed and confused by the inefficiency of the farming system, I went to see Sind's only large-scale capitalist farmer, a mango exporter of legendary wealth, to find out why nobody else was like him. I found him sitting on a lawn fringed by palm and avocado trees, Mozart drifting through the air, lecturing the three young Englishmen who had come over for Benazir's wedding on why Pakistan was a disaster. One had Raybans, one a trilby with the brim turned down, all had faces whose normal expression of arrogant boredom had been overlaid with polite interest that derived from respect for the wealth of their host, whose farm in the countryside, complete with swimming pool and jacuzzi, they had just seen. That's what it looked like to me, anyway; but perhaps it was just that I knew where they came from.

Rafi Kachelo is not worth arguing with. He is a tall, big man, too solid to be called fat, with a grey-bearded, heavily handsome face, and eyes that stare you down with no effort. His kamees, when I first went to see him, was done up with diamond studs chained together instead of buttons; that alternated with silver drops on subsequent visits. His watch looked as though it had been sprinkled with glue and rolled in a heap of tiny diamonds. He has absolute, unquestionable views, which need no qualification or support because he isn't interested in discussing them; and his speech bounces along fast from idea to idea.

I asked how much land he had; he *farmed*, he emphasised

carefully, 6,000 acres. Mostly mangoes, also lychees, avocados, bananas; and mostly sold to the Gulf. His principal hate was the kiwi-fruit.

He had switched from share-cropping to wage-labour fifteen years previously. I assumed his new capitalist ways meant more work. Not necessarily, he said; not if you have a system. And what, I asked, was his system?

'Bribery and corruption,' he said. 'You have to bribe the workforce. Every year, I sit down with the overall manager and the section managers, and work out what their target should be. If they miss their targets, they will suffer some cuts; if they pass them, they will get some bonuses.'

'And the labourers?'

'They get reports – on how many days sick leave they have had, how much work their families have done, several things. If they get good reports, they can make a good living.

'I insisted that my managers should have air-conditioned jeeps. You have to get people used to luxuries, you have to corrupt them. Money is the only thing that counts here. People talk about loyalty, but when they shake your hand, they're wondering what you can do for them.'

I asked him if other people in Sind went in for his sort of farming. Some in Punjab did, but not in Sind. Did he know why not? Of course: they were lazy and debauched. The feudal system was falling to pieces, but Pakistani capitalism was too inefficient to take over because the government was corrupt. And that, he said with humourless satisfaction, was why none of it would ever work.

He was, I knew, a sympathiser of Bhutto's, and openly close to Benazir. I asked him if the government caused him problems because of that.

'I don't crib,' he said tightly. 'I know the game. I don't say that Mr Junejo has taken my son. I met the kidnappers three days after they took him, and they said they were looking after him as I would. I met them at a senator's house.'

His thirteen-year-old son had been kidnapped a few months earlier. I began to understand the logic of Junaid's position. The kind of set-up in which you can raise a hundred armed men in half an hour means living in a primitive social system, ties down manpower, uses land inefficiently, makes for unrepresentative politics and impregnates government with nepotism and partiality.

133

Yet there are circumstances in which being able to raise a hundred men in half an hour could be a priority.

There aren't more Rafi Kachelos because so many landlords see the political power which the old system – combined with surviving tribal loyalty and the hold of the living saints – gives them as necessary and desirable. Their hold on their villages seemed to me both strong and weakening. But the Sindhi landlords' easy confidence was out of date. There were people moving in on them: soldiers, dacoits and an army of Javed Hashmis. The 1988 election astonished them. Sind's big landlords were almost all with the ruling party, the Muslim League's alliance. The voters, evidently fed up with being treated like battery chickens, threw them all out – including Illu.

I expected the tribal leaders – my next port of call – to have things better under control.

6

TRIBAL CHIEFS

THE DESERT IS like darkness: your eyes have to get used to it.

Travelling from northern Sind into eastern Baluchistan, culti-vation ends abruptly: a thick border of trees and grass holds back the frontier of the desert. The artifice is real, because the fertility is artificial. The fields go as far as the reach of the Indus canals.

On the other side of the frontier the train passes through yellow-brown desert, the colour of suburban brick. The horizon is flat as a ruler. In three hours you will reach Sibi. You reach for your book.

If you do not, your eyes begin to adjust to small differences. There is vegetation camouflaged against the earth: brownish clumps of some tough-looking weed whose only virtue is that it can survive. There is wildlife: I saw, hovering over nothing much, a sparrow-sized bird of prey, presumably the largest that can live on the tiny animals sustained by the vegetation. There are people: occasional distant clumps of square houses, the same colour as the desert, and lines of minimal tents, sticks bent in a semi-circle with brown material stretched over them.

Then you begin to see that the colour is not as flat as the land. By the train, it is the grey-brown of walnuts, graduating towards the paler, warmer brown of unpolished pine, brightening towards the horizon until, by the time it meets the sky, it is the colour of ripe wheat. Across the gradations are slight changes in texture that lighten and darken the colours the way wind and currents alter the surface-colour of water.

Evening drains the desert of brightness and the colours merge into a soft fawn. The sky, still blue at the zenith, slips down into pale grey which turns, towards the horizon, the same dust-colour as the earth.

Sibi is at the end of the plain, the last town before the mountains of northern Baluchistan. There was a dust storm when I arrived. After dinner, I and the civil servant I had gone to see wrapped shawls round us and walked out into the large, empty grounds of his house. The lights down the avenue were blurred with halos of dust, disappearing into the shrunken night. He showed me the mosque he had built at the end of the alley: plain white, a front with three columned arches, and arched wooden doors behind, answering the arches on the verandah of his colonial bungalow.

Akbar Ahmed is the commissioner of Sibi, and an anthropologist with impeccable academic credentials: Harvard, Princeton and Cambridge, and a list of well-reviewed books as long as your arm. His survival in the civil service is a remarkable tribute to his brains. Although an intellectual, he is regarded as an asset, not just because he writes about Islam and Islamic anthropology, but because his talents are recognised internationally. His book-launches, he told me, are big events, attended by ministers and ambassadors. His social pedigree is equally smart. Meeting his wife, you understand the meaning of breeding, in the nineteenth-century sense. The granddaughter of the last Wali of Swat, she has a calm, reserved beauty that demands no tributes.

Akbar Ahmed explained tribalism to me in his office, a map behind him and a pad in front of him. First he drew a square with horizontal lines in it: that, he said, was Pathan tribal structure, divided into layers of people of equivalent social status. For Baluch tribal structure, he drew a pyramid: on top was a single person, the sardar, and under him, layers of increasing numbers and decreasing status.

On the map, he divided Baluchistan into four zones. At the bottom was Makran, a political void, a land too vicious and rugged for anybody to have made much effort to run it. There were no strong sardars, he said, a few mullahs, and a strong showing by the left-wing Baluch Students' Organisation. East and north were the states, Kalat and Las Bela, which had kept their statehood over the centuries by allying themselves with the current superpower, and had never shown much inclination to oppose the Pakistani government either. North of them were the tribes, like the Marris, Bugtis, and Mengals, who had fought the British ceaselessly and, depending on the current state of tribal alliances, continued to oppose the Pakistani government: most of the guerrillas who had fought in the insurgency in the 1970s against the government had been Marris.

136

North of Quetta, up to the Afghan border, were Pathans, who worked hard and, apart from the occasional flirtation with cross-border Pathan nationalism, didn't bother anybody.

Akbar Ahmed had arranged for the deputy commissioner to show me round Sibi and its development schemes. The DC, a tall, uncertain Punjabi, said he had done well in his civil service exams, but somehow got stuck for eight years in Baluchistan. He had had to learn how to eat rice with his hands, but he still had a penknife with a spoon attachment which he took to villages with him.

Sibi, minimalist bricks, concrete and mud that suited a staging post between the mountains and the desert, seemed to be benefiting from the flood of development spending in Baluchistan. In the past few years government money had built the mosque in the commissioner's garden, a 100-bed hospital, a seventy-two-room guest house for Sibi Week, when grandees descend on the town, a park with a stage for the grandees to sit on, a fountain that did not work and a building in the park which the DC said would be a pagoda – 'red, like the Peking Café in Quetta'.

The DC was keen to take me to the seven-marla scheme, an idea of the prime minister's for handing out plots of land to the poor for them to build cheap housing. About three miles outside Sibi, near the model farm with its parched fields covered with a thin haze of wheat, two small identical houses, a couple of yards apart, appeared through a cloud of dust. In front of them was scrub, behind them mountains not quite obscured by the thick air. These, said the DC, were the model houses built by the government and given to poor people, to show others how to build themselves good cheap houses. One had been given to a widow, and one to a cripple. I asked him how the cripple got into town.

'That,' he said seriously, 'is a very pertinent question. Actually, they do not live in these houses. At the present time, there is no water, drainage, electricity or transport. But these will come . . .' We looked at the houses respectfully. They were nice houses, with still-bright red doors with shiny padlocks on them.

Baluchistan is Pakistan's soft underbelly, a permanent worry to the central government and to American geopolitical planners because of its vulnerability to Soviet penetration. Its hugeness makes it hard to defend and its position, stretching from the Afghan border all the way along the Iranian border to the sea, makes it strategically inviting. That wouldn't matter so much if the

Baluch were committed citizens of Pakistan; but its fiercely nationalistic people were, from the start, reluctant Pakistanis.

According to the Baluch Chronicle of Genealogies, the Baluch come from a tribe which originally migrated from Aleppo on the Mediterranean and also spawned the Kurds. There doesn't seem much evidence for that, but anthropologists are fairly sure, on the basis of linguistic evidence, that they were living on the edge of the Caspian Sea two thousand years ago. Their language, one of the Iranian group of the Indo-European languages, is most closely related to Kurdish. Still more obscure are the origins of the Brahuis, a section of the Baluch. Even the usually concise *Imperial Gazetteer of Baluchistan* toys indulgently with learned speculation on the Brahuis and their language. 'That the Brahuis are essentially nomads and flock-owners is well indicated by their proverb: "God is God, but a sheep is a different thing" . . . Like the Basque of Europe [the Brahui language] stands alone among alien tongues, a mute witness to ethnical movements occurring before the rise of authentic history.'

The British thought fairly well of the Baluch. Frontier and Overseas Expeditions tells us that 'the Baluch is less turbulent, less bloodthirsty, and less fanatical than the Pathan; he has less of God in his creed and less of the devil in his nature . . . Frank and open in his manners, fairly truthful when not corrupted by our courts, faithful to his word, temperate and enduring, and looking upon courage as the highest virtue, the true Baluch is a pleasant man to have dealings with. As a revenue payer he is not so satisfactory.'

General Jacob, commanding the Sind Irregular Horse, had a long-running battle with some tribes – the Marris and the Bugtis, particularly. In 1846, all Bugtis were deemed to be outlaws, and a reward of ten rupees was offered for the capture of one. Twenty years later, Sandeman achieved a sort of peace through his policy of boosting the authority of the sardars and making deals with them, to enable them better to govern their people. By 1876 the British had a treaty with the Khan of Kalat and the sardars, which enabled them to station troops in Baluchistan for defence against Afghanistan, in return for money and promises of non-interference.

The British were keen that the Baluch should join Pakistan; but the day after partition in 1947, the Khan of Kalat declared his state independent. Many sardars supported him, including Ghaus Bux Bizenjo, now at seventy the grand old man of Baluch politics, who made a speech at the age of twenty-nine which has caused many opponents since to accuse him of treason. 'We have a distinct culture like Afghanistan and Iran,' he said, 'and if the mere fact that we are Muslims requires us to amalgamate with Pakistan, then Afghanistan and Iran should also be amalgamated with Pakistan.' In 1948, the Army walked in and the Khan acceded to Pakistan.

Baluchistan brought Pakistan gas, coal and trouble. It provides eighty percent of the country's gas, which in 1980 saved $275 million worth of fuel imports, and most of its coal. The siphoning off of the province's riches is one of the Baluch nationalists' main complaints. They get a mere 12.5 percent of the well-head price (set by the government, at a rate the Baluch maintain is one of the lowest in the world) in gas royalties: the Canadian oil-producing provinces get forty-five percent. The coal mines are almost all owned and operated by non-Baluch.

The Baluch had more immediate grievances in 1958, when Ayub Khan amalgamated West Pakistan into one province, thereby denying their prized national identity. He threatened their traditional lifestyle by issuing orders for the surrender of unlicensed firearms, and the Baluch, led by the ninety-year-old Nauroz Khan, revolted. Nauroz Khan died in jail, and the Bugtis' sardar, Akbar, and the Mengals' sardar, Ataullah, were also imprisoned.

The extent to which the Baluch struggle is about maintaining the power of the sardars, as well as about national pride and independence, came out in a set of demands Khair Bux Marri, the Marris' sardar, put to the government in 1967. He was a Marxist, the furthest left of the Baluch leaders, yet he required the government to recognise that all minerals belonged to the sardar and the elders of that area, that the sardar and not the government should recruit the tribal levies (local militia) and members of jirgas (tribal councils), that the police and revenue staff should be withdrawn, and no roads should be built.

In the 1970 election when Bhutto swept Sind and Punjab, Baluchistan voted in a National Awami Party government, headed by Attaullah Mengal, with Ghaus Bux Bizenjo as governor and Khair Bux Marri as inspirational firebrand. Akbar Bugti was put out: he had supported, though he did not belong to, the Awami Party, and, it seems, expected a job. His brother compounded the insult by joining the Party and getting a ministerial post.

Bhutto's unwillingness to allow anybody but himself to wield power led him to sack the provincial government in 1973. A cache of arms discovered in the Iraqi embassy provided the pretext: the

National Awami Party, he said, was conspiring to start an insurgency against the government. The truth is still obscure. Selig Harrison, the American academic, suggests that while the more moderate nationalists, like Bizenjo, probably knew nothing about the guns, the extremists, like Sher Mohammed Marri, did; and that Akbar Bugti, who had found out, passed the word on to Bhutto. If so, Bugti got his reward; he was made governor.

Whether or not an insurgency was planned, the government's sacking was the cue for one to start. Guerrillas of the Baluch People's Liberation Front started to ambush Army convoys, and soldiers attacked villages. The fighting went on from 1973–7. At the peak, 80,000 soldiers were in action.

The war confused nationalist and left-wing motives. The real ideologues fighting the war were a handful of young men and women, many of them Punjabis, who, while studying at Cambridge, had imbibed a dose of Marxism. They were interested in the grievances of the proletariat, not the Baluch, but decided that Baluchistan would be the springboard for an armed insurgency against the state which would eventually spread across the country.

The Baluch 'left-wingers', like Khair Bux Marri, Ataullah Mengal and Ghaus Bux Bizenjo, were not noticeably socialist in their views. Their pro-Soviet ideology, it seems, sprang more from the need for Soviet support when Iran and, to some extent, America, were supporting the central government. It seems likely that the average Baluch – literacy rate in the province is six per cent – is moved less by socialist theory than appeals to his Baluchness and to his loyalty to his sardar. The nationalist element in the insurgency, thus, was central; the left-wing part tactical.

Zia, who certainly supported Bhutto's tough line on Baluchistan, was conciliatory when he took over. Baluchistan was a useful smear on Bhutto. He released the National Awami Party leaders who Bhutto had jailed. They were winded by the war, and silenced by martial law. Bizenjo stayed at home and started another political party; Marri left for Afghanistan with about 2,000 guerrillas; Mengal lives in the London suburb of Ealing.

The invasion of Afghanistan in 1979 led people who had never heard of Baluchistan to study the problem. Its heightened strategic importance, and the continual fear of a Russian push, supported by angry tribesmen, down towards the Gulf, focused foreign attention on the province. Zia's martial law governor, General Rahimuddin, decided to cash in. He suggested a special development programme for the area, financed by the foreigners. So the provincial government put together a lot of programmes in a hurry and took them to the foreigners, who came for official visits and signed cheques for more dollars than the Baluchistan government could manage.

According to the chief secretary of Baluchistan, Mr Poonegar, $5 billion worth of aid – $1,000 each for everybody living in Baluchistan – had been committed by the foreigners by the end of 1987. The rush was so great that the World Bank committed $40 million to one project without knowing the details. The money could be used as soon as they liked; the trouble was, Mr Poonegar said, they could not absorb it. They didn't want to employ engineers and teachers from other provinces, and they just didn't have enough trained Baluch to design the canals or run the schools.

The tribes were making trouble, too. The Marris would not accept development programmes, because Khair Bux Marri had told them not to. 'We had a beautiful scheme there,' he said sadly. 'A Kuwait Fund irrigation scheme. We'd done the study, everything was ready, then our man went to the Marri area, and they told him they'd kill him unless he left.' And the Bugtis? Interesting question, he said. Akbar Bugti did nothing to prevent development; but he had a suspicion that this was less a result of indifference than of a realistic understanding of the limitations of his power. Gas extraction, he said, had made a big difference to the area. Bugtis clamoured for jobs in the gasworks: as they made money and learnt to read and write, they were less bound to their old allegiances.

After his rivals left, Akbar Bugti took up the nationalist flag. His area is particularly sensitive since it includes the Sui gas field that supplies forty-three per cent of Pakistan's energy production: the tribesmen working there have taken to striking, which alarms the authorities. In these conditions, Bugti's loud anti-central-government speeches sound threatening.

But Bugti was suffering from the disadvantages of being an anti-government sardar. When Bugti was briefly governor under Bhutto, the Jam of Las Bela – whose delicious title means that if there were still a Las Bela state, he would run it – was his somewhat oppressed chief minister. The Jam got the Governor's job under Zia, and his erstwhile boss had a hard time. Politicians told civil servants to harass Bugti, and Bugti tribesmen complained that civil servants would do nothing for them. I decided that the Nawab was the person to explain tribal politics to me.

Leaving Sibi, I lost interest in the subtleties of the desert. The mountains were up there, in front, promising that the air would be clean of dust, that there would be small streams hidden among their jagged folds, and that their peaks would offer brain-clearing views of further mountains disappearing into blue.

We climbed into them along a dry river-bed. Then a trickle of water appeared and deepened into pure aquamarine, varying from pools of deep green to almost colourless where it bounced shallowly over rocks. I could see its coldness, and understand, in the dead dryness, that it was the most precious thing in the world. It was the absence of water that had made Baluchistan a country of tribes shifting constantly in search of a little more vegetation for their mangy animals, an untaxable land not worth conquering so not much governed.

Quetta was as dry as the mountains, but on a plateau patched with fruit orchards. The street life was like any other Pakistani street life, the sun making pyramid-shaped shadows from piles of nuts and dried fruit, and men frying round kebabs on flat iron plates; but here, even the kebab-firers had gloves on, everybody was wrapped in thick coats or blankets and men were selling piles of bright-coloured quilts by the roadside. The December cold was sharp-edged, flesh-biting, and the bright sun without strength.

The Nawab invited me to dine with him but, I realised as I put the phone down, had not given me an address. That didn't matter, of course; but I am still not used to seeing big people in small towns. The taxi driver nodded without comment when I asked him to take me to the Nawab, and bounced down a network of shrinking streets, to a small wooden door by a car-repair workshop, with a cigarette stall opposite. A silent servant, waiting by the door, let me in and disappeared.

The room was was small, with flat cushions on the floor around the walls, round cushions on them as back-rests, and nothing else in it except a blessed round iron stove, with a pipe going out of the window. I huddled by it, waiting.

The Nawab had the geniality of one who can afford it and the straight-backed bearing that is the result either of military training or of habitual dominance. Black eyebrows made his eyes fierce. His hair and beard were glossy white, and his moustache, curling upwards, implied a smile that wasn't there. His straight nose was too long for his looks to be ideal. His humorous good manners were made easy by years of unquestioned superiority.

He occupied one wall of cushions, I another, the stove and the door a third. Four men drifted in after him and squashed them-selves along the fourth wall. The Nawab introduced them: the grey, slight one by the door was a Hindu, an adopted Bugti and member of parliament; the thin, cunning-looking one was a nephew and, the Nawab said with mock-deference, a hajji, one who has done his pilgrimage to Mecca; the big burly one with a large head resting in a larger nest of beard was son-in-law, nephew and second cousin once removed; and, in the corner, was a Bugti academic who had recently returned from America and was teaching at the university.

I was curious about the tribal system: how they managed, for instance, one set of laws inside the tribal areas and one outside. Take adultery, he said: according to Bugti law, death was the mandatory sentence, and a husband's honour required him to kill a fallen wife. Bugtis living outside the tribal area had the option of losing their honour or being charged with murder; so such a man would probably take his wife into the tribal area and kill her there, or he could kill her and the lover and then escape. And, I wondered, was fornication also a capital crime? Of course, said the Nawab, and tried to count up the number of people whose right and duty it was to kill a fornicating couple. He got lost, and consulted the four men, who were sitting like birds on a fence, shifting their positions occasionally, but keeping their eyes on him. They came up with eight categories: the girl's and boy's fathers, brothers, uncles and sons.

I asked him if this was a good thing. The question did not seem to rate consideration: he shrugged, and said that these customs had taken a long time to develop. And blood feuds, I asked, did they still go on? Certainly, he said, with a certain relish, anticipating, I thought, my shock.

'We had a feud with one section of the Marris that lasted twenty years. A hundred and thirty people were killed. A couple of years back, we sat down with them and sorted it out with blood money in three days. Can you imagine a court settling all those murders in three days? We had a feud with the Jakhranis in which we cut each others ears off, and then started killing each other. We settled it last year. Two hundred and fifty people had been killed in thirty years.' He showed me a video of the reconciliation, attended by a baffled-looking friend of his from the *Financial Times*. Why, I asked, did they kill people so much?

'Diversion. There's nothing else to do there. We don't have videos in the tribal areas, people can't read.'

'Are you serious? Murder is a cinema-substitute?'

'Partly.'

'How many people have you killed yourself?'

'I've lost count,' he said. I decided that had to be play-acting. It must be fun, confusing foreigners with tales of ancient barbarism in elegant Aitchisonian English.

I asked him what nationalism meant to him. It was a genuine question, since it means nothing to me; but he looked as though I had asked him what water tasted like. At independence, he said, the smaller provinces swapped white colonialists for black ones – the Punjabis. So what did the Baluch want? Recognition of the rights of nationalities. Secession? Not necessarily. Money? If it were a question of bread, he said with disdain bordering on anger, we might as well be sheep and goats, and they could give us oats to keep us happy. No: the Baluch people should be allowed to run themselves. Which, I could see, would have certain advantages from his point of view.

Was there opposition to him from within the tribe?

'Of course. There is opposition to God.'

'But God gets the final say.'

'How?'

'Death.'

'I don't believe that stuff. After death, there is earth. Then the maggots get you. But my nephew,' he said with the relish of anticipated cruelty, watching the man curling his legs further under him, 'he believes in paradise. He has been on haj twice. You know what he is promised in paradise? Houris, ghilmans and sharab. Prostitutes, little boys, and wine. Very special prostitutes and boys,' he added confidentially. 'They have no openings.'

'No openings?'

'You ask him to explain it.' The writhing nephew tittered.

Behind the little room was a courtyard and a house, which I discovered when the Nawab showed me to the bathroom. There were three fat women and two fat boys in a pink room, watching television. He pointed them out as though describing kitchen appliances: the older one was one of his wives, the others his daughters, the boys his grandsons. He had thirty-eight grandchildren, he said with excusable pride. On the bed was a rifle; on the bathroom door a poster of Madonna.

The next evening, the audience had grown. A round-faced, humorous lawyer was there: he had been chief secretary when the

Nawab was governor, and was now in Islamabad. His elaborate deference to the Nawab was a joke, at which the Nawab took no offence; and he explained sardari politics to me as though the Nawab were a pickled specimen.

All this nationalism, he said, was the result of the crumbling tribal structure. The sardars could no longer rely on absolute loyalty from their tribesmen merely because they were sardars. They had to offer something else to build up new constituencies, and an ideology was the obvious option. Khair Bux Marri had opted for communism, and the Nawab for Baluch nationalism. Both had been successful. Khair Bux Marri called people to Kabul, and people from different tribes, not just the Marris, came. Nawabsahib's nationalism had won him a following in Baluchistan from beyond his tribe.

The Nawab made no comment, but started a game with another hanger-on who had appeared. He had been an official adviser when the Nawab was governor, because his family supported a Pathan nationalist party, so had to be brought within the fold of government. The game with Maliksahib, as they called him with mocking deference, was ridicule, and I was the audience. Maliksahib's fondness for government flags on his cars and houses was recalled. Maliksahib had been to jail for ordering a van load of canes for his tomato-plants: the police thought he was mounting a demonstration. Maliksahib had again been jailed for shouting obscenities about Zia's wife. Maliksahib told some of the stories himself, and giggled at them with the uncertainty of one who doesn't know if he is a target or a participant; but he had no option. I laughed helplessly, and later recalled the cruelty with distaste.

I went to Dera Bugti, the Seat of the Bugtis in the tribal areas, to see whether the sardar was still God. I decided he probably wasn't: there was too much money around. There were schools, roads, contracts, bribes, cash handouts − all the manna dropped by governments that makes people independent of the tribal fount of benefits. The notables I met, just below the rank of sardar, were keen to impress on me the decline in Akbar Bugti's position without showing disloyalty to the sardar. One of them pointed out that our meeting was proof of the sardar's decline. Twenty years earlier, if I had gone to Dera Bugti, I would have been allowed to see the sardar and nobody else.

But the thing that confused me was the gasworks. If Akbar Bugti was a determined nationalist, why did he not use the leverage he had over the government through the 500-or-so Bugtis who manned the Sui gas plant to gain concessions for his tribesmen and his province? I learned what seemed to be the answer by going there and meeting two Bugti tribesmen, Khair Din and Murad Ali, in the baked-mud Bugti colony that sprawled away from the company officials' brick and concrete houses. They were threatening to strike, and had just been to Dera Bugti to ask the Nawab for guidance. Had they managed to see the Nawab? No, he had been too busy. If he gave them advice, would they follow it?

'Wherever our Nawab goes, we will go.'

'Why doesn't he help you with your demands?'

'Our Nawab should not be begging for us,' said Khair Din indignantly.

The men in his union had been working for the company for ten, twelve and sixteen years. They earned 900 rupees (£30) a month. The old man in the shadow of the door had been a permanent worker, but was laid off sick and now earned 325 rupees a month handing out the wages from the contractor who hired out their services to the gas company. The contractor was the Nawab's brother-in-law.

'The Nawab's brother-in-law?'

'Of course.'

'Does it occur to you,' I said, trying to speak clearly through my laughter, 'that the Nawab might have a financial interest here?'

'Of course,' said Khair Din, laughing too. 'He is getting a commission. Why should he support us?'

'And you will do whatever he says?'

'Of course. He is our Nawab.'

'What if he told you not to strike?'

'He won't.'

'What if he did?' That was difficult. Khair Din paused, put the end of his green turban into his mouth and chewed it. Murad Ali glared at the floor. They spoke simultaneously.

'We would still strike,' said Khair Din.

'We might postpone the strike,' said Murad Ali.

Evidently the Nawab knew that he was no longer God – hence his calculated foray into moderate nationalism. As a new base for a political platform, it worked: in partnership with some of the old revolutionaries, he did quite well in the 1988 election. But Baluchistan's other tribes have, for the moment, been decapitated – either because the sardars are abroad, or because they are not serious about causing trouble. The frontier's tribes are more numerous and – increasingly – less easily controlled.

Under the British and the Pakistanis, government has had little power, legal or military, to compel tribesmen to do anything, so policy has had to be implemented through the regular application of money. When it comes to dealing with Pathan tribes on the north west frontier, policy has meant two things: persuading the tribesmen not to raid the settled areas, and playing the Great Game against Afghanistan and the Soviet Union. The job of the political agent, the man planted inside the tribal areas to hand out allowances and make alliances, was a dangerous one: in British times, three successive political agents in the South Waziristan agency were murdered.

Delving around in the catalogues of the India office library for something that would explain the tribal system in the frontier under the British, I found a dusty unpromising-sounding gem, the report of the North West Frontier Committee of 1924. The report itself was floridly dull ('India has indeed cause to be grateful that it is a race as manly and as staunch as the Pathan that holds the ramparts for her on this historically vulnerable frontier'), but the evidence, in which local civil servants and Khans tried to explain to ignorant Britishers how the frontier worked, was often funny and sharp. Mr Bray, head of the committee, asked Lt. Col. E. H. S. James, officiating revenue commissioner of the NWFP, what would happen if the government stopped doling out money to the tribes, and got the same reply that he might get today.

'If the sympathy engendered by the allowances were withdrawn, the situation would be impossible. The maliks would refuse to attend when summoned; they would encourage raiding in the tribe and turn to other rulers for allowances . . . Bolshevik money is being expended already, and if we do not maintain friendly relations with the maliks we would only throw them into the arms of our enemies.'

Frontier politics is played by different rules to those most politics are played by. Lt. Col. James tried to explain this to Mr Bray with a little story.

'I was riding along one day and I met a sepoy who was coming back on leave. I asked him if he had managed to save any money. He said he had saved about 500 rupees. I enquired what he was going to do with it. He said that he was going to buy a .303 rifle. I said the cost of a rifle is about 900 rupees, and that he had only 500 rupees. How could he get the rifle? He said: "Oh, it is very easy, there is no trouble about money. I will raise it by selling my wife." I told him that I thought that rather bad luck on his wife. He said "Oh! Once I get my rifle I will easily get my wife back again." That is one of the reasons why they like to have rifles.'

'After he gets back his wife, he will sell his rifle?'

'He will have both his wife and rifle.'

'What is the real object of arming themselves?'

'He can get other people's wives too, and property. Some of the property that he covets is in British territory.'

'He wants to rob?'

'I think that is very often at the back of his mind.'

'I am really perplexed about it. The thing is, we are supposed to have control over the tribes for the last so many years, and it is clear that they have at the back of their minds this unfriendly and raiding spirit, and we are continuing to make them allowances and treat them as friends, when we know that they are arming themselves to the teeth in order to molest British subjects . . .?'

Mr Bray hadn't understood that the Great Game was, and still is, one that three can play. The Pathan tribes have a long history of taking what they can get from rival powers intriguing in their area. If one side requires a semblance of loyalty in return for money and guns, that can always be provided; but if the other side offers significantly more, then the original allegiance can be forfeited. Mr Bray's dismay at the Pathans' apparent treachery would have meant nothing to them. Their loyalty was not to the British or the Russians, but to the Pakhtunwali, their code of law and honour, which laid down rules about the treatment of guests and women, but had nothing to say about staying on the side of the British if the Russians were offering more money, or not raiding property in British-administered areas.

Mr Bray had also failed to appreciate that the British did not – and the Pakistanis still don't – 'control' the tribes. British law did not operate in their areas, British administrators could not even enter some bits of the borderland, and when the British Army went to beat the tribes into submission it usually had a hard time. Politics had to be played through bargains between equals. Making the right sort of bargains with the right people was the skill of the political agents and residents, people like Mr Pears, the political agent in South Waziristan, who lived in extreme danger in the tribal areas.

Mr Pears was clearly having difficulties with the Mahsud tribe.

'They are not simply democratic . . . they are absolutely Bolshevik, the majority of them, and it is because of this anarchy among the tribe that the state of chaos has been created which has been such a calamity to us for the last 30 years.'

By Bolshevik, I suppose, Mr Pears meant unwilling to obey authority. There is an element of lawlessness about the Pathans, the other side of which is the attractive consciousness of their own dignity which made the British fall for them and despise the people further south who did what they were told. The Pathans are not quite leaderless, though. There are people who have some authority – maliks, who are recognised usually because their families are accounted important, or sometimes because they are clever, or pious, or rich, or have lots of sons. They are the people through whom the British dealt with the tribes, giving them allowances in proportion to their ability to influence their fellows.

The Pakistani government kept the system going, since it seemed a pragmatic way to run the area. New maliks are appointed, in addition to the hereditary ones; but they are useful only if they are listened to. On top of their special role of brokering between the government and the tribesmen, they get a further privilege: in the tribal areas, they are still the only people who are allowed to vote – a matter which causes some resentment among young men who see no reason why they should have fewer political rights than their counterparts in settled areas.

As Akbar Ahmed explained with his squares and triangles, these tribes are very different to the Baluch, who have one sardar whose authority is rarely questioned. The Pathan maliks do not have the power to order people around. Authority lies with the jirga, a tribal assembly made up of maliks, elders, and anybody who happens to be around when the jirga is called. It decides tribal policy – on war, peace, relations with the government and other tribes – and tries cases according to the Pakhtunwali, the main principles of which are honour, revenge and hospitality. All the tribesmen I talked to reckoned their legal system superior to that of the settled areas, which they thought slow, and often unjust because rich guilty people could escape justice by bribing judges.

A friend recommended me to Nadar Khan Zakakhel, a malik of the Zakakhel clan of the Afridi tribe, which lives along the border from the Khyber Pass westwards to the remote area of Tirah. He sounded the right man for me: James Spain, former American diplomat in Pakistan and writer on the Pathans, says that 'the Afridi . . . has . . . come to represent the archetype of the Pathan. To him can be applied a whole catalogue of contradictory adjectives: brave, cautious, honorable, treacherous, cruel, gallant, superstitious, courteous, suspicious, and proud.' The Zakakhel, he says, is considered the archetypal Afridi clan. 'It is reputed to be so untrustworthy that the other clans traditionally refuse to accept a Zakakhel oath in a jirga unless it is accompanied by the giving of hostages.'

Nadar Khan was one of the two main protagonists in a border battle just like the ones that were playing themselves out under the British Raj, a rivalry between Pathans which because of their location involved the governments of Afghanistan and Pakistan as well. Nadar Khan's rival was the principal Kukikhel malik, Wali Khan Kukikhel: the two were struggling for pre-eminence in the Khyber Agency. As though performing some weaving political dance, the two maliks switched sides in parallel; but it wasn't quite clear whether the governments were using them, or they were using the governments.

Wali Khan had his first bust-up with the Pakistani government in 1952, and got some of his villages bulldozed. He crossed over into Afghanistan, and stayed there until 1962, when the president, Ayub Khan, made peace with him and he got a seat in parliament. Nadar Khan, meanwhile, sided with Kabul and allied with people like the old Pathan politician Ghaffur Khan who opposed the Pakistani government.

After the Russian invasion in 1979, Nadar Khan returned, and was taken up by the Pakistani government. Wali Khan took the Afghan side and got all the support he wanted, in guns and money, from Kabul: the Afghan government was anxious to win supporters in Pakistan's tribal areas to make it more difficult for the anti-government resistance to operate out of Pakistan. Since the tribal areas' semi-independence makes it difficult for the government to operate inside their borders, Nadar Khan fought on Islamabad's behalf; and for months the road from Peshawar to the Khyber Pass was unsafe even for locals because of the two sides' reciprocal kidnappings. The Pakistani government's irritation with Wali Khan reached a peak in 1985: troops went into the tribal areas and bulldozed his and his supporters' houses.

Six months later, peace reigned once more. Wali Khan kept the guns the Afghans had given him, and in return for seventy-five million rupees from the Pakistani government agreed to stop making difficulties. But trouble erupted again over a road that the government was trying to build from Landi Kotal to remote Tirah, through Zakakhel land. When he was on the Afghan side, Nadar Khan had opposed it fiercely; but it had become his pet project now that he was with the government. Wali Khan Kukikhel mounted a campaign against it, though nobody I spoke to was clear whether this was because it was likely to mean government interference in the tribal areas, or because they thought only the Zakakhel would benefit from it. The Deputy Commissioner in Peshawar did not much care. He was fed up with the road.

'Every day, because of this road, I have had kidnappings, car liftings, rocket attacks, just to harass the government.'

I rang Nadar Khan and told him that I wanted to go to the Khyber Agency, but said that I would first have to get the government permission necessary for foreigners travelling in these sensitive areas.

'If you like you get permission. With me, is not necessary. I take you tomorrow at nine.'

Which he did, punctually, in a pagri with a gold-embroidered cap bound by a brown silk, gold-edged turban that rose in a stiff fan. Four gunmen, Kalashnikovs to their chests, stood to attention in the lobby of Green's Hotel. The receptionist looked up, momentarily surprised, then turned his polite attention back to a German with broken spectacles who was complaining about the state of his room.

One gunman got into the front of the Jeep, by the driver; Nadar Khan and myself climbed into the next row of seats, and three gunmen in the back. They sat silent, staring indifferently out of the window.

We drove north along the Grand Trunk Road out of Peshawar, past the university and the rows of big modern houses where the foreigners who look after the refugees live, past the 'Refugee Tented Villages' which are no longer tented because the refugees have built themselves a maze of mud houses covering acres, stretching for twenty minutes' drive along the road. The houses are the same, but the settlement like nowhere in Pakistan: in other mud box villages, some people have got rich enough to build themselves brick or concrete. We drove past the striped police barrier, where two policemen stood watching us but didn't stop us, past the smuggling supermarket at Jamrud, and on to a scrubby plain with the mountains waiting ahead.

Nadar Khan took his pagri off and replaced it with a mushroom-shaped wool Chitrali hat with a rolled brim, of the sort favoured by the Afghan mujaheddin. He was in his late fifties, I guessed, and, unusually for a Pathan, clean-shaven. His eyes were small and sharp above an oversized nose, his mouth thin-lipped and wide. His square jaw protruded slightly, reminding me of a pike, and made his smiles, however benign in intent, malicious. He looked like an experienced politician.

We passed a chain of donkeys led by a wrinkled brown man, with a boy with a small stick bringing up the rear.

'To Afghanistan,' said Nadar Khan, 'they go empty by road. They come back with so many things by hills.'

When we started up into the mountains, I could feel the gunmen behind me loosening up. They moved around on their seats, there were small bits of conversation, and occasional sharp laughs. They were on home ground.

The road followed a river-course. Above it, 'Wel Come to Khyber Rifles' and 'Happy Visit to Khyber Rifles' were written in white stones on brown and yellow sloping hill-faces. On the other side of the river was the railway, nestling into the hillside where the rock had been blown away to make a ledge, or boring through lumps of mountain, the tunnels finished off by stones chiselled into a neat circle, smart as the doorway of a country house.

We passed Shagai fort, an irregular fantasy in red brick whose odd shape was determined by the cliffs it hung on to. A couple of hundred feet above the road, at half-mile intervals, were boxes of yellow stone or brick, with horizontal slits in their four sides. The posts and the fort were built by the British to protect the road from Nadar Khan's family and friends.

'All British,' said Nadar Khan with an evil smile. I suppose he was pleased to have found me something to be proud about. Instead, I was full of historical pity for the men who had sweated with fear and heat in those boxes; but moved by and proud of that absurd, heroic railway. Any imperial power that could invest so much labour, capital, skill and pain into a railway going from Peshawar to Landi Kotal could not fail to impress, and could not fail to fail.

'There are muddy houses in London?' asked Nadar Khan.

'No,' I replied. 'It rains too much. You have been to London?'

'This year I was going, but there was some trouble with my road the government is building to Tirah. Maybe next year.'

I asked Nadar Khan what sort of trouble he had been having.

'These Russians and Afghans,' he said dismissively, 'They are making problems with their agents. They say the road will take away their freedom.'

The metal gate in a mud wall creaked open when the driver hooted, and we drove into a mud courtyard with a little lawn, a bed of pink flowers, and a tiny white mosque ahead of us. Nadar Khan gestured towards a pavilion beside it.

'Duke of Adambra, husband of Malik Elizabeth, drink tea there.'

He took me through the small wooden door into a walled garden, with a grove of shiny-leaved sweet lemon trees and rows of neatly-weeded beans, radishes, cucumbers, tomatoes and turnips. Through the next wall was another garden, with geometrical patterns of flower-beds overflowing with rose-bushes and olean-ders. I was touched by the pride with which he showed me his gardens. I had not imagined that Pathans would like gardens, though for no good reason. The emperor Babur, whose main occupation in early life was chopping off enemies' heads and building them into towers, was a passionate gardener. When he conquered India, he complained bitterly of their dearth.

Inside, the deep pink walls of Nadar Khan's house were blister-ing, and the red velveteen sofas and chairs were worn in places to pink. Water arrived, then fizzy drinks and raisins, almonds and pistachio nuts, then tea, then a round pink iced cake with icing flowers and silver balls on it, and a shiny pink ribbon round it. Nadar Khan prodded it.

'Sometimes, they come from Peshawar and stay in Landi Kotal bazaar too many days. This one is OK.'

He wrestled with the ribbon, then slit it through with the meat-knife beside his plate. It was midday, and I knew lunch would be coming soon; but there was no way I could avoid the lump of dry pink sponge on my plate.

The muscular young man who had brought the tea took our plates away again. Nadah Khan gestured towards him without acknowledging him.

'That is my son-in-law. Najibullah, malik of Afghanistan, used to do this for me when I was in Kabul.' He had been in Kabul, he said, off and on for twenty-four years. Najibullah's family had been friends of his, and since Nadar Khan was elder, Najibullah had to serve him. Nadar Khan had left for Pakistan when the Russians invaded.

'Communism,' he said, his jaw protruding even further than

153

usual, 'is against freedom. I can have so many things, but if I have no freedom I have nothing.' Oh yeah, I thought, appreciating the eloquent echo of the Letter to the Corinthians, but having developed a certain scepticism about the depth of ideological convictions in the subcontinent; what were his relations with the communist government in Afghanistan before the Russians arrived?

'That was different,' he said reproachfully. 'When I was in Kabul, we were with one side of the communist party, the Khalq. This means people. Now, after the Russians, it is Parcham side ruling. This means flag.' I was pleased to have my prejudices confirmed. The communist party, like Pathan tribes, clans, and families, was divided on no particular grounds other than that these people tend to divide.

The driver came in, took his shoes off, helped himself to one of my cigarettes and a handful of raisins and sat, legs crossed under him, on a cushion. It was a world away from the deference of Sind, Punjab or Baluchistan, which themselves seemed egalitarian compared to bits of India I had visited; I supposed it was part of the Pathans' 'Bolshevism' that status was determined more by age than by breeding.

Over lunch, conversation flagged. Nadar Khan's English was about as bad as my Urdu: a few minutes of pleasantries are easy, but for anything more serious new words have to be tried out and sentence-structure improvised to stretch a limited vocabulary. That requires more concentration than anybody is prepared to waste when there is good food to be eaten.

Half-way through a silence, Nadar Khan looked up. 'I have champagne!' he said. I waited to see if this would become clearer. He wiped his mouth, got out of his chair, and returned from an open door with a bottle with Russian writing and black foil around the cork. 'Russian champagne,' he said proudly. 'From Kabul.' He handed the bottle to me, then withdrew it. 'You will drink cold.' The son-in-law, yelled for, reappeared, took the bottle and put it in the fridge with the Pepsi Cola.

In the afternoon, Nadar Khan despatched me with a cousin of his, a small wiry man with a neat moustache who was an immigration officer at Tor Kham, the border post on the other side of the Khyber Pass. Rising out of the plain, the road narrowed to cling to the mountainside and the landscape erupted into peaks and gorges. Civilisation had been able to do nothing with these mountains, except cross them slowly and laboriously, winding up and down and round, as the mountains dictated. They were useful only to the Pathans, who understood that the worst that nature could throw up was the best defence system they could wish for.

As we twisted down from Landi Kotal (where the immigration officer would not stop: too dangerous, he said) a group of buildings, a queue of lorries and small crowds of people appeared at the foot of the pass. Tor Kham, said the immigration officer. Thousands of people, he said, Mussulman, Sikh and Hindu, crossed every day between Pakistan and Afghanistan.

'What for?'

'Some for work, some for family visiting, some for business.'

'What sort of business?'

'They bring grapes, apples, apricots from Afghanistan. In Kabul are the best grapes. Pakistan grapes are not good.'

'And air-conditioners?'

'Air-conditioners are going over there,' he said, pointing to the first set of hills to the right of Tor Kham, 'on the camels and mules. Also televisions, fridges, cloth. Because of these things, there is very much more business with Afghanistan than some time before.' I peered to the place he pointed at, half-believing him. As I looked, a chain of donkeys appeared in a gap between hills, black against the grey-yellow rock, heavily loaded and walking slowly, then disappeared again.

We edged past the lorries, which almost blocked the road, hooted our way through the crowds sitting, standing and chatting, and stopped outside an ugly concrete customs and immigration building. Opposite was the Tourist Information Centre, its windows boarded with wood and sheets of rusted metal. To the right was a wire-netting gate, with barbed wire on top of it and, on the other side of it, two Afghan soldiers in green, one lighting the other's cigarette.

As we returned, leaving the immigration officer at his post, I asked the gunmen if we could stop in Landi Kotal. Its bazaar is a major arms, drugs and smuggled goods depot. Understanding about journalistic tourism, they led me quickly down alleys past the amazed faces of kebab-friers and butchers framed by legs of meat hanging from iron hooks. We stopped by a row of men selling brown, shiny slabs of toffee. Hashish, said the gunman. Big business. And, I asked, was heroin for sale there?

'Not here,' he said. 'Heroin is not on roads. Heroin is in villages.' He gestured westwards, to the interior of the tribal areas.

The gunman strode faster down the alleys, so that I was skipping to avoid children and chickens, to a row of weapons shops. He picked up a Kalashnikov, and presented it to me in his two hands, like a garland. I asked the shopkeeper how much it was. Russian, he said, so 17,000 rupees. Five years before, they had been 35,000 rupees. And how much were Chinese ones? Not so much as Russians: 14,000–15,000 rupees. So many Chinese Kalashnikovs, he said, and everybody wants Russian ones. The gunman, bored of Kalashnikovs, found me a rocket launcher. I asked the shopkeeper if he had any of the Stinger missiles which the Americans had supplied to the mujaheddin. No, he said, his papery skin crinkling into a smile; but maybe he could get one. I asked how much, but he just laughed.

When I got back, Nadar Khan announced that I was to meet the women. I didn't know there were any in his house; I hadn't thought about it. He took me through yet another wall at the end of his house, into a mud courtyard full of women and children. He yelled at one of the women, and left.

They encircled me at a little distance, as though I might bite. One of the girls, her hair in tangles and her eyes bright with kohl ran up to me, pinched my leg, and ran back between the women, giggling. One of the women cuffed her and she howled.

The women were thick-limbed, with heavy faces and worn skins: peasant women. At first I couldn't see any young ones; it took a while before I could differentiate between faces and hands weathered by fires, wind, cold and hard physical work combined with child-bearing, and those worn by age. I was embarrassed, knowing that even if I could speak Pashtu I wouldn't know what to talk to them about. I wanted to go back to the familiar politics and comfort of the men's quarters.

Then one I hadn't seen came from the back, through the other women. Her skin was soft and young and she walked as though she should have been wearing high heels.

'Hello,' she said in clear English, 'I am glad you have come to visit. My name is Nihar Sultana.' She was Nadar Khan's daughter-in-law, from Peshawar. She had been to school there, and, since she was now in purdah and could not leave the house, was continuing her studies through the open university in Islamabad. She had done a course in English, and was now studying for her BA in economics.

She took me by the hand and, with the rest of the female and pre-pubescent population of the house straggling behind, led me into the courtyard where two women were cooking bread in a tandoor, slapping the rounds of dough on to the inside walls of the oven, to another courtyard with rooms off it, down narrow passages between the walls and into an overgrown garden, and back to her bit of the house, where we sat on a sofa by the television. For a bit, the children watched me instead of the screen.

The standard of teaching for the children was very bad, she said. The girls did not go to school, and the boys went to the mosque school, where the mullah knew nothing. I suggested she should teach them.

'Yes,' she said doubtfully; 'but my husband does not like. He says it is bad for the family.' I was silenced by the awfulness of seeing a knowledge-hungry city girl imprisoned by twelve-foot-high mud walls. Perhaps sensing this and wanting to explain, she took me on to the roof, the only place in their compound from which the landscape was visible. The sun had set behind the mountains to the west, and the sky was grey-blue at the edges, with a pink wash where the sun had been. The place was quiet, but for sheep and children's noises. I looked harder at the mountains, which resolved into three layers. Nihar Sultana brought binoculars. Through them, I could see a man with some goats on the nearest slope, the cutting edges of the mountain-tops, and the clear lines of small clumps of trees against the sunset.

'It's very beautiful,' I said hopelessly.

'Yes.' She smiled. 'More beautiful than Peshawar.'

I was glad to get back to Nadar Khan's bit of the house. The walls were as high, but they were the walls of a fortress, not of a prison. The champagne came out of the fridge, and Nadar Khan peeled off the black foil and pulled at the round plastic stopper. Nothing happened. He took a knife from somewhere about him, and was about to sever the head of the stopper when I grabbed the bottle from him and eased it slowly with my thumbs. It came out with a disappointing but professional hiss.

It was very bad champagne, sweet as rose hip syrup, and thick with a guaranteed hangover. Nadar Khan wouldn't drink any, but amused himself filling up my glass to ensure that I drank the whole bottle. My Urdu loosened up, and I asked him about maliks, money and the government.

The maliks got 3,000 to 5,000 rupees a month from the government, he said, plus extra money for special bargains; but many of

157

them were useless people, maliks on paper who had no money and no influence. There were some people, with so much money and some influence, now, who were not in the pay of government. What, I asked, was the money from.

'They are doing some trading with Hong Kong goods from Afghanistan,' he said evenly, 'but underneath is something else.'

People like himself and Wali Khan Kukikhel did not need the government, he said. They had enough money. Nadar Khan had his own business – though I was not clear what it was – as well as two houses in Kabul, the one we were in near Landi Kotal, one in Tirah and one in Peshawar. I asked him who was living in the ones in Kabul.

'You will laugh,' he said seriously. 'One house, near the Intercontinental Hotel, it is in the name of Najibullah's sister's husband.'

I began to see the point of Nadar Khan when he told me that a few months before, 1,000 people from the Khyber Agency had wanted to go to Kabul to fight for the Russians. Nadar Khan did not allow them to pass through his lands, which include a semi-circle around the Khyber Pass, and they did not go.

'I suppose your land makes you important to government?'

'Of course,' he grinned wickedly. 'Sometime before, Sardar of Turkey came to Pakistan. He wanted to go to Khyber Pass. But Turkey was in Baghdad pact, Kabul was against Baghdad pact and I was with Kabul. So he did not go. Then [ex-King] Daoud of Afghanistan, his brother came through Khyber Pass, had tea with me and went back. Government was very angry.'

I asked a retired political agent, the commissioner and deputy commissioner in Peshawar, and a political agent if Nadar Khan and his ilk were still a good surrogate government. No, said the retired political agent. Nadar Khan was still important, because he had kept in touch with the young men; but many maliks had not. The young men had taken the bit into their mouths. No, said the commissioner. The big money – business money, drugs money – had too much influence these days. No, said the deputy commissioner, who had been a political agent himself. The government had messed up a fragile system of political manipulation by using the Army too much. No, said the political agent. 'But what else have we got? It would take thirty-six Army divisions to control the tribal areas.'

Money and fighting have given Peshawar a split personality. Part of it is an Army town, built up by the British to protect the soft cultivators of the plains from the hard men of the hills and the unreliable Amir of Afghanistan. Mall Road is lined with trees and split down the middle by a band of neatly cut grass and tidy flowers; off it are Gunner Road and Artillery Road – all of them oddly empty. Smart soldiers stand rigidly, their eyes moving to watch passing women, and plump officers drive by in dark green Jeeps, watching the soldiers watching the women. Behind the trees are the high-walled haunts of the military. In the officers' bit of the military hospital, convalescents sit among marigolds and bushes with yellow trumpet-flowers.

That is British Peshawar, alert and armed to the hilt for fear of the Afghans. In Pakistani Peshawar the bazaars are booming from trade with the people the soldiers are protecting their country against. Smuggling brings cheap Russian goods and expensive Korean, Taiwanese and Japanese ones either by road and rail through the Soviet Union, or direct by plane to Kabul. From Kabul, they travel towards Pakistan on lorries, are transferred for the border crossing on to donkeys, which skirt round the post at the Khyber Pass. Then at Landi Kotal, just inside Pakistan, they are switched on to lorries or pick-ups and go to Bara or Jamrud, the big smuggling bazaars. From the south, they arrive in Karachi in transit for Afghanistan, thus avoiding Pakistani duties, and are shipped, legitimately, up north; but they never make it to Afghanistan. Fleets of lorries then distribute goods from Peshawar and Jamrud to the rest of the country.

A young journalist I knew was going to Jamrud on his motor bike to check out a rumour that cheap Russian bicycles were about to flood the country. He agreed to take me, but, since I did not have the necessary permission, made me dress in one of his sisters' slinky blue floral shalwar kamees and a black chador on top. I had to sit side-saddle, holding the chador, in the regulation manner, from the inside, trying to keep a large enough opening to see through while not exposing all of my western-shaped spectacles. It seemed easier to cover my face altogether, and watch the world through a black mist; but the journalist said that would not do, since the police would think I was a dacoit dressed as a woman. After that, I admired the women who perched on the backs of bikes, legs crossed as nonchalantly as though they were on a sofa.

Jamrud, just beyond Peshawar's smart University Town, where the foreigners live, and past a striped barrier marking the beginning of the tribal area, was a complex of shops in alleys and courtyards on two stories. Peering into the shops were family groups that might have been on an outing to a London department store, parents debating purchases and children sucking cold drinks from the stalls that had grown up around the complex to service the customers. All the riches of the East and the Soviet Union were there – round stand-up Russian washing machines for 900 rupees, Sony twenty-four inch televisions for 12,000 rupees, shops selling nothing but tricycles and toys, others with shelves full of floral-patterned vacuum jugs for keeping water cold in. Russian goods, said one of the traders I talked to, were getting increasingly popular because the quality had improved in the past couple of years. Perhaps, he said, it was something to do with glasnost.

The journalist found a friend in a dark little shampoo shop. He didn't know about bicycles, said the shopkeeper, fiddling with his empty light-socket, but would ask somebody who would know. He had his own problems – 120 tonnes of Russian steel and 1,000 bags of Russian sugar sitting across the border. He didn't understand why, but the customs people, who never usually bothered anybody that paid their dues, were making trouble, and he couldn't get the stuff through the border. He put a bulb in the socket, and the bottles of pink and yellow shampoo and vanity mirrors lit up like fairy lights.

The other source of new money around Peshawar is invisible. Poppies have been grown throughout the area that is now Pakistan for centuries. The British permitted it, licensed sellers, and taxed both the cultivation of the poppy (per acre) and the sale of opium, requiring merchants to bid for licenses.

Poppy-cultivation is now illegal in Pakistan, since, under an international convention, the Pakistanis opted not to grow their own. But heroin production around the frontier took off in the late 1970s, when American pressure was squeezing the far east's Golden Triangle. People in the area, defensive about accusations that their country's prosperity is ravaging the west's youth, say that suddenly foreigners – Germans, Filipinos and Americans – arrived with refining equipment, and showed the locals how to produce their own heroin and launch their poppy crop on to the world market.

According to 'Western diplomatic sources' in Islamabad, the production graph wobbles up and down. They say that its peak, before anybody started to try to control the business, was in 1979, at around 800 tonnes of opium (which refine down to a tenth as much heroin); but that by 1985 the campaign against production had got the figure down to forty tonnes. After the reinstatement of politics in 1985, however, the graph leapt once more because the politicians leant on the enforcement agencies to go easy. Anyway, the figures are very vague, and do not include production in Afghanistan – guessed at 300–700 tonnes – which is thought to be exported mainly through Pakistan. In 1986, Pakistan is reckoned to have supplied around 2.5 tonnes of heroin to America (out of its total consumption of six tonnes) and about the same quantity to western Europe (out of a consumption of five tonnes). Heroin seems to be a class-free business. Not only are there unknown tribals throwing their millions gaily around Peshawar; the son of the ex-governor of the frontier, a big landlord, is in jail in New York for smuggling, and at Lahore and Karachi parties you meet people who have friends or relations languishing in American and European jails.

There is now a great deal of money swilling around this once backward area, both from illegal and from legal sources. One result is social mobility. People with new money want not only to show it off, but to go into the business normally monopolised by old money – politics. Aspirants to political power need influence, both with the civil servants and with their fellow-tribesmen. The first can be bought; the second is usually inherited, but an upstart can win support if he can get the civil servants to do things for people.

Among the *nouveaux riches* of the tribal areas, people suggested I should meet the owner of the new English-language paper in Peshawar, the *Frontier Post*, a well-written independent-minded paper produced on the newest electronic equipment, with a lot of expensive syndicated material and an editor who had been brought in from one of the English-language Gulf papers. Nobody seemed to know the man's name, but there was a vague idea that he came from the tribal areas and an assumption that he must have lots of money since the paper must be losing so much.

He was called Rehmat Shah Afridi, and I found him in Lahore. He sent his brother round to pick me up in a grey Daimler which slid along the banks of the canal by the oleanders, way out of town past the university, and drew up beside a new white house and a new dark blue BMW. The house, white throughout, was like the plain rooms that Nadar Khan's women had taken me round, redesigned by an architect who took pleasure in knowing that his lines would not be blurred by elaborate furnishings. Rehmat Shah was curled up on a sofa, watching the West Indies vs. Pakistan World Cup match. I wouldn't have minded watching too; but he got up, shook hands, and twinkled at me with black eyes and a shiny reddish-brown moustache. He was handsome, in a boyish way, with curly hair, plump cheeks and a quick smile. He was thirty-four, he told me later, and had been married at sixteen.

I wanted to know why he had started the *Frontier Post*. Obviously a well-produced paper favourable to the government might be a worthwhile investment for a businessman; but the *Frontier Post* was the most critical English-language paper in the country.

It was thanks to General Fazle Haq, when he was military governor of the NWFP, said Rehmat Shah. Why him? In this country, he said apologetically, you have to have the government permission. General Fazle Haq thinks the frontier needs a news-paper, so he give me permission. Yes, but what was General Fazle Haq getting out of it? Someday, he said, General Fazle Haq wanted to be politician, and politicians want newspapers to write about them. (Sure enough, six months after I met Rehmat Shah, Fazle Haq was chief minister of the frontier.) And what was Rehmat Shah getting? A newspaper, he said, was good for education and the prestige of the frontier. Education was the biggest problem in his province, the most important thing for his people.

'I love to my country, I love to my people. I have a dream for my country, for my people. Now, there are so many things are bad, and the newspaper is the only way of showing wrong things about the country.' He picked up a copy of the paper and showed me its motto, a quotation from the Quran: 'And cover not the Truth with Falsehood, nor conceal the Truth, when you know.' He spoke with childish eagerness, smiling and frowning like a bad actor as the sense dictated. I believed every word; but I wondered why, since his English was so bad, he produced an English-language news-paper. He gave a text-book answer.

'Pashtu is provincial language. Urdu is national language. But Frontier is international problem, so we have international lan-guage newspaper.'

He reckoned he had lost around eleven million ruppees on his newspaper in a year and was still losing heavily. But he wasn't going to close: if he could get permission, which he didn't think he could because the editorial line was too critical, he would open a Lahore edition.

His family came from Tirah, where there were no roads and no electricity. One grandfather, a subedar, had won the Victoria Cross; the other had fought against the British. There was no land and no work in Tirah, so thirty years ago they shifted to Landi Kotal, then to Bara. They started a cloth shop in Landi Kotal, and these days, he said, he was in electricals and electronics, tyres, crockery, everything from Japan and Korea.

I asked if his father was a malik.

'No!' he said furiously. 'Not cheater, government-paid malik. You know, if anybody want to go for election, he pay 2,000 rupees to one malik. So maybe fifty lakhs [five million] for whole election.' In 1985, he said, he had spent lakhs of rupees for the government in the elections; and now the government was calling his father a Soviet agent. 'I gave this money to Nadar Khan for having jirga, but he is very big cheater. Many times I tell him, Nadar Khan you are big cheater.' And unlike the old maliks, who depended on their salaries, Rehmat Shah had the financial freedom to oppose the government.

'The government-paid maliks, they say their prayers five times a day, but inside they are black. They don't want education, communication. They want only for their own family. I told to the governor, we must have college in Bara tehsil: this is 1987, not 1947.' He had built a school, he said; but as I was writing this down (mostly because people usually like you to note their philanthropic activities) he put out a hand to stop me. That, he said, was between him and God.

We met again in Peshawar, and he drove me out to his house in Bara, just inside the tribal areas. The gold Mercedes bumped through the wooden stalls and mangy pye-dogs of the smuggling market. It stopped at thirty-foot-high walls, by an arched wooden gate between two crenellated towers. Roses climbed up the red brick. The walls enclosed seven landscaped acres, the lawns rising in slow terraces up to herbaceous borders and flowering trees. Beside a marble and carved wood mosque with a forty-foot minaret was a small pavilion with garden furniture. In front of the low house was a classical porch with a pediment and columns, where the Mercedes came to rest, although there was an underground car park with room for forty cars. Beyond the walled acres, Rehmat Shah was building another park for deer and peacocks, with a swimming pool and a squash court.

I was pleased and interested by Rehmat Shah. I was sure he was sincere in wanting all these good things for his country and his

163

province, and in his common Pathan passion for education. But the money was a different sort of money to that I had come across among most people I'd met. It didn't depend on land, or an industrial asset, or a constituency of people – the sort of money that ties people to governments.

Uncontrolled money can be put to all sorts of uncontrollable uses. Rehmat Shah – and, I'm sure, plenty of others like him – felt he had been mistreated by the government, and despised not just the government, but all the politicians. He was using his money in a way that was certainly inconvenient to the government. He could also, if he wished, use his money to undermine the government, or to steer people on some independent course.

The problem, it seemed, was that the frontier had been run through a system not of representation but of horse-trading. That was never easy, as the frustrated British political agent, fed up with the tribesmen's Bolshevik tendencies, testified; in the earlier days, however, the government was pretty sure which people to deal with, and the rest of the tribesmen were generally willing to go along with what the maliks advocated. But when prosperity created too many Rehmat Shah Afridis, and education and travel got ordinary tribesmen pondering the system, it was no longer working. Like the landlords, the tribal leaders still had a hold; like the landlords, they used, and were used by the other people involved in governing the country; but they were less in control, and therefore less use, than they were when everyone was poor.

Yet even when shaken by sudden windfalls of money, countrysides change at a measured pace. For a concentrated dose of a society's disturbances, you have to go to the towns.

7

URBAN UPSTARTS

WALKING THROUGH the bazaars of Pakistani towns I mourn for the infant Rudyard Kipling and all the little English boys who spent their first few conscious years amid that richness. A bazaar is a small universe of concentrated sensuality. The smell of horse-manure mixes with hot fat from spiced kebabs spitting on red coals. Yellow and orange pastries drip honey on to the streets, kitchenware stalls glisten with hoards of brass and stainless steel and the drains run blue with dye or red with the blood of sacrificial sheep. Tiny cupboard-like shops reach back into a darkness of shelves and jars of unplumbed promise, and each crossroads offers a selection of alleys, each leading to unknown excitements. And such a mass of people – eating, pushing, laughing, cheating, cooking, filling the bazaar to overflowing with life.

After a few years of wondering bliss, the bazaar boys were despatched to a cold country whose subtle differences of grey and green no child could be expected to enjoy, where it wasn't proper or even pleasant to play on the streets, and where they were imprisoned for the rest of their youth in disinfected boarding schools cleansed of affection and shuttered from the sun. The bazaar-smells would have grown fainter and fainter, and the colours receded into painful dreams of a possible return to paradise. The British have strange ways of showing their love for their children. Still, maybe if they had left Kipling happy, he wouldn't have produced *Kim*.

The small space of a bazaar encompasses more colour, smell, noise and business than is reasonable to imagine. No inch of street or stall is unused, and there are people in cupboards making bigger money than those in plate-glass-windowed offices. Maybe it's because of the overcrowding, but there's also an edginess to those towns that I have met nowhere else. In the bazaars, people jostle you: you never see the absurd skipping matches of London streets, where two people try to get out of each other's way. In India and Pakistan, they walk straight at you, leaving it to you to get out of the way or have your shoulder bashed. It certainly isn't innate rudeness, since the subcontinent is a polite place. There just isn't room. If you step aside on a pavement six people thick, you'll hit somebody else.

The overcrowding irritates. After half an hour in a bazaar, I'm ready to bite. You can see the effect of a life of it on rickshaw-drivers, who spend their days being jostled by cars, buses, buffalo carts and horse-drawn tongas, and therefore show no mercy to pedestrians. A good-tempered rickshaw-driver is a rare treat: most accept a passenger with a scowl and a slight jerk of the head towards the back seat. After a day in the heart of a subcontinental town – not in the high-walled, bougainvilleaed rich bits, but the bits where you are always fighting for room – you begin to understand how it is that, all over the subcontinent, these strange incidents take place when control snaps and thousands of people turn on other people – because they are Hindus, or Muslims, or because they speak a different language – and for a few hours or days murder them and burn their shops. Afterwards, when the glass is swept up and the bodies taken away, they go back to their rickshaws and cigarette stalls, and the bazaar returns to its habitual uneasy bustle.

Towns everywhere are more volatile than the countryside is because communication is easier. A scandal, a fight, a riot, spreads like warm butter. News and anger pass through the bazaars, and grow as they diffuse. Demonstrations are easy to stage – a few telephone calls can set one up – and difficult to disperse. The participants hard to catch. The police or the soldiers can charge demonstrators on one street, but there is usually a network of back alleys for them to slip down and regroup.

Trouble in the towns matters more than countryside disturbances. More people hear about it, get frightened, and wonder whether the government is competent to run the country. Offices and factories close and national income starts to fall. Businessmen begin to arrange that rather more of their money than usual should find its way into foreign banks, and the country's capital stock shrinks. Governments watch their towns as parents with irritable children that need to be prevented, through the application of discipline and sweets, from throwing tantrums.

Islamabad, the capital, doesn't count: it is a figment of bureaucratic imagination. Pakistan's real cities – Karachi, Lahore, Rawalpindi, Peshawar, Quetta – all share the bad-tempered vitality that makes subcontinental cities exciting and explosive. But Lahore and Rawalpindi, being Punjabi, are relatively cautious; Peshawar is absorbed in the opportunities for intrigue and profiteering provided by Afghanistan; Quetta is out on a limb. Karachi, Pakistan's only port, the centre of business and trade and provider of most of the government's money, with a population larger than that of Norway, Denmark or Switzerland, leads the country in violence and political volatility.

The earliest evidence of civilisation in the town that was to be the capital of the newly-created Muslim country at partition is a Hindu temple. The shrine to Siva, on fashionable Clifton Beach, is known as the Caves of Mahadeva and is mentioned in the Ramayana. But the settlement there was so tiny that its history is obscure. Until the eighteenth century it seems to have been a settlement of the Baluch Kolachi tribe; then merchants trading with the Arabs and the west coast of India from the Hub river, east of Karachi, found that their estuary was silting up. They moved to a place called Kolachi jo kun, the ditch of the Kolachi, which was provided with a pool of water, some tamarind trees and a sheltered harbour.

The British saw the point of Karachi's natural harbour, captured the fort on Manora Island in 1838 before they got the rest of Sind, and used the port to help them to supply their troops fighting the first Afghan war. The few buildings that survive from the early British days are the utilitarian constructs of an Army and a government in a hurry to establish its rule, without much time for the luxury of decoration. By the 1850s, the architects were indulging themselves in the Gothic monuments to the prevailing British fashion that still survive, grandly impervious to their incompatibility with their surroundings, all over the subcontinent.

At the turn of the century, Karachi's population was around 100,000. The city swelled with its growing importance as a strategic and naval base and, by 1947, it had 400,000 people. At partition, refugees were drawn to their new country's only port, and the population rose to over a million; it now has around eight million.

The refugees – known by the Urdu word for refugee, mohajir – still dominate the city as a whole. There are about 4.5 million of them, including the Bihari refugees who came from Bangladesh during and just after the 1971 war. There have been a few Pathans in the area for centuries, since the invasions of the Ghaznavids and Durranis; but the 1.5 million who now live there have mostly come, looking for work, since the construction of the Super Highway connecting Karachi with the hinterland in the 1960s. The 1.5 million Punjabis came in steady flow, over the years, as civil servants and skilled workers; but the influx of workers has increased with the economic boom brought by the Gulf money. The Sindhis and Baluch who were the city's original inhabitants number only around half a million.

Because Pakistan's relative prosperity has made it the local America, Karachi is stiff with illegal immigrants. Rich Iranians of draftable age flee across the Baluchistan border, stay in the Metropole Hotel and make plans to get to somewhere nicer. Poorer ones, mostly Iranian Baluch, live in Lyari among the local Baluch. The 100,000 or so Afghans have mostly arrived since the Russian invasion and live in settlements on the outskirts of town keeping themselves to themselves. Many of the men work as transporters. Karachi-ites, looking for scapegoats to explain the flood of drugs and guns that have arrived in the past ten years, and the riots of the past three, blame the Afghans.

Sri Lankans come to escape their civil war or just to work. Touts in Sri Lanka get deposits from them, and promise them fine, well-paid opportunities in Karachi. Often they find that they are cheap domestic labour, paid half what they expected; but they have too little money and too many financial commitments to get home. At the bottom of the pile are the 250,000-or-so Bangladeshis. Victims of the shortage of land and the economic stagnation in Bangladesh, they trek across India to get jobs in Pakistan. Fifty or 100 at a time try to cross the border. Often they are driven back by Pakistani border guards, and shot by the Indians when trying to re-enter India. If they make it to Karachi, they take anything they can get, for any money. The fishing industry absorbs a lot of Bangladeshis – deheading shrimps for export to Japan, for instance, at a wage of ten rupees a day. There is a thriving market in Bangladeshi girls. Men bring them over with promises of decent employment, then sell them either as prostitutes or as wives. The going rate is 5–10,000 rupees, depending on age and looks.

Karachi's odd history has determined its unusual geography. The old city, Lyari, where the original Baluch inhabitants still live is beside the port; the British built their courts, offices, barracks and parks to the south and east of the original settlement, and that remains the centre of town, with the Holiday Inn and the Sheraton, the Sind and Gymkhana clubs, and the business area stretching away to the west. But in the middle of all this are big settlements of poor and lower-middle-class people: the Lines Area, the old barracks bang in the middle of town, still houses the remnants of the 1947 refugees who set themselves up in the soldiers' quarters. Those who did well moved out, but more came and built houses among the barracks, creating a maze of little winding alleys. The commercial value of this central 700 acres is forcing change: it is now being redeveloped, and the poor residents shifted to distant areas more suitable to their income-levels. But 1947 colonies a little further away from the centre – like Bihar Colony, where a group of Biharis settled, and Liaqatabad, north of the Lines area – have survived, their populations more depressed and homogeneous than at partition because the educated and successful left for the nice middle-class areas being developed.

A little further out of town, colonies like Nazimabad were built for civil servants and professionals in the 1950s. Handsome land allocations allowed people more generous plots than in the congested Liaqatabad and Lines area next door. The richest preferred to get further away, though, and fled towards the sea to Clifton and Defence Housing Society, where Army officers who had been given plots sold them for huge profits. Those areas are still the poshest, the preserve of businessmen, professionals who have made a packet in the Gulf, Army officers, top civil servants and Sindhi landlords when in town.

Government planning to relieve congestion and the demands of Karachi's expanding industry created new poor colonies on the distant outskirts. People from the centre were shifted way out east, to Korangi. Next door, beside the industrial area, Landhi grew up, populated mostly by Pathan migrant workers from the frontier. The Pathans, who do most of Karachi's harder and nastier jobs, also colonised the Sind Industrial Trading Estate (SITE) area, the centre of the textile industry, over to the west beyond the Lyari river; their stronghold stretches south to Sher Shah Colony, where the scrap metal business they specialise in is centred. Refugees swelled the outskirts: the flood after the Bangladesh war in 1971 settled where they could, many in the northern township of Orangi.

Boomtime, driven by the petrodollar, came in the late seventies.

169

The city's middle-class suburbs stretched far north-west, towards the airport. Tall blocks of flats started going up, to accommodate the men who had taken white-collar jobs in the Gulf and come back with money to invest. More Pathans and Punjabis arrived to man the boom, and settled around the edges of the city in places like Punjab Town, to the west, and the North Karachi colonies, which is as far north as Karachi has gone so far.

More than a third of Karachi's population – about three million people – live illegally. They aren't impoverished squatters, of the sort whose shacks line the pavements and cram any available space in Bombay. Many of the houses in the illegal townships are better than the flats the Indian government provides its civil servants; but they are not supposed to be there, and if the law were implemented, they could be bulldozed.

Most of the illegal settlements in the past twenty years, and those now being built, are not the result of a spontaneous influx of people. You can see the difference, on the map, between the winding lanes and irregular groups of houses in areas like Lines and the straight roads and rectangular blocks of housing in the newer, well-organised settlements.

In the modern settlements, an entrepreneur takes over a bit of government land, having paid the authorities to turn a blind eye, and stakes it out into plots. He sells those, and sets up a builder's yard for people to buy the supplies from for building their houses. He arranges that water-lorries should service the area, and lobbies the municipality to provide electricity and piped water. These dalals, as they are called, have even been known to hire journalists to highlight the problems of the settlements they have established.

Orangi, the biggest illegal township, has nearly a million people. Its sporadic growth has mostly been determined by politics. The first flood came during the 1965 war with India, when people living around Maripur air base were evacuated to Orangi for fear of bombings. The Biharis, refugees from East Pakistan, were the next arrivals. Then, in 1972, riots around the province over language teaching drove mohajirs from the interior of Sind to Orangi: afraid to live among Sindhis, these people who had fled India in 1947 became refugees twice over. Economics has brought Pathan migrant labour to the township: they live, as though in the mountains of the frontier, on top of the hills that ring Orangi.

The names of the colonies in Orangi bear witness to its political awareness. Al Fatah was named when there was a surge of international support for Yasser Arafat. Yahya Colony became Hafeez Pirzada colony when the general was overthrown and Mr Pirzada became Bhutto's law minister. The language riots gave birth to Urdu Colony. I asked a resident why anybody should want to call their area Zia colony: because, he said, events there would get written up in the papers more.

Like the countryside around it, Karachi has its old political family. The Haroons, one of the country's most influential clans, came to power through the money and foresight of Hajji Sir Abdullah Haroon, who learnt business as a street trader when he was a boy and made millions out of sugar. He financed Jinnah, and started the Muslim League in Sind in opposition to Allah Bakhsh Soomro who was allied with the Hindus. The family's money and influence allowed them to dominate Karachi's politics for twenty-five years.

Their house is a monument to their political history. It is opposite the Holiday Inn on Sir Abdullah Haroon Road, a huge 1930s pink building, with rounded corners and balconies, surrounded by palm trees and a wall with broken glass cemented to the top. Hameed, the young (ex-LSE and Harvard) man who runs the Dawn group of newspapers, and Hussein, his brother, who was Speaker of the Sind Assembly after the 1985 election until he annoyed the government and was unseated, live there. Over Clifton bridge, towards the sea, lives their uncle, Mahmood, who returned to government as defence minister in 1988; the other surviving uncle, Yusuf, is in New York, looking after manifold business interests there.

Jinnah and his followers who came to lobby and plot against the recalcitrant Unionists of Sind stayed in that house, and it has never quite recovered from its past grandeur. Even the tiled floors are superb: some plainly elegant – smart white squares, with black triangular corners which form little black squares where the tiles meet – but in the abandoned central room, where the long dining table could fit forty, they blossom into art deco extravaganzas in black, white, and grey Carrara marble. You can hardly make them out, though, under the overcrowding of furniture whose inlay is so delicate that the flowers have stamens and the leaves veins. The tops of the furniture are covered with china and photographs: a bride in a high-waisted dress, the husband behind, pale in his black morning suit; Hajji Sir Abdullah himself, seated, stiff and black-bearded, and his soft wife (by all accounts a tough matriarch) smiling gently over his shoulder. In a cabinet are Raj toys: the ayah, the bearer, the dhobi and the English Sunday lunch in painted clay. I wasn't sure whether Hameed was showing it all to me out of pride or amusement. He and his brother have small, smart apartments on the edge of the house, independent of the history.

The Haroons were big enough at partition to make a difference to the Muslim League's finances, but by Ayub's time they do not figure on the lists of the richest business families. That's probably because they concentrated on politics: they quickly emerged as an urban version of the political landed families of the countryside and, as the first political family of Karachi, provided a chief minister of Sind (Yusuf), a governor of West Pakistan (Yusuf), two mayors of Karachi (Yusuf and Mahmood) and have held several ministerships. They also – thanks to the matriarch – married ruthlessly into the smartest landed families both in undivided India and subsequently in Pakistan.

Their business suffered from their politics. The family had difficulties with Ayub: according to Mahmood, when General Motors decided to pull out of Pakistan in the 1960s, it was practically decided that the Haroons should take over their assets. Then General Habibullah, whose son-in-law was Ayub Khan's son, stepped in and got the company. (General Habibullah denies that it was anything to do with his better access to the president: the Haroons, he says, were incompetent and indecisive.) Then, according to Mahmood, Ayub simply had Yusuf removed as managing director of the Intercontinental hotels, which had been set up as a joint venture between the Haroons and Pan Am.

Their problems with Ayub were nothing to those with Bhutto. Mahmood had supported Sheikh Mujib, who won a majority in the 1970 elections but had the disadvantage of being from East Pakistan, against Bhutto. After the split, Mahmood said, Bhutto had it in for them. He arrested Altaf Gauhar, now head of the Third World Foundation and then editor of Dawn. He cut the paper's advertising revenue, not just by removing government ads, but also by telling private companies to boycott it. Then the government, which issued newsprint quotas, started making it difficult for them to get paper. And, like everybody else, they had chunks of their empire nationalised.

A couple of decades back, their apparently unshakeable political base in Karachi would have been their comfort. But Karachi has gone beyond the stage where a family, however respected, has any serious political clout. The Haroons' electoral era was finished when they lost Lyari, the old city area bordering between business and slums, to an unknown PPP man in 1970. The whole city is now in the hands of the middle classes – first the Jamaat-i-Islami, to whom Hussein Haroon lost the mayorship, and now the mohajirs, who have no class and no history to offer, only belligerence and energy.

But the Haroons' newspapers, which were part of the cause of their troubles, are also the reason for their political survival. The Haroons still matter nationally. For a country whose governments have not paid much attention to basic liberties, Pakistan retains a surprising respect for the press. Its intelligentsia reads the papers carefully, looking for shifts in editorial position, or greater frankness, or speculating on the news between the lines. Not even the government thinks anybody believes the television, so it accords a certain importance to the newspapers and likes to keep in touch with the owners.

Until 1984, the Haroons seemed to be solidly with Zia – Mahmood was a minister in the martial law government. Then he resigned, for reasons unknown, and none of them had any job or affiliation with Junejo's Muslim League government. Everybody noticed, when Benazir came back to Pakistan in 1986, that Hamid was spending a lot of time at her house; he declared no party allegiance, but seemed to have become an unofficial adviser. Dawn began devoting a great deal of space to her activities, and, without risking a shift in position so drastic that it angered the government, made its approval of the PPP's bid for power clear enough to the readership. Well, said Karachi, perhaps the older Haroon generation has decided to bury past enmities and is gambling its political future on Benazir's prospects. But if that was the plan, the family changed its mind. When Zia sacked his parliament, Mahmood was back in government, with another ministerial job.

As the Haroons faded out of city politics, it wasn't the PPP who took over. Karachi was anti-Bhutto: he appeared to represent the Sindhis' interests, and it was a time of tension between the province's Urdu and Sindhi speakers. The mohajirs, who had come to Pakistan because of their religion, clung to it as their political identity. In the seventies, they were with the conservative religious Jamaat-i-Islami. In the eighties, something more important than party politics started happening.

On 15 April, 1985, a girl was killed in Orangi by a speeding bus. Crowds of young mohajirs came out on to the streets to protest

173

against dangerous bus-drivers, who are mainly Pathans. The police – who are mostly Punjabis – charged the crowds with sticks and teargassed them. A crowd of Pathans attacked a crowd of protesting mohajirs in Orangi, and street battles started around the township. In Liaqatabad, mobs of mohajirs burnt buses and attacked a police station. Policemen were doused with petrol and burnt to death. In two days of rioting, sixty people were killed. The city calmed down; but over the next year and a half, violence sporadically exploded and died, and around 200 people were killed.

In October 1986, busloads of mohajirs were going to a political rally in Hyderabad. They stopped on the Super Highway, just below Sorabgoth, a Pathan stronghold and the centre of the arms and heroin trade. Pathans fired on them, and six people were killed. Violence broke out around the poorer areas of Karachi, and a third of the city was put under curfew; even so, about forty people were killed in the next five days.

The government had no idea what to do, but yells of protest demanded that something should be done. In December, it decided to bulldoze Sorabgoth, which had become, to the mohajirs, the symbol of the Pathan gun-backed drug mafia. It was a secret operation, though residents saw streams of trucks moving out of the hilltop colony (which was reputed to pay a million rupees a month to the police and civil servants in protection money) the night before; still, the police got 185 kilos of heroin, 2.5 tonnes of hashish, one Kalashnikov, one other rifle and five pistols. Some 4,000 houses were bulldozed.

On the morning of 14 December, groups of Pathans at the bottleneck where the road from central Karachi enters Orangi, pulled motor cyclists off their bikes and beat them up. Then, at ten o'clock, at a call from a mosque in the hills above the township, Pathans wielding Kalashnikovs descended on Orangi's Aligarh Colony. Six hours later, after about 100 people had been killed, the police and Army arrived, and the mosque called the withdrawal. The assault, presumably in retaliation for the bulldozing of Sorabgoth, had evidently been planned: the attackers were sufficiently well-prepared to know which were the Pathan houses in Aligarh Colony and to avoid them. Another 100 were killed in the next two days.

Reporting at the time gives a good picture of what this does to a city. 'Transportation of goods to and from the upcountry remained suspended . . . Since Sabzi Mandi [the vegetable market] was almost closed because of shortage of supply prices of vegetables and fruit have increased by almost 50%.' A couple of railway stations were burnt and the 'majority of passengers cancelled their proposed journey by rail to upcountry owing to the law and order situation.' Even when the curfew was lifted, public and private transport stayed off the roads and the shops remained shut. The banks were barely staffed, and the factories in Site, Korangi and Landhi were closed; 'those who dared to come at their places of work indulged in engaging conversation with a few of their colleagues rather than working on their desks seriously.'

Nobody provided the Pathans thrown out of Sorabgoth with anywhere to live. They squatted in some half-built houses nearby, and when thrown out, rioted. They were given plots near an asbestos factory, where 'sources said that the final settlement would not take much time. The shiftees would soon start constructing their houses.' There was no water or electricity there, but the government assured everybody that they would be provided in the fullness of time.

The fighting went on through 1987, with 243 people (officially) being killed in smaller bouts. By 1988, the violence had matured further: in May in Orangi and North Karachi, people in cars and on motor bikes were shooting randomly at rickshaw drivers (who are almost always Pathans) and queues outside cinemas showing Pashtu movies.

Orangi is two different countries. Walking around the mohajir area, in the valley, the streets are busy with commercial life, shops selling electrical goods, restaurants, small garages, even women in the streets, their heads covered, their faces unveiled. The houses, in tidy, unpaved alleys, are neat and painted pastel colours.

Orangi's mohajirs may live in an illegal township, but they are educated middle-class people. Dislocation has pushed them down in the world: many of the Biharis from Bangladesh, particularly, were middle-ranking civil servants and white-collar workers. The literacy rate among the mohajirs in Orangi is eighty-one per cent, compared to fifty per cent in all Sind's urban areas and twenty-six per cent in the country as a whole. If you include the Pathans, Orangi's literacy rate comes down to sixty-seven per cent.

The township's geography is aggressive. The Pathans, either out of defensive instincts or through nostalgia for their mountainous homeland, live on the ring of hills around the mohajirs. Their settlements have become mountain fortresses of the sort you would

175

expect near the Khyber Pass, but not a few miles from American Express and Citibank. They control the only entrance to the colony from the centre of town, because the main road uses a narrow pass between their hills.

The Pathan areas feel like frontier villages. The roads are rocky and winding, and the streets are quiet. There are no women on them. There is more litter around, and the houses are in worse repair. They seem to belong to a wilder, less homely people. Some of the shops have closed down, because they tend to be kept by mohajirs, and mohajirs have moved out of Pathan areas as Pathans have moved out of mohajir areas. I asked a Punjabi I was with whether the Pathans were poorer than the mohajirs: no, he said, but whereas the mohajirs bought televisions with their money, the Pathans bought guns.

Evidently, though, the visible difference between people doesn't cause violence: it draws the battle-lines. Seeking causes, some blame the transport system, since bus accidents have sparked much of the violence. In 1984, there were 660 deaths on the road in Karachi – only a bit higher, per head, than in London, but odd in a country with only two motor vehicles per hundred people. Most of the accidents are caused by minibuses.

The minibus drivers, mostly Pathans, are dangerous. They can buy a driving licence from the police for 400–500 rupees (£13–£17), and, with a loan from one of the Pathan drug dealers or property magnates (who have also gone into money-lending) get themselves a bus. Interest rates are high, and the police also have to be paid for route permits, so the drivers, under financial pressure, drive fast, often for eighteen hours a day.

Backed by the money-lenders, the transport lobby is powerful. It demonstrated its muscle in November 1985, when, in reaction to the first lot of riots, drivers were being charged with 'causing death not amounting to murder' (section 304 of the penal code, maximum sentence ten years). The buses struck for two days, and the charge was reduced to 'accidental death' (section 304A, maximum sentence three years). People complain that the police avoid taking action against the drivers, partly because many policemen own minibuses, and some even drive them when off-duty. But the transporters deny that the police are on their side: according to the transporters' committee president, drivers who have killed somebody have to pay the police 15,000 rupees to be booked under 304A rather than 304.

The police are another target of mohajir anger. Traders are required to pay the police regularly under the 'bhatta' system of collecting from both illegal and legal business. Constables collect on behalf of the station house officer as well as for themselves. According to a *Herald* report, one SHO required his staff to bring him 8,000 rupees a day. One of his constables said, 'It was a terrible thana [police station] to be posted in. You literally had to fleece dozens of people a day to meet the target. Luckily, there were a lot of drug dens in the area'.

The opportunities for money-making are manifold. Petty laws — like those against street-hawkers — are not enforced for a small fee. The police can be hired to arrest or humiliate an enemy. They stop people late at night, smell, or say they can smell, alcohol on people's breath and demand money. Bribes from criminals are the best source of income: thus, corrupt policemen have an interest in ensuring that crime survives. In Lyari, the old city, an anti-drugs movement was gathering strength. One of its activists was shot by the police — according to locals, because they wanted to crush the movement.

Their ethnic make-up as well as their behaviour involves them in Karachi's violence. They are largely Punjabi: although constables are supposed to be recruited from among those who live in Karachi, non-resident Punjabis can easily buy a domicile certificate. Since the Punjabis have allied with the Pathans in the violence, the mohajirs maintain that the police have not only stood by during Pathan attacks, but have actually taken part in attacks themselves. In Orangi in January 1987, for instance, while a riot was going on a mile away, police broke into homes in a Bihari area, smashed furniture, beat up men and women and took some of the men away. They were held for between four days and two weeks. The Biharis said it was worse than Dacca in 1971.

The police and the transporters both fit into a general theory that some hold to — that the riots are the result of drug money muscle. The big Pathan dealers, they maintain, controlled the transport system through finance, and the police and the administration through payoffs; but, alarmed by the growing political consciousness and opposition to drugs in some of the mohajir areas, they felt the need to assert their power. The riots were organised to prove that the Pathans, being armed to the teeth, were ultimately in control of Karachi's ungoverned townships. That, of course, is a mohajir theory. The Pathans point out that, although the drugs

177

come from their area, there is no evidence that the big Karachi barons are Pathans.

Those who reject the conspiracy theory prefer to blame the violence on a large-scale collapse of the administration in the city that has driven its younger, more political residents to exercise their frustrations in beating up people from other communities. A report in the *Independent* in 1988 supported this view: 'People have been infuriated by water and electricity cuts which have disrupted life in the city in recent weeks . . . On Sunday, the police in some areas refused to come out of their stations to curb the unrest. Public frustration with the Karachi administration was so high that crowds, who had brought injured patients to the hospitals, started attacking government property and vehicles.'

Karachi's population is growing at six per cent a year, while the availability of amenities is increasing at 1.2 per cent a year. About thirty-eight per cent of houses have piped water, and about twenty-eight per cent sewage. The city produces some 1,200 tonnes of garbage a day, and there are arrangements for disposing of a quarter of it. The administration's failure leads to spontaneous privatisation. There is no machinery for the management of Karachi's 170 graveyards, so around half are being operated by freelancers who charge fees for burial, and half are being farmed or built on. One houses a martial arts club.

You can see the failure on the streets: taking a quick sample, I found that a third of the traffic lights were working. Not content to encourage citizens to have traffic accidents, the municipality seems to want to bury them: when I was there in mid-1988, the pavements of Dr Ziauddin Ahmed Road, from the Sheraton down towards the Bank of Tokyo and American Express, were perforated every twenty yards with open manholes, their covers nowhere to be seen. The unwary citizen would have plunged ten feet and dropped into sludge.

I picked through the cuttings files for small pieces of evidence of the state of the services. In February 1987, classes were suspended in the Urdu Science College because sewage lanes in the area had been choked for weeks and the overflow had flooded the playground. 'The Students Action Committee has threatened "other means" if the KDA did not resolve the problem within two days.' In August 1987 a newspaper headline announced 'Many Areas Stinking.'

The failure is partly to do with corruption. Rational schemes for

178

no-parking and one-way traffic systems are developed, but are abandoned because businesses club together to change the administration's mind. Plots of land reserved for 'amenities' are mysteriously commercialised; other plots, supposed to be sold to the public through ballots, end up in the hands of politicians and civil servants. The Auditor General of Sind found 'serious irregularities' in the accounts of the Karachi Development Authority which had, for instance, failed to charge businessmen for their water.

Nobody seems very concerned. I went to see the Karachi Development Authority — which, with control over the allocation of land in the city, is a hugely powerful outfit — to find out a little more about its operations. It was an instructive visit. The KDA's head, Mr Nizami, a fat man with a sly smile and a huge office full of silver objects, said, when I asked him about the illegal settlements:

'These things will happen! People move in, put a house up . . . on humanitarian grounds we cannot send them away.' I said I had heard it wasn't quite like that — that it was organised, profitable land-grabbing. He admitted that was the case, but these days, he said, there was very strict patrolling. The existing illegal settlements were being regularised, by order of the prime minister in March 1985 (we were then in December 1987). How many, I asked, had been regularised? He couldn't tell me. I should see the information department, he said, gesturing towards a man writhing silently in a chair.

And the transport system? What were they doing about that? There was a small deficiency, he conceded, but everything was going according to the last master plan of 1974, and the KDA was preparing another master plan. I should ask the information man, though, said Mr Nizami, gesturing towards the information man and the door.

Didn't the state of Karachi, I said, angered by his lazy complacency and ignoring the gesture, suggest that past master plans had failed? Not at all, he said with a fat smile.

'Our last master plan has been successful. Everything has been identified — the information department will tell you. Look at the other cities! Bombay, Calcutta, so many problems! Not only the third world — Harlem is in United States.' Mr Zaheer ul Islam of the traffic engineering department, was less complacent. There had been a lot of studies and plans, he said: there was the master plan, drawn up with the help of UN experts; a report in 1976 by the Rapid Transit Cell of the Ministry of Communications; another in

1981 by a committee chaired by a high court judge; and the most recent one in 1985 after the first riot sparked off by a minibus accident. They were all good reports, but they did not get implemented. Zaheer ul Islam was optimistic, however: they were setting up a new study, financed by the World Bank, so there was a good chance they might get some foreign money to implement it.

I asked if there was any evaluation of the achievements of the 1974–85 master plan. He said that he had worked in close co-operation with the master plan division, and none had been done. The deputy director of mass transit in the master plan department, however, told me there was an evaluation and found me a copy. The first page, which evaluated the six schemes for improving bus services, said enough: the number of buses had increased by thirty-three per cent, against a target of 400 per cent; the plan to make the bus service more competitive with rickshaws and taxis had made no progress; the project to improve the condition of the buses had failed, although bus fares had gone up; financial support provided to bus owners by the municipality had not improved services; the plan for providing operational and maintenance support to bus companies had made no progress; and there had been no substantial progress in training drivers. I wondered whether Mr Nizami had read the document.

Karachi has now taken two roads in response to forty years of the KDA and its ilk. They are quite different, but both are interesting, dangerous for the government and, it seems to me, the vanguard of Pakistani politics.

Doctorsahib isn't really a doctor, neither of the medical nor the Ph.D sort. Nobody's quite sure why he's called that, but he is, universally. He is Akhtar Hameed Khan, the grand old man of the subcontinent's co-operative movement, who must be nearly eighty now, but is still pushing his theories in the bits of the subcontinent where the government seems to have failed.

He studied at Cambridge, was an Indian Civil Service officer under the British, and decided to learn about life so became a locksmith. He ended up in East Pakistan, in a benighted district called Comilla in the west of the country, where he began a co-operative movement that became a Mecca for developmentwallahs. The principle behind it was simple: nobody was going to do anything for the people there, so they had to invest a regular few pence of their own to build roads, set up schools, bus services and, eventually, a bank.

Akhtar Hameed Khan was, on Bangladesh's independence, pronounced to be a CIA agent, and had to leave the country. But the Comilla co-operatives survived, and the principle was taken up by the new government as the basis for their first development plan. The government-sponsored co-operatives were a disaster, immediately falling into the hands of local big-wigs for whom they were not intended.

Doctorsahib's travels brought him to Karachi where, he decided, there was similar neglect and therefore similar need. I went to see him in the offices of the Orangi Pilot Project, a house in a backstreet in Karachi's biggest slum. The offices were full of posters, chairs, engineers plotting sewage projects for new streets, young men talking furiously in small rooms. They were, surprisingly, non-English-speaking: I would have expected that sort of project to attract more of the idealistic intelligentsia and fewer locals. Doctorsahib, tall, with a bony, intense face, was sitting on a chair too small for him engaged in passionate argument with an equally inflamed engineer. He turned his intensity on me for a couple of hours.

His project, he said, was to enable people in Orangi to build themselves sewage systems, and was explained by the past three hundred years of the subcontinent's history. Pakistan and Bangladesh, he said – not India so much, since the Indians had something like a government – had reverted to the eighteenth and early nineteenth century, when the rulers, the East India Company, were interested not in government but in pillage. Subsequently the British had built an administrative system that worked through impartiality and consensus: the civil servants would listen to the views of all the locals, including the bandits, weigh up opinions and make a decision. In Pakistan, though, the civil servants and the police had become employees of the bandits, so the decisions they made were not going to take anybody else's interests into consideration. In those circumstances, people had to take government into their own hands and build their own sewage systems.

It was heady stuff, touching earth occasionally in the administrative neglect of present-day Karachi, then taking off again into millennia of history – the discourse of a mind that likes big and colourful intellectual patterns, and has seventy years' worth of reading to draw on. It was convincing, too, particularly after I was taken round some of the streets of Orangi, and saw, between the neat concrete boxes, the building of sewers and septic tanks that

181

were the product of this conviction. Doctorsahib's organisation provided technical advice, but the building was done, or paid for, by the residents.

There seems to be more and more of it about. In 1984, among Orangi's 800,000 people, there were eighty-three registered community organisations: two years later, there were 178 of them – for education, sports, religion, cleanliness, theatre, drug eradication. The growth of self-help is not just restricted to the towns, either: it has, more slowly, started to take off in the countryside.

Its problem will be its success. No government can risk administrative – and therefore political – power sliding so far out of its hands in such a dangerous area as the Karachi slums. Probably it will have to be stopped – or maybe the government could just take it over, like in Bangladesh, to make sure that it dies a regulated death.

Karachi's other new phenomenon is, in a way, more optimistic. The Mohajir Qami Movement believes that if it takes over government, everything will be all right. It sprang out of a students' group in Karachi University after the Jamaat-i-Islami student wing, previously the preserve of mohajirs, was taken over by Punjabis. The party started in earnest at a mass rally in Karachi in August 1986; in December 1987, it wiped out the Jamaat-i-Islami and won the local elections in Hyderabad and Karachi, and Karachi got a twenty-eight-year-old MQM mayor.

The MQM is the logical result of the trend in Pakistani politics towards ethnic and regional splits. That shift is a practical admission that Pakistan has failed to build up a national identity. Everybody else is reaching for their regional identity, and the mohajirs, themselves a jumble of origins, have the common experience of dislocation to tie them together. They have a common material grievance, too – the quota system, which gives 'Urban Sind' (the mohajirs) 7.6 per cent of civil service jobs when it has around twelve per cent of the country's population. Since those who migrated tended to be the better-educated, mohajirs have taken a disproportionate number of bureaucratic jobs, but the quota system is pushing them out. In 1973, 'Urban Sind' had thirty-three per cent of top civil service jobs; by 1983, it had twenty per cent. Mohajirs, in the MQM's definition, are not necessarily Urdu-speakers, and not necessarily all those who came from India at partition. East Punjabis do not count, and Gujarati-speakers do. The line is an urban-rural one: the Punjabis were mostly villagers, and the Gujaratis town-based businessmen.

Although deteriorating services in the city help to explain the anger, there is much more to it. People in Karachi are certainly a lot better off than they were twenty years ago, but nobody protested then. The MQM is a second-generation party. The first generation of refugees, many of whom spoke Gujerati or Tamil, had even less in common than their children do. More important is the change in attitude. Refugees are often cautious, preferring to keep their political heads down and make good materially. The mohajirs' children are less willing to do this, or to observe the norms of respect that their parents accepted. Arif Hasan, an architect who has worked for years in Orangi, wrote of the typical young MQM activist:

'Sifarish, traditionally an honour for the one on whom it was bestowed, is a dirty word in his vocabulary, and he addresses his leadership as bhai [brother] and chacha [uncle], not as sahib, jenab, huzoor or saeen [respected sir].' In times of tension, he said, the administration used to restore order by summoning the 'notables' of the district and getting guarantees from them that disturbances would stop. That no longer works: the boys resent not only the rich of Clifton and Defence, but the whole system of patronage from which they are excluded. They therefore no longer listen to the local patrons.

Optimism apart, the MQM is a ghastly irony. Its members are the very people whose parents were the bulwark of the Pakistan movement, who left their homes in India because they did not want to be an underprivileged minority in a country with a divided population. They found that Islam, or whatever it was that led them to uproot themselves willingly, was not enough to unite their new country; and forty disappointed years later, they apparently feel they can get justice only by asserting their minority status and dividing the population further. The MQM's birth is evidence of the death of the spirit that created Pakistan.

The MQM was hard to locate when I was in Karachi after the 1987 local elections, because its leader, Altaf Hussein, was in jail, and most of its other notables were underground. I found a lawyer, Razique Khan, who had just won a municipal council seat – and, after I met him, became deputy mayor.

His telephone number started with unfamiliar digits which placed him in some distant area of north Karachi not much frequented by those with whom I had mostly been mixing. It took an hour to get there in a taxi, round a series of roundabouts surrounded by creeping circles of traffic with fewer and fewer cars and more and more buses and lorries. The further out we went, the worse the buildings: quickly put-up blocks and close-set rows of minimal housing, concrete spreading as far as I could see. It made no attempt to be anything other than a speedy way of accommodating a scary population growth rate. But I had to remember, coming from a country that reveres buildings and spends almost all its time inside them, that houses matter less when so much of life is lived in the streets. Going through north Karachi, it isn't really the ugliness of the houses that you notice. It is the bazaars with piles of quilts, the flower-sellers with garlands of orange and white flowers hanging from horizontal poles, the half mile of unpainted tin trunks, more trunks than I could imagine a country, let alone a city, wanting.

Razique Khan lived in Al Azam Square, not a square at all but an arrangement of blocks at right angles to each other, separated by tarmacked streets and mud alleys. We circled pointlessly, given vague, contradictory directions, with the rickshaw-driver muttering that women should know where they wanted to go. We were pointed by a man in a cowboy shirt down a long back alley with boys in new jeans playing cricket, stopping play grudgingly for the rickshaw. The girls were in clean white dupattas, grey kameeses and black shalwars. They clutched their books to their bosoms and picked their way round the small piles of rubbish. Meticulous personal cleanliness in a filthy environment still surprises me.

The passage that led to Razique Khan's block was covered in MQM Zindabad and I Love MQM sprayed over the Jamaat-i-Islami graffiti. An old man with a stick in one hand and a boy in the other was hobbling out into the street. He sent the boy off to show me the way; and the boy, without looking at me, scampered through the rubble and the motor bikes, up stairs with rubbish lodged in the corners, past balconies draped in washing, to a top-floor flat whose door was an old curtain.

Razique Khan wasn't there. His pretty, fat-hipped wife knew I was coming, sat me down beside a potted plant, called his office and pattered anxiously about the flat. On the wall was a cheap romanticisation of an ash-blonde woman carrying an ash-blonde child, a plaque advertising Happy Marriage and a print of a poor copy of a Gainsborough. Mrs Khan fluttered in with a trolley with a tea in it that would have fed six, and spilt a plate of bananas on the floor. A little boy with thick glasses and a squint came in, peering at me while Mrs Khan petted him. She pushed him towards me to give Auntie a kiss; but he just stared.

Razique Khan arrived, apologetically, after an hour. He had the squashy brown face and bridgeless, snub nose that can come from anywhere in eastern or southern India. He said he was from Bihar. The top of his head was bald, but the rest of his hair long, as though to compensate. He was fat, but it was an energetic fatness, that answered questions quickly and leapt up constantly to stop the telephone ringing. The people in his constituency were eighty per cent mohajirs, he said. Previously, the area had been a stronghold of the Jamaat-i-Islami, but they had been wiped out in the recent elections. His constituency was mostly slums (including one area whose Urdu name means Poortown) with all sorts of people living there – government servants, small shopkeepers and businessmen, clerks, labourers. Some of the areas, including Poortown, were illegal settlements.

'They have no programme, the Jamaat. They say pray to God and all will be well. But the young people, they like logical talk. They have some problems, they want some answers.' This, of course, was music to me and to the liberal and left-wing Pakistanis who fear more than anything the rise of the religious right.

Razique Khan was a little apologetic that his wife did not work:

'She is an MA, she might have given the lectures at a college, but she was nervous and prefers to stay at home. As a matter of fact, women in the subcontinent are suppressed. But we are becoming more like the West. This is a good thing.' Better and better. I was charmed by Razique Khan's sharp energy and quick laugh. His air of plump triumph, and the nervous satisfaction of his little wife, set him apart from the other politicians I had met. He was not performing a hereditary duty, a tiresome business necessary for the maintenance of position. He had just won the pools, got a new toy, or solved an insoluble equation: he had, coming from the nowhere-much of north Karachi, helped change the face of Pakistan. Razique Khan was having fun.

I forgot, while I was talking to him, that I thought I disapproved of him nearly as much as I did of the Jamaat-i-Islami. I cannot see it as anything but regression to vote for people because of what they are, not because of what they say. It takes me straight back to the years before partition when Indians, who had assumed that they would get their freedom as a united country, began to find their land splitting into Us and Them, which ended up as Pakistan and India. A high-up Pakistani with whom I had a conversation of astonishing frankness and gloom said to me 'Study the MQM

185

carefully. In it, you will find the genesis of the Pakistan movement.'

The MQM's success – it won eleven out of fourteen national assembly seats in Karachi in the 1988 election – suggests that Pakistan, which is moving so fast in so many ways, has got its politics stuck in a sort of neo-tribalism. However disrespectful the mohajirs are of sifarish, of the old networks of patronage, they are beginning to operate in the same way themselves. They are beginning to look like a huge braderi: voting for their own, demanding jobs for their own, closing their ranks against Them (the Pathans, the Punjabis, or anybody else who might seem a threat). That sort of politics must be regressive and inefficient; it depends on handing out jobs to Us and not to Them, which means the job is done worse than if it were given to somebody because he could do it; and it leads to mobs of Xs attacking a Y on the streets because there was a rumour that some Ys had attacked an X. To me, Bhutto's election was a step forwards, towards ideological politics, and it is up to this generation of politicians to decide whether or not he was an aberration.

8

POLITICIANS

IT WASN'T EASY to get into Benazir Bhutto's wedding reception. The wide streets of Clifton, the rich suburb of Karachi where she lives, were solid with traffic – chauffeured Mercedes and Toyotas with irritated guests peering out of their tinted windows, rickshaws overburdened with spectators, and police Jeeps hooting and flashing. In front of the high wooden gate of Clifton Gardens a crowd of three hundred yelled and shoved, intent on catching a glimpse of the beautiful woman who has taken up the political banner of her father, the executed prime minister. The security men were preoccupied trying to prevent the mob from breaking the gates down, so the guests had to squeeze in as best they could, clutching their jewellery and crushing their silks and their neatly-ironed shalwar kamees as they fought their way through.

On the other side were lawns and rosebeds stretching away into the darkness, with small crowds of people moving easily in the luxurious chill of the late December air. We stood spotting each other, exchanging small bits of conversation, interested mostly in who had been invited and who, if they had been invited, had thought it politic to come. The couple were on a dais in the middle of the gardens, invisible among the crowd of guests who pushed and pulled at each other's silks to get at them.

Everybody was there: Nawab Bugti, his white moustaches curling with excitement; Ghulam Mustapha Jatoi, the plump but edgy-looking former PPP leader, currently a prime ministerial candidate; Hameed Haroon scurrying from group to group. Junaid Soomro and Rafi Kachello were standing by the gate laughing at the rich people struggling in. The Russian and the Indian ambassadors were there, and the Indian film star, Sunil Dutt, who was splattered across the papers the next morning; also present, as they say, were Aveek Sarkar, owner of an Indian chain of newspapers, and his editor M.J. Akbar, both of whom had been refused entry to a press conference earlier in the day, presumably because the rest of the journalists were foreign correspondents so the guards thought it was Whites Only.

Suddenly a tadpole-shaped crowd flowed from the dais, Benazir and Asif in its head. Out in the street, I saw three Englishmen in morning suits following them down the pavement, with two small boys chasing after them, trying to grab their tails. That was the end of the rich people's wedding.

Down at the poor people's wedding, the huge square in the midst of the slums and bazaars of old Karachi was garlanded with ropes of lights in green and red (PPP colours) and little pictures of windmills and waterfalls in lights were pinned, like badges, to the buildings. Around the walled wedding-ground clustered the instant services that appear with any crowd – the sweet stalls, the kebab-friers, the chick-pea sellers, the men with toys and balloons hanging from a pole carried on their shoulder.

Reuters, the *Financial Times* and I found a crowd, which implied an opening in the wall. I shouted EXCUSE ME and the crowd parted, with mutterings of Memsahib. We squeezed through a gap between the wall and the wooden door which the security-men, Kalashnikovs over their shoulders, were pushing shut as hard as the crowd pushed it open, and into 100,000 people, seated at different levels. Almost everybody was sitting on the ground; the grander party workers were on a wooden platform; the happy couple was on a small dais surrounded by family and, in one of the little arbours, draped with strings of pink and yellow flowers, the Englishmen crouched in their penguin suits. With spotlights catching the gold decorations and jewellery, and bouncing off the silver foil that covered the wall behind the dais, the spectacle glittered.

The press was in purgatory with the smarter party people, on orange plastic chairs above the masses but below the bright glory of the wedding party. Between us and the waning smiles of Benazir and her husband, a plump man in a silver suit swayed as he sang passionately into his microphone. I asked the man next to me what the song was. It was a love song to a buffalo, he said. From behind me, gunfire cracked through the song, first a couple of separate shots, then long bursts. I turned and saw a man standing on the edge of our platform, his face set as though in anger or concentration, lit by the small flame from his Kalashnikov. 'They never used

188

to do this, you know,' said the man beside me. 'This is because everybody has Kalashnikovs now. It is a great disturbance when there is a wedding near your house. They go on all night.'

Hameed Haroon had had enough, and motioned me up and out. John Elliot, the *Financial Times*, came too. Hameed was a sizeable windbreak, but not large enough for the crowd outside. The memsahib was forgotten. Faces pressed in, and hands grasped any piece of flesh they could get. I saw, over John Elliot's shoulder, the face belonging to one of the hands, and did what I had longed to do for weeks: I hit the man full in the face, and registered with pleasure that he reeled back, clutching his eye. John put my arm into a lock and pushed me on.

The whole tamasha took place because of a dead man, present on the huge posters between the strings of coloured lights – fantasies of a father touching his daughter's bowed head, in a gesture of blessing and farewell. The Bhuttos are in politics for the same reason as the bulk of Pakistan's politicians: they inherited the business. They are a large, landowning clan from Larkana in Sind, on the Indus between Karachi and Sukkur. Zulfikar's father, Sir Shanawaz Bhutto, was one of the Sindhi grandees jockeying for power with Mohammed Ayub Khuro, Allah Bakhsh Soomro and Ghulam Hussein Hidayatullah in the province during the last days of the Raj. Zulfikar was groomed to go into politics, and became a minister in Ayub's government in 1958, when he was thirty-one.

Pakistan's hereditary politicians do one of two things: they either make themselves available to the government in power, or, more rarely, they build themselves a constituency around an issue or an ideology. The first route to power is the traditional one, taken by landlords and tribal leaders under the Moghuls and the British. The second is a novelty, born out of the ideas and ideals that were shipped into Pakistan when it was created.

Old-style politicians staffed the local boards and councils of the British, made up the Unionist party, joined the Muslim League and worked for the martial law governments. About seventy-five percent of the 1985–8 parliament was made up of the first lot, with forty-odd families ruling the roost. From Sind, five big families – the Pagaras, the Soomros, the Jatois, the Khuros and the Bijranis – had at least three members in the National Assembly or the Senate.

The prime minister, Mohammed Khan Junejo, never made any pretence of trying to rouse popular passions. He was the nominee of Pir Pagara, accepted by Zia. He cobbled together a party made up of other people like himself whose only strength lay in the loyalty they could command in their constituencies on the basis of tribalism and religion. In the absence of anything more appealing, they – or their cousins – could be fairly sure of being elected on their home ground. Their domination of parliament explains why it was such a disappointment.

When the parliament was elected, people expected it to be tame and corrupt, but there was nevertheless a bit of unrealistic optimism. Partly, that was because of the excitement of having any democratic representation after eight years of martial law; but it also sprang from a residual belief in parliaments. People knew that the combination of elections under martial law, the banning of parties, and their social set-up made it exceedingly unlikely that the assembly would be anything more than a buffer for Zia and a method of distributing patronage. But elections and parliaments still carry a baggage of ideas with them that cannot easily be reasoned away.

It disappointed the most cautious hopes. During its three years of existence, it did virtually nothing. It made a small gesture of independence in electing Fakr Imam as its speaker, but when Zia decided to get rid of him, submitted without a squeak of protest. Its only major pieces of legislation were the eighth amendment bill, which indemnified the martial law government of all its actions, and the speedy trials bill, which enabled the government to set up special courts manned by judges of its choice. The parliamentary committees which should have done the real work hardly met. It discussed at some length the questions of whether or not trousers were Islamic and whether or not a Chinese ladies' basketball game should be screened on Pakistani television (the players were wearing shorts); a day's session was spent considering the problem of a water authority engineer who had been insufficiently polite to a member of the assembly.

It did what it was expected to: it allowed its members and their constituents easier access to government funds and profitable enterprises. Each member of the national assembly was given five million rupees to hand out in development funds; the provincial assembly members got four million each. Gossip has it that more than 100 members were given free plots worth one and a half to two and a half million rupees; about forty members got loans of four to ten million rupees from the agricultural development bank for livestock development; and three members were given grants of land for the same purpose. There are profitable avenues in the government's gift – bonded warehouses, for instance, in which the goods that in theory travel from Karachi to Afghanistan are kept.

Straightforward profiteering is not, however, the purpose of hereditary politics. The aim is to stay on top. Money is one of the things that keeps you on top, but more important is to be able to command the support of more people in your area than anybody else can. That, in a tribal society, is the measure of success; and it remains important even in the minds of landlords with degrees in political science from British universities.

One of the ways of generating support is to be able to hand out jobs and opportunities for making money – the favours business. The politician and the constituent are the beneficiaries of that system: good government is often the victim. The adult literacy programme, a hopeless failure started with good intentions by Mr Junejo, was seen by politicians merely as a means of placating several thousand job-seekers. One politician I was touring with was approached by a villager who said, with a touch of requisite humility, that he would be eternally beholden if the man could find his brother some government employment. Of course, said the politician: the adult literacy programme. His brother could read, couldn't he? Yes, said the man hesitantly; but that wasn't quite what they had in mind. They were thinking rather more of something in customs.

People are also more likely to be in your camp if you can ensure protection for yourself, your relations and your constituents. People want protection from government and the police, and from each other. Being in politics helps a landlord ensure that his people are not harassed, and that their enemies are, through access to the ministries in Islamabad and the local civil servants' offices and police stations. That is both the result and the manifestation of power.

Hereditary politicians can do without power for a while on a gamble. Illahi Bakhsh Soomro put himself in the parliamentary opposition when he was not chosen to be prime minister. That was not too much of a risk, since it was not a real opposition, and he was not particularly vocal so was unlikely to be victimised; and by distancing himself from the prime minister, he put himself in a good position to be chosen for a big job when the next lot of tame politicians were brought in. Sure enough, when parliament was sacked in 1988, he went straight back to the cabinet.

191

But hereditary politics is a less secure business than it used to be. Years of military rule have shown that the old families may be able to provide their constituents with the goodies of government when the soldiers choose to let them – during Ayub's Basic Democracies, and Zia's flirtation with parliament – but that the politicians need the military more than it needs them. That was painfully clear after Zia's funeral. The politicians flirted with the soldiers, trying to look more appealing than one another in order to be selected as the one the military chose to put in power if there was to be a coup or rigged elections. Soldiers are unreliable patrons who sack their clients, as Zia did, without remorse; but the hereditary politicians looked as though they had no choice, for these days they cannot rely on the voters either.

The 1988 election proved that. The Muslim League and its allies still had all the advantages of being in government, and offered the choicest candidates. Still they were voted out.

Although constituents are happy to take the pickings of power, the politicians' cynicism and the poor quality of leadership that the hereditary system throws up has discredited them in the public's eyes. The old jor-tor (make and break) politics of the formation and splitting of alliances of clan and tribal leaders based on nothing but temporary self-interest may be the traditional political game; but the people whose support the landlords need are no longer compliant peasants.

Some are becoming middle class, some are getting educated, and all were promised something different when their country was created. Not that Islamic ideology wins many votes; but Islam brings with it an ideal of egalitarianism, of the equality of all men in the sight of God, that sits uneasily with the hierarchy which hereditary politics implies. And the very fact of creating a country on the basis of an ideal makes people susceptible to other, maybe different, ideals.

Offered an ideology that rings true, voters who would normally slide easily into the camps of one or other local landlord forget their old loyalties. That explains the second route that hereditary politicians, like Bhutto, sometimes take. They adopt an ideology, team up with people who are politically active not because they have a traditional claim to power but because they have ideas, and tempt the voters with a vision.

Despite holding a ministry in Ayub Khan's government, Bhutto established himself as the defender of the people against a coalition of Army, government and capitalism, the supporter of democracy against authoritarianism, the protector of the poor and scourge of the rich. His genius was his ability to recruit two sets of people, both crucial to his victory.

At an intellectual level, he appealed to an educated class frustrated by Ayub Khan's success at excluding it from politics through his indirect Basic Democracy electoral system, which left power in the hands of the brokers. With the help of J.A. Rahim, the brilliant ideologue who later became minister of industrial production and even later was sacked for being too left-wing, he wrote various pamphlets of analysis and policy whose tone and logic rang true to the students and the professionals hungry for political activity. The vocabulary – perhaps influenced by J.A. Rahim's stint as ambassador in Paris – was that current in radical movements throughout the world in the turbulent late sixties; but its survival in Pakistan, where 'vested interests', 'capitalism' and 'feudalism' are still part of conversation, suggests that Marxist analysis may have been better suited to such a country than to France, Britain or America.

It was convincing stuff. In 'Political Situation in Pakistan', written in 1968, Bhutto wrote that:

'The system adopted in our country is anything but *laissez-faire*; it is not liberal in any sense of the word. All the levers are so controlled by government that it can direct the flow of wealth into the pockets of whomsoever it pleases. Now, those who control the levers can also profit from the system to make themselves rich. In this way government servants, not to speak of ministers of government, form the managing personnel of the vast enterprise of getting rich through participation in authority.' Capitalism alone, therefore, is not to blame: it is government-directed profiteering, exacerbating the inequality perpetuated by an archaic social system:

'Observers from capitalist countries without deep insight into our conditions have been inclined to put the accent upon the familiar equation that money is power. This is true in Pakistan to some extent, but the real weight in the primitive structure which has supplanted the more evolved capitalist structure imposed by the British is in the equation that power is money . . . Power is money means that in order to become rich one must enjoy authority or be favoured by persons wielding authority.' Up to a point, true; and true and simple enough for any student to read it and feel that the author was not just against the rich and the powerful, but that he had formed a theory of the emergence of the rich and powerful and their stranglehold on the country which might provide for their replacement by something else. On solutions, Bhutto sank into slogans – democracy is our polity, socialism our economy and Islam our religion – but the analysis was powerful enough to win him the activists who devoted their spare time and their enthusiasm to the creation of the New Pakistan he promised.

At another level, he won The People in the Marxist sense – those without much money, influence or power over anybody except their wives and children, those with nothing to offer but their votes – by appealing to their self-interest and their self-respect. The traditional way of winning elections was to recruit the likes of Chandi, Shah Mahmood Qureshi or Illahi Bakhsh Soomro as candidates. They would bring their dependents and spiritual followers with them. Bhutto by-passed these people. During his nearly-year-long election campaign in 1970, he toured the country, talking to mass meetings of ordinary people, appealing directly to them for their vote. He was good at it: he was a crude showman, who, to make a point, flung his jacket into the audience for them to tear it to pieces, ridiculed his opponents, made bad jokes, played the question-and-answer audience-participation routine favoured by comedians and priests. It was all in crude feudal style, and not much approved by the refined middle-class ideologues who had joined up with him; but they appreciated the importance of his appeal to The People and they approved his message of basic economic rights. But the style of his approach was more significant than its content: Bhutto was the first politician to tell the poor that they mattered.

Some would argue Bhutto was bound to fail. With him, he had the students and trade unionists, professionals, small farmers and labourers; against him was a formidable opposition of land, industry, finance, religion and the military. The alliance of money and mullahs was partly what got him in 1977; but Bhutto, by destroying the constituency that made him, hastened his own demise, and in the process maimed the left. It has still not recovered, and Pakistani politics are still disabled as a result of his brutal reversal.

It was not so much the brutality as the betrayal that did the damage. I understood a little of that when I found a statement made by J.A. Rahim, Bhutto's ideological mentor in the early days, and a man who was respected and loved for his decency and his brilliance, after an encounter with the Federal Security Force, Bhutto's personal paramilitaries:

'Said Ahmed Khan [head of the FSF] hit me violently in the face

194

and on the body and was followed in the act by others of the FSF crowd. Besides being beaten by fists I was hit by rifle butts. I was thrown on the ground and hit while prostrate . . . My son tried to intervene to protect me and was himself assaulted by FSF men . . . I was dragged out by my legs, then thrown into a Jeep'. When he was released from hospital, the discharge slip mentioned 'multiple injuries'. Disciples who tried to see him when he was ill were threatened by the FSF. Many third world governments treat their politicians worse; but they haven't usually been popularly elected, and if they have, it is usually their opponents not their allies they beat up.

While destroying his left-wing base, Bhutto turned to the politics he was brought up to. The feudal families returned to the fold of government, joining the party in the mid-seventies, and getting their party tickets for the 1977 election. But the reversal was too late or too half-hearted. By then, Bhutto faced the opposition not just of business, the mullahs and the Army, but also of many ex-students, trade unionists and professionals who felt betrayed by his reversion to traditional politics – reliance on power-brokers and muscle rather than on systems and institutions. They joined the Pakistan National Alliance, a well-funded coalition of parties whose only aim was to depose Bhutto.

Benazir might have restored the self-esteem and dynamism of the left, but she chose another route. Although, after her return to Pakistan in 1986, she behaved like one with an ideological mission, her cry of 'Bhuttoism' had no ideological substance. Her approach harked back to hereditary politics and was coloured with what looked to some partymen like an excessive concern for western opinion. Yet she carried with her the ghost of her father's appeal: that, and her dogged bravery, set her above the others.

Benazir's dramatic homecoming demonstrated the huge public interest in herself and the party. The streets of Lahore were jammed with anything from 500,000 to two million people, and it took her car ten hours to travel the five miles from the airport to the town centre. People said she could, if she wanted, storm President Zia's citadel; and the enthusiasm was so uncontrolled that you felt the crowds might have torn him limb from limb at a word from her.

I went to one of the rallies early on in her tour, at Sargodha, a farming and mining town in the Punjabi heartland. I was with Ahmed Rashid, an energetic Pakistani journalist who writes for the *Independent* and the *Observer*. We sat on the covered wooden stand in the football pitch to wait and listen to my short-wave radio for news of the American bombing of Libya which a hookah-smoking servant at Ahmed's house had told us of. Another journalist came up to Ahmed with the stiff walk of one seeking a fight; but it stopped at shouting, before blows. Ahmed was a bloody white journalist, the man said, since he worked for British papers; and Benazir was giving interviews only to white journalists.

It was evening by the time Benazir arrived, and the ground had slowly been filling with people, like dark oil creeping over a surface. They sat on the ground surrounded by a circle of crude thirty-foot posters of Bhutto and muttered restfully to each other. As she walked on to the stand, the ground burst into yells, chants, pushes and small, sudden fights, as though disruption itself were a tribute to her. She quietened them with her hands and the chants subsided as she started speaking. She spoke not well – I was told that her Urdu was uneasy after so many years in London – and without passion or warmth, but with a hard conviction. Mostly the audience was peaceful, though near the stage, in the periphery of the spotlight, I could see a push turn into a punch, a security man run over and a scuffle between two people suddenly suck in another ten, swaying, but held up by the crowd. Then after two minutes of limbs and brandished lathis, the fight would stop as obscurely as it had started.

As she finished speaking, her press man, with whom I used to have cups of tea on the Tottenham Court Road during the days of his exile, shuffled me to the sofa where she was going to sit. The stand was shaking with the violence of its incumbents' desire to reach, touch, see Benazir. They pushed and climbed over one another, as I fought my way through and she slid calmly on to the sofa. I introduced myself nervously, shaken both by a crowd that seemed to be tipping over the edge of riot, and by her exquisite cool. She rearranged her dupatta and gave me her wide-mouthed, white-toothed smiled that combined glossy-magazine looks with a regal graciousness.

'Didn't we meet at Dominic's party in London?' Damn right, we did. But I didn't expect her to remember, since there had been an attendance of men in dinner jackets fetching her cigarettes and longing for her. 'And how is dear Dominic these days?' I had no idea, not having seen the man for some five years; but I assumed the requisite intimacy with his hopes and fears and we slid easily into a conversation of cocktail parties. The stand shook with increasing vigour, and the crowd seemed to be closing in on us despite the ring of security men beating the oncomers' heads with their lathis.

I spent two or three hours with Benazir that evening, and have interviewed her a few times since, usually in the large house in the richest suburb of Karachi, where you sit and wait for her in a banqueting hall observed by a life-sized portrait of Bhutto, watching a couple of gardeners tool around the edges of the lawn. Occasionally a smart young woman wanders through the garden from one bit of the house to another; but the rooms, built for crowds, speeches and arguments, their walls lined with chairs, waiting for suppliants, are empty.

Benazir isn't an easy woman to talk to: she has a powerful personality, but she is too tense to charm. She smiles politically, without giving the impression of small confidences that wins journalists. It is hard for her to be open, though, since openness and friendliness can be read as looseness, and the advantages that a beautiful female politician has in a sexually frustrated country can suddenly flip and become liabilities. As the distant object of a range of emotions from respect through adoration to lust, she has a lot going for her; as the fallen woman, betrayer of the honour of her sex and her male relations, she would be finished.

Her bravery and strength have struck me as outstanding. I guess they stem from an unquestioning, protective devotion to her father: an old Oxford friend of hers told me that at university she was a fairly ordinary student, going to student parties and laughing at student jokes, but that a whiff of criticism of her father, or even any of his policies, drove her to fury. I'm sure she wanted to win her duel with Zia, whom she saw as her father's murderer, partly because she wanted power; but she wanted power partly to prove her father right.

Yet despite her claim that 'Bhuttoism' is her creed she has, it seems, taken the opposite approach to that which brought her father to victory. She has junked ideology, promising no nationalisations and, at least when she talked to me, saying that land reform was unnecessary. She will not say that defence spending, the bugbear not only of the left but of most of the opposition inside and outside parliament as well as plenty of civil servants, should be cut. Before she went back to Pakistan, she made a quick trip to Washington and has refused, despite pressure from colleagues, to take an anti-American line on the Russian occupation of Afghanistan. Among the remains of the left in her party, and with the many Pakistanis who argue that their country is serving American geopolitical interests at great risk to itself, this would be hugely popular. She has, it seems, come to the conclusion that if she is to win, it will be through the good offices of the centres of power – business, land, the military and the Americans – and not as a result either of the wishes of The People, nor of hard work and organisation by party activists.

Her failure to take the line that won Bhutto his elections has lost her much support among the activists. You can meet them anywhere in the country. They will show you the scars from their days in jail in the early years of the Zia government, before it had learnt the advantages of tolerance, and tell you what it's like to be hung upside down. Many are still with the PPP, but many are now unenthusiastic, and others are looking around for different, more inspiring, political homes.

A year and a half after her return to Pakistan, I saw Benazir on a tour of the frontier. Her punctuality had not improved – an hour after the students' meeting was supposed to start, we were still waiting, and the bats were wheeling against the darkening blue of the sky. Aziz, a young journalist, and I tried to puzzle out the meaning of the red People's Student Federation banner that said in silver paint 'Your sovereignty ends where our threshold starts'. A thin young man bobbed through the trailing gold and coloured-paper decorations on the stand and tapped the microphone, sounding a boom around the crowded garden.

'That's the student's chairman,' said Aziz. 'He was always busy taking bribes from the vice-chancellor. Then when the new vice-chancellor came and wouldn't give bribes, he started making political protests and holding meetings.' Aziz, a part-time journalist, part-time office worker and union official who was also studying for a law degree, had no time for the PPP; his sympathies, muttered softly to me, were much further left. He had been too young for the heyday of the PPP, and in his view it had sold out long ago. He thought that the PPP student activists were just thugs who enjoyed running a gang; whereas he wanted real social change, change that would not be achieved by a party or through a system dominated by the feudals and the capitalists. It sounded familiar. He was the archetypal recruit to the PPP of 1968, and the kind of young man who had dragged it to victory; but it was no more for him.

'Quick, look!' he jumped out of his seat, pointing into the middle of the crowd. 'They're burning an American flag! I wonder what the guards will do.' I got up, but could see only a thin column of smoke. Benazir had banned the burning of American flags, a traditional PPP pastime, at her rallies, and those who indulged in it had occasionally been beaten up. It had become a game for the left-wingers to try to get a couple of flags burnt before anybody could stop them.

Somebody tried to rouse the chant of 'Zia, Zia, Out, Out' again. It had started as an aggressive bark, but after an hour and a half had gone limp. Aziz was silent, concentrating on a girl in green in the women's section opposite the journalists. She was chewing gum, stroking her hair and pushing her white dupatta off her head, then pulling it up, rearranging it, and starting again. One of the girls standing in the row between the gate and the stand to receive Benazir was pulling the petals off her bunch of flowers.

Half-speech, half-singing started to boom through the microphone, from an emaciated, bearded man with a visionary's eyes. It's poetry, said Aziz: Benazir is good, Bhutto was good, Zia is bad. He shrugged and smiled at the childishness of it all. He used to do poetry for Muslim League rallies, he said. I asked if he got paid.

'No!' he replied, shocked. 'My father was a Muslim Leaguer. I was happy to show I am patriotic to my country. Now,' he said sternly, 'I am not patriotic to Pakistan. Only to my soil.' He was silent for a while. 'Once,' he said thoughtfully, 'they paid me five hundred rupees. But that was a prize.'

Benazir arrived, suddenly. People were craning to see if the tripling of the crowd around the gate meant she had arrived, and then she was on the stand. The chants found their energy again: 'Benazir is coming, the revolution is coming', which, in Urdu, scans.

The size and the patience of the crowd surprised me. I suppose there were three thousand people there, adults as well as students. Before Benazir, they heard six untalented men speak. For forty minutes of seeing and hearing her, they sat for a good four hours. It wasn't just for the tamasha, though: it was also to do with the uncertainty. The people of Peshawar were there for the same reason that the rich of Karachi and Lahore bore themselves in the evenings with repeated speculations about the country's future that, taken to logical but inconceivable extremes, send them depressed to bed. Change and uncertainty keep people riveted to their politics.

Benazir's manner of speaking had improved a lot. She had not acquired passion, or her father's entertainer's skill, but she knew how to talk to the audience both as an older sister and as a martyr to a political cause. She started as sister, gesticulating with a pen in her hand to explain that Bhuttoism was not just a slogan, but an ideology for which people should sacrifice themselves, then her voice quickened and rose in pitch, and her body tensed and leant forward and her arms flashed out angrily as she attacked Zia, the government, her political opponents. Then she softened once more into her sister voice, became a little humorous, offered gentle advice to the students, and sat down.

It was only later that I saw how tight her control over herself was. She attended a dinner at Green's Hotel, given by an old cartoonist who lives there. He is a crumbled figure, destroyed by hard living, who mumbles and rambles and produces sharp, clever cartoons. I was worried about his speech, which somebody else read out in a crowded basement hall in the hotel, while Benazir sat in a pink chiffon dupatta, her head tilted to one side. The text drifted all over the place, with small unsuccessful jokes and unidentifiable references; then suddenly, underneath it, was a hard, open attack on Bhutto's treatment of the press in general, and a few journalists in particular which, the speech hoped, would not be repeated if Benazir ever came to power. Despite the ramblings and the idiosyncracies, nobody could have missed the point; and when mutterings started at the back of the hall, I worried that party people might break up the gathering.

Benazir had fixed her half-smile to her tilted face. She replied, this time in English, with grace, without anger, and without answering. She has learnt to use her fine, strong jaw-line and her long neck, challenging and taunting the audience with her chin in the air, then lowering her head and offering small jokes with a coy smile. She told us of the iniquities of the present government's treatment of the press, and we clapped; but the cartoonist had failed. He had wanted her to commit herself to the freedom of the press, so he could have something down on paper. People like him are less willing than they were to take things on trust.

Dinner, to which only party people and the smartest of the journalists were invited, seated forty people around long, white-clothed tables set in a square. When I got through the crush, Benazir was already seated, trying to spear a purple-dyed hard-boiled egg that slipped away from under her fork. The guests trailed in, sat tentatively, and waited for food. Benazir looked up, peered at me diagonally across the square and put on her glasses.

'Is that Emma Duncan?' I agreed that it was.

'How is Dominic these days?' I had half-expected attacks on my writing, but not this social ghost. I muttered excuses about my absence from England, don't get to see old friends much, you know. Since the rest of the table was taking its food in silence, I thought my bit of the audience was probably over; but the conversation went on, across the notables of the Peshawar PPP chewing at their kebabs and tinned Russian salad, through the matter of writing books (she was doing her autobiography), to V.S. Naipaul, the nature of his genius and the comparative merits of his studies of Islam in Pakistan and Iran. I had to catch a train to Lahore, so left, rudely, before the chief guest; but I was glad to get away from the silent, trapped audience to a conversation that would have suited a cocktail party better.

Benazir, I decided, would have made a good Mogul. There was an imperial ease in her dismisal of the existence of forty-odd people. On the other hand, I thought perhaps that was wrong. Perhaps it was a great unease, a knowledge that she could not manage a court as both king and jester the way her father had. Then I thought no: insecurity is the usual excuse for arrogance. She is a difficult woman to make out.

After her return, what had been the PPP split three ways, according to the main trends in Pakistani politics. One lot of hereditary politicians took themselves off, apparently to make themselves available to the Army should it need a new government in a hurry. Some of the left stayed nominally in the party, cohabitating uncomfortably with Benazir, but much of it drifted off either to try another party or to give up mainstream politics and try some grassroots activity. A third lot set about taking advantage of the rising nationalist feeling in the country.

The first group belonged to Ghulam Mustapha Jatoi, a big Sindhi landlord who ran the party in Sind while she was in London. He seemed to have difficulty adjusting to his inferior position after her return, and left to start the National People's Party with Mustapha Khar, governor of Punjab under Bhutto, a man known for his toughness with his enemies and his fondness for women. The party is weak on policy – nobody really knows what it is – and it is hard to find supporters around the country; but it is said to be well-financed through the support of businessmen who are still afraid that Benazir will retract her commitments to the private sector.

I went to see Jatoi when he was launching his party in Lahore.

Our interview was to take place in a rare old house in Lahore, of high ceilings and faded velvet curtains, the property of one of his rich supporters. Jatoi was an hour late, so I sat with an aide, trying to make out what the party was for. Who, for instance, was it going to appeal to? So many people, he said, who were not with the PPP and not with the government. For instance? Well, he said, businessmen, farmers, traders . . . most of the occupations in the country, it seemed. And of course, he remembered, the party was counting on its appeal to the religious conservatives who would not want a woman running the country. Sensing my suppressed sneer, he threw his hands up. 'Don't worry,' he said, 'I'm a progressive man. I drink whisky.'

I didn't get much more out of Jatoi, a plump man whose jaw-line has gone and who sat on a high-backed throne of an armchair like a tired king. He would prefer to be elected prime minister, he said, but there were circumstances under which he might be prepared to work with the government. It was hard not to agree with my friends in Lahore who concluded, the moment they heard of his move, that he was setting himself up as an acceptable alternative to the prime minister should Zia have felt in need of a change. He just kept missing it, though. By the time of the 1988 election, he had finally set himself up as the government alliance's strongest candidate. Then the Sindhi voters slung him out.

A few of the left-wingers of the PPP joined the parties that have been soldiering on since the birth of Pakistan. The National Awami Party, the outgrowth of the left-wing Pathan nationalist party that opposed the Muslim League around the time of partition, survived Ayub Khan, but not the Sino-Soviet split. In 1967, it divided, with Wali Khan, Ghaffur Khan's son, taking the pro-Moscow line.

Despite the division, the sixties were a prosperous time for socialism. It had international issues, like Vietnam, to protest against, and a healthy domestic opposition to economic inequality under Ayub Khan. The National Awami Party, however, did not enjoy many of the benefits: the activists were mostly creamed off by Bhutto. In Baluchistan and the frontier, however, the old left did well in the 1970s elections not so much because it was left as because it managed to combine its ideology with a mild form of Baluch and Pathan nationalism. Bhutto's imprisonment of the provincial government leaders in the 1970s heightened their popularity, but more because of nationalist resentment than because of support for their undiluted leftism.

Bhutto dealt such a blow to the left that its popularity since his demise has been based more on these provincial loyalties than on united Pakistani socialism. Much of the left, disillusioned with parties and governments, has taken up quiet, low-level activism that, at present, shies away from demagogic leadership and centralised organisations. It seems odd, in a country which seems to have enough inequality and enough education to sustain a revolution; but the left was badly burnt in the seventies.

A trade unionist in Karachi, a softly-spoken man with an over-intense stare, told me his life story. He had been a textile worker in Multan in the late sixties, and some student leaders arrived and persuaded them to strike. They occupied the old mill, took down the bell that summoned the workers, melted it down and sold it for drink. After that, the strike fell to pieces. But he started going to listen to Bhutto, and in 1971 . . . it was a kind of euphoria, he said, his eyes glistening with nostalgia. They had taken over a silk mill, and held the brother of the owner (the present governor of Sind) for ransom. Then they had taken over the textile workers' colonies in Karachi, banned police, political parties and prostitutes, and kidnapped a Karachi Development Authority engineer until they got a water supply laid. By October of 1972, they were all in jail; and they spent the rest of the 1970s in jail or underground.

He told me to come on an outing at the weekend. I would learn a lot, he said, about what people like him were doing these days. I arrived on time at his office; and since he was an hour late, I checked out his bookshelves. They were the shelves of international socialism, with books to help you know your enemy as well as your friend. Along with Marx, Lenin, Trotsky, and E.P. Thompson were Christopher Tugendhat on *The Multinationals* and the Price Waterhouse manual on corporation taxation. The noticeboard had a poster condemning the Thatcherite dismantling of the welfare state, a Namibia poster and a graphic in black on red of a woman tearing off her chador. On the door was a Free Nelson Mandela sticker.

Slowly the people for the trip assembled − a fisherman, a trade unionist from a gas company with curled white moustaches, a plump girl with a bursting smile who ran an International Labour Organisation-financed project in the village we were going to, her boss, who ran a co-operative movement with a network of projects in villages in Sind, a lawyer and his little son. The trade unionist I knew was last, apologising with a smile as though the apology were unnecessary.

Did I think, the gas man asked me in the Jeep as we rattled down the dual carriageway east out of Karachi, that Pakistani Islam needed to be seen in the context of Iran and Afghanistan, or by itself? The right answer was fairly obvious, so I said in context. He nodded seriously. Because, he said, Shia Islam is important to Pakistan. Sunni Islam is dominated by pirs and sayyeds, who are feudals. They don't want the system changed. Shiism is the Islam of struggle. In Iran, it has changed the society. But, I said, I know Shia feudals who don't want the system changed either. The gas man defended himself to general laughter. Maybe, he said; but lower and middle-class Shias are more revolutionary than Sunnis.

The fisherman was annoyed. Shiism is plagued by Imams, he said. Sunnis have nothing between themselves and God. Direct connection, he said, pointing upwards, and repeated it several times, so I should understand. I asked the gas man if he was a Shia. 'I was born a Sunni,' he said proudly, 'but now I am a human being.' Perhaps the gas man was right: the Jeep-load of socialists were all Shia except for him, the fisherman and I, although Shias are a smallish minority of the population. I asked how many of my companions said their prayers five times a day. Only my trade unionist at the driving wheel put up up his finger.

'You don't,' I said rudely. 'I've never seen you.'

'I don't have to be seen,' he answered quietly. 'I talk to God.'

'Drive more carefully,' said the girl. 'I'm as near God as I want to be.'

It took a few villages for us to find a tea-shop. Everybody agreed we should stop at a Baluch one, not a Pathan one because the Pathans used too much sugar. We made our way through the rectangular tables with piles of dirty crockery and water-glasses on them to an empty one: 'Shall we take one for the Sunnis and one for the Shias?' said my trade unionist, dismissing the argument by ridicule. But the fisherman, once agile boys with trays had brought thick milky tea and flat dry bread, with the air-bubbles cooked crisp and fragile as blown glass, wanted to keep it going. After all, he said, Sunni Islam was the first in Pakistan, because Mohammed Bin Qasim brought it. Rubbish, said my trade unionist. Shia Islam seeped in from Iran long before.

Tea and rotis (unleavened bread), said the gas man nostalgically. I lived on this for years when I was underground. The girl drew her black dupatta closer round her head, conscious of the tables of men around us. I found I hardly noticed their stares any more, but she wrinkled her nose in mock-distaste to mask her nervousness, and went back to the car. We stayed to finish cups of tea, a shiny brown skin hardening on them as they cooled.

There were twenty-five men waiting for us on orange plastic chairs under a canopy in a courtyard at the village. They were in a range of clothes that stretched from central Karachi to the depths of the Thar desert – anoraks, waistcoats and Sindhi shawls; embroidered hats, turbans, bare heads, and one flat corduroy cap. They were candidates from the local elections, some successful, some failed; and they had been called, my trade unionist explained, because they were the most active people in the villages and our team was hoping to put some ideas in their heads.

They listened, with this amazing Pakistani capacity for listening. There were two hours of speeches – explaining co-operatives and the virtues of fuel-efficient smokeless stoves, arguing that local elections were a means of restraining the people's national political aspirations, and explaining how the government abused the law. A man in the front row snored. My trade unionist told him to wake up, and he did. Mostly they watched intently, some nodding vigorously.

I asked the men afterwards what they thought of all this. We agree with these things, said a man in an orange Sindhi hat whose bulk and air of authority marked him out as a leader. They have spoken about our problems. I asked how people voted in the local elections – for braderi or for individuals? Both, said the man in the orange hat; but a man with a thin face, his skin folded into deep creases, said that the braderi was less important than before. In the last ten to fifteen years, people had become more interested in political parties. Why? He shrugged. People thought more about things than they used to.

I sat with the gas man on a charpoy at the dinner prepared for us round a fire, under the palm trees, at a nearby farm. I wanted to find out the nature of his politics, and felt like a spy. What did he think of the influence of foreign money in Pakistan? He could hardly disapprove of it, he said, when the ILO was funding the co-operative projects. Did he think Bhutto's nationalisations were a good thing? Terrible, he said. Bhutto did it not for socialism, but for power; and he closed his fist round his fingers. At independence, the country was left with three ruling classes, land, capital and the

Indian Civil Service. How did it benefit the people if property was taken from capital and given to the ICS? Power should go to the workers, not the civil servants. They had done it in the early 1970s, taken over factories and produced their own cloth. Then? He smiled, the firelight reddening his skin.

'The Army came in. We were jailed and tortured. But those were good times.'

On the way back, the fisherman started singing. It was an Urdu song; so we had to have Sindhi songs to balance it, then English songs from the foreigner. But we ended up with an Urdu song that even I could pick up, as easy as revolutionary songs always are:

The people of my village
Will get nothing without a fight
The people of my village
Come out and join the struggle
The people of my village
Bearing torches in the night.

Perhaps the quiet work that those people are doing in their villages will eventually bear political fruit; perhaps the Sindhis will eventually march out of their villages and demand liberation from the landlords and the capitalists. But it feels as though the left is still waiting for its wounds to heal. By far the liveliest political activity in the eighties has been generated by the desire to fight not the rich but the Punjabis. Several of the hereditary politicians, like Mumtaz Bhutto, a cousin of Zulfikar's who was chief minister and governor of Sind during the PPP government, have recognised this and joined the bandwagon.

Regional sentiment was there long before Pakistan was. As soon as the country was created, it emerged to irritate central governments. In theory, they respected it; in practice, they found it difficult to live with practically and disapproved of it ideologically. Not only did loyalty to a race or a language seem to contradict the ideal of Islamic unity which was the country's *raison d'être*; but the idea of greater regional autonomy was also anathema to the civilian and military bureaucrats who ran the country and whose professional upbringing demanded centralised authority.

It does get in the way of the running of the country. The best current example is the non-building of the Kalabagh dam. Pakistan is disastrously short of electricity generating capacity. The vast

Tarbela dam and the country's smaller hydro-electric generators are stretched as far as they can be, and Tarbela becomes less productive over the years as the water level slowly drops. In 1953, engineers selected Kalabagh, in the far north of Punjab, just on the edge of the NWFP, as the next most suitable site for a dam: but inter-provincial arguments have prevented it from being built. The frontier says that towns and villages around Nowshera and Attock will be flooded; Sind and Baluchistan say that the irrigation system planned around the dam will lower the water level and cause droughts further down the Indus; Punjab argues vainly that Pakistan must have more electricity generating capacity; nothing gets done.

Regionalism in Pakistan's early years climaxed in the Bengali uprising, but the war and Bangladesh's independence were not cathartic. Rather, they seemed to have set the country an example. The Baluch, during Bhutto's rule, suffered some of the same indignities – being governed by a foreign bureaucracy, having their local, popularly elected government sacked by the central government – and reacted in the same way the Bengalis had, by taking to arms. Military intervention, and the imprisonment and exile of their leaders, quelled them, but their failure to win either independence or greater autonomy does not seem to have discouraged the latest calls for autonomy, which come from Sind.

When the British seized Sind, the resistance against them was mounted not in the name of Islam but in the name of Sind. Hoshoo, the commander who led the resistance, raised the slogan of 'murvesoon, Sind na deshoon,' – we will die, but will not abandon Sind. The British recognised the importance of the Sindhis' identity, and decreed that their local language should be the official language of the province.

A fight against an outsider tends to unite otherwise disparate peoples, so the business of Sindhi nationalism was quietly forgotten, first in the struggle for independence against the British and then in the Muslims' battle against the Hindus. But, once the subcontinent was partitioned, Sindhi sentiment began to rumble. Under Ayub, who abolished West Pakistan's provinces and turned it into 'One Unit', it grew to a crescendo. That policy gave birth to radical Sindhi politics, which culminated in the formation of the Jiye Sind (long live Sind) party, whose slogan, Sindhu Desh (independent Sind) recalls the creation of Bangladesh.

The Sindhi movement is partly negative – against people it sees

207

as oppressive – but it is also positively to do with an idea of Sindhi nationhood which is both different from and opposed to the ideas of Pakistani nationhood currently being peddled. Sufism and poetry play an important part in this: their greatest poet-saint, Shah Abdul Latif, is a folk-hero. Sindhi writers and intellectuals I have talked to maintain passionately that the Sufi-influenced Islam passed down from such men is a personal, tolerant religion: it is concerned with internal peace, cohabits happily with Hinduism, and rejects the imposition of straight-jacketed, legalistic Islam favoured by General Zia.

The Sindhi movement's main visible target is the Punjabis. Sind's four million-or-so Punjabis started arriving more than fifty years ago. The British imported masons, carpenters, engineers and supervisors from the more modern province to build the Sukkur barrage and create an irrigation system around it. Competent Punjabi farmers were given some of the newly-fertile land; and Punjabis, better-educated than the Sindhis, got jobs in the police and civil service there.

During the sixties, as Punjab's agriculture became more capital-intensive, Punjabi workers and small farmers found themselves without jobs. Some of them moved to Sind as the construction of more barrages brought more land under cultivation. Large slices of that land were also given to Punjabi civil servants and Army officers. When Ayub's One Unit was disbanded, 17,000 Punjabi civil servants who had been working in Sind were incorporated into the new provincial civil service.

The Sindhis complain about being run by a Punjabi-dominated civil service, but it is Army rule that has heightened their sense of identity and grievance. The Army, heavily dominated by Punjabis with a smattering of Pathans, was, as far as the Sindhis were concerned, as much of a colonial force as it was in East Pakistan in the 1960s. And being in a somewhat foreign, hostile land, the Army exercised its power roughly in Sind. The antagonism culminated in the 1983 uprising, but the shock that gave the government did not lead the security forces to behave more gently. Subsequent anti-dacoit (and anti-left-wing) operations under the civilian government have paid little attention to Sindhi sensitivities.

A reporter from the *Herald* travelled around the interior of Sind in 1986, checking out statements put out by the police and the Army about successful operations by the security forces against dacoits. One claimed that 'some armed persons' had blocked a road, and that 'the law enforcing agency fired back in its defence resulting in two dead and four others injured'. In fact, three villagers had been killed two miles away from the road when, according to the locals, they were resting after a day's harvesting. One was an eight-year-old girl. Another announcement named two 'dacoits' who were killed in an encounter. One of them was eighty and blind. Some of the harassment seems to be intended to intimidate villagers into giving up dacoits they may be hiding; some is more to do with the grievances of local bigwigs. Each story of Army or police brutality is multiplied and exaggerated, sharpening the local resentment against Punjabi rule.

Pakistan's strange history makes the political configuration of Sind odd. The Punjabis are not the only target of Sindhi anger: the mohajirs are, in some places and at some times, more intensely disliked. In the urban areas, particularly in Sind's second town, Hyderabad, the mohajirs and the Sindhis are in direct competition with each other. The mohajirs, generally better-educated than the Sindhis, tend to have the better jobs; but because of the quota system for college places and civil service posts, the Sindhis from the countryside now have an easier time getting government slots, thus arousing the mohajirs' anger.

Even so, the MQM and bits of the Sindhi parties have made attempts to get together, seeing a common interest not just against Punjabis but against the Sindhi landlords. A slice of the Sindhi movement argues that the two groups have a common class interest, and therefore should be fighting together against economic, not ethnic, inequalities. That stand is, obviously, fiercely opposed by the landlords in the movement, who would do well out of the greater provincial autonomy they argue for – since they would run the province – and would suffer from a united left-wing movement.

One such is Mumtaz Bhutto, a cousin of Zulfikar's who was both chief minister and governor of Sind during the PPP government. Unlike Benazir, he has understood people's need for ideological inspiration and, in exile in London with Hafeez Pirzada, Bhutto's law minister, started the Sind Baluch Pushtun front, the party of the smaller provinces against colonialist domination by Punjab.

Mumtaz was sleek and fat with a black moustache and an expensive suit when I knew him in London. A couple of prison spells after his return to Pakistan thinned him down, and he now wears the populist politician's uniform, the shalwar kamees, and a grizzled beard. His house is pink silk with Chinese vases, statues and chandeliers, better suited to the London garb than the new man-of-the-people outfit. Mumtaz's father came in when I was last there: a tiny, frail old man with watering eyes and a string of garnet beads that he counted, muttering, like a rosary. 'Why are you speaking English?' he asked angrily. 'Speak Sindhi!'

Having left the PPP, Mumtaz is happily critical of the years in power. The story, as he tells it, is not unique: they went into office intending to bring about a revolution in the style and content of government, and found themselves operating in the same way as those they had replaced. Take the land reforms: they happened on paper, the zamindars retained control, the bureaucracy knew what was happening but took money to look the other way or to alter documents.

Mumtaz's solution, after he saw the strength of the 1983 movement in Sind, was to call for a break-up of the federation of Pakistan's provinces. 'Confederation' was what he wanted – powers over defence, foreign policy and the currency at the centre, the rest dealt with by provincial governments. 'The rights of the smaller provinces' was the slightly catchier slogan. He caught something, in Sind and Baluchistan, though his movement never took off in the frontier, and he did a bit better than people expected in the local elections in 1987.

There were two problems with his movement. First, he was an old-style politician, working through the power-brokers: his biggest successes in Baluchistan, for instance, came through his alliance with the brother of Ataullah Mengal, sardar of the Mengal tribe. Second, others, like the Jiye Sind, the Sind Awami Tehrik and the Hari Committees had got there first.

The grassroots Sindhi movement is vocal, confused and divided. Its problems spring not just from the usual Pakistani difficulty of too many leaders all wanting their name at the top of the list: there is a genuine ideological difficulty between those who see the rich as the biggest enemy, and those who think the fight is more against the Punjabis or the mohajirs. The second group seems to be winning; but meeting some of those involved it seemed to me that given a large enough grievance the two contrary visions of the world could probably shelve their differences and fight, temporarily, side by side.

Staying with Junaid Soomro in Shikarpur, I asked if I could meet some local radicals. Not really, he said: the left-wing and the nationalists were weak in this part of Sind, and there was nobody well-known in Shikarpur. I didn't want anybody famous, I said, just local activists. I wanted to see who they were and what they thought. He agreed, doubtfully, to see what he could do.

At the snap of feudal fingers, the men came. They started arriving half an hour after Junaid had sent a servant to collect them. Junaid went out into the street to do some business with a couple of the new arrivals. The others sat among the general audience that hangs around feudal houses, waiting to be summoned for interrogation.

A smart young man with shiny moustaches and good English from the revolutionary Watan Dost shifted on his seat, then leaned over to me to say that he was in a bit of a hurry. Fine, I said: let's go to another room, and we can talk. No, he said. That isn't possible. Why not? I understood, after a confused exchange, that it was impossible for him to leave the room without Junaid's permission. I went out in the street, found Junaid, and explained the problem.

'He isn't busy,' he said with a laugh. 'And if he is, it doesn't matter. He has to stay here until I tell him he can go.'

'You bloody feudal! I thought you were pretending to be progressive.'

'You see,' said the Watan Dost man, coming into the street. 'This is what we mean by oppression.'

The captive radicals were summoned to my bedroom, where they sat on beds and chairs, speaking when spoken to. Apart from the Watan Dost, we had the Hari Committee, the Communist Party, and Jiye Sind. Really, we needed the Awami Tehrik, the party that had taken over the 1983 movement, as well; but I didn't want Junaid to drag any more out of their homes at ten o'clock at night.

There were two men from the Hari Committee, one a doctrinaire with round, tinted spectacles and a maroon and blue-patterned Sindhi scarf. He didn't want to tell me anything. He was an intellectual sniper, lying on the bed and shooting occasional questions about Israel at me. His colleague, an electrician with a level voice, said he was a member of the Communist Party as well as the Hari Committee, and gave me a clear analysis of why the takeover of the Hari Committee by the Communist Party had weakened the former. It was, he said, successful in the fifties and sixties, in attracting peasants and fighting for their rights. But in the seventies, the Communists captured the central committee, stopped talking about the peasants' rights and told them instead about Marx, Lenin and the comprador bourgeoisie. Recently the Hari Committee, like the Communist Party, had split on the question of whether oppression of Sind by Punjab, or of the poor by the rich, was more important.

I thought he would make a good revolutionary. There was an unemotional calm about him, a quiet ruthlessness. Impressed by the clarity of his discourse, I asked him much education he had had. Primary school, he said: but he had been reading since. He had read all three volumes of *Das Kapital* in Urdu.

'I didn't know you could get it in Urdu.'

'Of course,' he said. 'They send them cheap from Russia.'

The Jiye Sind man was woolier, getting waylaid in his history of the movement by bits of political bitchiness. He was a teacher, fat and unshaven with a thick brown scarf around a thick brown neck. The party, he said, was started by G.M. Syed, a veteran Muslim Leaguer who now blamed himself for having assisted in the creation of Pakistan. Until Bhutto was deposed, the party reckoned that things could be done through the government; but since 1977, they had given up, and were demanding an independent Sind.

The Watan Dost man was very educated – a medical student, who left his course to do an honours degree in philosophy and then returned to medicine – and contemptuous both of me and of the rest of the company. His was a purely working-class movement, he said, based on a premise that nobody else in the room understood – that Pakistan was a new colony, exploited by multinationals, which needed a revolution to stamp out the comprador bourgeoisie. But training Pakistanis into socialism was a difficult business, he said: they were prepared to hear anything against Zia, but nothing against Allah.

We have not helped ourselves, said the electrician, implying that the Watan Dost man was an illustration of the problem. Always the left-wing and the nationalists have been fighting each other. This is not so much now, though: now we go to each other's meetings.

'There you are,' said Junaid, when they left after midnight. 'Those are our radicals. They have a long way to go, I think.' And he went downstairs, to pass the night talking to the watchmen in the street.

An opposition strategy meeting after the sacking of parliament in 1988 brought home to me the advantages to Zia of encouraging the growth of this menagerie of regional and ethnic parties. All the old parties were there, dominated by the PPP; and at lunch I asked whether they were going to ask the MQM, the newest, livest political force in the country, to join their campaign for more elections. How could they? asked the party secretary I spoke to. If they asked the MQM, they would have to ask the Pakhtoon Punjabi Ittehad, and the two would tear each other to pieces; anyway, the Sindhi nationalists were already with the opposition alliance, and they couldn't sit in the same room with the MQM. So, with a little bit of support and encouragement to ethnic and regional hatreds, the government succeeds in stunting the growth of national political cooperation. In a country which has already once split along those lines, that is a dangerous game.

The PPP's success in the 1988 election apparently narrowed those divisions in Sind. The unstoppable MQM won eleven out of fourteen seats in Karachi, but the little Sindhi and left-wing parties were wiped out. Yet the emotions were still there: the PPP had simply bagged them. Bhutto's Sindhi origins won his party the anti-Punjab vote; memories of his socialism brought the left-wingers; the revolt against the feudals swept in the rest because the biggest shots were with the government. The government alliance won no seats in Sind.

After the election, the game started again with an original twist. Punjab's provincial government, run by Benazir's opponent, Nawaz Sharif, decided that the province was an oppressed majority. Rumours circulated that Sindhis were burning the houses of Punjabi settlers in Sind. Politicians made rousing speeches warning that the Sindhi prime minister, Benazir, and the Pathan president, Ghulam Ishaq Khan, would drain their province of money. The Kalabagh dam, that centrepiece of provincial rows, reared its contentious head.

There wasn't any evidence that the new central government was likely to oppress the Punjabis; the opposition provincial government was just scared of being ousted. Inciting a little Punjabi chauvinism was a handy way of dissuading Benazir from asserting herself in the province. Having set her up as a Sindhi chauvinist, the provincial opposition politicians could then advertise any action of hers against them as an attack on the Punjabi people; and the Punjabis could be brought protesting on to Lahore's streets.

Us-against-them politics is easy, common stuff. It isn't peculiar to Pakistan: in the second half of the eighties it seemed to burst out all over the world. Westerners acquired a whole new vocabulary of mysterious minorities and provinces in Eastern Europe and Russia whose resentments against their neighbours or their governments burst out on to the streets. But for countries, governments and

213

people it is a wearisome and destructive sort of politics. Once regions, races or religions turn against each other governments forget about the everyday business of running a country: they have to worry instead about stopping people from killing each other and about preventing the nation from coming apart at the seams. In a country that was born by splitting India, and which twenty-four years divided once more, such fears are more than fantasy.

9

RELIGIOUS LEADERS

A LITTLE RELIGIOUS tourism illustrates the country's divisions: the philosophical and cultural arguments are all there in the buildings.

The Badshahi mosque in Lahore asserts the might of the one God, though the austerity of its vast red-stone courtyard and three white marble onion-shaped domes is softened by the delicate flower-inlay of white marble in red stone, red stone in white marble. The minarets are lotus-flowers, their petals opening to reveal the priest calling the faithful to prayer.

In the eye-wrinkling glare of noon, taking your shoes off at the door, you hop on the heat of the red flagstones. The white marble glitters with light. In the evening, the domes turn to white silk against dark blue, and the first star comes up, with absurd perfection, just between the left-hand dome and the minaret. There are always families there: city women in black, country women in peasant colours, children dragging the women back while the men stride ahead; families sitting round the white marble fountain in the centre of the red stone, enjoying the sudden, localised cooling of the air; families sitting on the grass in the little park at the bottom of the mosque steps, getting their chapattis out of their tiffin-boxes. They temper the mosque's intimidating formality with homeliness.

At the other end of the spectrum there is village Islam, an intimate, cheerful religion that thrives on the miracles of a local saint, not on the fearful omnipotence of God. I found it on an island in the Sindhi town of Sukkur, in the middle of the Indus. Except for the green triangular flag flying on the end of an unstable flagpole and streams of people entering and leaving, I wouldn't have known the shrine was there: it was hidden, on the edge of the river, in a grove of dark green trees. By the entrance were drummers, and a man dancing himself into a trance, stretching his thin stomach as he writhed over backwards, and rolling his eyes in a stage caricature of a madman. The families eating their rice lunches, and drinking out of great brass jars with brass mugs attached to them with chains, took no notice of him, but the women came close to me, offered me water and rice and giggled at me with sisterly solidarity.

The shrine was just a square building, the front wall built higher and wider than the others, curling into arches and points at the top and painted in blocks and stripes of green, red and yellow – pop art, or the exuberant drawing of a child with new crayons. Through the trees, where the branches grew low, was what seemed to be the holiest bit of the shrine, a red-painted cage of wood and wire-netting, that I was not supposed to go near. I couldn't work out the source of its holiness, but I could see a vase of marigolds in it. All around, under the trees and out in the light, were neat-edged paths and flowerbeds full of sunflowers.

The Lahore mosque was built by Aurangzeb, the last of the great Moghul emperors and a purist – or, some would say, bigot – in his religious views. While his predecessors had pictures painted of them surrounded by finery and nobles, his favourite pose was reading the Koran. He wanted to cleanse subcontinental Islam of the eclecticism encouraged by the emperor Akbar, and to conquer and convert the surrounding infidels.

The shrine in Sukkur was the shrine of a Sufi saint, and a neat little illustration of Pakistani Islam's failure to fit into the strait-jacket that Aurangzeb and his ideological descendants have prepared. The Sufi influence is the most important – and attractive – deviation in Pakistani Islam. The worship of saints seems odd in a religion which emphasises the direct connection between God and man, and denies the need for intercession. Like so much else in Pakistan, it goes with the hierarchical tribal society that existed before the country was created: the pirs, living and dead, were important people who would provide you with sifarish to God, as your landlord would provide you with sifarish to a minister. The Islamic ideal of a direct relationship with God – which corresponds, politically, to the belief that everybody should have access to and equal treatment from the government – was foreign.

The Sufis are central to Pakistan's literary tradition. Shah Abdul Latif, the Sindhi saint and poet, is probably the best-known of the country's poets, and certainly the best-loved. His memory and his writings are treated with religious reverence, and Bhutto, maybe because he appreciated the poetry, or maybe because he thought it politically useful to link himself to a Sindhi saint, used to quote him at length.

Pakistani Islam is polluted, or softened, depending on how you look at it, both by Sufism and by Hinduism. Even Aurangzeb was, no doubt unconsciously, tainted: lotus flowers on the minarets of that austere mosque in Lahore are a central symbol in Hindu art and mythology. Muslim ceremonies in bits of Pakistan, particularly Punjab, incorporate bits of Hinduism. Astrology, which has no place in Islam, is widely used in Pakistan: most of the people I have met regularly or occasionally consult astrologers.

The ancient richness of the Pakistani religious pudding was alien to a man like Zia. He came from a tradition of religious reformers and not from the class, as Bhutto did, that benefited from a hierarchical religion in which those at the top put those at the bottom in touch with God. Zia's sort sees such superstition as degenerate – as the 'jahaliya', moral chaos, that held sway in Arabia before the prophet came to sweep it away. Akbar Ahmed, the civil servant and academic, compares Zia to Aurangzeb; and certainly, the two leaders shared a conception of the importance of cleansing the faith and the people, as well as a certainty of their own righteousness.

It is as impossible to generalise about Pakistanis' attitudes to Islam as it is about Americans' attitudes to Christianity. There are people for whom Islam is the only solution to the political, economic and social problems of the country, who believe that Pakistan will never realise its full potential until the Nizam-i-Mustapha, the rule of the prophet, has been established. There are those for whom Islam is there, as the supreme good, in an undefined sort of way, who do not have much time for theological argument or legal systems, but would happily lynch anybody who spoke against the prophet. There are people who admit that they are Muslims just because they have been born to it, and who tell me that, whether I like it or not, I am therefore a Christian. There are atheists who do not believe there is sufficient evidence for the existence of God, and there are atheists who believe that religion is got up to preserve privilege; but neither lot would be likely to announce it publicly.

I can substantiate these generalisations only through bits of conversations I have had – the Army officer who said that of course he was a Muslim, but people's private behaviour was their own affair; the general who told me that naturally he would be a Christian if he were born in Britain – but would I please not quote him; the taxi-driver who said Islam? That's for the old men – Islam doesn't fill your belly; the doctor who said that Pakistan would never be a good country until it was cleansed of the filth of western influences and an Islamic regime came to power; the bazaari in Lahore who, when I asked him what Islam meant to him, looked at me in extreme puzzlement and said well, he was a Muslim, wasn't he?

It varies much throughout the country: the cities seem to have more fundamentalists than the countryside, and the north is certainly more religious than the south. Go out into Saddar Bazaar in Peshawar on a Friday afternoon, and the pavements are blocked with rush mats spilling out into the streets, with shopkeepers and customers saying their prayers. The mosque at the crossroads has a canopy in front of it, covering half the street, and under it 400 men sit, pray, signal to their friends and converse, while the invisible mullah's sermon blasts out of a loudspeaker. Yet in small towns and villages in Sind, Friday hardly seems to make a difference. A few shops are closed and there are slightly fewer people on the streets, but life does not seem to be disrupted by religious observance.

These days Islam has a power of veto. Thus, if something is publicly said to be unIslamic, it can be approved only if it can be shown to be in fact Islamic, or if the critic can be proved to be a bad Muslim. I suppose the word has the same function as unAmerican did in the days when people took such things seriously. Similarly, Islam can legitimise. If something is publicly said to be Islamic, it has to be shown to be unIslamic before it can be attacked. Thus, General Zia's Islamic laws were criticised not so much for being bad or unjust as for not being truly Islamic, and thus bringing the faith into disrepute. A lot of Pakistani newspapers carry strange columns by Muslim scholars, amid their editorial attacks on government policy, which look to me like insurance: once they have established their Islamic credentials, they can afford to take risks.

Some of this would be true in most Muslim countries today, but there are differences between the political pulling power of Islam in Pakistan and in the neighbouring theocracy, Iran. In some ways, the legitimising power of Islam is stronger in Pakistan, because there is nothing else to appeal to. Iran offers a glorious and powerful pre-Islamic past, embodied in Persepolis: being a Persian, a descendant of those who built a great empire, is a grand thing in itself. But Pakistan, carved arbitrarily out of the map forty years ago, has no ancient unifying glory to recall. Different bits of the country have different pasts: there is the Buddhism of the north, or, politically fashionable these days, the pre-Islamic past in Sind, a kingdom ruled by its own (Hindu) dynasty which was wiped out by the Arab invasion, but nothing that offers a national appeal.

Pakistan, a largely Sunni country, does not have the religious hierarchy that directed Iran's revolution. Sunni Islam has the village mullahs or maulvis, who look after the mosque and call the faithful to prayer, and the learned ulema, who are supposed to know their Quran, hadiths and sunnah backwards, and can pass judgement on matters of faith and law; but it lacks the pyramid of authority – the hojatoleslams, the ayatollahs and grand ayatollahs – that the Shias share with the higher Christian churches. The mullahs and ulema do not have a monopoly of religious clout: Pakistan has a disorganised collection of sayyeds, who command respect because of their descent from the prophet, and pirs – born out of the strong Sufi influence in subcontinental Islam – who are, particularly in the countryside, central to people's faith. They, rather than the sayyeds or the mullahs, are the objects of local adoration.

Religious authority is further confused by the variations in the faith. Some ten per cent or thirty per cent of the population, depending on who you believe, are Shia, and there are significant differences between Shia and Sunni law. Then, within the Sunni branch of the faith there are four schools of law and a variety of schools of thought, which sometimes get into political parties. The nineteenth-century reformist Deobandi movement, a traditionalist school which produced the puritans of subcontinental Islam, has turned into the Jamaat-i-Ulema-i-Islam. Its strength is in the frontier, among the Pathans, and in Karachi among the mohajirs who come from Uttar Pradesh, where the school originated. The Jamaat-i-Ulema-i-Pakistan, on the other hand, are a more easy-going lot, whose beliefs incorporate the Sufi saints and shrines which more mainstream Muslims find heretical.

The best-organised and strongest party is the Jamaat-i-Islami, founded in 1941 by Maulana Maudoodi. He believed that the subcontinent's Muslims needed to be purified of western influences, and that any Islamic state should be ruled by those with the theological learning and authority to be able to interpret Islam.

Maudoodi and most Muslim fundamentalists were against the creation of Pakistan, because they believed Islam to be supra-national. '"Muslim nationalism",' wrote Maudoodi a decade before partition, 'is as contradictory a term as a "chaste prostitute".'

All these parties dislike each other as much as they dislike secularists. So although they have certain common hates, they do not have common loves, and there is, therefore, no one group to which any political leader wishing to ally himself with the religious lobby can appeal. That is a comfort to the liberals and the left and, I suspect, means that Pakistan could never have the sort of religious revolution that homogeneously Shia Iran has had. Yet all over the country there are people who are important because of their religious credentials, who are used by the politicians and the civil service and who in turn use those founts of power.

Bhutto was one of their common hates. Some argue that Bhutto's open show of contempt for the mullahs was his biggest mistake. He had on his side a few with religious credentials, including an important pir, the Makhdoom of Hala, who was there at Benazir's wedding, and was with Bhutto mostly because of an ancient rivalry between himself and Pir Pagara. But Bhutto managed to antagonise most of the powerful religious people in the land. They hated his socialism, and attacked his womanising and drinking. He admitted the drinking, in a speech in Lahore: he said he drank wine, not people's blood – which, he implied, the mullahs did.

Despite the typical piece of clever, flip bitchiness, Bhutto did not disregard the power of religion. In some ways, he tried to cover his religious flank. His policy, he stressed, was Islamic socialism and it was he who, in 1973, made Islam the state religion. In 1976, bidding for leadership of the Islamic world, he held a tamasha on a grand scale in Lahore – an Islamic Summit, attended by the heads of state of the Muslim world.

His attack on the Ahmadis was also, presumably, intended to win him popularity with religious orthodoxy. The Ahmadis, a small and vulnerable sect, believed that a nineteenth-century religious reformer, Mirza Ghulam Ahmad, was a prophet. They say they are Muslims; but since they do not accept the finality of the prophet Mohammed, orthodox Muslims do not allow their membership of the faith. Bhutto was no religious dogmatist, but declaring the Ahmadis non-Muslims, which he did in 1974, probably seemed a cheap way to gain favour with those who otherwise disapproved of him.

Yet Bhutto's policy and personal morals remained vulnerable. Ranged against him in the 1977 elections he had the Jamaat-i-Islami, the Jamaat-i-Ulema-i-Islam, and the Jamaat-i-Ulema-i-Pakistan, as well as a collection of secular parties. The principal platform of this Pakistan National Alliance was that he was anti-Islamic: they called, predictably, for the Nizam-i-Mustapha (Rule of the Prophet), though not many of them would now claim that they achieved it by overthrowing Bhutto. Even after winning his election, he still felt vulnerable to their criticisms and, three months before he was overthrown, banned gambling, closed the bars and changed the weekly holiday from Sunday to Friday. It didn't help. The crowds still came out on the streets, their numbers undoubtedly swelled by the organising power of the religious parties during this brief period of co-operation.

In 1979, General Zia announced that he was establishing the Nizam-i-Islam. That led to more national soul-searching than any policy initiative since the country's creation. Those who supported it claim that it was what Pakistan was created for: what is the sense in having an Islamic country without Islamic laws? Those who opposed it dredged the speeches of Jinnah and other founding fathers to prove that they never intended Pakistan to be an Islamic state – a country for Muslims, yes, but a country ruled by a secular government in which non-Muslims would live with full rights and no interference on religious grounds. It is easy enough to quote Jinnah supporting this point of view – at the first meeting of Pakistan's constituent assembly, on 11 August 1947, for instance:

'You are free; you are free to go to your temples, you are free to go to your mosques or to any other place of worship in this State of Pakistan . . . You may belong to any religion or caste or creed – that has nothing to do with the business of the State . . . We are starting in the days when there is no discrimination, no distinction between one community and another, no discrimination between one caste or creed and another . . .

'You will find in the course of time Hindus would cease to be Hindus and Muslims would cease to be Muslims, not in the religious sense, because that is the personal faith of each individual, but in the political sense as citizens of the State.'

All the proof that the secularist could want. But Stanley Wolpert, Jinnah's brilliant biographer, asks 'What was he talking about? Had the cyclone of events so disoriented him that he was arguing the opposition's brief?' This was the man who, a year before, said he could not negotiate with 'higgling banias [Hindu shopkeepers]'; who had watched over 'the phoenix-like rise and regeneration of Muslim India from the very ashes of its ruination'; who said that India was made up of two – religious – nations that could never live together.

I suspect that he was not disoriented, nor was he so ill that he knew not what he said. He was, after all, a whisky-drinking, ham-sandwich-eating Muslim, trained at Lincoln's Inn in the legal system of a country whose church had long since kept its nose out of state business. In India, however, the connections between religion and power, strong under the Moguls and the Sikhs, had been fostered, not ignored, by the British; and Jinnah judged that when the British had gone, the religious minority would suffer political and economic discrimination. But, when he had won his separate country, his passion to secure his co-religionists' future was replaced by a determination to see that the political precepts into which he had been educated should be implemented in his country. Bizarrely, he wanted Pakistan to be a secular country.

The issue still bothers the promoters of the Nizam-i-Islam: President Zia made speeches attacking those who questioned Jinnah's commitment to an Islamic polity, and his government engaged in writing such doubts out of the schoolbooks. A directive from the University Grants Commission in 1981 said that the purpose of Pakistan studies textbooks should be:

'To get students to know and appreciate the Ideology of Pakistan, and to popularise it with slogans. To guide students towards the ultimate goal of Pakistan – the creation of a completely Islamised State.' According to one textbook:

'The All-India Muslim League, and even the Quaid-i-Azam himself, said in the clearest possible terms that Pakistan would be an ideological state, the basis of whose laws would be the Quran and sunnah, and whose ultimate destiny would be to provide a society in which Muslims could individually and collectively live according to the laws of Islam.' That seems as misleading as to say that Jinnah was clearly and consistently secular.

Shariat (Islamic law) benches were established in the high courts to check that no law was 'repugnant to the injunctions of Islam'; they were later replaced with a federal Shariat court. Bits of an Islamic penal code were introduced: the punishment for theft of goods worth more than 4.457 grammes of gold became amputation of the right hand at the wrist for a first offence, and amputation of the left foot at the ankle for the second offence. For the import, manufacture, transport or sale of alcohol by a Muslim, the punishment is thirty lashes; for drinking alcohol, eighty lashes. The punishment for adultery and fornication – which does not discriminate between rape and willing sex – may be stoning to death, a hundred lashes, or less; but it is hard to be convicted, as there are supposed to be four male witnesses to the act. As I write, though, a young woman in Pakistan has been condemned to death by stoning: claiming that she was divorced from her elderly husband, she had remarried, but her divorce papers were judged to have been forged. Maybe, like the blind girl who was raped and found guilty of fornication because her pregnancy was prima facie evidence of her guilt, while her assailants went free, she will be let off on appeal. Nobody has yet been stoned to death, though plenty of women have been lashed or imprisoned: according to a study, of the 160 women in Multan jail in 1987, sixty had been condemned under the adultery laws. Almost all of their cases were similar to that of the girl who had remarried thinking she was divorced.

The law which angered the women's groups most – and Pakistan has an active Women's Action Forum as well as the Pakistan Women Lawyers Association – was that on evidence. In certain circumstances, the value of a woman's evidence was to be considered half that of a man's. Although the law applied to a limited number of financial matters, the women felt that the injustice of the principle was more important than the breadth of its application, and protested loudly against it.

In accordance with the Quran's ban on interest, Zia announced in 1984 that the financial system had to be Islamised. The foreign banks reeled – domestic ones having been nationalised – took some lessons on Islamic banking, and adjusted. The new system required some new names for different sorts of loans, and increased emphasis on investment banking. According to a banker I talked to, 'there was a dangerous body of bearded men who had to put their thumbprints on the final documents, but the ministry of finance and the central bank had no intention of letting this place fall apart.'

While Zia's parliament existed, between 1985 and 1988, the Islamisation programme slipped. It was alien to the people who made up the parliament: their sort of Islam was the traditional, rural Islam, of pirs and shrines and poems. Purist, political Islam of the sort that attracted Zia made them uncomfortable. Apart from denying their claims to be living saints, it also condemned the British school of political and legal thought that they had been brought up with. With Zia's encouragement, the handful of Jamaat-i-Islami members introduced the Shariat Bill, which would invalidate all existing and future laws judged to be in conflict with Shariat Law. The parliament debated, stalled and sent it back. After he sacked the parliament, Zia passed it by presidential order.

When Zia sacked the parliament and passed the bill by presidential order, there was loud protest. Women's groups, particularly, demonstrated around the country, and got beaten up by the police for their pains. The Shias were up in arms, since they would in future be governed by the Sunni Hanafi school of law. The newspapers complained, the ex-politicians muttered. What the Muslim in the street thought, nobody knows.

Islamising the country was the responsibility of a select few bodies – the Islamic Ideology Council, the Federal Shariat Court, the Islamic University among them. I had seen a little of the work of the Islamic University in some papers from a scientific conference it had held in conjunction with a Saudi Arabian university. A furious physicist showed them to me. One said the earth did not fall apart because God had fortunately planted the mountains in it as roots to hold it together. A man from the Pakistani Council for Scientific and Industrial Research had worked out an equation for calculating the value of national *munafaqat* (hypocrisy). 'The West' got a score of twenty-two on a scale from zero, the ideal, to 100; Spain and Portugal, for reasons not explained, did better, with fourteen points. No score was offered for Pakistan, but the author claimed that 'a number of countries have become very rich in recent times and their wealth has given rise to . . . a munafaqat value ranging over fourteen as obtained for traditional societies of Europe.' He couldn't, of course, have been talking about their Saudi friends.

I thought I should visit the university, which is charged not only with furthering Islam in higher education, but also with training lawyers in Islamic law and bankers and accountants in Islamic banking. It sits under Islamabad's blue hills, beside the King Faisal mosque. Around the wide airport-terminal corridors were Chinese, Afghans, Africans, and few Pakistanis.

Dr Afzal, the rector, had floppy white hair and very thick bifocal glasses. His office was an academic's room, with tables covered in books and papers, and bookshelves on every wall which he would spring to and look up and down distractedly.

I asked him about the scientific conference. He showed me a letter he had written to my physicist friend in response to an article. It started, 'I agree that the conference was an exercise in futility' but went on to argue that co-operation with fundamentalists was better than confrontation. Then why, I asked, was it held? He became uncertain. Some people wanted it, and it turned out that the Saudi Arabian university was accepting and rejecting the papers. He had no control over it.

His unorthodoxy became clearer when we talked about interest. The thinking on this, he said, was defective. The Islamic laws were written hundreds of years ago, and the prophet was talking about exploitation of one person by another, not the operations of banks.

'Now the idea is developing that it is possible to reinterpret.'

'Developing among whom?' I asked. Among the students, among the people, he said. Not that they talked about it publicly. And was this, I asked, what was taught in his Islamic banking classes? Sometimes, he said with a laugh.

As we talked, he sprang up and down to his bookshelves, pulling out volumes and ruffling through to find quotations or essays he had written on the importance of science in education. I felt quite at home: I had been taught at university by people who moved and thought like him. But he was not the ideologue I had hoped for. I asked how a liberal like him, while cherishing the importance of doubt, was in a job whose purpose was to make national life conform with the certainties of faith. It was a sort of accident, he said apologetically. He had been Zia's education minister, then chairman of the university grants commission, and when the Islamic University had opened, somebody had to run it – the old, decent argument that somebody else would do the job if he didn't.

Did most of the teachers agree with him? No, he said, he didn't think so. The Jamaat-i-Islami had a fairly strong hold in the university; but he thought that Jamaat was probably on the wane. Why, I asked.

'A religious party is supposed to propagate a religion. But these people are more interested in power. They get involved in violence to grab power, then this discredits them with the people.' That, I thought, was a hope, not a judgement, born of his dislike of the Jamaat's approach to learning.

'You can't Islamise knowledge. You either use it or leave it alone. The Jamaat criticises these children's books that say a field is so wide and so long, therefore its area is so much: they say the books

225

should talk about the area of mosques!' He sent me to see a more orthodox member of staff, an economist called Dr Fahim Khan.

Dr Fahim was the first man to explain Islamic economics to me satisfactorily. Western economics, he said, was a description of how the economic system worked. The system could be described from different points of view, such as Keynesian or monetarist, which led to different prescriptions; but it remained a description. This was the problem with Islamic economics. The system had been in practice in Muslim countries for 500 years after the death of the prophet, and a diluted version had continued for another three hundred years after that; but nobody knew enough about it now to describe it properly.

What they had from the religious texts, he said, were the precepts of Islamic economics, which made it wholly different to western economics. Thus, property is never wholly owned: it belongs to God, and is held in trust on earth, so its temporary owner must follow certain injunctions set down in the Koran. He mustn't waste it, and he must share it with those who do not have any. Then, as an employer, he must pay his workers a fair wage, and he must give them reasonably good working conditions.

And was it, I asked, the responsibility of the state to ensure that the property-owners followed these precepts? Should they be legislated? Could a poor man take a rich man to court because he had not given away enough of his wealth? Certainly not, said Dr Fahim; and the extent to which state interference was justified was not set out in the Quran. Individual states should determine that. The point was, though, that if you had a community of true Muslims, they would do these things of their own accord, so you would have a truly Islamic economic system.

That seemed easy enough: if you had a country made up of unselfish, philanthropic people, you would have an unselfish, philanthropic economy. I asked him about interest, and he replied with some irritation that people went on about interest because it was the only part of Islamic economics that the foreign banks were involved with. The principle was that, in the matter of making money, there should be equal uncertainty for both parties. With interest, there was no uncertainty for the party lending the money, only for the person borrowing it.

And had they abolished unequal uncertainty? He raised his eyes to heaven and sighed.

'I am a government servant,' he said. 'I cannot comment on these things.

And the Khas Certificates, the government bonds which guaranteed the public a fifteen per cent a year return? Were they not interest-bearing? Dr Fahim was losing patience with our interview. The religious scholars said this was against Islamic principles, he said sharply, but the government had produced a justification: since the government does good to the public, and it needed the money, a guaranteed rate was permissible. For a greater good, a lesser good might be sacrificed. I thought it might be interesting to push him further, since we seemed to have arrived at a point where the Pakistani government was a greater good than Islam; but he seemed too unhappy already, so I left.

Five years after General Zia said 'I am today formally announcing the introduction of the Islamic system in our country,' he held a referendum. In December 1984, the public was asked whether it approved of the government's Islamisation programme. The general announced that, if the public did, he would consider it an endorsement of himself, and stay in power for another five years. Anybody found boycotting the referendum would be banned from standing for election for seven years, and anybody encouraging a boycott was liable to be jailed for five years. The government said it received 97.7 per cent approvals, with a sixty-two percent ballot, though foreign embassies with their spies out at the time reckoned it was more like ten per cent.

It is still unclear to me why General Zia went in for this Islamisation campaign. The foreign press and, more quietly, the more independent bits of the local press, attacked him for cynically using Pakistanis' attachment to their religion for his personal political ends by latching on to the legitimising power of Islam. The other explanation is that the president was sincere: that General Zia genuinely felt that he had a unique opportunity to make Pakistan a better, more Islamic country, and that he stayed in power in order to introduce his reforms, rather than vice-versa. Perhaps both are true; maybe military dictators, like the rest of us, can kid themselves that they do out of conviction what expediency dictates.

Either way, Islamisation has not been a great success. It is hard to find anybody in Pakistan, in the secular parties or the religious parties, in buses or shops or on the street, who has anything good to say about the policies, if they know or care about them. But Zia was at least more assiduous and successful in cultivating particular religious parties and figures than was Bhutto.

Zia was close to the Jamaat-i-Islami in his early years in power.

They, he thought, could be relied upon to support his Islamisation effort: the Jamaat had the ability to organise, they were implacable enemies of the PPP and, following Maudoodi's writings, they believed that elections were not necessarily a good thing in themselves – a point of view which might appeal to a military dictator. The Jamaat also had an alliance with the more fundamentalist Afghan resistance parties that had set up shop in Pakistan, and that connection could help both with intelligence and with policing the frontier, since they were well-armed.

The Jamaat does not have a large, amorphous group of supporters, the way political parties tend to. It has around 5,500 members and (it says) a million associates. To be a member, you have to attend weekly meetings and be prepared to give the Jamaat priority over your job and your family, if it should need your services. Few, therefore, are prepared to go as far as being members.

Organising protests is the Jamaat's strength. If a newspaper publishes a piece the Jamaat does not like, it may well find crowds of Jamaatis outside – or even inside – its offices. The *Frontier Post* reproduced Cranach's Adam and Eve in its arts section. Its offices were sacked, machinery was broken up, typewriters thrown out, not so much because the picture displayed nudity as because Adam, being a prophet, should not have been represented at all.

The Jamaat seems to have a lot of money, from the number of hospitals and colleges it has around the country, from the size of its Mansoorah complex in Lahore and the new centre I saw going up outside Peshawar. According to people in universities around the country, it uses some of its funds to help students pay fees and living expenses, which has given it a strong footing in student politics. That is important, since students have traditionally been at the forefront of anti-government protests. The Jamaat has also used its organisational abilities to effect in the trade unions, and has its own union of unions, the National Labour Federation.

Its special strength is its closeness to the Afghan refugees and guerrilla parties. It has an ideological alliance with the fundamentalist Hezb-i-Islami party of Gulbuddin Heckmatyar, which has been favoured by both the Pakistani and American governments. But the Jamaat has been working with all the parties, and in most of the refugee camps, as well as setting up its own hospitals for injured Afghans around the country. This has earned it not only the support of a well-armed group of fighters – according to a professor at Peshawar University I talked to, mujaheddin had been seen fighting alongside Jamaat students in a campus battle – but also greater hostility from Pakistanis who see the presence of the mujaheddin as evidence of Pakistan's subjugation to American foreign policy and the Jamaat as America's agents.

The Jamaat, in other words, is a properly organised political party, unlike most of the other parties in Pakistan. Its main problem is that people do not vote for it much. In the 1988 election, it won three seats in the 237-member national assembly. The rise of the MQM in Karachi, and the Jamaat's consequent defeat in a previous stronghold, has been a blow; but it has never relied on electoral success for its political influence.

I made an appointment to meet local leaders in Peshawar and was summoned to a Jamaati hospital. Walking into a hall past bandaged Afghans staring in hostile disbelief, I found a young man with a stethoscope and a white coat sitting in front of a map of Afghanistan, with a superimposed red tribesman driving a bayonet into a cobra. He wasn't the man I wanted, but we talked. He had been educated in Peshawar, he said, but the system of medical training in Pakistan was very like that in Britain because they used British textbooks. I took it as a small piece of irony that the Jamaat, with its hatred of the corrupt West, had to employ doctors brought up on our textbooks.

Dr Shabir Ahmed, the Peshawar leader of the Jamaat arrived, his face topped and tailed with greying hair. He shook hands with gloomy reluctance, sat down, had a small conversation with the doctor, and picked up a newspaper. After a couple of minutes I wondered if I should start our interview, but decided it was up to him; after five minutes, I thought he must be the wrong man. When Dr Iftikhar arrived and led the two of us up to a room littered with trays of medical equipment, I realised that Dr Shabir was the right man, but didn't want to talk to me. Dr Parvez came in through a back door, and we were quorate.

Dr Shabir said nothing and fiddled with a scalpel, while Dr Iftikhar took charge of things. He was small and restless, with bright eyes, skin paler than mine, and a flirtatious smile. His black hair was oiled down from a straight central white parting, and his neat beard curled and shone. He knew how to manage me, when Dr Parvez let him. Dr Parvez, who also worked in the hospital, had a long, curly moustacheless brown beard, thick lips and a wandering right eye. The eye was half-obscured by tinted glasses; but when he wanted to make a point, he poked his finger towards me and peered over the edge of glasses, unmasking his deformity. He spoke in a monotone, and drew breath not at the full stop or comma in a sentence, but at some unexpected conjunction of words. This made him hard to interrupt.

Dr Iftikhar explained to me the principle of the Jamaat: that, as Sayyed Maudoodi had said, Islam was concerned not just with personal life, but with all aspects of national life – cultural, educational, political. Members of the Jamaat believed that they should teach Pakistanis to live their lives in conformity with the laws and rules set down by the holy prophet (peace be upon him). And, said Dr Parvez, peering over his glasses, the Jamaat wanted to eradicate the corrupting influence of the West from Pakistan. The West had brought guns, heroin, alcohol, dacoity; thanks to the West, women walked immodestly in the streets. There were films and videos which taught people immorality. Even smoking was cleaner in pre-colonial days, when people used only the hookah which passed the smoke through water . . . Dr Parvez was into his stride. After a couple of attempts, I managed an interruption: didn't he think that Muslim society had faults? Wasn't he blaming too much on the West? Dr Iftikhar, playing with a paperweight on his desk, took over easily: of course, he said, the Pakistanis were also to blame. There were many good things to be learnt from the West, like punctuality (and he gave a bright little smile). Pakistan's ruling classes were to blame for adopting the bad things and not the good.

But that turned Dr Parvez on to another favourite subject; and he gave his lecture on the ruling classes. So we went on: as Dr Iftikhar would try to answer a question, Dr Parvez would take over with his tactless dogmatism. Dr Iftikhar gave up, and leant back in his seat, staring at the ceiling and pressing the bridge of his nose between thumb and forefinger. Dr Shabir cracked his knuckles.

I asked Dr Parvez about the attack on the *Frontier Post* office. 'That was a great thing,' he said. 'They deserved everything they got.'

'So you agree with the use of violence for political ends?' I asked, delighted. Dr Iftikhar leant forward and rested his elbows on his desk, hand across his eyes. 'That,' he said deliberately, 'was just some group of students. We have no control over them.'

Surely, I said, their failures in elections suggested that Pakistanis did not agree with them. Dr Iftikhar got an answer in when Dr

Parvez had only just started opening his mouth. Not so, he said, with a smile of sympathy at my ignorance. The number of members of parliament they had did not reflect their actual strength. Pakistan's elections were rigged by the ruling classes.

What did they think they had achieved in Pakistan? Well, said Dr Ifitkhar, with a modest smile, they had changed the way people spoke: people were now forced to speak in Islamic terms.

'Even the ruling classes, who do not believe in these things, they have to speak in our terms. Even Benazir Bhutto . . . I don't know about her personal life . . . she has to speak in this way.' He was right, of course: the compulsory vocabulary of Islam pervades all newspapers and political speeches. It was one of the things that I first hated about the country, because I knew half the people using those words didn't believe them; and I was horrified that an intelligent member of a powerful party should think that its success in forcing hypocrisy on the country was its greatest achievement. Either, to him, form was more important than content, or he was interested not in the nature of the Jamaat's achievement but in its ability to exercise power of any sort over the hated ruling classes.

As I left, Dr Parvez gave me a booklet advertising the hospital. It was a collection of pictures of the stumps left where limbs had been blown off, burnt-out faces before and after skin-grafts and children with tubes in every orifice. The pictures were captioned with quotations from Burns, Wordsworth, Longfellow and Shelley. 'I thought you were against western things,' I said to Dr Iftikhar, pointing to the quotations. He laughed.

'That is literature. You know people here like the poems of Shakespeare so much that they say he must have been a Muslim called Sheikh Zabir.'

After a four-year honeymoon, the Jamaat slowly fell out of government favour. Maybe it became clear to the general that a party without much support, however good its organisation, wasn't much use to him. More important, the party's failure in the 1985 elections – all the Jamaat leaders who stood lost – excluded it from a government formed under a prime minister from an opposite social and economic camp.

Hardly anybody had heard of Mohammed Khan Junejo when he was appointed prime minister. A little investigation showed that he was a Sindhi landowner who had been a minister of Zia's, and, most important, he was the nominee of Pir Pagara, reputed to be the most important behind-the-scenes politician in the country as well as one of its richest landowners.

Why, I wanted to know, was Pir Pagara so important? It was hard to get a satisfactory answer. People spoke of the Hurs, armed followers of the Pir's family, who would kill anybody for him, and die themselves, if necessary. How many of them were there? Nobody was sure. Maybe two or three thousand. But how could the devotion of two or three thousand people make somebody so important, unless anarchy reigned in the country? Well, they said, it wasn't just those people. The pir had followers all over, not just in Sind but in southern Punjab as well. If he blessed anybody with his nomination, that man would have the support of so many. Yes, but there were lots of other pirs in Sind – why was he so much more important than the rest? He was a bigger pir.

A friend gave me a book which, he said, would help explain the phenomenon. Called *The Terrorist*, it was the story of a Hur, Sainrakhio, 'translated and edited by H.T. Lambrick', an officer in Sind during the Hur rebellion in the 1940s. Lambrick said that he pieced the book together from various sources, including a manuscript supposedly written by the man who had the cell next to Sainrakhio's in jail. It's gripping reading: a boy's own adventure of hiding in ditches and crawling over sand-dunes to shoot policemen and soldiers, riding camels across deserts disguised as women, tracking and being tracked through forests, with occasional disparaging references to the new British officer, known as Limerick, whom the Hurs are evading.

The Hurs sacrifice all other pleasures and duties to their unwavering devotion to the Pir, illustrated by his first visit to Sainrakhio's village:

'I well remember the anxiety of my parents to produce an acceptable offering for Pir Saheb – the money was raised by selling the best of our few cattle. I was only a small boy, but soon partook of the feeling of restless expectation that was like a fever in the village. Every day news arrived how our Lord had advanced a further stage, and how each of the hosts, landowner-disciples to whom he had granted the honour of making the arrangements for his camps, had acquitted himself . . .

'I had never seen such a crowd as was assembled there and was astonished by the size of the camp. It was surrounded by canvas screens and within were numbers of tents and fine brushwood shelters specially built for the occasion . . . First we came to a bedstead covered by fine cloths; on this our offerings were to be placed. As we approached I could hear the tinkle and clash of metal. The women were stripping off their bracelets and other ornaments; there was a heap of them on the bed when our turn came. My father cast down fifty rupees which he had brought in a bag; my mother added her bracelets of chased silver, allowing the baby to touch one first . . .

'The disciples pressed forward to touch Pir Saheb's feet and ask his blessing, and as we drew near those behind escaping from control pushed on so hard that we thronged him, and the canopy-holders were almost swept off their feet. Pir Saheb began to shout curses on those who inconvenienced him, and to kick at the foremost, and order his men to beat them with shoes . . . My father tried to back away against the crowd that surged forward, but what could one man do? At least he and I did touch our Lord's feet, though not as reverently as we intended; my mother too held my little sister for him to bless, but was knocked forward on to her knees and so let fall the baby across Pir Saheb's feet as he struggled to free himself from the throng. So we were satisfied, and returned home with joy in our hearts.'

Pir Saheb announces that he is destined to be ruler of Sind, so Sainrakhio pledges himself to be a Ghazi, a fighting Hur, to help his Lord beat his enemies and rivals. During the swearing-in, the pir reads the funeral prayers over the young men. Sainrakhio is thrilled. From then, until his capture, he does no work except fighting: the Ghazis have all their needs provided for by the faithful in the villages. So Sainrakhio has meat, milk, honey and mistresses in villages all over Sind.

Politics and the outside world appear in the narrative, but have little effect on Sainrakhio. Pir Saheb tells the Hurs that the British are about to be defeated by the Germans and Japanese, and they are heartened. Allah Bakhsh Soomro, chief minister of Sind (great uncle of Illahi Bakhsh) is assassinated by Hurs for having shown disrespect to the Pir. The Army drops bombs and paratroopers in the desert, and slowly begins to gain ground against the Hurs, building up an intelligence network and winning defectors. There is a rumour – true, but Sanrakhio and his friends think it has been put about to confound them – that the pir has been put to death by the British. Sainrakhio will not give up: he wants to fight or die for his pir. During his band's last stand, his comrades make him escape with some vital information, and he cries in his disappointment at not being allowed to die with them. The shame of running away, he says, is the motivation for asking his cell-mate to write down his story. He wants to clear his name.

The Hurs eventually accepted that their Pir was dead, and his son, the present Pir, succeeded him when the Pakistani government welcomed him back from exile in 1952. His father's martyrdom swelled his popularity; and he turned out to be an astute politician. He likes horse-racing, ice cream and computers, on which he plays astrology and political strategy. He issues curious prophetic statements, in which he refers to killing as 'family planning'.

He got Bhutto's career started, employing the young man as a legal adviser and persuading Iskander Mirza to include him in a delegation to the United Nations. But they fell out when Bhutto rose too high, and became rivals. When Bhutto came to power, according to the Pir, he telephoned his erstwhile patron and said 'I will now deal with you.' The Pir was charged with subversion and treason, and his associates were imprisoned. He lay low, and kept the Hurs from attacking PPP people and thus antagonising Bhutto.

Revenge came soon enough. The Pir was one of the central figures in the PNA movement to overthrow Bhutto, and when Bhutto was due to be executed and others were arguing for clemency, the Pir said 'to show mercy to the wolf amounts to tyrranising the sheep: the sooner riddance from it is secured the better.' Zia took the Pir up because of his battle with Bhutto and his power in Sind. The Pir, happy to use and be used, called himself 'the GHQ pir'. He, Zia and Junejo, were described as the Father, the Son and the Holy Ghost – though nobody was quite sure which was which.

Pirsahib is refreshingly frank about his lack of ideology. He described the Junejo government, which he brought into existence, as 'a shareholding company'. Yet religion drew a clear divide between himself and the president. Although they both relied on Islam for their legitimacy, they came from opposed traditions, and their necessary antagonism came out over the Shariat bill, the proposal that all the country's laws should be vetted by a court of Islamic judges. Pir Pagara attacked the bill more outspokenly than any of the politicians. When supporters tried to burn him in effigy, it rained.

I tried hard to meet him. I rang him: he said gruffly that he was busy. I decided he should be approached in the local manner, through local channels, so I asked six people for sifarish. All promised me they would succeed, and all failed. I called him again. 'I will not give you the trouble of coming to see me,' he said. Nobody could understand why he wouldn't see me, but I thought it was canny of him not to. He probably realised that a western journalist might be shocked or amused by the scale of wealth and power generated by superstition; and would be tempted to make fun of his sainthood.

It looked to me as though Pirsahib was more powerful than he or his father had ever been. Landlord politics had done it. When Bhutto and his friends were in power, Pirsahib was out, but he still ran his own political party; and when Bhutto and his friends were out, Pirsahib was the biggest traditional leader in Sind whom the government could look to. I wondered, though, how many of his followers' children, angered by the blind loyalty of their parents and by Pirsahib's alliance to a government of rich Punjabis, wanted an end to the Pir's spiritual dictatorship. Plenty, it seemed from the 1988 election result. To the country's astonishment, the Pir was defeated by a PPP nonentity who got a huge majority.

Many such discontents, I suspected, went to see an old air commodore I met. I was led to him by frequent mentions of the movement he belonged to, the Tabliq. A general told me it was the fastest-growing religious trend in the Army; a frontier politician I met had spent half the previous year working for it; an atheist friend of mine had met the air commodore, been to a Tabliq meeting with him, and was impressed by the man and the occasion.

I found the air commodore, Inam ul Haq, at the library in Lahore where he worked, a building of classical colonial splendour built for the Lawrence brothers who ran Punjab. Its white columns and pediment, faultlessly maintained, glowed in the sunlight in the broad green park on the edge of the Mall. A thin old man with a long white beard and a briefcase was leaving as I arrived, and the attendant said he was Inam ul Haq. I ran after him, explained, and he turned and walked slowly back to his office. He had been going to lunch, he said, but it didn't matter.

He had talked to writers from England before. V.S. Naipaul had called him an air commodore with sad eyes: Inam ul Haq repeated it as though it were an insult. He gave me a book to read, and sounded as though he didn't much want to talk to me – because, I assumed, he felt that writers of my sort had neither the sensitivity nor the will to understand. But he was a gentle and polite man, so when I pressed him he talked a little.

Tabliqis, he said, met in mosques all over the country, in little groups. They stayed there for a few days eating simple food, studying, discussing and praying; and they knocked on doors in the surrounding area asking people if they would like to come to a meeting. The aim was to make Muslims better Muslims and they did not approach non-Muslims. It was mostly a movement for self-purification: 'We Muslims drink, we mistreat our wives. We give a bad name to Islam.'

They did not want power of any sort. There was no organisation, no propaganda, they avoided the newspapers and he didn't know how many followers there were. Many left, then repented and returned. He smiled slightly: 'The path to Allah goes like this,' he said, drawing a zig-zag on his desk. 'Saints can become topsy-turvy, dacoits can become saints. It is very strange.'

I was disappointed: I had hoped – for journalistic purposes – that the Tabliq would be a rival to the Jamaat and the pirs, sweeping away those loyalties into a strong new political movement. Yet the air commodore's pervasive gentleness was captivating, and I was puzzled by an almost Hindu element I thought I could sense in the emphasis on retreat from the world and self-purification. I didn't dare say that, but asked him if there was an element of Sufism in the Tabliq. Yes, he said, in its concern with love and brotherhood; 'but some of the Sufis want the joy without the discipline'.

He had got there through literature, he said. First, he read people like Oscar Wilde, then had a phase of Dostoyevsky and Tolstoy; and it was his love of books that brought him to the Quran. 'It is very captivating.

'I was always a misfit. In the Air Force, I couldn't fly, so they put me in the library, and in charge of education and motivation.' I asked why he couldn't fly, and he stroked his beard. 'It was the days of the RAF, and they said this was a drag'. He left me with a book, happy under ceilings built palatially high by an empire with money to spare.

The air commodore was the secularist's dream. He would shun the Pir's enjoyment of political power endowed on him by hereditary sainthood. Not for him the Jamaat's insistence on the indivisibility of religion and state. He would not try to force anybody to bow to his creed, nor would he use the movement's spiritual clout to make or break governments.

The air commodore and his fast-growing movement were also an interesting symptom of disillusion. They were, in a way, like the trade unionist and his little party of left-wingers who had given up on organised politics, or Akhtar Hameed Khan in the slums of Karachi who had given up on government. The Tabliq was catering to a need which, presumably, meant a failure on the part of politicised Islam: a longing for spiritual fulfillment untainted by Shariat bills or Kalashnikov battles.

10

CIVIL SERVANTS

IT WAS A source of resentment to the information secretary of
Sind, who had to vet me before I could apply to the home secretary
to visit a politician in jail, that his son, working in the private sector,
earned more than he did. Having established that we had a mutual
friend, an Indian consultant to the United Nations, we were circling
conversationally around each other, like newly-met dogs. Did he
wish, I asked, that he was a businessman? No, he said, with a
half-amused look that laughed, I thought, more at himself than me.

'There is more job satisfaction in the public sector. In this country
you can do nothing without the government. You want to write a
book about Pakistan? You must have permission from the government. You want to visit some politician in jail? You must ask the
government.' Or, as a friend who was thinking of leaving the civil
service put it, 'The only thing that really worries me is the idea of
being on the wrong side of the fence.' I never got to see the jailed
politician.

Although I now know the principles of dealing with the civil
service in Pakistan, I am bad at applying them. I forget, each time,
and rush in through the official channels; then curse myself as,
after the first few cups of tea and courtesies, my application
blunders into a quicksand of mislaid communication between
ministries and unanswered telephone calls.

If you wish to visit the tribal areas, the bit of the north-west
frontier normally closed to foreigners, you are supposed to get
permission from the home secretary (a civil servant not, as in
Britain, a politician) of the NWFP. I wanted to visit the political
agent of Mohmand agency, who had been recommended to me, so
I telephoned the home secretary's secretary and made an
appointment.

Being a foreigner and a woman, I had an easier time than most getting into the Secretariat. Dense and angry as a swarm of bees, Pathans crowded round the tiny semi-circular holes through which officials slip pieces of paper permitting the holder to enter the compound. Foreigners can slice through those crowds; and anyway, there is usually a separate, uncrowded, hole for women. I got my paper and waved it at a policeman at the entrance to the secretariat, who split the crowd with his lathi, and I passed through the iron and barbed-wire gate that protected the civil servants from the public.

The home secretary's secretary looked at me as though surprised that I had kept the appointment. He offered me a cup of tea, and I refused. With an air of weary resignation at the rudeness of foreigners, he motioned a peon to take me through to the next office.

The home secretary and I shook hands, and I gave my polite explanation of the innocuous book I was writing. He asked what I wanted from him. Permission to go to visit the political agent in Mohamand agency, I replied. The deputy commissioner, who I had met before and liked, strolled in, welcomed me with friendly surprise, shook my hand in his large one and sat down on a tea-stained armchair.

'The political agent's quite a good scholar,' said the DC. 'But he got the date of the death of the Fakir of Ipi wrong. I checked *The Times* obituary.'

'I will ask him to come to Peshawar,' said the home secretary.

'That's not much good to me,' I answered rudely. 'I want to see what your country is like.'

'To go to Mohmand you must get permission from Islamabad.'

'Please,' I changed tone quickly, trying to make an ally of a provincial bureaucrat who might resent the power of central government. 'You know what Islamabad's like. I'll have left the country before they give me permission.'

'You must apply to the ministry of information, Islamabad,' he replied, unmoved, with an expression that suggested he would like me to leave his office.

'Your predecessor but one gave me permission to go,' I lied. That was better.

'You know Jamshed Burki?'

'Of course,' I exaggerated. I had met him once, but knew that he was a professional high-flyer with snob value, being from a good family and Imran Khan's cousin.

'Then you can ask him for permission. He is in Islamabad now.' Check.

'But not in the ministry of information.' Check. We stared at each other. The DC laughed.

'You're a very cautious man,' he told the home secretary with a smile designed to irritate, lighting a cigarette as though it were a stage prop. The home secretary glared at him and said all right, he would ask Islamabad himself. I should get in touch with him the next day.

I rang him the next day, and the day after that, and every day for ten days. Usually he was in a meeting. Sometimes, he was 'out of station', an elegant evasion which smells to me of saddlebags and horses sweating through jungles. I could, I knew, turn up at his office unannounced, and annoy him until he gave me permission. Instead, I did what I should have done in the first place.

I went to see the deputy commissioner, waiting first in his secretary's office among the crowd of women with snotty-nosed babies and men slapping their forms emphatically on the man's desk to prove the importance of their visit. He regarded them with compassionate weariness, as though their troubles were so small and sad that his conscience forced him to take a philanthropic interest; but none of them got past him into the DC's office. Seeing me, he lifted his ancient black telephone, and I was admitted at once.

The DC, in the middle of a telephone conversation, motioned me to sit down. It was tantalising to overhear: the Swiss embassy, two people, six kilos, jail. I gave up trying to piece it together, and studied the dark-wood board above the DC's head with previous incumbents' names painted in gold Times Roman. He had had illustrious predecessors: Col. John Nicholson 1857, a soldier-administrator who inspired fear, devotion, and a religious sect called the Nikal-Seyni Fakirs, Mr O.K. Caroe C.I.E. 1930–2, later governor of the NWFP, and scholar of the Pathans, Iskander Mirza 1940–45, later president of Pakistan. The more recent ones hadn't lasted as long.

The DC put the phone down and swung round towards me. He was a youngish man with greying hair, a big Pathan nose, a twirled moustache, and the easy confidence of movement common among the Pathans, who know themselves to be better than other people. I asked about the telephone call. It was hashish, he said, picking up a pile of papers and beginning to sign them. Too many foreigners involved in this for his liking. Jailing foreigners was too compli-cated, with all the embassy business. One British fellow recently

240

had been caught with some heroin at the airport, and the DC had seen the poor fellow in jail. He was in bad shape.

'He was educated at Oxford, I found out. I have a weakness for Oxford, so I had a word with the magistrate, and we dealt with the law . . . very cleverly, I think. Nice man. He has an antique shop, and comes here to buy things with six or seven thousand pounds in his pocket.' I suggested that the man probably deserved jail. 'You haven't seen our jails. Putting you people in them is like passing a death sentence.'

A small, wrinkled Pathan in a dirty brown shalwar kamees entered and saluted energetically. Saying *as-salaam aleikum,* he reached over the desk towards the DC, who didn't appear to notice, took one of his cigarettes, and sat down. The DC asked me what I wanted, so I explained that I was finding some difficulty in getting permission to go to Mohmand agency. No problem, he said; but he would have to send me with an escort.

'These rules,' he said confidentially, 'are for your own protection. You can so easily get kidnapped in the tribal areas; and if I lose a British national, there's hell to pay.' So I went, the next day, with an escort which took me to Mohmand and left me with the political agent.

I won by applying a principle I knew quite well, but had ignored on my first application. The only way to get anything done is to apply not to the unknown man directly responsible, but to whoever among your contacts, or your contacts' contacts, is as near him as possible, either at the same rank or above, and preferably a personal friend of the man concerned. That person, with luck, should be able either to get the thing done himself, or to influence his colleague to hasten it.

A favour, once asked – particularly by a woman – is difficult to refuse. Civil Servants will happily hold up your business for months if they are required to do it merely because it is their job; but a personal request is hard to ignore, particularly if the applicant is a friend of the family, a co-tribesman, or an old school acquaintance. If the request follows a gift, or some hospitality, it has more force still. At most businessmen's parties I found a few crucial civil servants: the customs officer, the man whose job it is to allocate new building plots, the deputy superintendent of police. Business would not, of course, be discussed among the Black Label and the pastry and shrimp bouchées; but next time the businessman needs something from the policeman, the policeman will, if the trouble is not too serious, be obliged to help him out. In Punjab, the business of reciprocal favours is formalised enough to have a name: *vartan bhanji*.

Pakistani extravagance feeds, and is fed by, the favours system. The quality of the parties and the liquor matter: the more extravagant the dinner, the greater the host's justification for asking something in return. A Red Label party will not command so many favours as a Black Label party. Gifts have to be carefully chosen: the taste and cost of a series of presents will determine the civil servant's view of his relationship to the petitioner, and thus affect his sense of obligation to the giver.

A friend of mine visited a civil servant from whom she needed something. She discovered they came from the same village: her parents were the big landlords there, his family small ones. She (a pretty young woman – a relevant point) reminisced with him, as though they had grown up as childhood equals. She got her form stamped and, as insurance for the future, sent him a crate of mangoes from her parents' farm. Traditionally, feudals send each other boxes of fruit from their orchards, so to send mangoes to a petty landlord was to elevate him, by implication, to her family's status.

When I complained about the bureaucracy in Pakistan, people – particularly bureaucrats – tended to say that it was the fault of the British. They're partly right, though the Moguls, with their network of collectors, laid the foundations of the system. The British maintained and extended it. Their district officers – another name for the collectors – were the keystone of the administration, collected revenue, ran the police and were the chief magistrates of their districts.

It was important to the Raj that the judiciary should not be independent of government: unrepresentative rulers need to block challenges to their authority. But it seems odd that, once the foreigners left and the Pakistanis and Indians were ruling themselves, they should have adopted a system so open to abuse. Maybe they, like the colonial government, were more interested in executive strength than in impartial justice. They kept the district officers (by then called deputy commissioners) as their principal administrative and judicial tool. They also retained the élite guard, the Indian Civil Service, which in Pakistan became the Civil Service of Pakistan. In the colonial period, it was almost exclusively white; after the British left, it became a self-perpetuating club of the well-born established civil service families.

Although the commissioner is a grander man with a bigger house and a higher salary, the deputy commissioner is king of his district. For a journalist, the deputy commissioner's office is invaluable. Some DCs, if you turn up to see them, will chat about their area, the pros and cons of their job, and the interesting and alarming things going on. I once spent most of a day sitting in the DC Peshawar's office, as cups of tea and plates of biscuits arrived and disappeared and the clientele came and went.

The first arrival was a malik with a stiff grey beard, a pagri with a fine blue-and-white striped turban and a blue-and-gold patterned cap. He put his case, while the DC signed papers, then pulled his beard and watched with a sly, gap-toothed smile as the DC answered. He went out, and returned with four tribesmen in dirty shalwar kamees, as the DC explained that he was a powerful Afridi to whom the DC applied when he needed anything from that particular clan. He needed a favour from the DC: his tribesmen brought goods into town on lorries, and the police weren't letting them park in their usual place. Since the DC is, among other things, local head of police, the matter was sorted out with a telephone call. The DC smiled and got up to dismiss them. The malik grinned back, and the tribesmen wrung the DC's hand in unsmiling gratitude.

Next a huge man carrying his belly in front of him like a badge of status shuffled in and eased himself into the chair opposite the DC. He had dark glasses, a turban wound out of a scarf patterned with fruit and wore a v-shaped smile above a stiff, wavy beard that fanned out from his face like a peacock's tail. The DC rose and shook hands with him across the desk. Whether the deference was to his visitor's age, sanctity, or power, I did not know.

'This is our pope,' said the DC. 'You must talk to this man.' His visitor, he explained, was a leading maulana of the Jamaat-i-Ulema-i-Islam, respected by the masses and skilled at manipulating crowds. When there was some religious gathering that might turn nasty, say during the month of Muharram when the Shias were on the streets mourning for Ali and lashing themselves, the DC would ask the pope to preach last, and preach a sermon full of tolerance and jokes. In return? The DC helped him with his people's problems. He had come with ten small matters for the DC to sort out; but usually it was more.

I asked the pope whether there was more sectarian violence than there used to be. Yes, he said, thinking a little. Certainly. Why? Divide and rule, he said; we learnt it off you people. How did it work in practice? He rubbed his thumb against his fingers, grinning. 'They buy the mullahs,' he said, 'and the mullahs set people against each other.' The DC shook his head in irritation, muttering denials, and embraced the pope when he left.

A lanky man had arrived in the meantime, his shalwar kamees spotless, his hair slicked back in a manner that suggested larger horizons than Peshawar. He turned out to be an assembly member, who wanted to get a gun out of the police pound without the matter being recorded. The request was made with lengthy politeness, and the regretful refusal took longer still. The meeting broke up in warmest farewells. 'An old family enemy,' said the DC, pulling out another cigarette, 'From the same area as me. He's after my skin.'

'Aren't you worried?'

'I can make more trouble for him than he can for me,' he replied, laughing as though he had cracked a joke.

When I went to Lahore, I tried to do the same in the DC's office there. Even though I had made an appointment to see him, the men guarding his door stared at me suspiciously, and sent me round the back of the building to find a secretary who wasn't there. Reluctantly, they let me into a big office with a small man behind a large desk. He gave me tea and biscuits, watched me with wary eyes, and told me with great politeness that it would be better if I came back another day, since he was busy. Ever after, he was unavailable on the telephone. I shouldn't have been surprised: the DC Peshawar told me it would be so. The Pathan bureaucrats, he said, were the most accessible, because they ran their offices like the tribal jirgas they had been brought up with. The Punjabis used their powers to keep people out.

Since independence, the bureaucracy has mostly been run by mohajirs, who tended to be better-educated than those living in the land they migrated to, and by Punjabis, because of their numbers. That is one of the reasons for anti-government regional movements: people don't like being run by foreigners. In Sind, the frontier and Baluchistan, Punjabis are as foreign as mohajirs. It's like being run by a colonial power, people say to you, only this time the colonialists are brown.

It's more than anti-colonial resentment, though: it's resentment against anybody who has great power. The civil servants are seen — not by themselves, but by many others — as the bosses. They can, at will, make people's lives profitable or impossible, by issuing licences and permits, imprisoning people and fining them. They can collect money, spend it and steal it.

You hear the resentment from the man in the bazaar as much as from the intellectuals. The first will say that the bureaucrat is king; the second, meaning the same thing, that Pakistan has been run by a military-bureaucratic complex which has held power, occasionally allowing the politicians to play some superficial role, since the creation of the country.

There's something in this – more than there is in the countries where governments are run by politicians who are in power for a number of years, and get to know a bit about how to govern. In a country where ministers are usually either soldiers, who are generally uninterested in making budgets and setting cotton-prices, or they are in or out at the will of a soldier, the civil servants become particularly important. Pakistan's symbol of bureaucrat-rule is Ghulam Ishaq Khan, a severe old civil servant who was an assistant secretary under Ayub, a secretary under Yahya, secretary-general for defence under Bhutto, finance minister and then chairman of the senate under Zia. He has undoubtedly had a greater influence on the serious business of government – the collection and spending of money – than anyone else in Pakistan's history.

Ishaq's power was no secret, but, until Zia's death, it was background. That crisis forced him into the foreground: the constitution said that the chairman of the senate should replace the president in the event of absence or death, so Ishaq slid quietly and easily into the job. There was no showmanship or drama; and the absolute naturalness with which he conducted himself in his early days in office only confirmed the view that the bureaucrats are the real rulers.

Take the 1987 budget, which was withdrawn after the proposals for a new, hefty excise tax closed the country's shops and brought the shopkeepers on to the streets in protest. The finance minister, Mr Yasin Watoo, an old professional politician who was secretary-general of the PPP and switched to the Muslim League, was not known for his fiscal expertise. The budget, according to bureaucrats and ministers I talked to, was therefore put together by the governor of the central bank, the head of the planning division, the secretary of finance and Ghulam Ishaq Khan. One of the latter's enemies – of whom there are many, even in government – was bouncing with glee at the budgetary disaster. Just goes to show, he said, what happens when you leave policy-making in the hands of those who have no political feel.

Bhutto understood the political mileage to be made out of the public's dislike of the bureaucracy. His attacks on them make him sound like Mrs Thatcher:

'No institution in the country has so lowered the quality of our national life as what is called naukershahi [*nauker* = servant; *shahi* = rule]. It has created a class of brahmins or mandarins unrivalled in its snobbery and arrogance, insulated from the life of the people and incapable of identifying itself with them.'

He sacked 1,300 civil servants in 1972, thereby terrifying those who remained. In 1973 he abolished the Civil Service of Pakistan, automatically getting rid of the system by which the best jobs were reserved for this well-connected group, introduced 'lateral entry' of people from other walks of life into high-level jobs, and deprived the civil servants of the constitutional guarantees which had made them virtually unsackable. Some of those who were sacked were political enemies; some of the lateral entrants were political friends. 'Most fundamentally,' wrote Professor Charles Kennedy, an American academic, 'Bhutto's policies served to increase the politicisation of the bureaucracy.'

The reforms helped persuade the bureaucrats to do what the prime minister told them. Of course, collaboration between the bureaucracy and those affected by some of Bhutto's measures – land reform, for instance – ensured that they were not as effective as they might have been. But the threat of possible dismissal now hung over the civil servants' heads – and still does – to increase their enthusiasm for implementing the policies of the government in power.

At first Zia reckoned that the civil servants must be the puppets of Bhuttoism, as Bhutto had imagined they were the pawns of the military. A civil servant I know remembers that, 'Soon after taking over, he assembled the top-level bureaucrats in an auditorium. He said words to the effect that the civil servants were sabotaging his mission. It was so tough that even General Chisti [a ruthless soldier and prime mover in the coup] told him to go easy.' Zia's subsequent order that civil servants should wear shalwar kamees instead of trousers and shirts in the office was at once a petty irritation and a clear statement of his disapproval of their westernised life-styles and aspirations. He earned their gratitude, though, because he sacked hardly any; and Zia and the bureaucrats soon began to get along. As a soldier said to me, 'They are bureaucrats, and we are military bureaucrats. We have a lot in common.'

I went on a drive around a bazaar with a civil servant and after some minutes worked out what was odd about his driving: he stopped at traffic lights. He said he had got the habit during his education in London, and had never lost it. His suit was impeccable, the lawn which stretched away from the colonnaded verandah of his government-provided white colonial bungalow was neatly mown, and the tea-trolley was heavy with fruit-cake. There was something quietly sad about him, as though whatever was wrong was too big to be worth talking about.

The military government had not been too bad, he thought. You could argue with those people on the level. 'They spoke the same language', said his wife, smiling at the cake as she cut it. His experience of political governments was unhappy. During the campaign before the 1977 elections, some PPP people, along with a top civil servant, came to the division where he was commissioner, arranged a meeting with him and the deputy commissioners and said that it would be a good idea if the opposition candidates lost. He and the deputy commissioners conferred and decided they were not prepared to fix the result; since it was a few days till the election, it was too late to sack him. I asked if that sort of stuff had gone on during the 1985 election. Of course, he said; but not so much, because Zia's position was not at risk.

He was not happy with the results of electoral politics, though. One of his jobs was to monitor the politicians' spending of the four to five million rupees they each got for development in their constituency. The politicians would decide on a scheme, and the provincial government transfer the money for it to the district councils.

'At the moment there is no accountability. I've heard that these politicians appoint their own contractors. And I've heard that they get fixed commissions from the contractors, though I have no proof for this. Of course, substandard building is happening.' He said I should look at the highway north of Islamabad: built a few months before, and already subsiding. I did. He was right.

A commissioner I had met invited me to dinner, but I got no further than his office. His wife was ill, so his cook had sent food. A tall thin servant, who saluted and said Good Night as I arrived, brought in saucers with fish kebabs, and chicken sandwiches with tomato ketchup. The commissioner, a clever man whose despair was tinged with humour, said that the politicians weren't too hard to manage. 'They depend a lot on the civil servants. They have too much of clutter on their radar. We have to help them select the targets.' He was supercilious about the politicians, but not as infuriated as most civil servants I met. I suppose it was an ideological decision, for he was more worried than most about the ease with which the civil service adapted itself to martial law. 'When a decision is taken by a military regime, it's usually very sound from the civil servant's point of view and the martial law point of view. But the third party, the affected people, are not consulted. And,' he continued with a sort of tired anger, 'you think why the bloody hell can he give this order? Just because he has got a gun?'

Bhutto's government certainly increased the civil servants' insecurity, but it also expanded their power. Nationalisation naturally does that: suddenly textile mills, chemical plants, ginning mills and a host of unfamiliar businesses are in the civil servants' hands, and more civil servants are needed in the capital to liaise with the ones in the chemicals plants. At the same time, modernisation tends to increase the field of government's operations: with each new electricity or water connection, and every public sector school or health clinic, the civil service has more to do.

The Water and Power Development Authority started life in 1958 with a handful of employees. It now has around 130,000 and is using up some forty per cent of total development spending, and the management system is still the same as when it was first established. One of the team of consultants and foreigners who are trying to reform it said that they found, in the Wapda offices they moved into, a set of tyres. One of the employees, sufficiently senior to have a car, had got a new set of tyres on the company. But he was still responsible for the old tyres, which were in his name, so he had to take them wherever he went.

Wapda is a dirty word, not just among administrative reformers, but also to the public. The opportunities for making money are enormous. I was given figures of twenty-six per cent and thirty-five per cent for the amount of electricity that is lost between generation and transmission. Most of that, they say, disappears through the birds' nests of wires you see attached to the electricity poles in the cities, and the Wapda inspectors are paid not to notice. But those figures exclude the electricity that is lost through a clever system described to me by one of the reformers: a government agency is overcharged for electricity and complains, the meter is checked, the money reimbursed, but meanwhile the electricity, which goes down on Wapda's accounts as having been billed, is sold to somebody else. The reformer I talked to could think of no Wapda official who had been held accountable for the disappearance of electricity.

The areas which governments are particularly keen to control are riddled with regulations that give the civil service, or its masters, a stranglehold. Ayub's Press and Publications Act is a fat book which has done a lot to help governments control newspapers. In order to start a magazine, an applicant has to have his form cleared and stamped by, in turn, the city magistrate, the local police, the city magistrate, the provincial press information department, the chief minister's office, the provincial press information department, the federal press information department, the intelligence bureau, the federal press information department, the provincial press information department, the deputy commissioner and, once again for luck, the provincial press information department. Applying for a newspaper is more complicated.

The more regulations there are, the more money there is to be made. Prohibition has increased the financial benefits to the civil service, since the import of alcohol is now very big business. A civil servant friend recounted seeing a man at a party in a suit obviously worth many hundreds of dollars, with the fattest cigar he had seen, who drove off in a Mercedes. He was baffled to hear that the man worked in the meteorology department, until somebody explained: he was the man who put out gale warnings to the coastguards when a whisky ship was arriving.

Accountability may be limited; but civil servants keep their heads down in case they irritate those higher up. It is, people told me, increasingly difficult to get civil servants to take decisions because of their fear of retribution. According to a senior bureaucrat, this tendency is reinforced by the ministers, who want to draw decision-making powers towards them:

'The concessions to sell cigarettes on railway stations used to be granted at a very low level. Then the railway minister sent out written orders that, since there was corruption at lower levels, he would take the decision himself. Of course, he made a bomb.'

But if the politicians start taking on the civil servants' more lucrative jobs, the civil servants complain that they are becoming politicians. Sitting in the office of the DC, Peshawar, I heard him make a curious telephone call, cajoling somebody to come round to his house on the grounds that 'I just want to get rid of these goondas [thugs].' Putting the phone down, he turned to me.

'You asked me once what my job was. Too much of it, these days, is political. There is so much distance between the politicians and the people they are ruling, with this non-party system, that I have to fill the gap. Look at this university campus. There are goondas from all these parties that have no representation – the People's Student Federation [PPP], the IJT [Jamaat students' wing] the Pakhtoon Students' Federation. They all have guns and shoot each other. Now the politicians in power are all Muslim League: they have no hold on these people, so I have to go in, try to make some compromises, get some order. This fellow on the phone is the head of the Democratic Students' Federation. It's very left-wing, not so big, but very well-organised. So I ask him round in the evening to see if he can help me.'

The grouse of the civil servants – and the political opposition – is that the ministers and members of the assemblies not only expect the civil servants to do their dirty work, they also want them to win the elections for them. Governments – not just in Bhutto's time, and not just through the crude ballot-box-stealing methods – seem to use the civil servants in elections as though they were part of the party machine. There were plenty of stories of it during the local elections which were happening when I was in the country: deputy commissioners passing information about candidates to the government, the use of police and government vehicles for campaigning, the changing of constituency boundaries.

The most popular method of disarming the opposition is to disqualify its candidates. This can be done with little difficulty on, apparently, the thinnest of grounds. The decision is made by the commissioner. Nawab Akbar Bugti provided me with a sheaf of disqualifications signed by the commissioner of Sibi. I assumed that the Nawab was annoyed with the commissioner because the Nawab's son, who was a candidate, had been disqualified because he was under age.

Noorhan, son of Jani Khan Kirmanzai Bugti, appealed to the commissioner against his disqualification as a candidate by the Assistant Political Agent of Dera Bugti. But his political ambitions remained thwarted:

'The nomination papers of the appellant were rejected by Returning Officer on grounds of his being a problem for civil administration and supporter of Marri Farraris [fugitives] and also does not enjoy good reputation. Although the appellant denies of above allegation, but he could not produce any solid proof in support of his contention . . . Appeal rejected.' Similarly, Pir Muhammad, son of Lal Han Bugti, had his appeal against disqualification rejected on the ground that he was 'problem-creater for civil administration and that he instigated the labourers at Pirkoh Gas Field to create lawlessness. The appellant could not prove his innocence'; and Rindhan, son of Habib Sohbazai, lost his chance of politicial stardom 'on grounds of his being Notorious person and giving shelter to Marri Farraris'. Who needs to steal ballot-boxes?

This kind of election-fixing is cause and effect of the politicisation of the civil service that Professor Kennedy complained of. It isn't just American academics who worry: plenty of Pakistanis are concerned that the civil service should be used to crush legitimate opposition. It's unjust; it's against the rules; but, as people point out, the British started it. The reader may recall the commissioner of Lahore's casual report during the 1857 revolt: not much going on, he said, 'with the exception of the summary execution of a Meerut butcher who . . . made a very dubious and threatening speech to the Bazaar sergeant'. The difference, and the reason why the civil servants of the Raj are held up as administrative paragons, is that although they used their position to squash opponents of the government, they did not much discriminate between browns. In Pakistan, the civil service is also used to carry out powerful people's vendettas.

Politicisation of the civil service is a difficult spiral to get out of. One government turns the government machinery against its opponents; then when the opposition comes to power and has the tools in its hands, those who lived well under the first government will be made to suffer.

The civil servants, blamed for cowardly subservience to the informal pressures of politicians, argue that the politicians make the rules: if they discriminate in favour of their friends, the bureaucrats are powerless. Down at the Karachi Customs House, that most lucrative and important of bureaucratic postings – customs provide sixty-eight per cent of government revenue – the deputy collector of customs was complaining about legislating preferential treatment for successful lobbyists. His anger may have been pre-emptive. Journalists are mostly interested in customs in Pakistan mostly because the officials are reputed to make so much money.

He slapped on to his desk the Customs Tariff Book of the Central

Board of Revenue. Around fifty-two per cent of imports, he said, were exempt from duty, and another thirty per cent were on a concessionary rate of twenty per cent. Some of those were government imports – service uniforms, power equipment, and suchlike – which seemed reasonable. What he was incensed about, going through the book was, for instance, the order in 1979 that 'the federal government is pleased to exempt the joint chiefs of staff and chiefs of staff of the three services from the payment of duty on a car': the duty on a Mercedes, he said, was 500 per cent, which would come to around two million rupees. Then, 'the federal government is pleased to exempt from whole of customs duties and sales tax all articles of household and personal effects of the Ruler of any Gulf Sheikhdom who is in possession of residential accommodation in Pakistan'. Possibly the government was keen to encourage the hunting of the rare great bustard, for which pastime the sheikhs visit Pakistan. Less easily explained were the exemptions for individual companies – 'exemption on one hundred and eighty units of autoairconditioners imported annually by Bukhari Engineering Corporation' – which presumably argued some effective lobbying. There were 100 pages of exemptions in the book.

'I don't know who pays tax,' said the deputy collector, shutting it. 'Anybody who is anybody can get an exemption.'

Down at the docks, past the lumpy plastic and hessian sacks of vegetables being loaded on to wooden launches going to the Gulf, the pounds with rows of dusty cars in them, and the acres of piled containers that make ports look small and lifeless, was an assistant collector of customs in a small bare room. He had dyed black hair, and a gold ring with *Amir* (rich) engraved on it. There were three men with him.

'They are informers,' he said as they left and he called for tea.

'What do they inform on?'

'Misdeclarations. They are private people. Our people who are supposed to inform us do not. Private people are better, because we pay by results out of some secret funds.'

He must be an important man, I said: did a lot of people want to make friends with him? So many people! His hands flung wide, then he passed me eight unopened envelopes. 'These have come today only. You will find I know none of these people.' I opened them: they were all printed in gold on white or red, wedding invitations with receptions at the Karachi Development Authority officers' club and the Sind Club. I read the names on the ones printed in English to him: never heard of them, he said.

Customs are the main target for corruption jokes, but the police get blamed for everything. They are at the sharp end of the civil service, where the pressures concentrate. The police are the people politicians most often need – to put people in jail, or to get them out, to see that a charge is dropped, or that one is got up. It is the police who have to try to manage the result of the failure of politics – riots – and the police who either control or make money out of crime. The police have the most opportunity for taking the public's money in return for not enforcing the law. And, of course, it is the police who get blamed for the riots, the drugs, the victimisation, the corruption and most of the much-discussed ills of Pakistani society.

The press cuttings file gives some idea of how people see the police. January 14th, 1988: shopkeepers in Rohri went on strike because 'police in Rohri subdivision is reportedly providing shelter to anti-social elements, including some known dacoits, murderers'. January 19th: Sind's inspectors general of police called for serious action against the Eagle Squad paramilitaries who had allegedly deprived a factory owner of 5,000 rupees. January 21st: the traders of Harunabad went on strike against the 'alleged atrocities perpetrated by the local police on the students, businessmen, citizens, journalists, workers and advocates'. January 25th: the president of the Karachi truck-owners' association said that the Gadap police station was the most profitable in town: truck owners gave it 400,000–500,000 rupees a month.

If money gets stolen, it is not surprising. Constables' pay starts at around 700 rupees (twenty-three pounds) a month. A deputy superintendent (DSP) asked me whether policemen were well-paid in Britain. Yes, I said: better than teachers.

'Here they are paid like sweepers. I have some private means, but people who do not, they must indulge in some funny business.' Still, jobs in the police are in demand. The DSP said it was because 'People with my mentality – rural people, from small landlord families – we like to put on uniforms and have this authority.' But an assistant superintendent (ASP) who was giving me a lift to a Lahore police station where I had an appointment, had another theory:

'You see, this is a third world country. In your country, the professionals are the élite. Here, it is the nuisance value that counts. Police has a lot of nuisance value.'

For a policeman – but perhaps not for a Pakistani policeman – he was keen to talk politics. He cursed the new civilian government: 'We work better with martial law than with civilians.' As we spoke, his telephone rang, and I could hear a loud female voice squeaking out of the earpiece. The policeman listened silently, grimacing at me, said it was very difficult for him to do anything, and put the phone down. 'We are a bureaucracy, you see, and the Army is a bureaucracy. Now when we have the politicians–' and, on cue, the phone rang again. It was the same squeak. The policeman said sharply that he would check, and put the phone down quickly enough for her to take it as an insult.

'This woman is a councillor. She has rung up four times today. She wants me to release somebody who has been arrested. How can I do this? And today, three ministers have telephoned me with some request. This does not happen in your country, I think.' That sort of interference, I was told, was the reason why nobody would take the job of Inspector General of the Punjab police. It had been empty for months, but those in line for it were not willing to face the difficulty of reconciling the requirements of the politicians with the requirements of the job.

An ASP was sitting silently in the DSP's office, his elbows on the arms of the chair, his hands knit, staring at his knees. He didn't react when the DSP told me that he was 'a very beautiful officer'; and when he was told to show me round his beat, got up without looking at either of us. He drove through Lahore, glaring at the traffic as though it were responsible for his gloom. Suddenly he said.

'Our police force, you see, was created by British for strengthening government. In Britain police force was started as service to public. This is very big difference. Our police is force, not service. It is not interested in the public welfare.' The radio blurted out sharp phrases, and he spoke back at it.

'I think in England, if a baby is crying in the house, the police will come and help the mother. Here only they are interested in the lawnorder, not the crime.' I asked what the difference was. Crime, he said, was against the public. 'Lawnorder is like just now on radio they tell me that some students are in Regal Chowk making some protest. That is lawnorder.' That was clear enough: lawnorder was against the state.

He drove down backstreets and, by a stack of building materials, turned into a courtyard lit by streetlights with a tiny mosque in the middle surrounded by a square of small houses. It was, he said gloomily, where he had made a successful raid the week before against some heroin dealers. It wasn't his area, but some locals had come and complained that their police 'had not been dealing with this matter properly'. Two men came out of one of the houses and stared suspiciously at the Jeep, their faces green under the street-lights. The ASP shooed them away and drove off.

They told me there was a Britisher, Niblettsahib, in the police, so I rang him. L.S. Niblett had retired at the rank of deputy inspector general, but was still in charge of the control room. He lived in a police flat in a red-brick block opposite the Plaza Cinema with its forty-foot posters representing passion, evil and innocence in lurid colours. He was a sharp, perky little man, with a quiet Anglo-Indian wife in a floral 1950s dress; and the television with the children's photographs, the plastic water-filled dome on the mantlepiece with the Virgin Mary in it surrounded by pink plastic flowers, the Father Christmases among the fawns and ducks in the cabinet might have been suburban London thirty years ago.

He was born in Delhi, where his father was in the police. He didn't know why he had opted for Pakistan. Hardly anybody had, though he remembered two other old Britishers in the Pakistani police. When they had retired, the Nawab of Kalabagh had given them adjacent houses on the Indus, and they dressed for dinner every night – you know, said Mr Niblett, making a little bow-tie gesture under his chin. I asked him if he had been back to England since independence. He said no, indifferently; and I realised later he had probably never been.

'What men the Punjab police used to be!' People, he said, used to come from Calcutta to see them. They were bigger in those days and they never lost a street battle. Now the food was adulterated and milk watered down, so Punjabis were weedier; but the trouble had really started when they insisted on employing matriculates. These days they had all the equipment they could wish – full riot gear, Chinese semi-automatic guns. Compared to the British police, they were paramilitaries, really. But they hadn't the discipline to face a crowd any more.

'Of course,' he said with a certain pride, 'the British crowds have never thrown bricks like the crowds here. Sometimes the Mall is so covered in bricks that the police vans can't move.' The seventies was his favourite period: he remembered those street battles against the anti-government protesters with nostalgic relish. 'What

255

a time – every day we had action. There was always something happening.' But never, he said, had he obeyed an illegal order – when they were torturing people, or shooting suspects in cold blood. He'd never done that, and he was proud of it.

A young man bounded through the door from the stair, in a blue and orange track-suit, and demanded tea from his mother. He paced around the room as we talked, moving restlessly, picking things up and putting them down again, turning the television up and down. He was large, dark and colourful against the grey propriety of his father.

A phone call came from a businessman whose story Mr Niblett told with great amusement. He had been on a bus in Sind, and the police picked him up as a terrorist suspect. They beat him and his friend up for two weeks, until they were recognised by the magistrate and sent back to Punjab. It had cost the man 35,000 rupees in treatment at Nawaz Sharif's hospital.

The son was shifting on his chair. 'What about our land, Dad?' He appealed to his mother and myself. 'You know this man wants to give us a plot in Murree?' His father looked uncomfortable, as though he didn't want to have this argument again, particularly in front of a guest.

'Son, you know that here nobody ever gives you anything for free.' The son, whose temper seemed as unpredictable as his movements, sounded angry.

'Come on, Dad,' he nearly shouted. 'What can you do for him? You're retired now.' But the father stayed silent, and the son sulked.

Policing Lahore is a picnic compared to Karachi. That uncontrollable city is not only more criminal than any other in Pakistan, it also has by far the worst lawnorder problem. The ethnic riots that have been going on since 1985 have, at times, stretched the police to exhaustion. The opposition sometimes argues that the Army puts people up to it in order to destabilise the civilian government and bring about the reintroduction of martial law, or that the government started it all to set the city's political factions against each other, thus preventing them from uniting against the real enemy. Maybe the politicians are enjoying it, but the police are not. And at the same time, the dacoity of Sind stretches into urban banditry – commonplace crime and violence that had led the richer citizens to arm the chowkidars at their gates – and the drugs trade, local consumption as well as export, concentrates in Karachi.

256

I found a senior policeman on the verandah of this police station, looking for all the world like a nineteenth-century DC waiting to receive petitioners from the village, except that he was in one of the nastier areas of Karachi. He was a tall, languid man called Iqbal with a manner that would have done well in a Noël Coward play. As I sat down and lit a cigarette, he began a lazy discourse.

'Whatever the reputation of the police, we are not as fascist an organisation as . . .' and he paused with a smile, 'I would like. We are hampered at every step from implementing the law as it stands. There's a certain amount of third degree, I wouldn't deny that. But the general condition of our police stations is that anybody in custody immediately feels tortured.' He talked as though releasing anger, so I smoked some more and let him run.

'Every year, 250,000 people come into Karachi who are of no fixed abode. So land grabbers, strong arm men, drug pushers, arms dealers have a hell of a time. Respect for the law is dying. The whole machinery of justice is breaking down.' I was used to a general discontent among civil servants – and the Pakistani tendency to exaggerate – but this seemed interestingly extreme. I asked him how much ordinary crime had increased in the past five years. Twenty or thirty times over, he said. There weren't any figures, but that's what he'd guess. I gaped, and he smiled with half his mouth. 'It's so easy. The police are soft, the machinery of law enforcement is soft, and there are so many weapons.' At Benazir's wedding, he said, there had been 500–600 armed private citizens. When the crowds at the gate got too forceful, they shot into the air – and sometimes at the balconies. A woman had been killed and five people injured. 'There was no case, nobody arrested. That's the level of enforcement. Of course,' he said, as though the conclusion were self-evident, 'nobody wants a good police force. The feudals and the Army, which is the government, don't want one: then they might be subject to the law.'

A policeman carrying a pile of cardboard lunch boxes approached and, from a respectful distance, asked us if we would join him for a bite in his office. The lunch boxes and five policemen were arranged around the edge of a desk piled with papers; somebody found a saucer for our bits. Iqbal dipped a piece of warm fried fish into the green chutney provided in plastic packets and chewed at it, pulling long bones out of his mouth. 'Terrible food,' he said. The policeman who had provided it, a large man with a small moustache, looked up. 'Tolerable food,' said Iqbal, chewing. 'Everything all right?'

The big policeman shrugged. A bit of a problem at the Habib Plaza, the smartest new office complex in Karachi. A group of students had had a dispute with the bank and had threatened the staff. The management had persuaded five of the leaders to negotiate, but the DC turned up and had the rest arrested. The leaders said it wasn't fair, and came back with another three busloads of students. So, I asked half-joking, the place is under siege? You could say so, said the big policemen, and went back to his chicken tikka.

This man, said Iqbal, pointing at a muscular young policeman who grinned at being singled out, is a big bandit. His latest gag is to fix a machine gun to his motor bike. Seriously? I turned to the young man, hoping that he would tell me whether or not I was having my leg pulled. Only a light one, he said modestly. We wiped our hands on coloured tissues.

Iqbal had some work to do across town and I went with him in the police Jeep.

'Look at this street,' he said, as we edged forward in the traffic jam. 'Cars parked in the middle of the road. It screws up the traffic, but we don't do anything about it.'

'Why not?'

'It's not worth it. We'd get a call tomorrow from the employer, he'll say why are you harassing my driver, he'll accuse us of taking bribes from his competitor . . . Look at that policeman!' He pointed at a fat-bellied, grey-haired man gesticulating at the cars. 'There's a traffic jam, and what does he do? He blows his whistle.'

He pointed out the shining new brass lettering, with the Sind police insignia, outside the police station we were visiting. It was made out of used tear-gas shells, he said. The compound was half-colonial – squat whitewashed buildings with colonnades of arches making courtyards with thick old trees making sunshades over them – and half in the new subcontinental institutional style of yellow concrete boxes that stretches from Madras to Peshawar. The sky was turning pink: against it, above the black trees, wheeled a spiral of buzzards.

With some pride, Iqbal showed me the refectory. Its walls were chemical white; the lights were bright; men in their shalwar kamees sat at dark tables with their orange vegetable mush and rotis on metal plates. In the kitchen was a queue of men with their plates, a man with a tub of vegetable stew, and another in charge of the hole in the ground that was the bread-oven. I watched him slapping in the dough and taking out the cooked rotis spotted with browned air-bubbles. He gave me a suspicious look, then, realising that his art was appreciated, smiled and performed with an exaggerated flourish.

The police, complained Iqbal as we drove back, got the blame for everything. Take the riots: everybody said that the police had done nothing for so many hours during the massacre of mohajirs by Pathans after the bulldozing of the Pathans' drug-and-arms market at Sorabgoth. But what were they to do? There were a few hardly-armed policemen in the area, and hundreds of Pathans with Kalashnikovs storming down from their stronghold in the hills above Orangi. Were the police supposed to stand in their way? I couldn't answer, but casually mentioned a story I had read in that day's afternoon paper – an investigative piece, unusual in the Pakistani press – listing a number of heroin traders and their hang-outs which, the journalist said, the police knew about. Iqbal picked up matches one by one, and, breaking them, threw the bits angrily out of the window.

'Do you know how many cases there are against these people? This Malik Salim – there are fifty or sixty cases against him. Go and ask the courts why they don't convict him. These journalists are helping the dealers when they say police are corrupt. These men aren't angels, you know. You have to use certain strong-arm methods against them . . .' The non-sequiturs, produced I suppose by his anger, sounded like the policeman's permanent dilemma. He was blamed either for not catching the criminal, or for roughing up suspects.

But he was right, I thought, I should go and see the courts. For while the police are accused of violence and inaction, of personal corruption and of pandering to the vindictiveness of politicians, they cannot be the scapegoats of last resort. The police are the enforcers, not the guardians of the law; thus, when the state is allowed to misbehave, it is not their fault so much as that of the courts.

The legal profession in Pakistan is remarkable for the courage with which some of its practitioners have stood up against oppressive governments and the ease with which others have succumbed to them. Jinnah, after all, was a lawyer – one of the best the subcontinent has produced – and his cold analytic skill in negotiation was certainly partly responsible for the creation of the country. At times when the country has risen against the government, the lawyers' associations have usually been in the forefront of protests, high-court barristers being arrested and beaten in their black suits and white ties. More formally, the bar associations have often passed critical resolutions – in 1977, for instance, demanding that all lawyers removed from their posts for political reasons should be reinstated.

It surprises me how annoyed Pakistani governments have been by legal harassment. There is a residual respect for the law, even among those who break it: they would rather not be seen to be breaking it. So, when Fakr Imam, the Speaker of the National Assembly, suspected that the formation of the prime minister's Muslim League in the assembly was, according to one of the president's orders, illegal, and referred the matter to the election commissioner, there was a stink. Obviously the prime minister was in power, so he could do it; but he and those around him were concerned to do it legally, so the president passed a retroactive order which made it legal.

Thus even in a country that has mostly been run by generals, the opinion of the courts still matters. I think respect for the law goes back to the British days: although the Raj had few qualms about squashing, by legal or illegal means, challenges to its authority (lawnorder), in civil cases people usually got quick, fair trials. That has left a residue of faith in the legal system which compounds the disappointment when justice is not done.

I went along to the Lahore High Court to find out about some of the laws which successive governments had passed to make the job of controlling their opponents easier. The court, in imperial-Mogul red stone, dominates the Mall. In the front are lawns and hedges, at the back car parks and lawyers' offices. I timed my arrival for the morning coffee break. The courtyards were filled with small groups of lawyers and clients on chairs, and in the school refectory of a coffee room, men in black jackets, black ties, white shirts and striped trousers argued around the long tables. I found some people I knew – Malik Qasim, the white-haired head of an anti-government splinter of the Muslim League, who was exercised about the slow progress of his petition to the High Court on the illegality of the government's Muslim League; Aitzaz Ahsan, an ebullient, successful pro-PPP barrister who, when I had last seen him, had been deep in discussion with Imran Khan about a case he was fighting for the cricketer over a dispute on sports equipment advertising; and Afzal Haider, a former president of the Lahore Bar Association whom I asked to help me. He ordered me a cup of their coffee, a sort of extra-creamy cappuccino, which I spilt on his striped trousers.

Afzal Haider has a handsome, hawkish face, oiled hair with a thick white parting, and a formal nineteenth-century sort of politeness. He took me over to the committee room, and called a servant in a white jacket, who returned with a pile of books. There was section 144, he said; but that was provided by the British. Dating from 1898, it allowed the local magistrate – the DC – to ban assembly and the distribution of leaflets. And swimming in the canals, said a languid young lawyer who was leaning on the window-sill listening. But there were plenty of others, he said; there was the law making it legal to hold a suspect for detention for a year, which Zia had, by a Martial Law Order of 1977, extended to two years. And then, said another man who had sat down, there was the presidential order of 1982 which introduced trial in camera for political prisoners, plus special laws of evidence which shifted the burden of proof on to the accused.

As lawyers had drifted in, a little group had gathered around the bench. What about the laws to make the courts more malleable, somebody suggested. Quite, said Afzal Haider. The 1973 constitution allowed the president to transfer a judge from one high court to another, with his consent and in consultation with the chief justices of the two courts. Zia had decided that, for a two-year transfer, no consultation was necessary, the judge could be sent to any court (not just a high one) and if he refused, he would be deemed to have retired. And, to ensure insecurity of tenure, during most of Zia's years in power there has been an acting, not a permanent, chief justice of the Punjab High Court.

There was a slight hush as a small man with a painful-looking red eye came in. Afzal Haider whispered that he was Mr Samdani, former Justice Samdani. He was one of the few judges who had refused to take an oath on Zia's provisional constitutional order, and was therefore a respected man. The intelligentsia's basic complaint against the judiciary these days is that, having taken an oath on the 1973 constitution which made the imposition of martial law illegal, most of it had no apparent difficulty in swearing on the provisional constitution of the man who had declared martial law.

The courts legalised Zia's martial law in the Nusrat Bhutto vs. Chief of Army Staff case. Soon after the coup, Bhutto's wife took Zia to the Supreme Court for violating the constitution, which says that 'any person who abrogates or attempts or conspires to abrogate, subverts or attempts or conspires to subvert the constitution by use of force or show of force or by other unconstitutional means

261

shall be guilty of high treason'. The court decided that 'necessity can be accepted as a justification for an extra-legal act, in certain conditions'; and that in 1977 'a situation had arisen for which the constitution provided no solution ... acceptance of the changed legal order is not so much on account of its efficacy as such but rather on necessity in the sense of *id quod alias non est licitum, necessitas licitum facit* (that which is otherwise not lawful, necessity makes lawful)'. I liked the Latin, but it sounded to me dubious as a principle, since a principle as flexible as that can be stretched to include all manner of evil in all sorts of circumstances.

So I thought I'd ask the chief justice of the Lahore High Court, Mujadad Mirza, about it.

Mr Mirza's telephones contrasted oddly with his office. While the room had the ponderous air of thick dark velvet, he had one telephone in pastel blue plastic and one in pink. But Mr Mirza, a comfortable man, seemed at ease with the stylistic conflict. He shook my hand warmly and called for coffee and sandwiches. I was enveloped by his nostalgia for London, and, apparently, included in it. He had read for the bar at Lincoln's Inn, living in Golders' Green, and walking at the weekends on Hampstead Heath. Twelve years after he had left, he had returned and walked around Lincoln's Inn Fields. He looked at the sun on the grass, saw that the trees it was coming through were a little bigger than he remembered, and was glad to be alive. I felt friendly too, by then: I like people liking my city.

What, he inquired pleasantly, did I think people's impression of the judiciary in Pakistan was? I said I thought people's views were a little confused, since the judiciary's existing members had taken an oath to a martial law regime that had abrogated the constitution which . . .

'The constitution was NOT abrogated,' he said without warmth. 'It was . . . kept in abeyance for some time. You see,' and he crossed his legs with an air of informal confidentiality, 'every country passes through the mill at some time. But that, hopefully, is a closed period now.' I suggested that some people felt the judiciary were in part guilty for not standing up to the vagaries of governments.

'The judiciary did pass through horrible storms and hurricanes. But the institution survives, and is working for the people.' Hadn't it been permanently harmed, I wondered, by the laws which had been passed to make the judiciary more malleable?

'Those are not in good taste, I would say. Not in good taste.' And the martial law courts, to which the government could refer any case it wished? Weren't they an encroachment that the judiciary should have protested against?

'I don't think a judge should be sensitive to that extent, that he should mind about this sort of thing.' The angrier I felt, the more complacent he seemed to become. Then, I said, did he feel that the Army's assumption of power was legal although, according to the constitution then in force, it was not?

'Quasi-legal, under the circumstances,' he smiled. 'The doctrine of necessity.'

'But who determines the circumstances in which necessity justifies violating the constitution?' The judges, of course. Which leaves it up to people who he thinks should not be too sensitive about small matters like the introduction of martial law courts, who consider laws designed to weaken the judiciary's independence merely in bad taste, and who are satisfied with quasi-legality.

But I knew, as I wandered back along the carved-stone walkways to the lawns, that it was silly to be angry because the man had been to Lincoln's Inn and should have known better. Nobody in particular is to be blamed for the subversion of laws, and constitutions, and systems, or for not standing up to people who take them into their own hands. The odd people are those like Mr Samdani, the president of the bar association with the bad eye who had refused to take his oath. I was ashamed of my self-righteousness: it was a luxury born not of personal uprightness but of the knowledge that where I came from there were very few occasions in which somebody like me would have to choose between my conscience and my comfort. I would probably never have to know the bad news.

The strangest part in Pakistan is the combination of cynicism and deep-rooted faith in the law. People went on challenging the legality of Zia's rule (partly, perhaps, for publicity). Aitzaz Ahsan had a petition in the high court claiming that Zia should be liable to prosecution on the grounds of being a 'trespasser *ab initio*'. The precedent was the case of the six carpenters in England in 1609, when Chief Justice Coke ruled that the carpenters, who ate, drank and had a brawl in a tavern, were guilty of criminal trespass because, by violating the terms of entry, they were 'trespassers *ab initio*'. Zia, Aitzaz argued, had violated his terms of entry because that original supreme court judgement legitimising his coup said that 'the period of constitutional violation should be as short as possible' – and it had not been.

263

People like Chief Justice Coke are to blame for the perverse faith in the courts. Too many Pakistanis have been brought up to believe that the courts are more than the servant of the man who has just taken power. Some of them judges, many are lawyers, and plenty are private citizens. So although, in the really big decisions, the chief of Army staff is going to win, there's always an uncertainty – and, more important, a belief that he shouldn't.

If the courts have lost some of the essential ingredient that justifies their existence – their independence – they are the only state employees to have shrunk in stature and importance. The police may find crime and riots less controllable, but their field of operations has expanded far into the private sector – into protecting and carrying out crimes as well as harassing civilians. And the bureaucrats, willingly or not, have found themselves taking on the jobs of the politicians.

Most of these changes in the political boundaries can, in the end, be put down to the men who are taking up more and more of the map – the soldiers.

11

SOLDIERS

IT SEEMED elaborate to drive twenty miles out of town for a conversation, but there was a logic to it. The Army officer I had arranged to meet didn't want to see me in the barracks because he was afraid of the security services, or in his house because he was afraid of his wife. I didn't want him to come to my hotel room, because, although he seemed decent enough, letting unknown men into your hotel room is a risk similar to drinking unboiled water – to be taken in emergency, and at your peril. I was amazed he was prepared to talk to me at all, since it was entirely against the rules, but I was still unused to the power of sifarish: I had gone to him with a recommendation from a mutual soldier-friend.

'Sooo . . .' he said. 'Well, I tell you. I have a bungalow some distance out of town. I'll pick you up at six and drive you there.'

He arrived looking jaunty, in blazer and cravat. As I got into the car, he handed me a large brown envelope, addressed to himself, marked Personal and Strictly Private, with a square bottle in it – Johnny Walker, the currency of social exchange. He was more than jaunty, I thought: he looked mischievous, and that, for him, was the point of the trip. Taboos and rules have their uses: a soldier taking a girl out for a drink in Aldershot wouldn't be having nearly as much fun. He put a Lionel Ritchie tape on, and I wondered whether Lionel Ritchie knew how big he was in Pakistan.

He drove impatiently through the rickshaw-clogged streets, and fast when we got on to the straight open road, curling out to overtake maize-laden lorries and buffalo carts. Sensible people, he said, got their drink from the Tribal Areas. A litre bottle of Stolichnaya cost 150 rupees there (slightly under half the London price), and even whisky was cheaper there. For somebody like him, there was no difficulty in transporting it around the country, for no policeman would dare look in his boot.

We turned by an open-fronted shed with a single light-bulb that could only be a cigarette stall. Wages are cheap enough and the population dense enough to support commercial life that to a westerner appears absurd: imagine an English country lane with a shop selling only cigarettes open at night. We bumped down the small road, and the vegetation grew better-tended: the track passed down an avenue of eucalyptus then through an orchard of slim young fruit-trees. The bungalow appeared at the end of a neat lawn.

There were no servants to be seen, yet it was evidently servanted. In the hall were two pairs of black and two pairs of brown hunting boots, shining softly with frequent polishing and held up with old-fashioned wooden boot-trees. We settled at a table, and an intuitive servant appeared with glasses, soda, ice and savoury and sweet biscuits.

The Army had never been against drink, said the soldier, settling down to a whisky the size they pour in prohibition countries. 'If a man drank, but he was a gentleman – a professional, straight, not a thief – the jawans used to say he was a good chap.' But this Islam business had hit the Army as much as the rest of the country. You couldn't do it publicly any more. 'Awful people, these mullahs. Of course we can't say anything against them.'

The Army was changing, he said, as Pakistan was changing. The officer class wasn't what it used to be . . . though most of the higher levels would still be from the English speaking schools. And, thank God, the Army had avoided this obsession of Zia's about imposing Urdu on everybody: training was still in English.

I asked if there was corruption in the Army. He poured another whisky thoughtfully and topped mine up. 'There's no smoke without fire. It's got into the marrow of the people in this country. But it can't be accepted from a soldier. You can't trust your life with somebody like that. I say if a general is corrupt, line him up, shoot him.'

He got on to martial law before I asked. What I needed to understand, he said, was that the politicians pulled the country to pieces because of their factionalism. The Army was the only institution in the country still, touch wood, free of that, and so it had no option but to move in when things went wrong. Mistakes had been made, though. The Army hadn't done what it should have done during the last martial law.

'What should it have done?'

'Drastic surgery.'

'Oh what or whom?'

'Oh, you know. The drug dealers. In Malaysia, they shoot them. And the civil service and the politicians. Made an example of some of the high-up people. Instead, we wasted our time with this Islam business.' The Koreans, now, they had made good use of martial law. They had got their economy together, and had built an Army bigger than the Pakistani one. The economy was the key to it, and Pakistan's Army had failed to get it moving. What the country needed, he said, was a good leader. It hadn't had one since Jinnah. Britain had a good leader, and look what she had done for the country. Margaret Thatcher – the only man in Europe. Leadership, leadership: that was the key. Of course, democracy was desirable; but those politicians . . .

I wanted more, and encouraged us into another whisky. But he didn't want to talk politics any more. He wanted a chat, like the fellow in Aldershot taking a girl out, he wanted a bit of a laugh and a flirt. So we talked London, and shops, streets, theatres and hotels, and London against New York, and the Americans against the British. The servant brought pakoras, kebabs and a tiny saucer of tomato ketchup to defend our stomachs against the alcoholic onslaught.

When the bottle was two-thirds empty, I decided we had drunk enough, and that I would get no more out of him, so he wrapped the bottle in its envelope and we made for the car. Back on the main road, the car started thudding, and he stopped. Puncture. I laughed tipsily, but he was suddenly serious, and got out of the car to rummage around in the boot for a tool-kit. The moon gave us a little light. He said he always had a driver to manage these things, and wasn't sure if there were tools. He found the jack, jacked the car up, and straightened himself, puffing hard. Our problem, he said, was that there was no wheelbrace. The house might have one, but it was four miles back. The evening was quiet but for the frogs, and the air had an edge of chill on it.

As we wondered what to do, two tractors approached simultaneously from opposite directions. Both were piled with men returning to their villages after a day in the fields. Both stopped, unloading a dozen men, turbanned and bare-headed, who stared curiously at me and my officer. Some wandered around us, as though we would be more easily comprehensible if seen from all angles. The officer asked if anybody had a spanner, and there was discussion with the tractor-drivers. Nobody had one; nobody knew where one could be got.

A man came up close to me and, mimicking drinking with his thumb in his mouth and his fingers curled in the shape of a bottle, demanded *sharab*. I looked behind me into the passenger seat, and saw that the envelope had been taken off the bottle. Edging round the car, I put the envelope back on the bottle as unobtrusively as I could, and my bag on top of the envelope. Looking up, I saw that my officer had come over to the passenger side of the car, while the tractor men had massed on the other side. They were arguing over the bonnet. The men had, while I was worrying about the bottle, changed from curious disparate individuals into an angry collective. They wanted drink, they told the officer: he had been drinking, he still had some drink, and it was their turn now. The men behind were pressing forward, and some were beginning to edge round the front of the car towards the soldier.

Without looking at me, he said 'Pass me what you find under your seat.' I felt, and there was a pistol in a case. I handed it to him, and he put it on the bonnet. There was a tiny indecision on their collective face; the impetus failed momentarily; then they pressed on, and their mutterings rose. Give us your sharab. We want some sharab. The officer eased his pistol out of the holster and waved it at them, telling them to be off; he didn't point it at them, but gestured with it as though to emphasise his words. They hesitated again. The muttering subsided, and after a second of indecision they turned and got back on their tractors, which drove off in opposite directions into the night, leaving us once more with the frogs and a flat tyre.

The wheelbrace was there, of course, wrapped in plastic in a crevice in the boot. Huffing and puffing, the officer edged the bolts off one by one. His shirt was taut against his plump back, and the patches of sweat were spreading from under his arms and sticking the polyester and cotton mix to his skin. I feared for his heart. But the wheel was done, and he stood up, triumphant, dishevelled and wheezing slightly, his once-neat hair sticking to his forehead like seaweed.

The incident had made him reckless. On the way back, I had to hold the whisky bottle on my lap so that he could take swigs from it in the darkness between the headlights of oncoming cars, while he told me old stories of drunkenness in battle. I thought that either the man was a risk-taker for kicks, or he had astounding confidence in his ability to get away with things. Maybe the latter was truer. With a gun to protect him from the immediate demands of importunate peasants, and the Army to protect him from the rest of the country, he was safe from most eventualities. He would face serious difficulties only when the balance turned; and those peasants, after their second's hesitation, no longer drew back.

The Pakistani Army is used to government, and that experience has made of its officers something more than professional soldiers. They have a sort of gaiety that comes from a confidence in their ability to have things their own way. Their importance – acknowledged by others as well as themselves – makes their voices a little louder and their presence a little larger than other people's.

I have some acquaintance with subcontinental generals, because my landlord in Delhi, and all his friends, were retired generals; but they, conversing in modest south Delhi houses over whiskies and sodas about the price of rail tickets to Bombay and the fortunes of their fellow-officers' children, had the small financial and personal worries of any group of retired professionals. They spoke of things going on in the world with a bemused nervousness. Their opposite numbers in Pakistan – with whom they had served during the Second World War – had larger houses and cars, and the gracious self-importance that comes from having exercised power. National affairs were an interesting challenge, not a source of bewilderment, because they had come to be part of the generals' jobs.

Pakistan's Army has had time to acquire the habit of power. The country has been run by three generals: Ayub Khan (1958–69), Yahya Khan (1969–71) and Zia ul Haq (1977–88). But even in Bhutto's time in office, the Army had the opportunity to taste the pain and pleasure of rule: in Baluchistan, when the Army was trying to control the insurgency there, it was effectively in power, and in 1977, during the PNA movement, Bhutto declared martial law in certain cities, and the soldiers were sent out to bring order. They managed it in the end, but not quite the way Bhutto had intended.

As usual, the British can be blamed for setting precedents. When, as happened with monotonous regularity during the Raj, sectarian riots or protests against the government went beyond the point which the police could control, the Army would be called out in 'aid to civil power', to sort out the disturbance and then go back to its barracks. It wasn't a popular practice among the officers, who worried about using Indian soldiers against their own people. The best-known abuse of the system, in the Jallianwallah Bagh massacre in Punjab in 1919, when General Dyer ordered troops to shoot on protesters in a walled courtyard and 379 people were killed, was a watershed of anti-British sentiment.

The new Pakistani government continued the practice. When things started getting nasty, the soldiers were called in to sort out the messes made by the politicians. Not surprisingly, the view grew among the soldiers that if some higher quality person or institution were in power, the messes might not happen in the first place. From there, it is a short step to martial law.

The British are also blamed by Pakistan's intelligentsia for militarising the country. The Punjabi Muslims and the Pathans were both, according to nineteenth century theory, 'martial races': good at fighting and good at obeying orders, unlike, for instance, the over-educated Bengalis. The area that was to become Pakistan was therefore the Army's principal recruiting ground; and within that area, three districts in Punjab – Rawalpindi, Jhelum and Campbellpore – were the core soldier-producing districts. The land in those areas was arid and unirrigated, so there wasn't much else for local boys to do except join the Army. The Baluch, who had been favoured as soldiers by the British in the nineteenth century, were sent home because of their inconvenient habit of disappearing without leave. 'Baluch' regiments continued to exist, but they had no Baluch soldiers in them and the Baluch still do not go into the Army.

The skewed recruitment policy had two consequences, which persist. Pakistan's Army, at partition, was disproportionately large for the country which, with a population an eighth the size of India's got eight infantry regiments, six armoured ones, eight artillery while India got twenty-one, fourteen and forty. These days, it has around 480,000 soldiers to India's 1.4 million. While India's army would find it virtually impossible to sustain martial law in a country of 800 million people, Pakistan's can manage 100 million without too much difficulty.

The pattern of recruitment means that it is not a national Army. According to Stephen Cohen in his excellent book on the Pakistani Army, at partition seventy-seven per cent of the recruits from what was to become West Pakistan came from Punjab, twenty per cent were from the frontier, two per cent from Sind, and almost none (0.06 per cent, to be precise) from Baluchistan. The proportions

270

remain pretty much the same, since the sons of Jhelum followed their fathers in to the Army, and the Sindhis, who were judged not to be a martial race, never took to fighting. These figures reinforce themselves. Because the Army is Punjabi the Sindhis don't think of joining it. Punjabi soldiers swear there is no discrimination against Sindhis, but that they have no opportunity to prove this since the Sindhis don't join up.

Skewed recruitment matters, particularly when the Army is running the country. It isn't just the principle of 'colonial' rule by the Punjabis that the smaller provinces object to: they also want their slice of the cake. Government is seen as a money-making business, and if the Punjabis are governing Sind they must be ripping off the Sindhis.

The recruits may be from the same place as 100 years ago, but the changes in the Army since partition, or the phases it has been through, are evident to any older officer you talk to. The Pakistani Army has, after all, been through three wars and three periods in power in the past forty years, as well as shifts in alliances, equipment and ideology.

The crop of generals now retiring were mostly trained before independence, and thus are imbued with a larger dose of Sandhurst-style Army spirit and mythology than the younger officers. By and large, they are men with a commitment to the idea of 'professionalism', without much ideology, but with a gut suspicion of Hindu India confused by friendships with Indian contemporaries.

The rising generals are what Cohen calls 'the American generation': the men who were young officers in the 1950s when the Americans started to flood Pakistan with equipment, many of whom were sent to America for training. From the way the people who went to America talk about it, it sounds as though there was a genuine warmth of friendship between them and their hosts. That trust was destroyed, probably forever, when the Americans cut off spare parts and supplies to Pakistan in the 1965 war with India. After that, the Pakistanis lost faith in the Americans and started diversifying their supplies.

The seventies were the Army's darkest days. Under Ayub, it had failed to control the country, and had to give government back to the civilians. Much more painful to the national psyche, it had lost Bangladesh, and lost it in a messy, brutal war in which the Pakistani Army raped and murdered its fellow countrymen to the horror not just of the outside world, but also of some of those West Pakistanis who heard about it and believed. The Army that crawled home from Bangladesh and from India's prisons during the early 1970s was a loser, and a dirty loser at that. Nobody wanted to join up after Bangladesh: soldiering seemed no longer to be an honourable profession.

The Army's self-esteem returned, through the seventies, as the wounds healed and Pakistan quickly shoved aside unpleasant memories. Zia, as Bhutto's chief of staff, improved morale: he promoted education in the Army, both boosting the level of general training at home for officers, and sending more of them abroad. As discontent and disruption grew and Bhutto imposed selective martial law, the generals began to talk once more of civilian incompetence, until, in July 1977, they took matters into their own hands.

Power is good for self-esteem. During the last decade, the armed forces have got richer, too. Anecdotes relate how officers in charge of martial law courts profited from their powers. Better documented is the shuttle to the Gulf, where the Saudi Arabians have been employing around 40,000 Pakistani soldiers (rotated every year or two) to augment their tiny armed forces. The Pakistani soldiers had a bonanza: pay in Saudi Arabia was ten times that in Pakistan.

Over time, the kind of people becoming Army officers changed. The British, although they had a sort of scholarship system for bright boys, wanted officers from the rich landed families (Zia was a notable exception). But those families have turned against the Army, preferring to send their spare sons into the civil service or, at a pinch, business. Officers therefore come increasingly from the small landlord families or the shopkeeper class, which is generally less imbued with British-style liberalism, more consciously Islamic and more anti-left. These days, although you meet old generals at the better sort of party in Lahore, you don't meet young Army officers the way you still do among the British gentry.

General Fazle Haq would certainly get an invitation, but more because power confers class than because of birth. His family was modest, but he did well in the Army and ended up as Zia's military governor – absolute ruler – of the NWFP. He had a period of oblivion, out of power because he had fought a rash war inside the tribal areas against Wali Khan Kukikhel, but was brought back as chief minister after Zia sacked his government in 1988. He quickly, and fairly successfully, converted himself into a politician: the Pathans like a strong man.

He lives on the edge of Defence Society in Peshawar, the area where soldiers get free or cheap plots, with three armed guards in front of his house and another six sitting and lying on charpoys by the brown tents on the other side of the road. The garden is large and neat, with a cage of little white birds bobbing and squeaking on their perches under the shade of the fruit-trees around the lawn, and a wire-netting enclosure with a hen looking after three pea-chicks. 'Silly girl,' said Fazle Haq, coming out of the sliding glass doors to his study. 'She thinks they're hers.'

He's a big man, bulky without looking fat, with black hair and eyebrows, and a grey quarter-inch long military moustache. I supposed, since I kept meeting these moustaches, that they were a way of avoiding shaving the upper lip while not indulging in the vanity of a moustache; but like so many sensible fashions, they have become a badge of period and profession. On the pannelled wall of his study with its old-fashioned flap-top desk and squashy sofa and chairs is a life-size portrait of himself in fatter days: authoritative, martial, and not much fun.

In fact, Fazle Haq is fun. He has the ebullient charm of one for whom things have gone well. He talks a lot, and peppers his talk with *risqué* stories which he chuckles at. He is not a man given to false modesty, discretion or reticence: he gave me a brief, damning account of the social pretentions of the smarter local families along with his version of their origins. He moves restlessly while he talks, sitting on the sofa with his legs tucked under him, then uncurling them and crossing them. His hands are always in use. For a gesture of contempt, the right hand is lifted to forehead height, as though to catch a ball, then twisted quickly to face backwards, as though flicking the matter or person into the oblivion in which it belongs.

He was commissioned, he said, in 1946, and paid 420 rupees a month. Most people then were from good families, though a few were from the lower classes. They weren't terribly well educated – A-level sort of standard. After partition, they suddenly got top-class brains coming in, because people were giving up their careers to go into the Army and help protect their country. The 1965 war led to another rush of good people, but after that there was a big expansion in the Army, which meant pulling in all sorts of people, and after that was the humiliation of the 1971 war.

'Usually, the best go into medicine, the next into engineering, the third into the civil service, then the duds say we'll have a fling at the Army.' I asked him why he joined up. He grinned, half with pleasure at the thought of times and illusions past, half because he knew I'd be amused.

'It was the glamour, my dear. The glamour of the uniform, of hunting, shooting, polo.' I struggled to find a question that would give me a feel of it.

'What did you . . . talk about in the evenings?'

'The officers would be talking about the regiment in the most glowing terms, and the British officers who were killed, and the tent-pegging trophy we had won. We talked of the sports . . . not to speak of the women and booze. And we would be discussing India, and how those regiments were getting along.

'The mess was like a family. Every night you were dressed up, two nights a week in tuxedos. The ties were very difficult to tie. Breakfast was a no-speak affair, dinner was a rowdy affair, with drinking at the bar. Then after dinner, the pipers would enter and play Cock O' the North, and somebody would rise and say The Queen . . . and Pakistan.'

After a while, he said, the social life began to dwindle.

'Whisky became expensive, and anyway Pakistanis aren't clubby types. They like to spend most of the time with their families.'

I asked whether, in those halcyon early days, everybody drank. Not everybody, he said; not even half. Probably thirty percent drank. 'Zia ul Haq never drank. And, when the time came for night prayers, he would go over into the corner of the mess and bend over in those tight uniforms you could hardly move in.'

Islam is certainly a bigger deal in the Army than it was in Ayub Khan's days. Zia pushed it hard. He wrote in 1979:

'The professional soldier in a Muslim army, pursuing the goals of a Muslim state, CANNOT become "professional" if in all his activities he does not take on "the colour of Allah".' Faith, thus, is a necessary condition for professionalism, according to Zia; yet to most of the generals I talked to, who didn't want to be quoted on their views on Islam, this was a dangerous travesty.

Zia did his best to bring young officers up believing both that Islam is central to soldiering and that one of the jobs of the Pakistani Army is to protect Pakistan's ideology. Islam and ideology feature increasingly in the training of officers, and the attitude of Zia and his ilk to the Army's job was well-expressed by Lt.-Gen. (Rtd) Ejaz Azim, in a strange article in Lahore's English-language

274

paper, the *Nation*, which started an unprecedented argument in print.

General Azim was upset about a recent announcement by the prime minister that in future the generals would have to make do with Suzukis instead of the grander cars they had been getting.

'I and some of my retired colleagues,' he wrote, 'have been following with growing consternation and concern the attempts at "general-bashing" on matters totally unrelated to their sphere of activities. It has well-nigh become fashionable to lay the blame on the generals if the crops have suffered damage due to the untimely rains or if there was a drop in remittances from abroad.' He went on to explain the Army's great responsibilities:

'Ours is a national Army. It is the repository of the nation's confidence which has charged it with the sacred duty of defending its physical borders and its ideological frontiers.' Who says? Wrote one or two of the respondents. The argument was brought to a sharp close: the corps commander Lahore, I was told, thought it had gone far enough, and told the paper to wind it up – a matter, one might argue, totally unrelated to his supposed sphere of activities.

I read these pieces, all stuck in a big leather-bound book of clippings, in the airy offices of the *Nation*. After 20,000 words or so, I burst out laughing, and the girl reporter who was bringing me a cup of tea looked at me curiously. I had just realised, I said, that in all these words discussing the role and reputation of the generals in Pakistan, the name Zia ul Haq had not been mentioned once – at a time of unusual press freedom, when the papers abused government policies, and accused ministers of corruption. She passed on, with an ironic smile more, I thought, at my amusement than at its cause.

Army politics, for the observer, is rather like eastern bloc politics because its processes are harder to divine than in a democracy. Everybody knows that Mrs Thatcher and Mr Lawson are having a row, either because they give public statements ('I am in total agreement with the chancellor/prime minister . . .') or because journalists have been told in off-the-record briefings. But in systems run by the Army or the party, where the press addresses peripherals and steers clear of fundamentals, observers have to glean much from tiny signals and barrack- or committee-room gossip. The hours of speculation this involves is, initially at least, interesting; and in some ways the obscure system is more educative than the open one, since instead of having the facts and their possible consequences spelt out in the newspapers or by opposition MPs on the nightly news, people have to work things out for themselves. Partly for that reason, there is more, and better, political conversation in Lahore than in London.

People don't despise the soldiers. The generals may not be remarkable people; their attitudes to governing their fellow-countrymen may be despicable; but it is hard to sneer at those who ultimately run the show. The generals, however, despise politicians. They have to: it is their excuse, and possibly also their reason, for taking over government. They are convinced that the politicians cannot manage politics and merely endanger the unity of the country by playing on divisive forces like region, race and class, to build up support for themselves. They know that the Army is the only united institution in the country, and that it is therefore sometimes forced to take over in order to try to stop the politicians' arguments pulling the country apart.

One of the images soldiers use about the Army and politics is applied particularly to Bhutto's war against the separatist guerrillas in Baluchistan: if you use a stick too often to beat people with, eventually the stick will turn against you. Not an elegant image, perhaps, but its force has lodged it in the brains of several of the soldiers I talked to. If the Army is required to aid the civil power too much, it will come to the conclusion that the civilian is no longer competent to hold power. Given the history of Pakistan's civilian governments, the argument has a certain validity; but looking at the history of the military governments, it's not clear that they've done much better. The generals are against martial law now, of course . . . but, at the time . . .

General Wajahat Hussein is a tall man with abrupt movements, perfect suits and a voice better suited to Aldershot than Lahore. He doesn't look like Zia's sort of man: not surprising, therefore, to learn that he was sent off to be ambassador in Australia soon after the coup in 1977. Ambassadorships are recognised as one of the more tactful ways of getting rid of dissenting or dangerous generals.

'I feel,' he said, deliberating, 'that interference with politics by the military is not right. That is why this country has not settled down.' So why, I wondered, had the Army stayed in control for so long?

'Power.' He stared at me, and I stared back. 'Power. There have been very few instances in history of people handing over power

276

voluntarily. I said this to Zia. He told me, in 1977, that he could take over any time he wished. I said I know: getting on the tiger is easy. Getting off it is more difficult. He put his hand on his heart: he said it will be ninety days, and then I will be out.' That tiger image, too, had stuck. I heard it again and again, mostly from doubtful soldiers. It sounded like a phrase from a mess argument on what the Army should do, that had been handed round, polished, and put back on the table.

There was a general I wanted to see, one of the most powerful men in the military government. I had no sifarish, and couldn't get him on the phone. So I screwed up my courage, went to his house and waited in his chowkidar's plastic chair while my card was taken in. Trying to dull my embarrassment, I watched a cockerel picking seeds out of the flowerbed by the side of the house. The chowkidar came out and jerked his head towards the house.

Stumbling as I introduced myself, I promised not to name him. He watched my nervousness with slight amusement and offered me an apple. They had tried, he said, to put the politicians back in, but the politicians just wouldn't play ball. The PNA was afraid that Bhutto would win an election, then after Bhutto was killed . . . things were a little unpredictable,and Zia had started this Islam business. He and other generals, he said, had slowly worked on Zia . . . 'drip, drip, drip' – to bring back the politicians, and by 1985, they had to have elections: 'the pressures had built up. The Army said Zia should get out before it was disgraced.'

'Pakistan has never had normal politics. It's always been palace intrigues – Ayub, Yahya, even Bhutto manipulated things to stop Mujib taking over.' But democracy would take root, he said, eventually – so long as the mullahs were kept out of politics. 'I don't know how those Jamaatis ever got involved in government. They're totally fascist. Islam is a secular religion: it recognises all others, and the mullahs have never understood that.' There was a contained energy, and a quiet cleverness about the man; and all he said about the Jamaat pleased me. Yet I forced myself to be sceptical: however appealing a proponent of democracy and secularism he sounded, he had been one of the mainstays of a military regime with theocratic tendencies. I wondered again, though, when his son drove me home. The boy was studying in college. Wasn't he going into the Army? No, he had wanted to, but his father wouldn't let him. Why not? My father, he said carefully, doesn't think the Army is a good career any more.

But these days, the Army offers all sorts of careers. During the years of military rule, its tentacles have crept into areas of life that in most countries would not be considered Army business. On a flight from Islamabad to Karachi, I sat next to a tall thin man in a checked shirt. He offered me a Marlborough in his long fingers, I offered him a Gold Leaf (a local brand). I lied, as I often did, about my travels: I said I was researching a guide book, and showed an interested ignorance of the workings of the country. He was a colonel in the Army, he said; he had spent some time on the president's personal guard.

'One day, I was in the room alone with him, and he asked me if I drank. I do, but I said "Oh no, sir." Then he asked what I thought of the laws on drinking. "Well, sir," I said, "I think it's up to people what they do." But Zia said, "I have been put here by the grace of God. I want to make Pakistanis better people. If you have children, you don't always let them do what they want. So I think it's my job to bring some discipline."' The colonel smiled in amusement I was supposed to share. I was horrified.

'But he's talking about adults.'

'You can't argue with a senior officer.'

'Do you agree with him?'

'No. I keep telling my wife – we don't get on too well, she's a very headstrong woman – that if she forbids the children to do things all the time, they'll still do them but they'll tell lies.' I asked the colonel what he was doing these days. Working for intelligence, he said. There were a lot of problems in Sind, and he was on an undercover operation in Hyderabad, pretending to be a businessman. Did he have an office, I asked, and headed writing paper and business cards? Of course. So what did he do when somebody tried to place an order with him? No problem, he just quoted them an unreasonable price. And what, I asked, were the problems in Sind? A lot of dacoits, he said, and some leftists and nationalists. The dacoits were partly being encouraged by the landlords, but they had got out of control. And some of them were taking help from Russia and India.

'Is there any evidence?'

'Some . . . how would they get these sophisticated weapons they have?'

'Buy them?'

'Maybe, but I have done some studies. The price of a Kalashnikov in Peshawar used to be 50,000. Now you can buy it for 17,000, even on instalments. That's cheaper than in Russia. What would you think if you could buy that shirt for one pound in England, where it is made, and fifty pence in Pakistan?'

'Are these leftists a danger?' I meant to sound moronic: I didn't want him to think he risked an argument.

'Not really. Put me in power and I'd finish them off in two days. But the government seems to want to go easy on them.'

Maybe he wasn't an Army intelligence officer: maybe that was his way of impressing girls. But he got the colour of the waistcoats of the attendants in the presidential palace right, and the level of a lieutenant-colonel's pay.

If he was, he was a little bit of evidence of how close some of Pakistan still was to martial law. The soldiers wandering around the bazaars in the towns of upper Sind were part of the local scene, like the chaiwallahs and the drugs police. The towns' inhabitants no longer remarked on them, but to an outsider, they were a surprising sight, buying their cigarettes and trundling behind bullock carts in their Jeeps. It seems logical that, if the soldiers are permanently on the scene to ensure that 1983 doesn't happen again, so are the officers like my thin colonel, dressing in civvies, avoiding taking orders from the unsuspecting public and sending their subordinates to join and spy on left-wing organisations.

The Army seems permanently to run the edge of government, the bit of lawnorder which is seen as a possible threat to the regime. That isn't a problem for many soldiers, like Lt.-Gen. Ejaz Azim, contributor to the *Nation*. If the Army is not just protecting the country's physical frontiers from external enemies, but also its ideological frontiers, presumably there are internal ideological enemies of Pakistan from whom the Army needs to protect the country even when martial law is not in force. The result, of course, is that the Civil Intelligence Directorate is no longer the country's main watchdog. The Inter-Services Intelligence is the organisation the government relies on, and sensible civilians fear and respect.

It's not an easy organisation to find out about. Politicians told me that ISI officers would occasionally visit them to check out their opinions about the way government was going, and about some of the people Zia had picked. According to one who said he saw them fairly regularly, the director-general of the ISI had to see either the president or the prime minister every day.

I found an ex-ISI officer who was a little more forthcoming than others. The ISI's job, he said, used to be external intelligence and counter-intelligence – what the Indians, the Afghans, the Iranians and the Russians were up to – and keeping an eye on the forces. Baluchistan had involved it more in internal intelligence, because the insurgents were getting help from outside: keeping an eye on the Afghans' and Russians' activities meant watching Pakistanis. 'We used to investigate the Russian network in our spare time as a hobby. Intellectuals were in it, journalists were in it, students, poets, businessmen. I don't think there was a civil service department the Russians didn't have a man in.'

Then the ISI took sole charge of the Afghan guerrillas, which was a huge operation. All the money, guns and other aid that went to the Afghan guerrillas went through the ISI. The ISI received the weapons consignments, broke them up and divided them among the mujaheddin groups favouring, according to Pakistani policy, the religious fundamentalists. I checked this with what are called 'Western diplomatic sources', who agreed, but said that the ISI also had a hand in the mujaheddin's military operations: as well as getting regular handouts, the mujaheddin alliance's military committee would meet an ISI team and agree on a set of operations, and ISI officers would sometimes go inside with them. The ISI thus had tight control over the guerrillas: those who did what they were told got more weapons.

The PNA movement that overthrew Bhutto was not, said my ISI officer, within the organisation's sphere of interest. It belonged to the civilian intelligence directorate, and anyway, Bhutto had his own intelligence outfit because he didn't trust the existing one. During martial law, though, the ISI's role had expanded considerably. Being the soldiers' own intelligence service, it was more familiar to the generals than the intelligence directorate, so Zia used it as his main source of internal political information.

Beyond intelligence-gathering, the Army is expanding into a range of non-military areas. The soldiers have always had their allocations of cheap plots in the cities, and in areas that become fertile through irrigation – the barrages in Sind being the largest and most-resented example. And they have the Army Remounts Corps, the organisation which runs estates all over the country that were once used to house spare horses. But other peripheral bits of the military empire are growing fast. The National Logistics Cell, for instance, expanded dramatically in the early 1980s. It has sole charge of the road transport of shipments of food and necessities for the Afghan refugees, as well as the arms for the mujaheddin. But these days, transporters complain that it is now encroaching on private sector business which they reckon is legitimately theirs. In a country where the Army has such influence in so many fields, the private sector may find it difficult to compete with military ventures: businessmen are aware that it is better to be on the right side of the military.

As a charity for the families of ex-servicemen, the Fauji Foundation does not sound like a power to be reckoned with. I asked Mr Pasha, the smooth besuited finance director who I went to see in its white offices in Rawalpindi surrounded by pink rose bushes, whether it was the largest industrial enterprise in the country. He became quite coy. 'I do hope not . . . but I'm afraid I think people say we are.' They have a polypropylene bag plant, a plant for metallising paper, a packaging unit, three sugar plants (they are the country's biggest sugar producers); they run an oil and gas field on the Baluchistan border, produce liquid petroleum gas, make fertiliser, metal containers, microelectronics; they process maize and have an experimental farm developing improved seed for sugar.

There is nothing obviously political about their businesses, yet according to the graphs on Mr Pasha's wall their fortunes have followed politics. During the 1970s, their turnover, profits and assets stagnated. In 1978–9, assets were 986 million rupees. By 1985–6, the latest year that Mr Pasha could produce, they were 3,473 million rupees. Profits had increased seven-fold. Mr Pasha was understandably proud of this: 'We are working in a noble cause.' But there could be other reasons for their prosperity: according to Stephen Cohen, rumour has muttered of the Fauji Foundation's involvement in importing equipment for the nuclear weapons programme.

The outlets for the foundation's profits – 637 million rupees in 1985–6 – seemed a little thin, given the scale of the enterprise. It has scholarships for ex-servicemen's children, cottage industries where wives are taught handicrafts, and a nursing school. It does not pay pensions, which come out of another fund. It doesn't look after the ex-airmen's families: they have their own huge Shaheen Foundation. I left with the suspicion that there were probably informal outlets for their earnings as well.

While military businesses expand, the soldiers are also spreading into civilian organisations. Ex-soldiers have been recruited into the civil service since Ayub's time, and Bhutto increased the number of jobs available to them by allowing the military to participate in the lateral recruitment programme into the civil service. But under Zia,

281

the recruitment of soldiers and ex-soldiers rose noticeably. At top grades in the federal civil service, ten per cent of places are now reserved for military officers who are retired or on secondment. The career civil servants are, of course, infuriated. They find themselves losing promotions to soldiers younger than themselves who continue to enjoy the benefits – cheap plots of land, the excellent military medical service – of being in the Army. And, since the military men never become part of the civil service tribe, the civilians suspect them of spying and reporting back to the ultimate authorities.

Military men also get important jobs in the nationalised corporations like the airline, the steel mill, the fertiliser factories. I decided to visit the new head of the Water and Power Development Authority, only to find that he was one General Zahid Ali Akbar, who, rumour had it, had been expected to become the next vice-chief of staff. His failure to get the job was put down to General Zia's concern for his own future: General Zahid Ali Akbar, people said, was too obviously ambitious.

I found him in the rather New York Wapda building in Lahore, all atrium and glass. In the waiting room sat sad men with their briefcases, chain-smoking and not being called. The attendants, in white pagris and red coats, looked like hotel doormen. One of them beckoned me into the general's absurdly large office. Behind the yards of plate glass looking over Lahore's parks, the evening was turning from orange to purple. On the window-ledge, black against the sky, was a ballet of pigeons landing, flying off and bobbing up and down.

The general was an extremely handsome man, large-framed with a pronounced bone-structure. His confident smile was immediately attractive; but once I understood that it was born from a habit of unquestioned command, it became smug, and palled. He answered my questions quickly, not giving me time to think; and with each answer, threw a self-congratulatory smile at a silent hanger-on, lying on a sofa in the corner of the room, who nodded appreciatively. His new toy, which he said was going to solve many things, was the computer on his desk. He tried to get it started, then yelled for somebody who got it to flash up 'For the exclusive use of General Zahid Ali Akbar'. It was going to centralise operations, so there would be less corruption. Why, I asked, was there so much corruption?

'There is none in Wapda now.' By then, I was more interested in him as a general than as an expert on water and power generation.

'And in the country?'

'There is more now. Politicians are more corrupt. There was more still under Bhutto's government.'

'At least he was accountable because he was elected.'

'He became a dictator. Maybe you can say that Zia ul Haq . . . But I tell you this, I promise you this, <u>if Zia ul Haq goes, there will be martial law again in six months.</u>' He pointed at my nose, in imitation of the Kitchener poster. 'I am a serving Army officer . . .'

'You're *serving* – I thought you were retired. This is odder and odder.'

'Why?'

'Well . . .' I floundered, 'this is a civilian operation, why should it have a serving soldier running it?'

'Ask the government.'

'You must have some idea.'

'It was an entirely political decision. Mr Junejo said he wanted a general.'

'Why should he want a general?'

'He needed the right man,' he said, producing his smug smile.

'And he couldn't find one among a hundred million civilians?' He shrugged.

'Don't think I'm happy about it. I used to stop work at two, play golf for two hours and go home at four. Are you going to publish all this?'

'Of course. This was an interview.'

'I shall lose my job.'

'Tough.' <u>Overconfidence in others makes me belligerent.</u> It may be that his air was a professional technique, but if so it was an effective one. Faced with him, a man with an aura of authority surpassing that of all the politicians I had met put together, I could see why people obey soldiers and leap to attention when they come into power. I imagined it would take either a strong natural dislike of the manifestations of authority, or principled courage, to tell General Zahid Ali Akbar where to get off.

The most important civilian position that had been militarised was, of course, the presidency. I had been trying to piece General Zia together for a long time before I went to see him. The clues were thin. There was this smile, on television, a huge rectangular smile that bared a set of polished teeth standing to attention to the camera. The frightening smile was still there, but ten years' of power had done his interview technique no end of good. His hands used to wring themselves incessantly in his lap in a painful imitation of a Dickensian moneylender, and the smile used to be one of cringing apology. The hands were still, now, and the smile amused itself.

Then there were the things that people said about him. At least he's a sincere Muslim. He's the biggest hypocrite of them all. He's a very humble man. He's the most cunning politician we've ever had. He isn't corrupt. He has fostered corruption in others. He's a good listener. He brought back decency to this country. A man who genuinely hated him, politically, said he was a nice man. The only disinterested person I've met who actually said he liked him (politically) was a Karachi taxi-driver because, he said, 'In time of Bhutto, there is too much prostitute, alcohol, drugs. I like these things, but I do not like them openly. President Zia is same as me.'

One of my friends does an imitation of the voices of men like Zia, who Arabise their grammar and speak Urdu with assumed Arabic accents. Arabic, the language of the Quran, is holier than Urdu. Another mocked the way he stood, hands held in front of him as though to protect his private parts. But neither of them would seriously ridicule the man himself. His achievements were too remarkable: he executed the prime minister who promoted him and got away with it, he confounded those who said he was a little second-rater put there because Bhutto was sure he wouldn't give any trouble, he disproved those who said he was the front man in a coup run by more serious people, and he stayed in power for eleven years.

A trade unionist told me a story to make me understand the difference between Zia and Bhutto. He was at a conference which Zia opened. Zia shook hands with all the participants, and as he came past, my friend asked for a word with him. He was summoned afterwards, and told Zia of a friend of his, a political prisoner, who was sick in jail and whose doctors had told him he needed to go abroad for treatment. Zia was concerned. He would see what he could do, and took my friend's name and address, saying that he would be in touch.

And was he? I asked. No, said the trade unionist; nor, as he had expected, was his friend allowed to go abroad. Bhutto wouldn't have helped either. The difference, he said, was that if he had spoken to Bhutto, he would have been picked up and thrown in jail

284

himself within an hour. At least Zia's sort of repression was a little more discriminating.

Zia's most successful tactic was his personal touch. There were the handouts – not of money, but of London hospital charges for the sick son of a civil servant, of a university place for a struggling boy, of a house for a poor old widow. I asked Mahbub ul Haq, the planning minister, for an example: immediately, he told me of the joint secretary in the planning ministry who was going to retire. Zia found that the civil servant had a handicapped daughter – as Zia himself did – went personally to the man's house and asked how he was going to look after the girl. The civil servant didn't know; so Zia said he would give him a small plot of land in a market on which he could put a shop. The secretary came to Mahbub ul Haq in tears of gratitude. Mahbub ul Haq was amazed: he had never even known that his underling had a handicapped child.

The stories got about. To me, they sounded cheap, dangerous popularity stunts: a country whose government was degenerating into a network of who-knows-who needed not individual exceptions and personal kindness, but systematic application of the rules. By the same token, however, the stunts worked. Pakistan esteems personal contacts, gifts are a sign of respect not an attempt to corrupt, and patronage and loyalty are powerful political tools. Zia's technique, therefore, won him more praise than scepticism.

I was to meet the president at his Rawalpindi residence, and was alarmed to hear, on the morning of my appointment, that the city's roads were likely to be blocked by protest marches for most of the day. What they were protesting about I never discovered, nor did I care much: I was just worried about making it on time. But urgent phone calls from the president's military and press secretaries told me the venue had been changed – not, they assured me, because of the protests. Islamabad would be more convenient.

Duller, though. I would have preferred Rawalpindi, because 'Pindi is the soldiers' city. Since British times, it has been the prime military recruiting area, the headquarters of the Army and its peripheral activities like the Fauji Foundation and the National Logistics Cell. In the back streets which soldiers wobbled down on bicycles under the trees spilling over from the walled gardens, the houses' name-plates advertise colonels and brigadiers. There, I could have seen the president on his own territory.

The presidential palace in Islamabad lies flat and white on ground just higher than the rest of the city, winged by the senate and the national assembly. It doesn't look Pakistani, and isn't. It was built by a foreign architect, and has an openness at odds with a country as dusty and private as Pakistan. Whenever I am in Islamabad, bits are still being built on to it or repaired: with its scaffolding and its isolation from Pakistan's crowds, it looks as though it is waiting for a tenant.

Plump soldiers guarding it peered through the window of my battered taxi and checked me against their lists. One, with unPakistani ceremony, led me into a hall that seemed a caricature of presidential palaces: red carpet, matching attendants with red waistcoats and brightly-polished brass buttons, chandeliers, floor-to-ceiling mirrors all the way along that multiplied me and the attendants to infinity. I could imagine the pleasure of striding down that hall followed by a trail of attentive retainers, and knowing it was all for me. The constant reminders of one's own importance must be part of the attraction of power.

Upstairs was more businesslike, with the fawn carpet and wood panelling of an expensive hotel suite. They put me in a room of pale flowered sofas, vases of flowers, *Time*, *Newsweek* and *The Economist* neatly laid out, and a glass of fresh purple pomegranate juice brought by an attendant with its own tiny doily under it. The president's military secretary came in, made small familiar jokes about an article I had written which hadn't been allowed into the country and told me where I should sit when I was taken in to see the president. I became nervous.

The president was small, dressed in a black sherwani and flanked by ministers and advisors. They, more than he, alarmed me: I had been promised an interview alone with him. He and I shook hands – which, I was told, he did with foreign women but not Pakistani ones – and I examined his face for clues. It was too odd to read: that smile, again, which might have been laughing at me, eyes round like a child's but sunken deep in dark sockets, and skin strangely unlined for a man of sixty-four. We sat at opposite ends of a sofa in a room designed to dominate Islamabad. The city, below, was bright with sunlight and blurred by a haze that might have been mist but I knew to be pollution.

Ranged in a semi-circle round us were Mahbub ul Haq, the planning minister, Sahabzada Yaqub Khan, who had just resigned as foreign minister after failing to get himself elected as head of Unesco, Dr Afzal, the rector of the Islamic University, and Brigadier Salik, the president's suave press secretary. On the table in front of us was a tape-recorder. The audience horrified me: I knew that I would worry about making a fool of myself, instead of concentrating on trying to understand the president.

I asked him about his origins. He leant forward slightly, over the hands folded on his lap.

'I am from a family which I'm proud to say was not rich, nor a high middle-class but an average middle-class family.' It was an ideal story: father a minor civil servant with six sons and two daughters, one of whom died very young of TB. Zia was the eldest son, and a boy scout at school. His father gave the children whatever he could afford, and at the age of thirteen, Zia was sent away to live in a hostel and attend the government high school at Simla. He then went to St Stephen's College, the best university college in Delhi, where he joined the officers' training corps. He liked the uniform.

'My aim was to become a judge, but it was too long to wait. I decided to join government service – the civil service. Then in 1944, the government said it would select future civil servants out of those who had joined the Army, so I joined up.'

He was among the last lot of officers, with the last lot of equipment, to leave India: he didn't go until 17 December, 1947. His family had to leave their home in Jullundur, in east Punjab, earlier in the year, and he still regretted not being with his family to help them move. His grandmother had died in the refugee camp. 'Thereafter,' he said, 'my time in the Army is a story of love, love with the profession.'

I asked if he minded if I smoked. Not at all, he said: he used to smoke very heavily. When he was a boy, his parents didn't allow it, so he used to hide in the shed at the bottom of the garden then clean his teeth and chew a couple of cardamoms. As sins go, that seemed to me uninteresting; but any disobedience brightens the story of a model boyhood.

I asked him the question I was most curious to hear him answer: I thought I knew what he would say, but wondered how he would put it. Was Islam a sufficient national identity for a country? No, he said, to my surprise.

'Islam doesn't bind people through geographical boundaries. To be a Muslim is to be international, and not a nationalist in the restricted term of nationhood. We consider the Islamic Umma as one body, forty-four countries, one faith.' What, then, was the *raison d'être* of Pakistan?

'This was a political campaign. Men like Mr Jinnah saw an uncertain future for Muslims. This minority had been given the country for 1,000 years, then the British looked after both communities. But when they were to leave, the majority would be ruling. Mr Jinnah saw how biased, how parochial the Hindu mind was.' My original question still remained. Islam might be reason enough to create a country, but what, then, was to keep it together? It wasn't a matter that seemed to worry the president.

'You in the UK are still Irish, Scots, Welsh. There are many ups and downs through which we have to go, in our political structure, our Islamisation of the country. You can't say Islam is not a binding force, because we are not actually practising it.' Faced with this unworried illogic, I gave up. Surely, I thought, a man running half a country which fifteen years ago was split in two should be thinking harder about these things? And shouldn't I argue that he was contradicting himself about the role of religion? I didn't, suspecting that I had come across what my Oxbridge Pakistani friends had always warned me of: somebody who didn't argue in the if-not-A-then-B manner I had been brought up with, who relied on force of personality and rhetoric. On the other hand, I thought, perhaps he just doesn't believe what he's saying. Maybe he's getting into a bog by trying to humour my secularist tendencies. I tried another route. Wasn't Islamisation divisive, since there were so many schools and sects of the religion?

'There's no such thing as Islamisation.' I noticed a start of surprise in the audience. It was just, he said, that a country created in the name of Islam was trying to keep up with those values:

'From a situation in which the British governed India by religiouslessness,' Secularism, muttered Brigadier Salik at his lap, 'No,' said the president firmly, 'religiouslessness, it will take us a long time to develop our values again.' But Islam, he insisted, did not believe in putting women in burqas and keeping them at home. That, I thought, was throwing buns to the bears of the western media.

The religion itself was not divided: different routes had emerged over history, but the fundamentals were the same. 'Say at Muharram [the Shia month of mourning], some large procession is going by, and some people get beaten up. That is not because of religion, that is politics. A society that has been kept under pressure . . . goes very fast when it is released.' But, I persisted, those beatings up might not be because of religion, but religious differences were the trigger.

'That,' he said with a marginal loss of serenity, 'is vested interests.

Shias are only five per cent of the population [lower than the lowest estimate I had ever heard anyone offer]. The minority is always better organised, more conscious of its rights. So some individuals would always try to create a rift.' I was glad I wasn't a Shia. 'Anyway,' he said with a restoration of the smile, 'this is politics, not religion.' That jarred horribly with everything I had ever read about the Muslim fundamentalists' attitude towards politics.

'But you,' I spluttered, 'are the man who is trying to unite politics and religion.'

'Of course,' said the regiment of teeth, standing to attention. I liked that, and enjoyed an answer which sounded to me as though he had either placed himself in the category of the people he had been condemning in the previous paragraph or merely contradicted what he had just said. I didn't press it, in case he changed his mind, but said that even on the few laws which he introduced to implement the principles of Islam, there were arguments: just that morning, for instance, I had read a piece in the government-owned *Pakistan Times* arguing that Islam did not sanction stoning to death for adultery. There was a simple enough answer to that:

'The dispute on stoning to death has been the creation of those who do not believe in the fundamentals of Islam. It is my belief that I should abide by the Quran and its interpretations.' Or, more generally, if you disagree with me you are wrong. Angry, I supposed that his assumption of infallibility extended from beliefs to actions. How, I asked, I hoped acidly, did he justify the disrepair into which Pakistan's education system had fallen during his time in office? Spending on education had fallen and literacy was apparently stagnant, with female literacy in the countryside falling slightly. Zia's hands rose from his lap in a small manual shrug and the smile spread.

'It was just one of those things. A very unwise policy. I didn't think of it at the time.' I told him I found this disarming: what was I to do with my follow-up question with statistics proving the decline of educational standards in the face of his denials? He laughed, and the audience echoed him.

'When you are at fault, you should accept this. I bungled up.' It was charming, of course, but awful. When you have total power, when nobody can hold you accountable for your failures, there is no need to lie about them. Democracies, not dictatorships, call for dishonesty. What a luxury that must be, I thought: how many western politicians would like to shout Yes! I blew it! if they weren't sure of losing their jobs.

The audience had swollen for lunch: Attiya Inayatullah, a beautiful advisor on family planning to the Bhutto government and then to Zia, arrived, along with Mahbub ul Haq's clever economist wife and a genial Sartaj Aziz, special advisor on agriculture and ex-international bureaucrat. The round table was loaded with silver, crystal filled with Coca-Cola and a central rosebed.

'Presidential roses flower all year round,' said Zia, sitting down next to me.

Nervously I ate all my bread. The bearers brought me more, and I ate that too. Effortful smallish talk started over the green soup so I decided to kill it. I turned to Zia:

'The thing that I'm really curious about is how you have survived so long.'

'By the grace of God,' he replied with a mischievous look.

'I'm afraid that doesn't answer an agnostic.'

'By the love of the people . . . well, if not their love, then their greater dislike of something else.' Mahbub slid in. 'Since I'm sure the general doesn't want to blow his own trumpet, I can say that the people wanted a period of normality and quiet. They wanted good government. And, I think I can also say that the president has restored decency to the country.' The chicken arrived – those ubiquitous subcontinental chicken cutlets, which must be a legacy of the Raj but these days wouldn't dare raise their greasy heads in a London restaurant.

'Why did Bhutto die?' It says much for Zia that I asked him without much trepidation. The people who went on about his humility are very wrong, unless they meant something else, something that I suspect made him different from Bhutto: he showed none of the insecure man's desire to overawe. He made you feel you could say anything to him, and he would consider it politely.

'Two things. You know, when he was arrested, he was taken to Murree – not to jail, to a nice bungalow. Then he was released, and he came to me. He said Zia, you have the power but I have the brains. Together we could make a great team. I said nothing doing.

'Then, the other thing, he was tried for murder. I have always believed in the rule of the law. And the supreme court, the judges he had appointed, passed the sentence.'

'You could have commuted it.'

'I have *never* commuted a death sentence.' It sounded as though he were saying he had never told a lie.

I asked about nepotism, the business of giving the job to your clan member of your brother-in-law's brother. Zia countered with a competent little story about Montgomery favouring a friend's relation; but Mahbub agreed with me as strongly as he could in the circumstances, 'and it is getting worse now the political government has come in. But,' he gave a little shrug. 'we are a developing country.' I had heard that too often, and had written it off as an excuse, not an explanation. Still, Mahbub said, people in Pakistan could rise by merit:

'Look round this table: we're all middle-class or lower-middle-class . . . except one.' All eyes turned on Yaqub Khan's long elegant face and aquiline nose. He blushed all the way up it, threw his head back and laughed with everybody else.

That lunch helped me understand why the military manage to go on running the country. It was brilliantly done. The guests were, as Mahbub pointed out, the stars of the Pakistani meritocracy, which was likely to impress me far more than a tableful of the standard hereditary landowning politicians. Attiya Inayatullah was the perfect advertisement for Pakistani womanhood under an Islamising military government: her clothes and punky hairstyle would have done credit to any glitterati evening, her manners to anybody's dinner party, and her intellect to an Oxford high table. On top of all that, she was pushy, in an impatient, Thatcheresque way, leaving one in no doubt that the Muslim woman need not be a retiring flower. Each of the people at that table could have talked long and well about almost anything, yet each had a speciality, ready to pull out particular bits of information if gaps in Zia's knowledge required it. They did it with perfect politeness, appearing merely to expand on what he was saying rather than to answer the question for him. And he dealt well with them, deferring occasionally to deeper knowledge while never allowing anybody to doubt who was in charge.

And the presents! Normally I don't accept presents from people I'm interviewing. If by mistake or out of embarrassment I do, I give them away, to *The Economist's* charities board or a convenient taxi-driver. Usually I don't want them anyway. But Zia, as we left the lunch-table, presented me with an enormous pile of books, some of them signed by himself – picture books on Pakistan, books on Islam, an illustrated translation of Iqbal's poetry, serious books on

Pakistani politics. Among them was Stanley Wolpert's biography of Jinnah. You only can buy pirated copies in Pakistan: the legit ones were impounded because the book includes an anecdote about Jinnah's fondness for ham sandwiches. I was offered a legit copy.

'But general,' I said, 'I didn't think this was available in Pakistan.'

'It's available with me,' he said mischievously.

Now, I'm not quite sure whether books count as a bribe. Obviously you can't sell them for much, and they are an improving sort of thing, not like being given a crate of champagne. But, as they had presumably anticipated, I wanted that pile very badly. Zia made it worse: I was welcome to refuse them, he said, solicitous of my conscience. I didn't.

After that lunch, I thought I understood Zia better, too. He was a happy man who would never have a sleepless night nor yearn to share his problems with a shrink. He had no doubts, and he would never feel guilty. Nobody was going to shake his faith that his decade had been good for Pakistan, that he was the leader Pakistan needed after Bhutto's corrupting influence, and that his version of Islam was the right one to impose on the country. If anybody disagreed with him, that was fine, because they must necessarily be mistaken.

Understanding his certainty helped me to sort out his motives for taking power and keeping it. I decided that, as far as he was conscious of his real motives, reforming Pakistan through establishing Islam as the basis of the law and government was probably high on the list – not just, as so many of his opponents claimed, a cynical pretext for staying in that soulless luxury hotel of a palace. But, whether he admitted it to himself or not, I guess that he found that power was fun, and that he liked to watch himself growing into his position of supremacy.

Why the Pakistanis had let him stay there was a more difficult question. They're not a quiescent lot: political anger has brought them out on the streets to destroy two governments. While journalistic generalisations about public opinion are always suspect, I was constantly surprised by the number of Pakistanis who said, without any specific grievance against Zia, that martial law was a Bad Thing.

Obviously there are lots of reasons, to do with the memory of Bhutto, and economics, and fear, that have for the most part kept the crowds off the streets. But I think Zia was a major one. He made himself virtually invisible. Going round the offices of civil servants, businessmen, intellectuals, religious leaders, soldiers, I never once saw Zia's picture. Only Jinnah's sombre hollow-cheeked face graced their walls. I asked Zia if it was policy: it was.

How dictators are seen to live appears to be a factor in their survival: there is a positive correlation between ostentation and overthrow. Imelda Marcos need not be dragged into the equation: Ayub's children were visibly making money and Ayub used this position to climb. Himself from a fairly humble background, he married his children off to Pakistan's top families. People didn't like that.

Except for the handicapped daughter whom Zia took to receptions with him, hardly anybody knew who his children were or what they did. I asked around; eventually a minister's wife told me that he had three daughters and two sons, one son in the Bank of America in Bahrain, and one son a doctor. The eldest son is married to the daughter of one General Rahimullah, but the minister's wife couldn't think who the other children were married to. Zia certainly did not use his position to drag himself up the social ladder. Rather, he said he was proud of origins that would (if he were not powerful – power has a certain social cachet) ensure his exclusion from the best social circles.

Mahbub's word 'decency' stuck in my mind. Worldwide, it is a virtue of the lower-middle classes, who prize it more than they do freedom, originality, passion or even, probably, justice. As Thatcher and Reagan have had plenty of support for their efforts to start rolling back some of the liberal legislation of the 1960s, so Zia's concern with 'decency' might well have dulled the objections to his government among those who heard stories of Bhutto's women and drink, and shuddered. I asked Attiya Inayatullah about this, as we drove the next day into the hills above Islamabad and sat on chairs overlooking the bright, hazy city, while the man from the tea-shop brought us lunch.

'He shares the morality of middle-class people like me,' she said, her bright red lipstick melting into the tiny wrinkles around her wide mouth. I decided she was extremely attractive, but that her face was too strong to be beautiful. 'He's shy with women. He's not a . . . disco person, and nor am I. I don't wear jeans in public. You might catch me in jeans, listening to disco music at home, but that's a different thing.' So decency might include hypocrisy: it justified being one sort of person in public, and another in private. Presumably, if Bhutto had been more discreet about his women, his affairs would have been decent. I asked Attiya what decency was. She thought for a while.

'They had key clubs in Bhutto's time – you know, where everybody puts their car keys in a bowl and the women go home with whoever's keys they pick. And these days, drinking is less. Of course people do drink in the towns . . . and in the villages they have their local makes. But less of it is seen. Also now, there are more families together, walking or picnicking in the parks. Zia, you know, is more like the people. He's humble, not showy. He doesn't mind shaking the hand of a poor man, so other people are becoming the same as him.'

His death was a shock but not a surprise. For a long, long time people had been saying that his luck must run out and that by allowing the Americans to saturate Pakistan with arms he was inviting some unimaginable violence. But his astonishing success in confounding politicians and predictions had mesmerised people, and they had ceased to believe what they said.

The manner of his death suggested a badly-written script. The man had to go for the plot to move on, but the writer had run out of ideas. The country was not going to revolt; the man's cunning meant that he would always be able to deflect attempts by other generals to edge him out; the only solution was that contemptible cop-out, the *Deus ex machina*.

More interesting was the way the plot began to move afterwards. Very swiftly it became clear that the generals' view of their job had altered during his time in power. They were no longer just sentries patrolling the boundaries of civilian life. They were inside the compound, privately, making their political calculations, promoting people, discouraging people, prodding the president. If the politicians and the electorate behaved themselves, then certainly they would be allowed to look after their own affairs – so long as they did not interfere in the Army's. But the generals would be the judges of the civilians' behaviour: if it was childish, violent or politically suspect, then, regretfully, the generals would have to take over again. The Army had, quietly, turned into the country's biggest political party.

12

BEGINNING AGAIN

IN THE WEST elections are as bland and distant as a television chat show. In Pakistan they are street theatre with audience participation. The scarcity value heightens the excitement: everybody turned out to watch the 1988 show because, they said, they weren't sure when there would be another performance.

Some friends of mine borrowed a first-floor office on a crossroads in British-built Lahore. It had high windows and a carved-wood balcony under which Benazir's last and biggest procession was due to pass. Below were knots of policemen leaning on their sticks and chatting. Groups of men sat on plastic chairs outside the street restaurants slopping up stew with torn-off bits of flat bread while the chefs squatted on platforms above them stirring greasy, spicy meat in huge pots or turning orange chickens on spits. The PPP's green, red and black banners spanned the street. The crossroads was decorated with bright film posters of fat-thighed women and fleshy-faced bandits and candidates' posters in the same school of portraiture: plumping out the faces, doubling the chins, and lending a twist of lascivious brutality to the lips. Some perfectly harmless-looking candidates I knew were painted as overweight thugs.

We, of course, did not go down to the street for our food. It was brought up the ancient dusty staircase from one of the restaurants by a thin boy. The balcony on which we stood and chewed our chicken-legs was in the same style as those that Mogul emperors lean out of in miniatures. But while they were handing out judgements to the crowds below, we were watching what kind of judgement the crowds would make on the tamasha the PPP was laying on.

People began to form a thin lining to the procession's route.

295

Some carried banners and flags, most wore a folded cardboard party-hat in green, red and black. Suzuki trucks began to crawl down the road, each sardine-packed with people and flanked by marchers throwing thick handfuls of leaflets into the crowd. The men from the restaurants began to leave their plates and drift over to the roadside. The police, grossly outnumbered, forced themselves on to the road edge and tapped a few shins with their sticks. As the spaces between the vans filled with people, the procession slowed to snail-speed and the shouting rose.

Then round the corner came a lorry fronted by a fifteen-foot picture of Zulfikar Ali Bhutto in a Mao cap, followed by another lorry carrying his daughter. She stood in its open top, turning, waving and smiling, surrounded by hangers-on who also waved and smiled in recognition of the crescendo of adulation roaring through the street. The lorry crept purposefully. The driver must have been steel-nerved, for there was a permanent wedge of young men squashed between the front of the moving lorry and the unmoving crowd. They always just pushed and squeezed their way out before being crushed.

A couple of women on our balcony leant over like pop groupies and yelled 'Bhutto! Bhutto!' making victory-signs at the crowds; but they were drowned by the ambient noise. I asked the girl standing beside me in an embroidered kashmiri shawl whom she was going to vote for. 'The other side,' she said with an apologetic smile. 'My family are rather big business people, and we do not trust the Bhuttos.'

Our air-conditioned Pajero slipped in between a couple of the painted and steel-frilled buses. Each was topped with fifty or so people waving, singing and dancing, like too many cabaret girls sprung out of a birthday cake. The procession edged its way down on the road towards the railway station and the old city where Benazir's great rally was to take place. The buildings got shabbier and older, with carved balconies and classical balustrades, little arched windows and thick, studded wooden doors in arched doorways.

'I've never been here,' said one of the Lahore housewives in the Pajero in a tone of touristic interest. We were in one of the most historic as well as one of the main commercial areas of the city, and just next to the railway station. Perhaps it wasn't that surprising, though: Pakistanis do not seem much stirred by history. The commerce there was grubby, small-scale stuff that her family would long ago have graduated out of. And if she wanted to travel long-distance, she undoubtedly went by plane.

The buses and Suzukis, lorries and Pajeros crept to a stop; only the motor bikes and cycles, edging their way between the vehicles, were moving. The symphony of horns (with voice accompaniment) soon stopped: everybody realised that something important had stalled the procession. Benazir was having a rest.

Small entertainments sprang up quickly in the interval. In a space between two lorries, a crowd cheered on two acrobatic dancers who rolled their stomachs, their hips and their eyes at each other. On the edge of the crowd, three small boys practised the same dance, giggling and wiggling. The usual salesmen with sugar-cane and spiced peanuts and lentils in newspaper cones moved in to take advantage of the captive market. On top of Benazir's lorry, three of her young candidates – an accountant, a lawyer and a man of property – were keeping the entertainment going while she was away. They chanted and threw rose petals on the crowds and the crowds chanted back. The floodlights meant for Benazir lit their smiles, inflated by a brief taste of back-street fame.

The election brought an unusual burst of optimism to the Pakistani political landscape. Getting there at all felt like a major democratic achievement. After eleven years of Zia and three of his limp, handicapped parliament, nobody really felt that proper party-based elections would ever be allowed to happen. People argued that the Army would be bound to stop it, if only to prevent a Bhutto getting to power again; that the people who had been around Zia and feared a Bhutto victory would be bound to incite the Army to stop the election happening.

Those worries were quite realistic. Six weeks before the election, in Hyderabad in Sind, carloads of unknown gunmen in several parts of the town simultaneously started shooting at passers-by. They mostly shot Mohajirs, and the killings started off killings of Sindhis elsewhere; but it did not look like Karachi's usual ethnic violence. The scale, organisation and anonymity of the operation led plenty of people – including me – to believe that it was arranged by those who wanted violence to spread throughout the province and the Army to move in and cancel the election.

The Army did not move in; and once it had resisted that level of incitement people began to believe the election would really happen. The posters and banners came out, the candidates got on the road and the slogans started to fly. It looked just like a normal election campaign: nasty, personalised, and no more intelligent than the one that the Americans were having at the same time. People began to talk as though they were soon going to get an ordinary, dull sort of government, just like the ones you get in other countries where they have election campaigns.

Being Pakistan, of course, it was a little peculiar. Both the PPP and the Islamia Jamhoori Ittehad (the Islamic Democratic Alliance – the remains of the Muslim League and some odds and ends) were looking over their shoulder all the time at the Army. When IJI politicians talked to me, I could tell that much of what they said was intended for the soldiers' consumption. Benazir gave a press conference at seven in the morning, after a rally which ended at four. Perhaps exhaustion made her frank: asked if it was possible to cut the defence budget which was eating up thirty-five per cent of all government spending, she said with a smile; 'If you want to invite martial law.'

Then the choice of candidates was, by any other country's standards, odd. Both parties' candidates were, in Punjab at least, the same people. It was all the old families again. Many of Benazir's candidates were people who had been with her father, had abandoned the opposition for Zia's parliament, and, now that the odds seemed to be on the PPP again, had switched once more. The big families, unsure of the outcome, mostly covered themselves by providing a candidate to both parties. The parties saw nothing odd in this, and accepted the candidates offered to them by the best families: they were too uncertain of themselves and their country to choose candidates for their loyalty and their energy rather than their saintly origins and tribal clout.

In Pakistan the rules for elections, parliaments and government do not look unlike that of many western countries that cobble together their governments out of class and ideological alliances; yet it is all the other things that make up Pakistan's political culture that determines who gets to be a prime minister, a minister, or a member of parliament and what they do with the job when they get there. How, for instance, was a journalist to explain to a foreign audience that Mr Junejo, the quiet, rather fey Pakistani prime minister shaking hands with Mr Reagan on his visit to Washington and begging for an Awac or two was only there because he was selected by Pir Pagara, a man whom, to several thousand armed Sindhi peasants, is something like God incarnate? Pakistan's layers of history mean that to try to understand the country through official organisations, like parliaments, ministries, courts and chambers of commerce, would be like trying to get an idea of the geography of a country from a railway map. The lines would be clear and straight enough, but without the towns, the roads, the rivers and the hills, they would mean nothing.

Certainly, the courts, the ministries, the police, the businessmen are there. Even the parliaments are sometimes there. They have their limited freedoms. But the bounds within which they work are set only partly by what is written down on paper, and what is learnt from books about how they should work; they are also set by things – informal things, because they do not fit into the theories – that are not there in other countries. The accumulation of land over centuries has created a group of people who can – informally – make those institutions work in unfamiliar ways. More than that, the memory of tribal allegiances that held people together in protective alliances before there were governments to regulate behaviour make those institutions behave in particular ways; and an idea of spiritual authority peculiar to that piece of land gives some people an importance that cannot be nailed on to an office door or gleaned from a bank balance.

Pakistan's politics have worked badly because people who claim to be playing by one set of rules are in fact quietly playing by another. That started before Pakistan was created: it was set up as a democratic Islamic country with a Bengali majority and a minority of West Pakistanis who had a sense of racial superiority and more firepower and were not going to be run by a Bengali. Islamic unity and democracy were at once submerged: the West Pakistanis spent two decades trying to avoid a proper election. When they had one, and got a Bengali majority party, they applied their firepower to East Pakistan and the country ceased to exist.

Bhutto, the only democratically elected prime minister, gave the country its first decent constitution and promised his followers a 'New Pakistan'. Yet, once in power, he behaved like an Old Pakistani – a Sindhi feudal lord loosing his paid gunmen on his enemies, or a Mogul emperor piling up the skulls of the soldiers of rival armies. He was toppled partly because people had, initially, believed him: they thought that he was offering them a country in which state power was no longer to be used for the settling of tribal scores or the elevation of an individual to one of those jewel-encrusted balconies that the God-kings sat on in the sixteenth century.

Even Zia, having changed the rules so often himself, had people hoping again. That unimpressive parliament which was elected in 1985, without any of the real opposition in it, might have slowly grown, over a number of elections, into a sovereign body whose continued existence was taken for granted. But, although there was hope, there was also a knowledge that the parliament wasn't for legislation, or for producing a government. It was the emperor's court, enabling the nobles to enjoy the benefits of access to government and to shore up their popularity in their villages by distributing the patronage that emanated from the court.

When Zia sacked the parliament he made the clearest statement yet of the balance of power in the country. He had no excuse for getting rid of it, other than that the parliament had been what anybody with a knowledge of how the country works should have expected it to be; yet, one hot May evening, he told it and the government to pack its bags. With hardly a squeak of complaint, the politicians went their ways, ready to return when summoned once more by the soldiers. Then, with his death and the 1988 elections, people began to hope again: perhaps they were being given once more the chance they had lost in 1977.

It wasn't the same chance, though, because the map had changed in the years under Zia. Although, by the time of the election, everybody seemed to be trying to forget that he had existed, the country the politicians were fighting over was a different country to the one which Bhutto had lost to the Army.

Although both parties chose candidates from landed families, the election still proved how the landlords', the pirs' and the tribal leaders' grip is slackening in some parts of the country. The grandest families in Sind were all with the IJI: the PPP was stuck mostly with second and third rankers. The PPP had an undiluted victory: the biggest shots, whom everybody assumed were guaranteed winners, were all wiped out. Pir Pagara lost to a small local landowner who, in a fit of humorous self-confidence, registered himself under his alias, Mr Parrot. Pagara's enemies chortled with delight: the biggest Pir in Pakistan was beaten by a parrot.

In Sind, the collapse of the police force and the erosion of the landlords' power – partly the result of the saturation of the country with weapons intended for the Afghans – created a vacuum which the Army, apparently willingly, filled. It became the law and the administration. I didn't understand this from the figures people gave me on the deployment of soldiers in the province, or the

300

numbers of cantonments being built: I realised it when I saw the Army trucks waiting on the corners of small Sindhi streets, and the soldiers wandering through markets with an indifference that suggested their presence was natural and inevitable.

The Army's hold on all sorts of unexpected areas strengthened during Zia's years in power. The Fauji Foundation's mysterious growth has made it probably the biggest industrial empire in the country. The military's control over the shipments of arms to the Afghan rebels has made the Army's National Logistics Cell the biggest freight transport outfit in the country, and led it to expand its operations into the private sector.

Even as the 1988 elections were being held, nobody who thought or wrote seriously about these matters argued that the Army had really withdrawn. They accepted that government would in future have to be an implicit partnership between the prime minister and the chief of Army staff; and that any prime minister who did not understand that would not last very long.

As the Army's hold strengthened, so that of other groups and institutions weakened. The courts' independence has certainly been eroded, particularly in the past ten years. In order to be fairly certain that, in the most important cases, a decision would go in favour of the Army, the military rulers had to emasculate the courts. The requirement that judges should take an oath on the (dubious) provisional constitutional order, sorted the judicial sheep from the goats, ensuring that the more reliable and obedient sheep remained in control of the courts. By keeping acting, rather than permanent, chief justices, Zia had added a spice of insecurity to the judges' lives.

Whatever else Zia's parliament achieved, it proved how little a collection of elected representatives can do to alter the life of a country. The same could be argued of the British parliament; but its peculiar method of organisation does produce parties which produce governments. The government, while Zia's parliament was alive, was not that of the result of the assembly's choice, but of the calculations of Zia and Pir Pagara.

That parliament's failure does not determine the performance of future elected bodies; but it helped wear down people's thinning faith in politics and in institutions. Other failures have generated a similar disillusion: the failure of the civil service to provide the people of Karachi with a liveable-in city, the failure of the police to enforce the law impartially, the failure of the courts to uphold the constitution. By allowing themselves to be bullied or bribed into acting as the servants of politicians and generals, these mainstays of government have lost the trust of those whom they should be serving.

That growing, widespread cynicism is leading people to turn away from the regular institutions of government. A foreign banker told me that, in the past five years, several of his respectable clients had put on their payrolls gangs of armed men whose job it was to extract payment from other respectable businessmen. They felt they had no option: the courts were not going to convict the debtors, so harassment and kidnapping of relations was the only sure way of getting paid.

The armed men who travel with landlords in Sind and the frontier, and the armed guards at the doors of rich houses are symptoms of the ultimate failure of a state: an inability to protect citizens which leads citizens to buy private protection. But there are subtler manifestations of the retreat from collective, institutional life. Those left-wingers who were trying to teach the Sindhi peasants about smoke-free stoves, cooperatives and ideology had given up, temporarily at least, on the business of electoral politics. Their experiences with Bhutto had taught them that it isn't worth involving yourself in national political life when you risk the anger of a feudal landlord with the resources of the state at his command. The little groups of people in Karachi who are building their own sewage systems or starting their own schools have given up hope that the state will provide for them, even if they do pay their taxes. The growing thousands of followers of the air commodore's Tabliq are after some sort of spiritual satisfaction not to be gained from the parties and pirs who have allowed themselves to be used by generals and politicians. The businessmen who went into politics in Ayub's days learnt a sharp lesson under Bhutto and have, with a few rash exceptions, stayed out since.

A different set of cracks is appearing all over the country – and particularly recently and violently in Karachi. The business of who you are – a Punjabi, a Sindhi, a Pathan or a Mohajir – is another result of the failure of nation-building. Those groups of young men, waiting on street corners for the next battle or the next police charge, have turned themselves into small tribal armies because the government seems to belong to other people. It may belong to the Punjabis, or the soldiers, or the landlords – all they are sure of is that it isn't them. The rise of the MQM suggests that some people still believe it can be won back through elections; the gangs on the streets mean that others don't.

Military coups and failed politics have deprived Pakistan of the political leisure to work out how to integrate its different histories. It may be that the idea of Islamic separateness that brought Pakistan into being needs to be worked into the system of government. Perhaps there is room for an assembly of learned clerics of the sort that would appeal to religious leaders. I doubt it – elections do not favour the religious parties, and Zia's attempts to force Islam on to the political system did not meet with enthusiasm – but if a parliament were allowed to grow and change, it might decide to become something like that.

It may be that elections and parliaments are compatible with Pakistan's ancient network of tribalism and sifarish: that the assemblies should just be regarded as a means of distributing government money and jobs, and policy should be formulated by civil servants. It's plausible, though it doesn't sound particularly efficient or equitable, since not everybody will have their patronage-funnel and civil servants do not generally have sensitive political antennae. But it might gel into a workable system.

Perhaps, if a parliament were allowed to work uninterrupted and had to put itself up for re-election, and if the courts were allowed to get on with their business without being interfered with by soldiers, Pakistan's government would in the end resolve itself into something similar to India's or Britain's. It would only take a little luck and a little forbearance on the part of both politicians and soldiers.

At the time of the 1988 elections, optimism was high. It seemed that at last there was a chance of such a parliament setting itself up. With Zia gone, the country was able to pay its dues to Bhutto by voting for his daughter. After eleven years in power, the Army seemed prepared at least to take a back seat. The religious parties were routed in the election, and already there was a sniff of secularism in the air.

People who had hated Benazir's father for betraying their hopes and despised her for abandoning his ideology suddenly forgot their old vitriol. They voted for her, attended her rallies and cheered her. She was the embodiment of that fresh hope. She was young, she was female: whatever else, she was as different as she could be from the uniformed dictators and grey-bearded mullahs who had had their way for too long.

I sat through most of the night with some friends watching the election programme on television. One of the girls shrieked as it started up; 'The PPP must have won! The announcer isn't wearing her dupatta!' – the modest scarf compulsory for public women during the Zia years. The election programme had the spontaneity and amateurishness born of inexperience. When the male announcer spoke the female one inspected her fingernails, swept her hair back from her forehead and chatted with somebody off-camera. Blurred bodies occasionally passed between the camera and the announcers, who asked them testily to get out of the way.

My friends were more interested in the snippets of change. 'They're flirting, look they're flirting!' somebody shouted. Sure enough, the female announcer simpered as the man charmed her with some significant new result. One of the commentators quoted George Bush: 'The people have spoken', and one of my companions said it was the first time that The People had been mentioned on the official media for eleven years. But they were most excited when the announcer wound up the programme with a quotation from Pakistan's best-known poet, Faiz Ahmed Faiz – a Communist, who had been wiped off the nation's official memory under Zia.

When Benazir won nearly twice as many seats as the IJI – though not an overall majority – the liberal intelligentsia was delighted. Plenty of people weren't, though – like the men I met under a canopy at the headquarters of one of the IJI candidates. I asked the small crowd that surrounded us why their side was insulting the Bhutto women (a euphemism: its slogans ranged from the straight 'We don't want to be ruled by women' to one suggesting that Benazir had sexual relations with dogs).

'The problem,' said one of the men, shrugging his shoulders apologetically, 'is that although I myself am an MA, there are so many illiterate people in this country, and . . .' Another face poked out of the crowd towards me;

'We don't want to see their bloody faces,' he sneered.

The soldier and the businessman were not too happy, either. We were sitting in the businessman's bar, the walls behind the shelves mirrored to reflect the crystal glasses, golden whisky-bottle and dark mahogany of the counter. The soldier had invited himself round to the businessman's for a drink; the businessman sprang up with nervous frequency to refill our glasses with too-large whiskies.

'I'm not against Benazir,' said the soldier, 'but don't ever tell my Army friends I said that. The trouble, I say, is these goondas [thugs]

304

in her party. But then,' he went on with a laugh, 'all these damn politicians have their goondas, don't they?'

'I think so,' said the businessman politely, his fingers running over the patterns on his glass as though he had something on his mind. 'Do you think that she will go in for this revenge business? Some of us, you know . . . not that we were with Zia . . .'

'They had better be careful,' said the soldier, suddenly serious. 'Zia was a gentleman, a very humble chap. Next time, it might be horrible.'

INDEX

and businessmen, 85–6, 88–9, 90;
and the civil service, 246, 248, 281;
and education, 25–6; executed, 68,
290; and Islam, 220–1; landowner
support, 66–7, 105, 195; populism,
46, 62–3, 102, 105, 192–4; socialist
measures, 65, 85–6, 205;
mentioned, 2, 70, 100, 127, 172,
217, 269
Bhutto family, 100, 189
Bijrani family, 189
Bizenjo, Ghaus Bux, 138–9, 140
braderis, 102–3, 205
Brahuis, 138
bribery, see corruption
Bugti, Nawab Akbar, 139, 140, 141–6,
187, 205
Bugti tribe, 136, 138, 141, 143, 145–6
business, businessmen, 77–97; see also
economic affairs

Chandi, see Hussein, Abida
Chinyot, 85
civil service, bureaucracy, 42–3,
238–53, 264, 281–2
class, social, see social class
clothes, fashion, 46
Comilla, 180
Communist Party, Communism,
153–4, 211
Congress (Indian political party), 59,
100
constitution, 65, 71–2, 261–3
consumer goods, 44–5
co-operative movement, 180–1
corruption, bribery, 41–3, 50–1,
178–9, 266, 282–3
customs and excise, 45, 251–3
Cyrus the Achaemenid, 55

dacoits, dacoity, 121, 124, 127–8,
208–9
dalals, 170
Darling, Sir Malcolm Lyall, 103
Dawn group, 31, 32, 172, 173
Dawood family, 84, 88

death, funerals, 20–1, 113
Deobandi movement, 219
deputy commissioners, 242–3
Dera Bugti, 145–6
desert, 135
Douie, Sir James, 100–1
drink, see alcohol
drugs, heroin, 39, 43, 78, 155, 160–1,
174, 177–8
Dutt, Sunil, 187

Eagle Squad, 34
East Pakistan, see Bangladesh
economic affairs, 37–44; under Ayub
Khan, 62–3; Islamic economics,
226–7; see also agriculture; banks;
business; industry; landowners;
wealth
education, schools, 25–7, 51, 289; see
also universities
elections, 8–9, 99, 117–18, 125–7,
130, 131–2, 230–1, 250–1, 295;
1969, 64; 1977, 67, 221; 1979
(local), 69; 1985, 71, 72, 163, 231,
247; 1988, 73, 118, 134, 146, 186,
192, 214, 229, 235, 295–8, 300,
303–5
electricity, 206–7, 248–9
Elphinstone, Mountstuart, 57
English language, 14, 26–7, 29, 266
exports, 39

Fahim Khan, Dr, 226–7
Fakr Imam, 52, 115, 190
families, notable, 48, 52–3, 83–5, 87,
100, 189, 192, 298
family life, 20–1
Fancy family, 84, 84–5, 87
farming, see agriculture
Fauji Foundation, 281, 301
favours, 44–5, 52, 191, 241–2
Fazle Haq, General, 2, 69, 162, 272–4
Federal Security Force (FSF), 66,
70–1, 194–5
firearms, guns, 34, 257, 294, 302
Frontier Post, 161–2, 228

Jatoi family, 100, 189
Jewna, Shah, 110
Jinnah, Mohammed Ali, 59, 60, 77, 88, 221–2, 288
jirga, 149
Jiye Sind party, 207, 211, 212, 214
judiciary, law courts, 116, 242, 259–64, 301
Junejo, Mohammed Khan, 2, 71, 100, 125, 189–90, 231–2, 298

K2, 5
Kachelo, Rafi, 132–3, 187
Kahuta, 8
Kalabagh dam, 206–7
Kalat, 136, 138
Karachi, 3, 34, 49, 167–86, 256–9
Karim family, 84
Kashmir, 4, 57
Keshowlal, Mr, 130–1
Khalil ur-Rehman, 31
Khar, Mustapha, 201
Khilafat movement, 13, 59
Khuro family, 100, 189
King Faisal mosque, Islamabad, 1
Kipling, Rudyard, 4
Kochanek, Stanley, 89–90
Koh-i-Noor, 56
Kukikhel, Wali Khan, 66, 150–1, 202

Lahore, 3, 5, 51, 167
Lakhani, Sultan, 90
Laksons, 90
land tenure, revenue, 100–1
landowners, landlords, 40, 97, 100–34; see also families, notable
language, 25–30; see also English; Urdu
Las Bela, 136
Las Bela, Jam of, 141
Latif, Shah Abdul, 208, 216–17
law and order, 33–6; see also constitution; judiciary; police; riots
law courts, see judiciary
Lawrence, Henry and John, 57
Liaqat Ali Khan, 60

Mahbub ul Haq, 62, 69, 83–4, 106, 285, 286, 290, 291
Mahmud of Ghaznavi, 55
Mairaj Mohammed Khan, 65, 70
Makran, 136
maliks, 149, 157–8, 163
Manora Island, 5
Marri, Khair Bux, 139, 140, 145
Marri, Sher Mohammed, 140
Marri tribe, 136, 141
marriage, 19–20
martial law, military rule, 8–9, 67–8, 69–70, 71, 72, 192, 266–7, 269–70, 272, 276–7; opposition to, 89, 261, 292
Maudoodi, Maulana, 219–20
Memons, 83, 84
Mengal, Ataullah, 139, 140
Mengal tribe, 136
Mirza, General Iskander, 61–2
Mirza, Mujadad, 262–3
Moguls, 28, 47, 55–6, 68
Mohajir Qami Movement (MQM), 182–6, 209, 214, 302–3
mohajirs, 34, 91, 167–8, 209
Mohenjodaro, Indus Valley civilisation, 54–5
money, see economic affairs; wealth
Movement for the Restoration of Democracy (MRD), 70, 71, 124
MQM, see Mohajir Qami Movement
Mujib, Sheikh, 63, 64
Multan, 114
Muslim League, 59–60, 61, 64, 104, 118, 192
Muslims, 13–14, 58–61, 85; see also Islam

Naidu, Sarojini, 59
Napier, Sir Charles, 57
National Awami Party (NAP), see Awami National Party
National Logistics Cell, 280–1, 301
National People's Party, 201–2
nationalisation, 65, 85–6, 205
Nauroz Khan, 139
Niblett, L. S., 255–6

Nizami, Mr, 179
Noon family, 100, 105
North West Frontier Province
(NWFP), 4, 66, 147
Northern Areas, 4
nuclear weapons, 7, 8, 281

Orangi, 169, 170–1, 175, 181–2

Pagara, Pir, 67, 69, 189, 231–2, 234–5,
298, 300
Pakhtunwali, 148, 149
Pakistan, 3–10, 15–17, 218–19;
British rule, legacy of, 14–15,
100–2, 122, 122–3, 138, 147–9,
152, 167, 207, 242, 251, 260,
269–70; founding of, 6–7, 13–14,
60; history of the region, 54–9;
hypocrisy in, 13–14, 24–5, 231;
official language, 14, 27
Pakistan National Alliance (PNA),
67–8, 70, 195, 221
Pakistan People's Party (PPP);
established, 62–3, 65–6; in 1969
elections, 64; Bhutto's purge of, 66;
Zia and, 68, 70; landlord support,
105; disillusionment with, 198; split
after Benazir Bhutto's return, 201;
in 1988 election, 118, 214, 295–8,
300
Paleejo, Rasul Bakhsh, 212–14
parliament; in Bhutto's constitution,
65; under Zia (1985–8), 71–2, 125,
189–91, 223–4, 300, 301
party-giving, 45
Parvez, Dr, 229–31
Pasni, 7
Pathans, 7, 60, 91, 136, 137, 147–58,
174–8
Peshawar, 7, 158–9, 167, 218
pirs, 103, 110, 216, 219, 232–4
Pirzada, Hafeez, 209
PNA, see Pakistan National Alliance
poetry, Urdu, 28
police, 33, 34–5, 116, 127, 176–7,
253–9, 264

politics, politicians, 29–30, 115–16,
189–214, 277, 299–300; Army and,
276–7; see also martial law;
businessmen in, 88–9, 96–7; civil
service and, 247–8, 249–50;
landlords, 100, 102–3, 104–5,
111–12, 118, 123–4, 125–7, 131–2,
134, 189–92, 195; a policeman's
view of, 254; see also constitution;
elections; Pakistan People's Party;
parliament
Poonegar, Mr, 141
PPP, see Pakistan People's Party
press, journalism, 30–3, 111–12,
161–2, 172, 173, 200, 249
Punjab, 4, 5, 26, 101–2, 114–15, 118,
122, 123; British rule in, 57–8,
59–60, 104
Punjabi-Pakhtun Ittehad, 91
Punjabis, 91–2, 208–9, 244, 270–1

Qadeer, Dr Abdul, 8
Qasim, Malik, 260
Quetta, 142, 167
Qureshi, Makhdoom Sajjad, 2, 109
Qureshi, Shah Mahmood, 114
Qureshi family, 52, 100, 105, 114, 115

Rahim, J. A., 193, 194–5
Rahimuddin, General, 140–1
Raj, British India, see under India and
under Pakistan
Ranjit Singh, 56–7
Rashid, Ahmed, 195–6
Rawalpindi, 167, 285
Razique Khan, 183–5
regionalism, 206–7, 214, 244; see also
nationalism under Baluchistan and
under Sind
riots, violence, 33–4, 174–5, 256,
302–3

Saigol, Naseem, 87–9
Saigol, Rafique, 88–9
Saigol family, 84, 87–8

Sainrakhio, 232–4
Salik, Brigadier, 286
Samdani, Mr, 261, 263
Sarkar, Aveek, 188
Saudi Arabia, 7, 272
savings, 37
Sayyeds, 16, 103
schools, see education
servants, 44
sexual behaviour, 21–3
Shabir Ahmed, Dr, 229
Shafi, Tariq, 91–4
Shafi family, 91–2
Shakespeare, William, admired in
    Pakistan, 231
shalwar kamees, 1, 46
sharab, 23
sharecropping, 122–3, 128
Shariat Law, see laws under Islam
Sharif, Nawaz, 2, 80, 94–6
Sheikh family, 84
Shivaji, 56
Sibi, 136, 137
sifarish, 51
Sikhs, 5, 56–7
Sind, 4, 5, 101–2, 118–34, 218, 300–1;
    agriculture in, 122–3; British
    capture of, 57, 207; nationalism,
    separatist movement, 26, 207–14
Sind Baluch Pushtun front, 209
Sind Club, Karachi, 49
Sind National Alliance (SNA), 213
snobbery, 48–51
social class, 48–53, 78, 82–3
social life, 44
Soomro, Illahi Bakhsh, 2, 125–30,
    131, 134, 191
Soomro, Junaid, 118–21, 123, 187,
    210–11, 212
Soomro family, 100, 119, 189
Sorabgoth, 174, 175, 259
Soviet Union, 147; see also under
    Afghanistan
Spain, James, 149–50
Sufism, 103, 110, 208, 216–17, 236
Sukkur, shrine at, 215–16
Sultana, Nihar, 156–7
Sumar, A. K., 88

Swat valley, 5
Syed, G. M., 212, 214

Tabliq, 235–7
tamasha, 127
taxation, 39, 40, 41–2, 106
Tehrik-i-Istiqlal, 66
telephone books, 32
Tiwana family, 100
transport, traffic problems, 49, 173–4,
    176, 179–80
tribal areas, tribalism, 4, 82–3, 102,
    104, 136, 141, 143–4, 145–51, 158,
    164; difficulty in visiting tribal
    areas, 238–41

Unionist party, 60, 104
United States of America, 7, 70,
    197–8, 228–9, 271, 294
universities, 34, 228; Islamic
    University, 224–5
Urdu, 25–30, 60

Valika family, 87

waderas, 119, 122–3, 124–5, 127–8,
    130
Watan Dost, 211, 212
Water and Power Development
    Authority (Wapda), 248–9, 282–3
Watoo, Yasin, 245
wealth, 43–51
White, Lawrence, 84
Wolpert, Stanley, 221
women, 17–19, 77–8, 223
World Bank, 80, 105, 141

Yahya Khan, General, 63–4, 269
Yaqub Khan, General Sahabzada, 2,
    52, 286

Zaheer ul Islam, 179–80
Zahur, Arif, 77, 78–82

311